I0565089

A Good Death

Helen Davis

TP

ThunderPoint Publishing Limited

First Published in Great Britain in 2014 by
ThunderPoint Publishing Limited
Summit House
4-5 Mitchell Street
Edinburgh
Scotland EH6 7BD

Copyright © Helen Davis 2014

The moral right of the author has been asserted.

All rights reserved.

Without limiting the rights under copyright reserved
above, no part of this publication may be reproduced,
stored in or introduced into a retrieval system, or
transmitted in any form or by any means (electronic,
mechanical, photocopying, recording or otherwise),
without the prior written permission of both the
copyright owner and the above publisher of the work.

This book is a work of fiction.
Names, places, characters and locations are used
fictitiously and any resemblance to actual persons,
living or dead, is purely coincidental and a product of
the author's creativity.

Map Copyright © GEOATLAS-GRAPHI-OGRE/shutterstock.com
ISBN: 978-0-9575689-6-9

www.thunderpoint.co.uk

TO DAD

Glossary of Spanish and Quechua Terms

ayahuasca (i-a-was-ka): the sacred plant used in Andean rituals to create a hallucinogenic trance

ayahuasquero (i-a-was-kero): shaman adept in the preparation of ayahuasca for use in rituals and healing

brujeria (bru-hair-ee-a): black magic

cholo: derogatory term for a working-class man

coca (co-ka): leaves of the coca plant chewed like tobacco for pain relief, as a stimulant, to overcome tiredness.

curandero (coo-ran-dare-o): healer, shaman

cuy (coo) negro: black guinea-pig

espanto (es-pan-to): fear, horror

gringo: white person

huaca (waaka) de la luna: temple of the moon

indio: Indians of Central and South America

laika (lay-ka): used variously to denote witch or sorcerer

maca (ma-ka): stimulating drink usually served hot like coffee or hot chocolate

mestizo: mixed race: Spanish and Andean forming an upper tier of Peruvian society

ñaqak (na-kak): evil white man from native folklore who sucks the fat from the bodies of Indians

pischtaco (pish-tak-o): Quechua term for ñaqak

pisco: grape brandy

queros (qware-oss): descendants of the Incas

San Pedro: Saint Peter, associated with ayahuasca

susto (soo-sto): when the soul leaves the body as a result of intense fright or shock

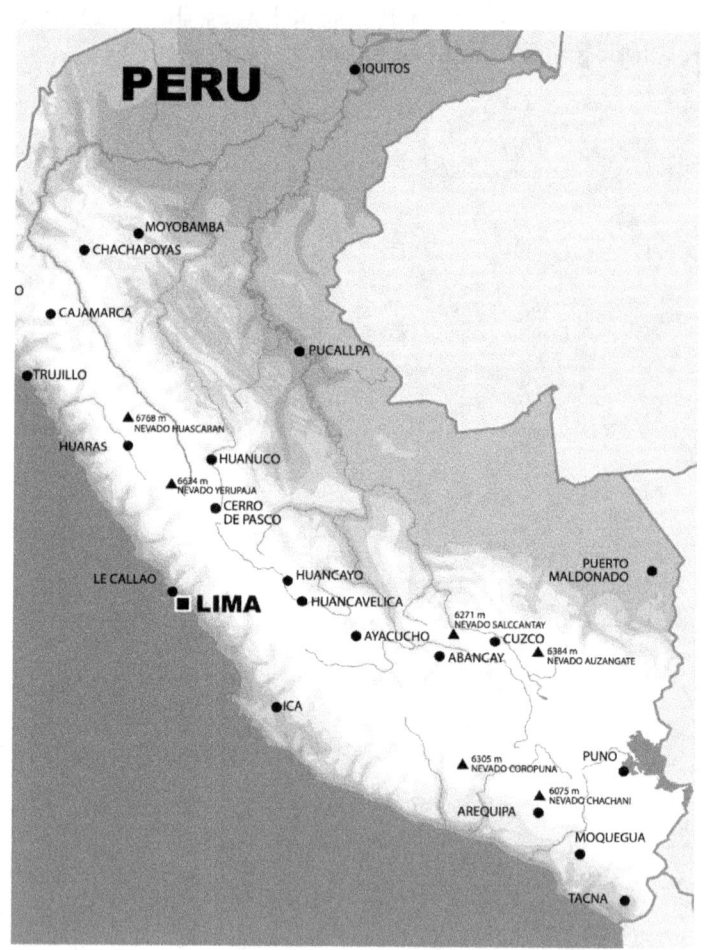

PART I

1

'Are you going to be much longer?' Theo's sing-song lament echoed behind us. 'Sophie's turning positively blue!'

Of the four of us only Sophie reported symptoms of dehydration. Just a mild headache and the beginnings of a sore throat. It wasn't severe enough to warrant an emergency descent, but it prevented her from climbing any higher.

'Damn it all,' Helena said under her breath, trying to buckle the flysheet too tightly.

'Need a hand?' I asked.

Theo had taken charge of the cooking and seemed intent on nursing Sophie. I thought it made a pleasant change from flirting with our local guide and couldn't see the harm in it. In fact relations between them seemed to have cooled quite a bit over the last two days. I might have felt sorry for Wamani had he betrayed the typical signs of a wounded male ego, but if anything he seemed even more full of himself. Perhaps Theo had let him down gently.

'Do you still think we can make the summit?' I kept my voice light and focused on the task at hand. Helena scowled.

'I think we should go for a quick ascent,' she said. 'I don't trust the weather no matter what *he* says.' She jerked her head in Wamani's direction. He was talking to Sophie who frankly looked done in, his arms extended like a proud father showing off his first-born.

I pulled a face. 'What *is* he doing?'

'His usual *the spirit of the mountain has blessed us so far* routine I expect.' Her breathing came more sharply between gritted teeth.

'Are you all right?'

'Fine. Sorry.'

That took me aback. I couldn't recall ever having heard her apologise. Not in the three years I had known her. Not even the first time we'd met when she nearly knocked my front teeth out – *Goodness that was a silly place for you to stand* – during our first week at Cambridge. Now in our final year, having studied and climbed together, I thought I knew everything there was to know about my friend.

I gripped her gloved hands and stilled them.

'You're frightening me. What's the matter?'

'I don't know. It's this place maybe.' She looked at me, her red curls pushed back behind her ears like a schoolgirl and I swear I felt a chill finger run down my spine when I saw the apprehension in her eyes.

'We don't have to go any higher,' I said. 'Theo says she's not bothered about the summit and Sophie's better off resting where she is.'

Helena fastened the last buckle, her mind made up.

'It's fine,' she said. 'We'll be fine. Just don't leave me alone with *him*. One more crack about me and Sophie and I swear I'll thump him right between the eyes.'

That was more like it.

'Well,' I allowed myself a smile, 'he did say drinking ayahuasca would show us all our true nature. He's just rather pleased with himself, that's all.'

'Smug bastard,' she muttered under her breath.

We pitched camp by dark and bedded down. I needed sleep but my mind was still trying to make sense of the night of the San Pedro ritual. It was as if my memory had become a snow globe that got shaken up whenever I closed my eyes. Faces, shapes, sounds, colours all swirled about. The order of events kept shuffling around. There were gaps and smudgy recollections which could have been real or imaginary. It was important that I remember; the trouble was I couldn't remember why it was important.

Resigned to a sleepless night I listened to the sound of the others slumbering next to me and summoned up images of home instead: England on the cusp of summer, lengthening days, warmer nights. This would be our last term. Finals were just around the corner. I held on to the fact that my life had a schedule: examinations, career, marriage to a tall, dark, faceless chap with good teeth then three children, a boy and two girls because even though my own brother was the best in the world, I had always felt the lack of a sister. I kept my dreams of a starry future close to my heart like a winning hand before the final play because at twenty thousand feet nothing is certain.

***

It had been a good week. We made base camp within five days of leaving town and steady progress thereafter, breaking for much needed rest and an opportunity to adjust to the increasing altitude.

It was, after all, only two weeks since our arrival in the Andean settlement of Cuzco, bustling, dusty and crowded with Quechua traders from all over the region.

For thousands of years Cuzco had been a capital city, the gathering place for prospectors and pilgrims, merchants and shamans. The Spanish conquered and rebuilt in their own image, using stones from nearby ancient sites. They created elegant colonnades and whitewashed buildings with pantiled rooves, bestowing enormous colonial charm in the process.

There was no doubt that to the European eye, superficially at least, Cuzco was seductive.

The trickle of backpackers and trekkers in search of high peaks and mystic adventures had swollen to a deluge by the late 1970s. When we arrived in Peru the year after the Falklands Crisis, we brought hard currency and expectations of hot water and electricity.

We arrived on a blistering afternoon in April, dusty and tired after the long bus journey from Lima. It was market day. Llamas and mules laden with sacks of corn and maize ambled through the paved streets. On every street corner Quero Indian vendors traded tobacco and gossip for alpaca fleece, woven cloths and goat's milk cheese, indifferent to the civilised architecture around them. Cuzco opened her arms to them all like a Madam with a toothless grin, ready to prostitute her own daughters if necessary, and certainly not for a handful of pesos.

Once settled at our hostel Helena elected to sort through the equipment. Sophie was on laundry detail so that left me and Theo to do the donkey work.

'Don't promise anything.' Helena was speaking to me but looking at Theo.

'Relax,' said Theo, trying on her new sun-glasses which still had the label attached.

'You're bound to be an obvious target,' Helena continued. 'We have our own alpine gear remember. We don't need half a dozen Indians to carry your luggage. This isn't San Tropez.'

Genuine Cuzco porters were renowned for their skills and fortitude, able to carry three times their body weight in rugs, canvas and ironware. Local guides were also in demand.

'I get it,' Theo pouted.

'We're not hippies remember.' Helena was not going to let up. 'We're here to climb. It's the highest peak in the Cordillera Vilcanota and it's going to be difficult enough without any . . . ' she searched for the right word, '. . . complications.'

'I *know* Helena. God.' Then turning to me, 'Please can we go now, Miss?'

I raised my eyebrows at Helena. It was no good. It was just one of those cases of the girl can't help it.

'Oh, *you* talk to her.' Helena pursed her lips together.

Helena's words were still ringing in my ears as we picked our way through the piles of coloured textiles and hand-woven garments that littered the stone streets. But shopping for a local guide was not on our agenda. It was simply a matter of picking up a few supplies: it would be four or five days at least before we could make a start. Plenty of time to scout for a guide.

'It's quite warm isn't it?' said Theo, tripping over the leg of an Indian woman sitting with her wares on the pavement.

I pulled Theo upright before she could do more than glare at the woman and linking arms, marched her on to the main square where we were quickly swallowed up in the crowd.

'Do you think you could have worn something just a little *more* revealing?' I said, conscious of the hostile glances and furtive words uttered in our wake.

'God, I'm desperate for a cigarette. Just hold on will you?' She wrestled free and clamped a cigarette between her lips whilst ferreting about in her jacket pockets for a lighter.

'Oh for God's sake,' she looked around at the bemused locals. 'Georgie don't just stand there. Ask one of them for a light.'

I sighed. Once Theo had decided to down tools for

a nicotine fix it might be another fifteen minutes before I could get her moving again. Smoking was a performance art, much like everything in Theo's life.

My broken Spanish was hilarious enough to persuade a squat Quero woman to volunteer the loan of her thin cheroot. Theo took a drag and coughed, to the delight of the local Indians who clapped her on the back. She gained a light and sucked in her face, exaggerating the cheekbones I envied before breathing out a plume of smoke. She combed her fingers through her long blond hair, establishing her space, enjoying the attention. She would not be rushed.

'Why don't you just relax George? Have a puff.'

I shook my head and frowned. *Just remember that this is a holiday.* The trouble was that in Theo's company I felt like the maid of all works rather than a partner in crime.

'Helena can be such a drag. Why do you let her talk to you like that?'

I did a double-take in spite of myself.

'She was talking to *you.* I'm not the one who got caught in the toilet with a member of the cabin crew.'

The cheroot woman's husband proffered a couple of knitted ponchos. Theo gave little nods and a broad smile as they chattered away with their unintelligible sales spiel.

'Oh but he was rather cute.' She smiled in her conspiratorial manner. 'Not that I would expect Helena to understand, her batting for the other side.' She fingered the tassels on one of the ponchos. 'Anyway,' she said with finality. 'Helena thinks it's just about sex with me. She's wrong, but I can see why she might think so. It's because she's so frustrated.'

I couldn't disagree there, but hoped that the situation with Sophie would resolve itself soon for both their sakes.

'The thing is Georgie – and I really want you to remember this – the thing is that brains in a woman are never enough in this life. If you really want to get on, you have to have men on side, powerful men.' She saw my look of disbelief and shook her head sternly.

'I know what I'm talking about.'

'I daresay you do.' I looked over the ponchos and smiled wanly at the cheroot woman.

I don't know why I thought Theo might have behaved herself abroad any better than she did in college. Helena pretty much despaired of her. Sophie, a product of her convent education, was always ready to forgive. I must admit that secretly Theo was everything I would have loved to have been, but dared not even try.

'Where men are concerned, you have to be fearless and charming and never ever let on that you need them, emotionally that is. Hefting furniture about is fine, or running about on a pitch. It keeps them from thinking too much.'

I wondered, not for the first time, whether the women of Theo's year group mostly hated her because they envied her freedom or because, politically incorrect as she was, men found her utterly disarming. Not that I hated her. Not then.

'Grotesque aren't they?' She beamed at the couple who evidently took her admiration for encouragement and pulled out more woollen items for Theo's approval.

'C'mon,' I said pulling at her arm.

'Muchos gracias!' She blew them a kiss as I led her through the narrow walkways between the stalls in search of bottled water and a pharmacy.

2

It was on the evening of the following day that the four of us felt more human. We took a stroll into the quieter districts after dinner and found ourselves in the San Blas district around ten o'clock. We happened upon an archway between two stone buildings, above which a brightly coloured hand-painted sign boasted the best maca tea in town and cool-cool beer.

'I'm parched. Let's stop,' said Theo, pulling me and Sophie along with Helena trailing behind.

Through the open wooden doors, the cafe courtyard was whitewashed and spotless. The bare red earth had been compacted into a hard level surface that was dotted with dark wooden tables and benches. Overhead the proprietor had constructed a makeshift pergola, a lattice work of plastic vine leaves garlanded with strings of fairy lights to provide local colour. It was not, however, a place for locals. The obligatory soundtrack of panpipe music echoed from a battered cassette player on top of the deserted bar. We strolled over to an empty table, grateful for once to be left to ourselves.

Theo spotted him first, a tall darkly featured man of about thirty wearing aviator shades sitting in a corner sipping an espresso. At first glance he seemed to exude the quiet authority of a man used to getting his own way. His profile was handsome. He turned his head in our direction and there was a moment's hesitation. His expression was unreadable and I wondered if he might be a famous actor trying not to draw attention to himself. I lowered my gaze. He uncoiled his long limbs, before standing to remove his sunglasses, and crossed the courtyard with a leisurely stride, making directly for our table with a dazzling smile, his hand outstretched in welcome.

'Forgive me, ladies.' It was a cultured Spanish voice, sonorous, authoritative. He was of the mestizo or misti, the upper social class in the Andes. He wore chinos and a dark blue linen shirt, an alpaca scarf or chalina draped casually around his neck and a matching chuspa, the small ubiquitous woven pouch used to carry supplies of coca leaves.

Helena and I exchanged glances, but Theo was, as ever, quick to size up the situation and held out her hand to grasp his in welcome.

He sat down without waiting for an invitation, leaned forward confidentially and gave us his most winning smile.

'I am delighted to make your acquaintance, my name is Wamani José Fernandez.' He produced business cards which he handed around to each of us as he spoke. 'And I am at your service.'

Theo giggled. 'Well, that's a lovely thought,' she said, winking at the rest of us. 'Is this your café?'

'It belongs to a cousin of mine,' he said as if to suggest that the cousin in question was lucky to be entrusted with such a venture, but that his own interests ran to far more important matters.

'Before we talk business,' he continued, 'I think we should have some drinks.' He called out and within a matter of seconds a stocky figure appeared from the back room behind the bar, bearing a laminated menu.

Our new found compadre gave him short shrift, firing a volley of instructions in Quechua to the poor man who looked nervously over his shoulder and responded meekly. Wamani waved his hand dismissively, called him *cholo*, and the waiter disappeared, red in the face.

'These indio are a stupid, lazy people,' he added as if

for our benefit, though I felt a twinge of embarrassment. 'It is my pleasure to make you welcome in my country.'

My first thought had been that he merely wished to practise his English but his confidence in his surroundings and his command of the language suggested that this was not the case. His gaze alighted on each of us in turn and I felt myself blushing. His eyes were deep brown with large black pupils and the skin around them crinkled into tiny laughter lines when he smiled, which he did, often. He was smiling at me now with undisguised appreciation. It was so totally unexpected that I suddenly wondered if Theo had somehow put him up to it – just to see my reaction. I fumed inwardly before realising how insane that was. She couldn't possibly have known he would be here, and besides, why pass on the opportunity to have him herself? Much taller and lighter skinned that the waiter, more European in his bearing, he was a world apart from the other Quechua speakers we had so far encountered. I felt a knotted warmth in the pit of my stomach and the telltale slip of arousal between my legs.

The waiter reappeared carrying a huge tray with bottled water and maca, nuts, tamales, a bottle of pisco and five glasses.

Wamani ignored the waiter as he placed the tray on the table with hands that quivered slightly. Our host then peeled a single dollar bill from an inch thick wad in his wallet and handed it over to the waiter who kept his head down the whole time, nodding in a way that might have denoted gratitude or embarrassment. It was impossible to tell.

'Please, take a drink with me. That is what you say in your country, isn't it? "Take a drink"?' He poured five shots of clear liquid and held them out.

I tried not to look at Helena, but Theo had already grasped a glass and was sniffing the liquor like a connoisseur.

'Thank you.' Sophie hesitated slightly then smiled politely and held her glass against her chest like a holy relic.

I took a glass and felt his fingers brush against mine. I avoided his eye.

'It's *have* a drink actually,' Helena said, accepting a glass and staring back at him.

He nodded his head to one side and shrugged. 'Of course. You are English. Very precise. A toast.' He raised his glass. 'What shall we drink to?' I had a feeling that this was a rhetorical question, one that he had prepared and delivered many times over with young women from faraway places.

'To Friendship and Life and all that She can throw at us,' said Theo gaily. I scowled at her. That was our mantra – just the four of us. Nobody else.

Wamani's eyes widened. 'Very good,' he said. 'To Friendship and Life and all that She can throw at us.'

We clinked glasses awkwardly. Theo giggled and threw back her head exposing a long neck and pearly teeth. She swallowed and flashed a beautiful smile which had the desired effect. He raised his eyebrows in admiration. Helena sniffed her glass and belted it back, not to be outdone. Sophie sipped her drink tentatively. I took a gulp, felt the fumes hit the back of my throat, scorching my tonsils as I swallowed it down, and started coughing inelegantly, ruining the moment.

Wamani leapt to his feet and stepped around the chairs to kneel beside me. He curved his arm across my back, the other hand holding my shoulder. Theo made little *ahhh* noises like I was a pet lamb. 'Georgie's not used to strong drink,' she said firmly, taking the opportunity of Wamani's change of viewpoint to slowly uncross and re-cross her legs.

'I'm fine,' I said, sounding hoarse like an old man.

'George?' He did a double-take. 'You are called by a man's name?'

I shook my head. 'My full name is Georgina. In English it gets shortened to George or Georgie.'

'Or Gina,' said Sophie helpfully.

He let his hand slide against the small of my back. The sensation was delicious and all the more frightening for being unseen by the others.

'George-gina.' He rolled my name around his mouth. 'You are sure that you are ok now?' he said, and his voice was soft and grave.

'Yes.' I arched myself forward away from his fingers. 'Yes, I'm fine.'

He stood again and returned to his seat.

'Mister Fernandez.' I was grateful that Helena was now assuming control of the conversation. Goodness, how formidable she could be. No wonder she and Sophie's mother clashed so. Her grey-green eyes saw everything. 'Are you from Cuzco originally?'

Wamani's eyes flickered slightly at the formality of her tone. He seemed to give due weight to her question and acquiesced with the ghost of a smile. Of course. She wanted to know if his intentions were honourable.

'This is my birthplace. I have travelled in the States, Europe, Asia, but I always return to *this place*.' He tapped his chest. 'My home. My first love. My country.'

'What do you do when you travel?' Sophie put down her glass and folded her hands in her lap, composing herself as if she were stuck on a long train journey with a tiresome companion and determined to make the best of it.

'I am an adventurer, Señorita. Though some would

say I am nothing but a rogue and a villain.' He winked at her and I was amazed to see Sophie's cheeks colour; she dipped her chin slightly.

Theo leaned in, stretching her perfect legs out in front of her. 'How wonderful,' she breathed, holding out her empty glass and giving it a little shake.

Wamani obligingly refilled her glass and topped up his own. Though I did not fully understand at the time, he was savvy enough not to offer more where it would have been refused. It was psychology of the highest order. Generous and divisive at the same time. He played us all: weighing us up, establishing the hierarchy, isolating the weak link, sensing the fault lines and the handicaps of our class, education and background. He played us like the hustler he was. We knew it, like the casual on-lookers hooked by the antics of a street magician, playing Find the Lady, losing coin after coin, but we were helpless to resist. Quite simply we were no match for him. It was a slow, seductive surrender and we were all equally to blame.

'May I ask you a question?' He seemed to consider carefully his next move. 'You are all friends together. You are perhaps students at one of the universities? Oxford I think, or London?'

'Cambridge actually.' Helena again.

'Ahh. Very beautiful.'

Helena rolled her eyes. 'I don't know if you mean the university or *me*, but I'm afraid I'm definitely not your type.'

'You are a goddess,' he said simply. 'A mountain lion, a beautiful woman. In my culture we admire such women. Such women are not a *type* – they are magnificent!'

'Good Lord,' Helena laughed, but I could see she was not entirely unmoved by the sentiment. 'You have enormous charm, Mister Fernandez,'

'Wamani – please.'

'Very well. *Wamani*. Tell me, is it your habit to buy drinks for all the customers?'

'Only the goddesses,' he smiled.

There was a slight pause. Helena looked nonplussed. Theo let slip a small giggle. I followed suit and before long, Sophie, Theo and I were giggling like half-wits. Helena scowled at the three of us but it was no use. Wamani's mouth curved into a knowing smile as if the point were immaterial, but he must have sensed a kind of victory in that moment. He waited until we had regained our composure.

'This country,' he began, his voice warm and serious. 'This part of the Andes is very special. Cuzco is the heart of my people's traditions. This is a land of magic and mystery.'

Theo raised an eyebrow but something in his tone seemed to reach deep inside me and touch a tiny tingling nerve.

'Many come to study with the wise shamans,' he continued. 'I myself have studied some of the greatest medicine with descendents of the Inca masters.'

'Where?' I asked.

'Here. Cuzco is the centre for curanderos – healers, wise ones who know the secret of San Pedro.' He reached casually into his woven chuspa and pulled out a handful of coca leaves. 'Regular tourists tend to stay in Lima. Of course Lima is a beautiful city, with many wonderful things but it is only when you go about with the people, when you talk and share with the ones who have lived here all their lives,' he looked at each of us in turn, '*then* you start to feel the *soul* of my country; *then* you start to feel *alive*. Please,' he gestured for each of us to take a coca leaf to chew.

Theo looked a little unsure but to my surprise Sophie popped hers straight in her mouth and started to chew. Helena and I did likewise. It tasted like tea leaves. After a couple of minutes my mouth felt a little numb.

'This is a spiritual place,' he said, placing his hand over his heart, his brown eyes searching and humble. 'You understand?'

He disarmed me utterly. There was something undeniably thrilling about this man. He seemed to combine the two essentials most lacking in the English male undergraduate species: machismo and passion.

Wamani grinned at Theo. 'You smoke cigarettes?' he asked. She nodded. He shrugged his shoulders. 'This is better for you. Please – try. You English drink tea for a pick-me-up; here we chew the leaf of the coca plant. It is medicine for the body and soul.'

She took a leaf and started to chew.

For a few minutes we chewed the coca. I felt my edges softening. I looked at Helena who had a slightly glazed look on her face. Then Sophie broke the spell. She smiled warmly at Wamani and helped herself to a glass of maca tea.

'Were you expecting us?' she asked.

'There does seem to be some confusion,' said Helena, although I could see that she too had dropped her guard somewhat.

'I am here to meet you,' he said, hands wide in a gesture of welcome.

'Oh dear,' said Sophie. 'I think we must be talking at cross-purposes. I think you must have us confused with another group entirely.'

Wamani looked at each of us expectantly. 'You are not the *Forrester* party?'

'No, indeed, we should have introduced ourselves properly.' I felt somewhat embarrassed.

'How very strange,' he exclaimed, his smile extending from cheekbone to cheekbone. He raised his eyes heavenward and muttered what looked like a prayer. Then he looked penitent and took us further into his confidence. 'I saw the four of you come in while I was waiting for this group – the Forresters. I arranged to meet them in this very cafe. I wondered where they could possibly be. The cafe directions are very clear. This is a good road. But,' he sighed, 'it happens all the time.'

'What does?' This was quite a performance, but Sophie was always polite to strangers.

'Tourists coming from the United States or from England make a booking and then they do not honour the agreement. I have made arrangements, paid for excursions on their behalf but,' he gestured with his hands, 'it sometimes happens that they do not turn up, and then . . . ' he shrugged his shoulders and left the rest unsaid. 'But now it seems my prayers have been answered. It was my dream that guided you to come here to meet me instead. The money does not matter,' he said and stood up. 'This has been very special for me.'

'Oh no, wait,' said Theo, not about to let this attractive stranger get away in a hurry. 'Whatever do you mean about your dream?'

'San Pedro appeared to me last night.' He put his hands together in a gesture of prayer. 'He showed me four beautiful women, two were golden-haired like the sun, one was dark as the night and the other had fiery red hair and flashing green eyes. These are the Goddesses of my Faith. I have waited all my life to have such a dream. For such a dream I would gladly lose all my money!'

We all looked at each other. Theo and Sophie were fair-haired, I was dark and Helena, a redhead. It was such a blatant come-on that we might have all fallen about laughing, but for the sheer boldness of his approach. Besides which, we were four and he was only one. There was nothing to fear. It was one of those moments where good old-fashioned English common sense flies out of the window. I think it was probably also the case of female hormones clouding intellectual judgement.

'Look, it's awfully decent of you but shouldn't we at least pay for all this?' I indicated the tray in front of us.

'No, it's my pleasure.' He shook his head. 'I will pay at the bar, and I wish you all a good day.'

He had barely gone four steps when Theo spoke up on our behalf.

'Look here, what exactly had you planned for the other party?' she asked.

Helena shot a glance at me then at Theo, but it was too late.

He turned on his heel and shrugged his shoulders.

'They were engaging me for the length of their stay. Interpreter, guide, companion. I have arranged a tour for them to meet a local Shaman – very secret, very magical.'

'Well fancy that,' Theo nudged me with her elbow.

Helena tried to wind up the conversation. 'You've been awfully kind but I think we ought to settle this bill.'

He spread his hands. 'As you wish.' He sat down once more, which I could see was not what Helena had in mind at all.

'The thing is,' Sophie's voice was suddenly very clear and distinct and took all us by surprise. 'What we really need is a reliable guide.'

Theo grinned as Helena bit her tongue.

'I am here to do your bidding,' he said. 'What is the purpose of your visit?'

'We plan to climb Ausangate,' said Sophie.

'Are you serious?' He seemed quite shocked, and

uttered a little laugh. 'Ausangate is the home of the *Apu*. It is the most sacred peak of all. You understand that to climb Ausangate is a sacred pilgrimage? In fact this is the meaning of my name.' He smiled broadly. 'Wa-man-i. It means sacred mountain. Who better than myself to guide you? This is surely Fate!' He slapped his thighs with both hands. 'San Pedro has sent me here to find and protect you. It is not safe to climb the mountain alone. You must prepare. You must ask the spirit of the mountain for permission to climb. Not all are successful. It is dangerous. Many strangers perish because they do not make the right ceremony.'

Sophie's eyes were shining. My own heartbeat had quickened at the mention of the *Apu*. Even Theo was stilled in a moment of quiet reflection. 'Oh Helena,' I prayed silently. 'Please say yes.'

Helena's steadfast gaze was unwavering and she seemed about to speak, but then Sophie put out her hand to gently touch her shoulder. No further persuasion was necessary. We all knew she wouldn't deny Sophie.

'So, it is settled!' Wamani clapped his hands together. 'It is destiny that we should meet here. I know of a delightful hacienda in Chincheros where you can stay. Not expensive. The owner is a cousin of mine. He will make you a very good deal.' We protested feebly at such generosity. 'No, I insist,' he continued. 'There are many bandits around. It will be no trouble, no trouble at all. I will treat you as my own sisters. You will be much more comfortable and safe with me.'

And that is how we met Wamani in the Spring of 1983. I dare say the Forresters never existed. Of course we insisted on paying for the drinks and after an appropriate show of declining, he graciously permitted us to settle the entire bill.

PART II

1

Nearly thirty years later I found myself on the road to Helena's farmhouse in Cambridgeshire. Fenland stretched in every direction. Driving the last five or six miles through flat arable country seemed to spell out the whole truth for any lone visitor to see: here shall ye come and no further.

I wound down the window and breathed in the fresh peaty tang of autumn as if it alone could cleanse my blood of the grey fumes of North London.

Helena cut a tall figure striding along with gun cocked, a brace of pheasant over her shoulder and Ralph, her sleek chocolate Labrador, trotting to heel. Dressed in her customary grey cords and green waxed jacket, with her russet hair and high cheek bones she embodied the very essence of Hesiod's Gaia, steadfast goddess of the Earth. This was her land, passed down through generations of her father's family.

I couldn't imagine keeping sane this far from the city. But Helena's home with Sophie, born of the long acquaintance they shared first as undergraduates, then as lovers, had yielded a warmth and comfort that even now, driving towards the dark, I felt as palpable as a beacon guiding me home.

I slowed the car down to a crawl to keep up with her.

'Good timing,' she said. 'Sophie's taking a bath. God knows why – she's only been here half an hour. Says she needs to get rid of the *stench* of small boys.' Sophie had found her niche teaching mathematics to junior public school boys in King's Lynn.

'No sign of Theo yet?'

'Nope. Phoned to say she'd be a bit late. Traffic must be bad.'

Our weekends together had an established routine: just the four of us, no work, no make-up, no men.

Lots of alcohol, laughter and good food. Some walking, a bit of wildfowl shooting and plenty of hot baths.

In short, it wasn't *lemon*.

***

My induction into Sophie's private language had begun on the occasion of our first meeting during Fresher's Weekend at Clare. The college was in the habit of hosting a Parents' Buffet which I had been silently dreading.

My mother and father were trying not to feel out-classed. The only remedy for their discomfort seemed to be a rehearsal of the domestic mini-opera for three voices that had dominated the household ever since I had received my letter of confirmation.

My mother commenced with the overture, *Why on earth couldn't you have applied to Oxford, it's barely an hour up the M40?* This was succeeded by her aria, *You will promise to eat properly*, swiftly followed by my father's deep baritone, *Don't forget to write to your mother or she'll drive me mad with wondering*. My response to these entreaties and demands usually involved a lot of eye-rolling and caustic whispering. There were other variations of course. But on this particular occasion I could have happily knifed them in the guts.

My father was a self-made man, determined that I should have the opportunities never dreamt of by him or my mother when they were my age. But my grammar school education had not prepared me for mixing with the élite classes of my own generation.

I was eaten up with vicarious embarrassment. Why couldn't I be the progeny of the glamorous couple with ski tans conversing on first name terms with the Master, or the fabled younger sister of one of the Junior Fellows? I didn't really appreciate what it cost my parents either. As far as I was concerned my father was blustering and foolish, my mother simpering and weak. I hated them both in that selfish, vicious, naive way that only children at an immature stage of development can, and I couldn't wait for them to leave and let me make my own way, without them.

I was about to settle for a salmon vol au vent when I observed a slender reed of a girl with a jaw line that could cut through butter, standing by the canapés. She was wearing a knee-length yellow silk dress with a little cashmere cardigan. Her angel hair was tucked neatly behind ears that my mother would have described as 'unfortunate'. This exaggerated her rather pointed features. And yet there was a soft, sad look about her. A female Bambi. No question. I looked around for Bambi's mother, but the girl seemed entirely detached and completely unselfconscious.

She leaned forward and whispered, 'Awful isn't it? Absolutely *lemon.*'

'Is it?' I asked, tentatively, unsure whether I had heard her correctly.

'Frightful. I'm Sophie.'

'Georgina. How do you do.'

'Lovely, thank you. Let's find something *jammy.*'

Sophie's whole world fell neatly into nursery categories of *lemon* and *jam. Lemon* was boring and conventional. *Lemon talk* was small, mediocre or boorish. *Lemon* could be a person as in 'oh he's an absolute *lemon'* or a place, a thing or an action. Helena, same staircase, my fellow student of Classics, and by nature more given to analysis than either of us, sought to introduce degrees of lemon-ness and so our language evolved to include *juicy*, a much used adjective to denote boring, *citrus* for deadly dull and of course *curd* for the most interminable and excruciating circumstances such as luncheon with tutors, phone calls from parents or tea with the Monsignor.

Jam, at the other end of the scale, was tops. *Jammy* covered much of our extra-curricular pursuits and proved a more than satisfactory descriptor until early one morning in Lent term, fagged from dinner and dancing and feeling utterly replete, Sophie declared her night to have been *tarts all round*. Thereafter our vocabulary exploded on the jam front with jam-*fest* meaning holidays, jam-*pot* for someone bohemian and mad but utterly gorgeous and irresistible and jam *sandwich* which only Theo, first violin of our little quartet, ever claimed to have experienced, drawing snorts of derision from Helena (definitely cello). I suppose I thought of myself as second fiddle in those days, and never more so than when the conversation turned to sex and boys.

Cambridge had been pretty jammy for Helena and Sophie (unmistakably flute), but mostly juicy for Theo with her succession of jam-pots who quickly lost their allure and were down-graded to citrus. Age had not withered her in that department.

***

Now, nearly thirty years on, we were middle-aged and although Theo never stopped talking about sex, it was something of a foreign country to me. I had long since given up the very idea of finding either passion or romance, in or out of marriage. The tall, dark lover with

22

good teeth had never materialised. I had long since settled for an older, separated, rakish companion; children had never been an option.

I parked my car on the edge of the road in a passing place, letting the engine idle for a moment or two while Helena caught up.

Ralph got up on his hind legs and poked his head in through the open car window for his regular greeting. I stroked his soft, warm head and tickled his ears.

'Sophie's on chilli duty. I'll be along in a tick.'

Ralph's breath was fogging up the side mirror. 'I have pisco as requested.'

'Weather's set fair for tomorrow.' She grinned broadly. 'I hope you're up for some serious sport. There's a definite drop in greylag this winter so it's every woman for herself.'

'Must be global warming,' I teased.

'My money's on this bloody coalition,' she half-joked. 'Just another EU quota gone up the spout.'

And then before she could really get into her political stride I revved the engine and slid the clutch into first gear.

'See you at the homestead.'

She waved. I drove off, following the road and then making a turn into the last twist of dirt track half a mile up to the farm where lights were already blazing against the darkening sky.

***

Black Farm consisted of an imposing grey flint and stone farmhouse with a huddle of outbuildings to match.

The large, north-facing kitchen was as ever the most welcoming room while the upper floors of the old house with its gables and wainscoting, yawned and creaked like an old lady's corset. Helena's three great uncles had grown beet at Black Farm for fifty years. Helena, an only child, inherited the farm after the last of the male line succumbed to pneumonia.

She was brought up in Hampshire by doting grandparents on her mother's side, never having met her father's extended family until a letter postmarked Ely arrived on her sixteenth birthday. She'd never received a letter like it before. The paper was faded but of a fine grade and smelt of soil and old cupboards. The handwriting was cursive and childlike as if the writer had taken special pains to make a good impression. She thought carefully about her reply. She drafted her response several times in the back of her school rough book before committing herself to the final wording in a note-let printed with a seasonal floral arrangement that she sealed with red wax and an embossed 'H'.

She had no desire to hurt anyone.

Helena rarely spoke of her early childhood but I had gleaned a few facts; orphaned as a baby, privately educated, she had received the benefits of an ample, comfortable, middle class life. She was truly grateful. But curiosity about her father's relations grew and grew. It was as if she had suddenly found a way into the forest and couldn't resist embarking on a quest of her own. She announced one breakfast her intention to catch a train to go and visit her remaining two uncles. Telephone calls ensued and a plan was made. Helena duly travelled up to London where she met her cousin Christian who was to escort her on the tube as far as King's Cross.

Helena described that onward journey as the most important of her life. 'It was an epic venture,' she confided one night to me as we strolled back to Memorial after dinner.

She had no idea of what her great uncles would look like, or how to recognise them. In her imagination they were knights of the Round Table and she was

Guinivere, ready to escape into a new world of adventure. When she dismounted from the train she looked excitedly up and down the platform. When the station had all but cleared she saw two lean stooping men in their sixties standing against the wall sporting newly cut thick white hair and worn shoes polished brightly. They smelled of *Old Spice* and mothballs. Their suits, though clean and freshly pressed were about two inches too short in the leg and their ties were of a lurid 1950's style print. They had the same piercing blue eyes and when they spotted Helena they smiled shyly like schoolboys on a first date.

That was the beginning of her adult life. She returned to Winchester in time for the new school term but from then on the majority of her holidays were spent at Black Farm. She cast off stockings and skirts and put on jumpers and jeans. Her great uncles bought her a set of overalls which were always neatly washed and folded ready for her return. She learned to plough and sow seed, to harvest and lay up stores. She slept in her father's old room, still filled with his toys and books. Like him she excelled in Latin and come the day her housemistress quizzed her on her plans for the future, Helena declared her desire to follow her father's example and go up to Cambridge.

There was something deeply rooted about Helena. I put it down to her farming background. Being close to the earth. Having a pragmatic philosophy about life and death. I thought it part and parcel of her seasonal routine on the farm. Cycles of growth and natural decay. It seemed a good foundation for someone attuned to the Classical mind. She was always the most stable and reliable of our company. Helena didn't get flustered or agitated when things weren't right. It seemed to me that she was truly stoic in temperament. It wasn't that she didn't feel deeply, simply that she understood how a surfeit of passion might render a person vulnerable, and idiotic things might result. If something was difficult she just worked harder at it, embodying her old school motto *Per Aspera ad Astra*. If ever she felt pain or disquiet, she kept it well hidden. At times it felt like she was in locum parentis. Theo was by far the more experienced but carnal knowledge is no substitute for maturity though at eighteen they can seem to be one and the same thing. Helena never seemed to suffer from self-doubt whereas I was riddled with angst of an unspecified but tenacious variety. But of all of us it was Sophie who touched Helena's heart the deepest.

Sophie was sitting in pyjamas, her bed socks warming on the rail of the battered enamel range. She was curling a strand of still-golden hair around her finger and gave a sudden jump when she spied me coming into the kitchen.

'Georgie!' She threw her arms around me and kissed me on the cheek. Her smile was tender and sad as she stroked my arm.

'What a lemon, eh?' I smiled back at her but she wasn't fooled for a moment. She pulled me into an even tighter embrace and held me as if I would sink to the floor.

'You'll make me cry,' I sniffed against her shoulder. She rocked me gently then gave a little snuffle and slipped her hands into mine.

'Better off without him. Look at me and H, happy as a couple of larks! I tell you Georgie, forget men – find yourself a Yummy-Mummy instead.'

Still so girlish, I thought. Sophie never seemed to get any older and her sunny outlook couldn't be overshadowed. Loving was Sophie's great gift to the world. Yet it rankled sometimes just how much Helena had protected her over the years. I chided myself for being jealous when I knew perfectly well that their relationship had cost Sophie dearly. In her family's eyes she had forsaken God, so they in turn had forsaken her.

'Let's make chocolate with marshmallows. You saw H on your way up? Here, you must be done in. Ooo lovely, pisco! Is that from the same little chap in Clerkenwell? Have a brandy. Do you think Ralph's looking a bit fat?'

She chatted away, busying herself with a pan of milk whilst I let the brandy do its work. A pleasant warmth gently seeped through my limbs and my mind settled itself in recollection of better times. Balmy evenings spent on the Cam. Helena demanding the death of Clytemnestra. Sophie and Theo making impassioned pleas for clemency. Myself caught up in the question of Agamemnon's guilt.

Did the Gods look down upon us with stony-faced indifference even then?

***

I was glad Theo was late. I wasn't ready for the onslaught of questions regarding my famously moribund career. It didn't matter, of course, in terms of the day job. Publishing was riding high on the new wave of Scandinavian crime fiction. Editing manuscripts in translation was a blessing compared to fielding chick-lit offerings. Then out of the blue two poems from one of my early collections had been selected for a new anthology. Suddenly there were rumours of an imminent comeback. There was every danger that a Sunday supplement might start taking an interest. Daniel had wanted to celebrate with champagne and sex. He just seemed a teeny bit too pleased and surprised and when pushed, he admitted to having called in a few favours. There was no harm in asking for a bit of help. Writer's block affected just about everyone. All I needed just now was a bit of a push, a couple of interviews. He'd line someone up for me, find me a new agent. I had instead hit the roof and told him to fuck off back to his wife.

The flat suddenly seemed unbearably empty, the silence mocking me as if to say, well I hope you're satisfied. I soldiered on steadfastly for a couple of weeks, refusing to call or text him. The trouble was I missed the silly bugger like hell. But I didn't want to be forever on the reserve list, wheeled out whenever a sub-editor wanted to run a 'whatever happened to?' feature because they were a bit short of real scandal. What exactly was the statute of limitations for 'promising'? At what point could it safely be assumed that whatever promise had been spotted in a 'rising talent' was not going to actually manifest? That my potential had indeed left the building? Remedy to feeling like a complete failure: Girls' Weekend. No work, no make-up, no men. At the first whiff of success I had, as usual, run away.

The back door opened suddenly and Helena and Ralph breezed in trailing mud. The smell of wet dog in a warm kitchen arrested me. Sophie pounced on him with a large, mud-stained towel and rubbed his fur briskly, uttering little affectionate noises that Ralph clearly recognised whilst Helena deposited her firearm in the gun cupboard under the stairs and slumped in an arm chair to take off her boots.

'Righty-ho, I'm off for a hot bath. Sophe – give the chilli a stir will you? She's been making corn bread and tamales too, for tomorrow. I'll take a brandy up.'

It was about an hour later that we heard the sound of an engine. We made our way to the front of the house, Helena still towel-drying her cropped red curls. As the beam of headlights swept into the driveway

Helena pulled open the front door whilst Sophie and I peered out into the semi-darkness from behind the curtains in the front room.

'Oh Lord,' Helena muttered under her breath.

'Who on earth is that?' hissed Sophie.

A stranger had hauled himself out of the front passenger seat and was taking in his surroundings. He looked up at the house, hands in pockets, stifling a yawn, his breath forming a small cloud of vapour. Theo was foraging in the backseat of her husband's Volvo estate, talking to herself. Douglas must be away on business. He'd never normally let Theo drive The Beast unsupervised. She emerged at last, up-do in disarray, laden with three Merlots, a bottle of Courvoisier and a guilty smile. She must have driven straight from work judging by the high heels and tight red woollen twinset.

He was medium height, stocky, mid thirties, wearing the uniform of journalists and redbrick academics: black drainpipe jeans and jacket, creased white, open-neck shirt, grey scarf, lozenge-shaped black-rimmed glasses and two-day-old stubble. He had a worn leather satchel slung across his shoulder and that stooping gait associated with lugging too many books around campus. Not a journo then. I tried to picture him in his natural habitat, leading seminars on Visual Culture at a former polytechnic. Saturday afternoons of his youth spent flogging the Socialist Worker outside Camden tube station. He seemed more physical than meta-physical, his shaven head no doubt intended to suggest a rogue-ish sexuality. I suspected a latent rage that could only find expression through juggernaut sex. In my line of work I frequently came across academic defectors seeking to migrate across the border into fiction, each one convinced of their outsized talent, each one chafing against the bonds of political correctness. The thugs of

Postmodernism. Voluble, bullish, ready to sell their firstborn for tenure. Unrecognisable to the working class generation of unemployed, disaffected miners and dockers who had begot them. They were a breed apart. Classless and rootless, they nonetheless channelled an aggressive masculinity – a sense of entitlement – which would have been better discharged on the football terraces than in the lecture halls of middle England.

Theo, public relations agent to half of London's television and theatre producers, had a knack for seduction and a penchant for articulate, angry, younger men. 'Posh totty', she whispered breathless and pink to me one night as we jostled our way out of the Union after a particularly brutal pasting, she in pursuit of the shaggy-haired interlocutor who had so brazenly asserted Lawrence's right to 'fuck middle-class mores'.

'The foot soldier of the Great Class Struggle can't resist the idea of unbuttoning a nymph of the Bourgeoisie,' she giggled adding, 'Here, be a darling,' thrusting her coat, bag and gloves at me then applying a little gloss to her lips, sashaying purposefully after her intended for the night, turning to bequeath me a superior smile and a dirty wink. I dutifully returned to college, and wondered, not for the first time, whether I would ever drop my drawers.

I didn't realise it at the time but Theo was that exceptionally rare creature, a woman unafraid of men. Witty, arch, funny, she genuinely liked men and they seemed to adore her. The ancient Greeks had four different types of love and although Theo clearly was adept at all manner of erotic love, it was in the sense of philia or philos that she truly excelled. She felt a kinship with men, a complete equanimity in their company that I could never muster. This was a trait that put her at a considerable advantage later in life but at that time, the early 1980s, it wasn't deemed cool to be so sexually adventurous.

Theo didn't care. She walked into Boots as cool as you like to buy condoms over the counter. She looked after herself. She kissed but she never told. Many had good cause to be grateful to her. She had an eye for potential. She could turn a fumbling, hesitant, gangly youth into a sex god over the course of a weekend. She didn't date men as such, never looking to hitch herself to anyone in particular. She didn't cut up rough when a chap decided it was time to settle down with the right sort of girl. In fact she regarded such a move as proof of her success, like a sort of erotic Mary Poppins, and moved on to the next. She was generous too. She enjoyed sex and felt no shame in it. She was breezy and good-humoured. Had she lived three hundred years earlier she might have been a courtesan of great fame. Of course the feminists of our cohort despised her twice over. She made sex a part of her life in the same way others included orange juice or a high fibre diet. To her, sexual appetite was an indicator of health and well-being. Good sex was akin to aerobics and much more fun. It provided excellent cardio-vascular exercise and made the eyes bright and the skin glow. She never got attached because she knew that her own happiness did not depend on any other human being. The secret of her success was that she never gave her power away and had the feminist contingent been less obsessed with denigrating the opposite sex, and condemning her by extension for sleeping with the enemy, she could have been a remarkable role model. She was unfazed by the slanders routinely made against her by members of the moral majority, the sporty girls who despised her beauty, the blue stockings intent on establishing their intellectual superiority, the debutantes with standards of etiquette to maintain, the politicos for whom sex was enslavement, and the sanctimonious God squads terrified of her corrupting influence.

She won them over in the end. As the final Trinity term loomed a trickle of maidens started to flow through Theo's rooms seeking advice on how to give and receive sexual gratification. It wasn't necessary to be a virgin after all. The rules had changed and the same chap-lipped Anti-Nazi League, Socialist Workers' Party feminist conspirators who had shunned her, were now in awe of her considerable experience of the male undergraduate population, and eager to make amends. The May ball might be the last opportunity to do the deed and if well accomplished, might even secure an engagement before going down for good. Ha-ha.

Above all, Theo was the friend to whom I played second fiddle, so it fell to me to cover her indiscretions, mollify her latest conquest if it became apparent that she had no further use or interest, and to testify to her sobriety and conscientious scholarship. But that was then, and this was now. Everything changed after Peru. Nothing was the same after Ausangate.

'Just so long as he doesn't smoke,' I said as Sophie pulled a face.

'Well I'm not dressing,' she said bluntly. 'It's just too bad. He'll have to suffer me in PJ's and have done with it.'

'Hellooo!' Theo tottered forward on too-high strappy sandals like an overweight gazelle. I was amazed to see her looking a little bit haggard. Generally she had flawless skin with the rosy glow associated with screen sirens and television advertising. The secret of her youthful complexion was doubtless the result of artful surgery but clearly she'd not had any work done for a little while. Poor Theo. Was age catching up with her at last? She winked at me. Was this her idea of a joke? Norma Desmond and her thrusting young stud? This was not the weekend I had had in mind.

'This, my Darlings, is Matthew Boyd. Mattie, these are my special friends that I have been telling you about, Helena Copeland, Sophie Thompson-Moore and Georgina Marsh.'

Theo's new talent nodded, shaking each of us by the hand in turn. His grip was firm and dry.

'That's quite a welcome,' he grinned lasciviously, taking in Sophie's pajamas. She coloured instantly.

Helena ushered them down the hallway towards the kitchen. 'Well, this is a surprise. Matthew – welcome. Sophe – a bottle of the good stuff if you please. George, nice glasses on the top shelf.'

***

We ate quietly, our coded response to Theo's transgression. She, however, was not in the least bit repentant and kept up a steady flow of anecdotes including the indiscretions of an A-lister known for the sanctity of her marriage and the latest instalment of a bitter rivalry between two ageing queens that could only lead to carnage at the BAFTAs. I bit my tongue. Over cheese, as if saving the best till last, she expanded upon Boyd's prowess in the field of intellectual endeavour. He was, she declared, a Marvellous Find, quite wasted on students. His grasp of post-Marxist deconstruction-thingy was without parallel. According to Theo, he was going to rock the ratings. Forget all that star gazing with Cox the boy wonder, here was a real man to wet the gusset. Real-politick for the modern woman.

'Goodness, what a juicy idea,' smirked Sophie.

I kicked her under the table. Helena considered her empty glass for a moment. I looked at Boyd but his face remained calm as if he had heard it all before. I wondered then whether he fully believed Theo's hyperbole, or whether this was all just a bit of a game to him. He looked at me and I half expected him to raise an eyebrow as if to share the joke or to make some self-deprecating gesture, but he didn't. And then I realised that whatever Theo thought of his potential was nothing compared to his own self evaluation. It was etched on his face. *You'd better believe it.* When finally called upon by his mentor to say something witty and arresting, he dabbed his lips with his napkin and made some cursory remarks about Gramsci's attitude to women. It was all rather over my head, but Theo kept up a good show of interest with doe-like eyes and judicious nodding between sips until it suddenly dawned on me that she really was in earnest. As our guest got into his revolutionary stride I felt all my usual disdain for her sexual antics drain away. She seemed completely smitten. By coffee I was ready to sign over all my worldly goods to the proletariat just to shut him up but the combination of brandy and red wine had the desired effect. Like warm syrup trickling through the veins it calmed and revived us in equal measure.

Theo beamed at Boyd and gave him a lascivious wink. He seemed strangely detached. I wondered if they'd had sex yet. Something told me *not yet.* I hoped to God that this was not going to be the venue. I glanced across at Helena, but she didn't look up.

'I hear you girls were all at Cambridge together.' Boyd reached into his breast pocket for cigarettes. 'Sophocles and out-door pursuits,' he mused. 'Seems an unlikely combination.'

'The Greeks invented the Olympics,' said Helena. 'And this is a non-smoking kitchen,' she added.

'Where did you study?' asked Sophie, politely

steering him away from a potential argument.

'Leeds for my first degree.' He left the cigarettes on the table as if to suggest that Helena had not had the last word on the subject. She bristled.

'Really?' Sophie persevered. 'What was your subject?'

'Art History.'

'Ah.' Sophie put on her 'pleasantly surprised' face that was usually reserved for parents' evening.

Helena did her best to conceal a smirk and passed me the wine bottle. In our day Art History was for pretentious thickos who could neither sculpt nor paint, nor subject themselves to the rigours of a Classical Tripos. But nowadays it was all the rage. Ever since it had become the choice of young, handsome Royalty.

'Then film school of course.' He took possession of a wine bottle and emptied the last of the contents into his glass without offering it round.

'Of course,' Sophie nodded with a pleasant smile designed to pacify.

Theo picked up the conversational baton and tried to run with it.

'Matthew's quite the innovator. He's won all sorts of prizes for his new film style,' she gushed.

'It's not a style, sweetheart,' he said, his tone suggesting that this was a perennial mistake made by mere earthlings.

'No? Well, whatever,' she said making a laughing noise that somehow turned into a piggy snort.

He fixed his gaze on me as if I alone were capable of understanding though I hadn't given him the slightest encouragement, and frankly couldn't have cared less.

'Style is a bourgeois concept,' he began. 'Superficial, vain, elitist, totally immoral. The great documentary film-makers of the twentieth century saw the lens as a scalpel: incising, revealing, paring back the skin of society to reveal the truth. But,' he sat back and spread his hands in a gesture of seemingly open enquiry. 'What is truth?'

Theo's eyes widened as if to say *I told you he was really interesting.* I rolled my eyes.

'Doesn't that rather depend on your philosophical perspective?' I ventured.

'Exactly my point!' He suddenly snapped forward in his seat jabbing his finger in a manner that made Sophie flinch and caused Helena to draw in her chin.

'Philosophy has failed. Politics has no moral centre. Look at the internet. Let's face it, with modern technology, reality becomes whatever you want it to be. I could film this very conversation and re-present it in any number of ways using digital technology. Reality is whatever I choose to make real. Truth,' – he looked round triumphantly – 'is dead.' He took a great swig of wine.

Theo's jaw had fallen slightly open.

'Now take religion,' he continued.

'Oh God,' Helena sighed under her breath.

He ignored her. 'If God is real then He must be the source of all truth. But if truth is dead, then God is redundant. After all, what's the point of a God that deals in relativities? Suddenly there's no such thing as right or wrong. You'd have to start dealing in half-measures and percentages. At the very least He's *im*potent rather than *omni*-potent.' He laughed at his own little joke, picked up another bottle and helped himself to more wine.

I cast a sly glance at Sophie who continued to listen politely. How could she bear the insufferable ape? Still, she must have to endure all kinds of stupidity in her line of work. Teaching must make you infinitely patient.

'Actually,' she cleared her throat. 'The Catholic Church has always been rather good at quantifying sin.

The half-measures you speak of wouldn't phase a parish priest. How much for a white lie to your mother? Two hail Marys. And of course there is a great deal of difference between mortal and cardinal sins.'

Boyd smiled indulgently.

'Which is bloody ridiculous,' he said swinging his wine glass in her face for added emphasis, 'if you think about it: repeat these words and bingo – you're saved! There will always be room for the Absurd of course. The vast majority of people in the world can't live without it – whether it's the notion of absolution or *Strictly Come Dancing*. Millions of people trying to find the meaning of life, and settling for game shows and sequinned romance instead. We each of us choose the manner of our own enslavement. Mankind has always enjoyed a great capacity for fantasy. '

'You think God is just fantasy – a mass delusion?' Theo was catching on at last.

'Of course. If God really existed he'd have made his presence known to all of us by now. He'd have his own chat show for one thing. I take it you're a good little Catholic girl.' Boyd tipped his glass in Sophie's direction.

Helena shifted in her chair.

'I was brought up a Catholic,' Sophie said.

'That sounds evasive.' He cocked his head to one side. 'Lapsed then I take it?'

Sophie poured herself a drink.

'Then you'll know exactly what I mean,' he continued. 'All lapsed Catholics share the same dirty little secret.'

We all looked at him sharply. When Sophie refused to take the bait he laughed. 'He let you down didn't He?'

There was a weight to those words that Boyd himself didn't even recognise. There was a shift of mood, almost like a drop in temperature as if one minute we had been sitting in sunshine and now a grey cloud had passed in front.

'Yes,' she said simply. 'I suppose He did.' Sophie contemplated the glass in front of her. 'But I still believe there is a higher power beyond our everyday experience, forces that operate whether we believe in them or not,' she said.

Theo looked uncomfortable. I wasn't surprised. She'd obviously been spilling the beans to her young prodigy and I wasn't going to let her get away with it. Helena's expression was much more difficult to fathom. She seemed exasperated, but with whom I couldn't tell.

'And as for confession,' she carried on, 'it might seem absurd to you but, well – in my experience absolution doesn't come easily. You have to feel contrition. The words must have meaning. That's the difference. Without true feeling a person can never become fully aware. Nor can they be forgiven.'

There was something in her tone that seemed to give Boyd a moment's pause.

'Ah. I suppose that's courtesy of the famous Female Intuition. Highly subjective. A bit too' – he groped for an appropriate put-down – 'touchy-feely for me.'

Sophie carried on, though I could see she was struggling to maintain her composure. 'It's your digital technologies that make the world subjective – everyone cocooned in their own little universe, plugged into iPods, devoid of any real empathy, any true connection to others around them,' she said with feeling.

I looked at Helena but she kept her eyes fixed on Boyd with a blank expression.

'Well, I suppose that's all very politically correct,' he answered, taking another slug of wine before sliding the empty glass towards Theo for a re-fill. 'But if there *is* a God and the only way to discover him is by navel-gazing, why doesn't He make it easier for us? Come out from the closet? No – I'm afraid any notion of an existence beyond what we can see and grasp in this world makes no sense to me.'

'There are more things Horatio than are dreamt of in your philosophy,' I murmured.

'Perhaps,' Boyd shrugged. 'But Hamlet didn't sleep well, did he? I, on the other hand, sleep like a log.' He winked at me. 'Especially in the arms of a beautiful woman.' I stared at him, then turned my head slowly to glare at Theo. If Theo hadn't already slept with him, surely she wasn't pimping on my behalf? Her cheeks flushed a little.

'I think,' Sophie said slowly, 'that if I were a deity, I'd wake up every day hoping against hope that humanity might find me. Perhaps it's not God's fault. Maybe it's us. Maybe we're looking in all the wrong places.'

'Or not looking at all,' Helena said, catching my eye.

I took a sip of wine and waded in.

'So, you think that the truth is just what we make it – reality is totally subjective? *You* don't believe in the Divine so humanity must have made Him up. It sounds to me like you have a very tightly woven, utterly subjective universe wrapped around you. Isn't it more likely that you are simply living in denial?'

He grinned at me and shook his head.

I followed up my temporary advantage. 'People who go around trying to persuade others to their point of view are usually running away from something aren't they? Perhaps you're afraid deep down that one day you'll wake up to find God speaking directly to you? Aren't you just terrified that He exists and that's why you go to all the trouble of trying to prove otherwise? Suppose He suddenly manifested right now, and asked you what the devil do you think you're playing at?'

There was a fractional intake of breath. Theo laughed loudly. 'Goodness, how serious everyone is tonight!'

She tapped her wineglass with a perfectly manicured finger and changed tack.

'I was an English student. Sophie read Maths. Georgie and Helena did Classics together. I remember there was a production of *The Oresteia*, I think it was. I was quite the drama queen in those days – '

'You still are, but we love you anyway,' said Sophie.

'Wasn't that Angelica what's-her-name's big moment?' asked Helena.

'No, you're thinking of Babushka.'

'Who?'

'You know, the one who thought she was Kate Bush with all the hair? I'm sure she played Iphegenia.'

As they reminisced Boyd turned his head towards me and his eyes were sharp. 'And you were a wordsmith of great promise, I hear.' I tried to ignore his use of the past tense and fought an impulse to look away. Mistaking my silence for acquiescence, he expanded on his theme.

'Skiing is more my bag. I always find it easier to think clearly above the tree line. I would have thought being on top of a mountain – the Alps or the Andes for instance - would inspire you to write all kinds of stuff.'

I stared at him. The Andes – what the hell? I wondered then if he realised how much he was turning the knife. Peru was not up for discussion. Not with any of us.

And certainly not with a complete stranger. Theo had been careless. Pillow talk no doubt. I made a mental note to have it out with her later.

'Not much opportunity for mountaineering round here though, is there?' he added lightly. I shot him a look. Blast Theo. Damn and blast her.

'She married an investment banker and then took him for everything he had when she found him shagging the au pair across the ironing board,' said Theo.

'Golly, the things you know about people!' Sophie poured some more wine. 'Do you know something, I don't miss it at all, not one little bit, being in the thick of it so to speak. I mean, it's fun to hear the odd smidgeon of gossip every now and again but other people's lives are so tawdry when you get up close.'

'That's just the way Theo tells it,' I said, savouring this small opportunity to put her in her place. 'There's always the other version to consider.'

'Like what?'

'Let's suppose for a moment that Mrs Investment Banker is performing a noble deed. Her husband has become so outrageously self important and got away with all manner of criminal negligence, salted away a vast fortune from bonuses and share dealings – '

Boyd let out a snort. 'Good luck to him!'

' – then,' I glared at him. 'The final insult! He seduces the au pair, a beautiful, innocent girl far away from her home and family. He taunts his wife. His overweening belief in himself has reached its zenith. His wife rises up like Athena and smites him down like a sacrificial bull.'

'In Islington?'

'I'm just saying that sometimes things aren't as they appear.'

'Nobility in violence,' said Helena.

'Dulce et decorum est pro Domina mori,' I sniggered.

'Audaces fortuna iuvat,' she declared solemnly, and seeing Boyd's blank face added, 'Fortune favours the Brave.'

'Amen.'

'Well I just think that it's better not to know sometimes,' said Sophie. And then without missing a beat, 'We get along just fine down here on the farm. Do you know the Fens at all, Matthew? It's a far cry from London, but we like it.'

Helena squeezed her hand and stood up to fetch another bottle of pisco.

Theo finished her wine and refilled the glass. 'Matt, why don't you tell them about your new project?' He opened his mouth but Theo continued, 'Matt's book as a drama-doc. Or a documentary-drama. I never really know the difference.'

'How about a docu-soap?' I chimed in.

'Or a game show,' said Helena.

'I'll name that revolution in four,' I quipped.

'It's going to be utterly compelling,' Theo finished, glaring at me.

'How thrilling,' said Sophie. 'What's it about?'

'Trotsky's life in London. Looks like the BBC might pick it up.'

'How lovely,' Sophie beamed at him. 'Wasn't he the one who was put on a sealed train?'

'You're thinking of Lenin,' said Helena, bottle in hand. 'Trotsky got an ice-pick in the neck.'

'I think you'll find it was an ice axe,' I said quietly.

'Ice pick, axe – whatever. He's already caught the eye of a couple of commissioning editors.' Theo leaned towards him and rubbed his arm in a way that seemed to denote ownership. He, however, seemed unmoved.

'Most people are fascinated by the Mexico years though, aren't they?' I said. I imagined some hard-pressed BBC accountant putting a red line through Boyd's original treatment. From palm trees to Clerkenwell in a single stroke.

'That's been done to death,' he said, 'if you pardon the pun. What most people don't realise is that Lenin established a revolutionary Russia right in the heart of

St Pancras and Bloomsbury, long before the October Revolution. Of course the buildings are still there – the Sidmouth Street flat used by Martov, even Holford Square. But nowadays these areas are upmarket, bourgeois. In Trotsky's day they were filled with shabby boarding houses, underground print works and gambling dens.'

Theo gave us a conspiratorial wink.

'Mattie's been living a double life in the East End consorting with all manner of n'er do wells. All in the interests of authenticity – isn't that right?' She clasped her hands together and wriggled her hips in her seat.

Boyd shrugged his shoulders in a gesture that seemed to mock Theo whilst at the same time avowing the truth of her assertions. What a prick.

'That must be quite dangerous,' said Sophie.

'I think you have to get your hands dirty if you're going to really bring a story to life,' he said.

'Like method acting? You re-live the life of a Marxist revolutionary by hanging out in seedy bars, secretly filming conversations?' I asked, trying to keep a straight face.

'Something like that.'

Helena stuck out her bottom lip. 'Nice work if you can get it,' she drawled.

'You must be sure and tell us when it's going to be broadcast,' said Sophie pleasantly.

'You don't have a television Sophe,' I laughed.

'Oh.' she thought for a minute. 'I'm sure someone at school could tape it for us and then perhaps we could watch it at yours sometime?'

I shook my head at her with a smile. 'The whole digital revolution has just passed you by, hasn't it?' It was quite beyond me just how nice Sophie could be. Even to arseholes like Boyd.

'As for the BBC, nothing's settled,' he said smugly. Then he looked at me squarely. 'I want to keep my options open.' He lit a cigarette and let the words hang in the air. Helena coughed. Sophie frowned slightly.

'You don't think working with a bourgeois public service broadcaster might compromise your integrity?' I said.

He curled his lip. 'It's the message that counts. Sometimes you have to shake hands with the devil to get what you want, as I'm sure you ladies' – he winked at me – 'are well aware.'

Helena's jaw tightened. I cast a glance at Theo who was already up on her feet wrapping her arms around Boyd's shoulders from behind. It was only then that we realised how far gone she really was.

'A toast,' she slurred. 'To all of us. To Friendship, to Life and all that She can throw at us.'

'To Friendship, to Life and all that She can throw at us,' we echoed.

'Let's have some music,' she drawled. 'I'm in the mood for something smoochie and decadent.' Sophie and Helena started to clear the table.

'I'd prefer it if you smoked outside,' said Helena.

Boyd shrugged his shoulders and stubbed out his cigarette on an empty saucer. Helena gave me her *are you all right?* look and I nodded almost imperceptibly. He stood up and let Theo drape herself around him.

'Okay Princess,' he grinned, 'let's see what we can find.' Theo giggled as he slapped her bottom and hoisted her against him. He pushed his thigh between her legs and lifted her so that her shoes barely touched the ground and walked her like a drunken marionette down the corridor to the sitting room. Theo was cackling with delight.

'What the hell was that all about?' Helena put her

arm around Sophie.

'Why has she brought him here? Not exactly a jam-pot, is he? Gives me the creeps,' said Sophie.

'She's plastered,' said Helena.

'He's not,' I said curtly. 'He knows exactly what he's doing.'

'He was making a play for you,' said Helena thoughtfully.

'I can't imagine why. He's got her eating out of his hand. Who needs a publisher when you've got a publicist?' The strains of a Frank Sinatra number were coming from the sitting room. 'Do you think she's ok?'

'Nothing a strong coffee won't fix.'

There were whoops of girlish laughter now and the rumble of a male voice crooning along to *Strangers in the Night.*

'Poor Georgie, this isn't what we had in mind at all, is it H? I think the sooner they crash out the better.' Sophie poured hot water into a large caffetiere.

'Coffee first,' said Helena, making her way down the corridor with a tray of cups. 'Stiffen up the sinews and all that.'

'In a minute,' I said slowly. The first little worm of fear had started to uncoil in the pit of my stomach. There was something about Matthew Boyd that didn't seem quite right to me. I didn't trust him. I certainly didn't like him and it was clear to me that he knew it.

***

Theo seemed to have fallen asleep on her feet. Boyd continued to shuffle round the sitting room like a window dresser with last season's mannequin. Helena tapped him on the shoulder and offered to help relieve him of his burden, whereupon Theo came to, snapped her head up and pleaded for another round of *I Did It My Way.* Boyd managed to prise her fingers from around his neck and she fell back onto the sofa. He dropped down beside her and leaned forward to take off her shoes so as to avoid her feeble attempts to pull him into an embrace.

'For God's sake leave the poor man alone,' said Helena. Sophie poured coffee. I helped myself to a cup and settled in a low armchair. The room smelt pleasantly of wood smoke and bees wax. I don't believe the rooms had changed much since Helena inherited the house. Furnished with dark brown oak and the odd bit of utility furniture, gilt-framed watercolours of farming and hunting scenes, scuffed chesterfield sofas and wing back chairs, it had the feel of a gentlemen's club in urgent need of restoration. Table lamps and a couple of fraying kilims softened the overall feel but there was no hiding the fact that neither Helena nor Sophie paid any heed to the popular obsession with design interiors. Indeed, television was considered a bore. The sideboard still housed a gramophone. Helena had inherited her uncles' collection of 78's. Some evenings we were treated to Soviet recordings of Tchaikovsky or Bartok that made the beams vibrate.

Helena loved to experience music out loud. She couldn't understand the modern compulsion for headsets and earphones. Music should be a shared, almost physical bond between people. She once had us listen to the entire *Ring Cycle* in one day. Theo kept disappearing upstairs, complaining of a weak bladder. Sophie made sandwiches and flasks of coffee to keep us going. But I was rapt. Something shifted in my relationship with Helena that was not evident at the time, but it marked a change of mood between us. Henceforth, I found myself resonating on a different frequency as it were. Theo was still, nominally at least, my best friend. But with Helena I felt a deeper kinship born of our mutual feeling for the music. It carried with it a sense of purpose. But what that purpose was, we couldn't tell. Not until much later.

The alcoves on either side of the inglenook were lined with bookcases crammed with cheap paperback crime thrillers, farming memoirs and cricketing almanacs. Helena adored Agatha Christie and Dick Francis. As a crime fiction connoisseur with a gun cupboard, an array of farming implements and a disregard for all things politically-correct we often joked that she had all the credentials to carry off a jolly good murder, not to mention plenty of land for safe disposal of the body parts. *Wouldn't that make me a prime suspect?* she would reply with a raised eyebrow. Ah, the double-bluff. It can't possibly be Farmer Copeland, Your Honour, because she *is* the most likely suspect.

Piles of *The Field* and *Country Life* spilled from the low walnut coffee table onto the floor. Ralph had taken up his position on the ottoman next to Sophie so that she could feed him titbits. Helena didn't approve but it was an age old argument between them that was usually settled by Ralph decamping to the kitchen like a sulky teenager. Dogs are sensitive. They can't stand to hear the parents argue.

'Do you think she's all right?' Sophie said to nobody in particular.

'She'll pass out in a minute,' said Helena, adding 'with any luck,' under her breath. We sat in companionable silence sipping coffee as Theo drooped. Boyd wedged a cushion behind her head and shortly after, to the relief of all, she began to utter little snores. I regarded our sleeping beauty.

'Do you remember her wedding?' I said.

'Which one?'

Theo had married the same man twice. Douglas was nothing if not persistent. His first courtship had been romantic and swift, resulting in a bohemian rush to the registry office and the birth of twins seven months later. Two years after the inevitable divorce, he had wooed her back with the promise of an open relationship so long as the boys could remain blissfully unaware of their mother's 'needs'. Theo had been as good as her word ever since.

'The second one, at that ghastly hotel in Maida Vale.' On the occasion of Theo's second wedding I had made the acquaintance of the man who would turn out to be the great love of my life. The only problem being that he was already somebody else's.

'Ooo, with the pianist in the gold lame suit.'

'And that funny man with the splangly waistcoat who you thought was her father – '

' – but was actually the master of ceremonies for somebody else's reception.'

Sophie giggled. 'Whatever made you think of that?'

'She just looked so happy then and I was so jealous.'

'You never wanted to get married,' said Helena.

'I might have done.'

'You told us you never ever wanted to get tied down, that marriage was legalised prostitution,' laughed Sophie.

'That sounds like the kind of thing I would say.'

'Well then.'

Theo shifted position in her sleep, pressing her rump against Boyd's flank, her knees tucked up under her chin. He gave her bottom a playful spank and let his arm rest on her hip as he sipped his drink. Ralph lifted his head and looked at Boyd then Helena as if to say, *I'll bite him for you if you like.*

'Do you think she can hear us?' I said.

'They say it's the last sense to go.'

'That's when you're dying, Sophe.'

She blushed a little. I bit my tongue.

I think we were all thinking the same thought when Helena turned her attention to our guest and said, 'I must admit we weren't expecting two of you. Theo's bed is a single, I'm afraid. I can make up another guest room in a tick.'

Boyd smiled. 'I'll be fine with the sofa once her ladyship has gone up. But does anyone have a charger for my mobile? It died rather suddenly just after Theo picked me up.'

'It's no trouble.'

I exchanged glances with Helena as she headed for the stairs. Perhaps he and Theo weren't an item after all. And if he wasn't here for a dirty weekend, why on earth was he?

'Are you both staying tomorrow for the shoot?' asked Sophie, stifling a yawn.

Boyd looked non-plussed. 'Have you done any shooting before?' I asked. 'Wild fowl, pheasant, duck, that sort of thing.'

'No.'

'Oh.'

Another silence ensued. Boyd seemed entirely unconcerned.

'It's early to bed and early to rise for us I'm afraid, but you can lie in as long as you like.'

Theo's head lolled against the arm of the sofa. I wondered, not for the first time, how was it possible for a grown woman to make such an exhibition of herself. It never seemed to occur to her that she might not be safe. The trouble with Theo was that there was always someone there to look out for her. She never worried about what might happen because Douglas or me or whichever boy she had in tow would always sweep her up and kiss it better. She never knew what it was to fall spectacularly on her arse and have to clear up the mess.

Guilt was beyond her.

At nineteen she had taken up with Brian Woolcot, a tall, loose-limbed member of the Dampers Club who introduced her to pot. They'd punted up to Granchester for tea and were almost home and dry when Theo decided to swim back in her underwear. Brian got the shock of his life. In his befuddled state he thought she had been sucked under by aquatic aliens. His pole got stuck and snapped off. She clambered out of the filthy green water wearing a lacy bra and a half slip. It was by the most enormous stroke of luck that she was discovered by Giles Gibbon, a terribly sweet boy with a bit of a crush. He came banging on my door to tell me that Theo was 'swimming on the lawn'. I dropped the Peloponnesian Wars and scooted out with a dressing gown and a straw hat to find her stretched out on the grass covered with blanket weed, eyes round as saucers, doing the breast stroke. If we hadn't managed to smuggle her back in, she would have been sent down for sure.

Completely undaunted by her experience she worked her way through two packets of Jaffa cakes and a rather nice Dundee cake sent up by my mother. It was only the munchies that put her off smoking dope. She didn't want to get fat because then nobody would shag her. I told her she was shallow, that men of our generation were far more interested in a woman's mind than her looks. Of course, I was wrong about that. It turns out that I was wrong about a lot of things.

Sophie stretched her arms above her head and asked me if I wanted tea or coffee in the morning. The house had several bedrooms but only one bathroom and an outside lavvy just beyond the kitchen next to the coal bunker. At Black Farm we followed the same rota as during our second year when we shared digs. Helena, up first, would bring Sophie a mug of tea before using the bathroom, then knock on my door whilst Sophie showered and I in turn woke Theo. Sometimes Theo's bed was empty. I didn't mind because it gave me longer in the tub. Tutors, however were less forgiving. At least those she hadn't slept with.

I took the tray back into the kitchen and decided to make a start on the washing up. Helena reappeared a few minutes later with a blanket and pillow.

'I can't see Theo moving much before morning. I'll tuck her up. Don't bother with all that now.' She hesitated at the door. 'Have you heard from Daniel at all?'

I felt my cheeks redden. I know she meant well, but I couldn't look at her. 'It's over,' I said.

'He phoned me a couple of weeks ago,' she said quietly. 'Said he was worried about you.'

I stared at her. 'What the hell did he mean by that? I break up with him so there must be something wrong with me? Why's he phoning you? You've never liked him.'

'I don't like that he's married.'

'Separated.' I stacked the plates on the draining board. 'You don't seem to mind Theo breaking her vows every other Thursday.' It was a lame argument. Douglas was sweet but chose to ignore his wife's indiscretions as long as they were superficial, transitory and conducted in London rather than on his own doorstep. I loved Theo – sort of. I liked Douglas immensely. He loved her and she was very fond of him. I thought it rather odd though that she should have the family car for the weekend. Somehow that was crossing the line. It pained me to think of Douglas checking the oil filter and tyre pressure, completely unaware that his wife was chauffeuring some jumped-up, redbrick, pseudo-intellectual prick about the countryside.

'He told me he thought you might be having nightmares again.'

I felt hollow inside. I didn't answer.

'Are you?' She sounded concerned but I wasn't ready for another lecture. I tried to divert her.

'I suppose he told you about the book deal.' I looked at her when she didn't reply. 'You think I should have taken it, let him mould my life. We've always despised women who rely on men to do that!'

'Look, Daniel's no Svengali and he wouldn't be with you if you were some nymphet. You have something that's entirely your own. He can see that, we all do.' She paused. 'You know he always phones me to check you've arrived safely, don't you?'

But not this time.

I remembered the last occasion I had run away from Daniel, some ten years before. Drunk and wretched after yet another row about moving in together, I had phoned Theo. Within an hour she'd booked us internet flights for an impromptu holiday.

'Thailand?' Daniel's mouth turned up at the corner into that familiar crooked smile, half tease, half sneer to cover his own embarrassment.

I rotated my coffee cup in its saucer by fractional degrees, as he digested my news the following evening in the refreshments room at Marylebone Station, our usual Friday night rendezvous.

'I thought,' he hesitated, coughed, a small laugh escaping him. 'You and I,' followed by a deep sigh and then in a quieter voice, 'For Christ's sake, what the hell do you want to go to Thailand for?' His brown eyes were angry now. Angry because of what? Because I hurt him? Because I let him down?

'Are you trying to make a fool out of me? Is that it?

Is this your way of punishing me?'

I stared at him, numb from the heart.

'Yeah, of course, this is all about *you*,' I snapped.

'Keep your voice down!' More harsh now. He knew the moment had passed. I wasn't about to succumb to another distant promise. I'd called him, raised the stakes, answered his bluff with one of my own and he couldn't buy himself out of this one. I had all the cards and he knew it.

'When are you going?'

'Tomorrow.'

'*Tomorrow*? Christ, what about *us*? I thought we might spend time together over New Year, maybe go away somewhere just the two of us.' He was so indignant, I really think he was starting to believe his own fiction.

'You told me you had to see the kids. You said you'd be stuck in town all through the holidays, so I made other plans.'

'For fuck's sake, you're just doing this to annoy me.'

Yeah, just to annoy him.

At Bangkok station, barely two days later, I scrawled 'I miss you' on a cheap postcard. Theo was already boarding the train and shouting for me to hurry up. No pen to hand, all I had on me was a greasy eyeliner pencil to make my mark. And as soon as I dropped it into the letter box, sank back into my seat and felt the train jerk forward, I knew it was a lie. A maggoty worm of a lie to reel him in.

What I wanted then was for us to live together. Conducting an affair might have been thrilling at twenty-five but at thirty-five it just felt degrading. I wanted him to choose me. I wanted us to belong to each other. I needed something to show for all the effort I had invested in him. If not a diamond, then at least an address.

Thailand started out well enough. Theo's plan was to take the overnight train to Trang, then a ferry to one of the smaller islands. We departed late afternoon, stowing our rucksacks at the end of the carriage, each retaining a small overnight bag to see us through till morning. A tall brown-haired man of European complexion wearing a cream linen suit sat diagonally across from me on the other side of the compartment, his arms and legs folded neatly, his concentration fixed on a small volume of poetry. Theo and I opted for backgammon. The train lurched and rattled through the outskirts of the city until tin shacks gave way to lush forest and paddy fields streaked with crimson in the dying light.

At six o'clock the waiter brought us menus. He shuffled back and forth in his starched uniform snapping gate-legged tables into position, laying chopsticks, napkins, water glasses, toothpicks, soy sauce and small ceramic bowls. Within minutes we were feasting on steaming bowls of rice, succulent beef spiced with green chillies, lemongrass and coriander, sliced chicken and fresh ginger, garlic prawns in coconut milk with sweet red chillies and kaffir lime leaves. Cold beer scalded our throats and the world blurred pleasantly as the food warmed our bellies and we slouched, legs outstretched on the scuffed leather seats. The colonial past still echoed in that third class railway compartment, on the night train to Trang, gateway to the South China Seas.

At ten o'clock the waiter reappeared with a metal key and respectfully asked us to move to one side whilst he expertly snapped metal grilles across the windows and lowered the overhead bunks, transforming the carriage into a sleeping compartment. Sliding between thin sheets I felt like a sardine in a canning factory. We trundled through the warm night over wooden bridges and metal viaducts, through villages and rainforest until dawn.

Over breakfast we plotted our route island by island. Mr Linen-suit opposite seemed rather distracted and kept looking at us over his newspaper. Theo was oblivious. As the train pulled up at the end of the line he seemed intent on following us. We disembarked and I headed for a small roadside café that advertised bottled water on top of a large chest freezer. When I looked back over my shoulder to speak to her I saw that she was still standing some fifty yards back at the side of the train, hands on her hips as he remonstrated with her. She shook her head and strode towards me whilst he stood, suitcase in hand, like a travelling salesman who'd just lost the deal of the month.

'What did he want?'

'Nothing. I think he thought we might be up for sharing a taxi to the ferry.'

I stopped dead in my tracks.

'Did you have sex with him?'

'No!'

'You *did*, didn't you? I don't believe it! How, when – where on earth?' I broke off as I pictured the sleeping compartment. Only midgets could have achieved coitus in the coffin sized bunk beds. 'Not in the toilet, please God tell me you didn't have sex with that man in the toilet!'

'I did not have sex with that man!' Theo hissed. 'Keep your voice down.'

'What's that, the Clinton Defence?' I shouted, 'It all depends on what you mean by *sexual relations*?' She had the good grace to go pink.

'It was just a hand-job.'

'What is *wrong* with you?'

'What's wrong with *me*? What's wrong with *you*? When's the last time you had a decent shag, or a book signing for that matter?'

I stared at her open mouthed. 'So are you telling me that you gave that man head – don't even try to deny it – there's no way he's all hot and bothered over just a hand-job – just to prove a point?'

'Isn't that why we're here?' she screamed back at me. But not this time.

Helena was waiting for a response. The washing up was mostly done. Pretty soon I wouldn't have any excuse not to turn and face her. She wavered. 'Whatever you said to Daniel, however angry you feel, I can't believe he just suddenly stopped caring, not after all these years.'

'Did he phone?'

'No. I left a message on his voicemail.' She tried again. 'It's been such a long time, I just think you should let him in.' She paused. 'It's nearly thirty years. Wamani was a long time ago – '

I cried out as a broken glass-stem bit into my hand. The blood dripped into the bowl turning the soapy water pink.

'Do you think I don't know that?' I snapped at her. Helena was suddenly by my side, ushering me away from the sink, wrapping my hand in a tea towel to staunch the bleeding.

'Don't you think I'd give anything for it not to matter anymore?' I was spitting mad. 'I wish I *could* speak to Daniel. I wish Theo wasn't such a tart, I wish I could write again, I wish I could go back to the beginning and make everything okay, but I can't!'

'I'm sorry, I'm sorry.'

I felt my head spin as Helena gently sat me down at the kitchen table.

'It's ok,' she muttered. 'Let me have a look.' The cut wasn't deep but it was stinging like hell. I heard footsteps in the hallway and Sophie appeared. 'Get her a brandy,' said Helena reaching for the first aid box.

'It's not serious,' I said, but no-one was listening.

'I think it's time we all turned in,' said Helena. 'Breakfast at five?' I nodded. Sophie gave my arm a squeeze. 'Will you be able to shoot?' I nodded again.

I saw Boyd leaning against the doorframe, hands in his pockets, watching me curiously. Why didn't he just leave us alone and go to bed?

Helena spoke to him briskly, 'Help yourself to breakfast in the morning. We should be back around ten.'

'Do you need to get back to London?' asked Sophie diplomatically. 'One of us can drive you into Cambridge tomorrow afternoon if you like.'

He didn't answer. Instead he said evenly, 'Theo's awake. I think she's going to need a bucket.'

2

Saturday morning I lay in the narrow bed of the little, yellow guest room on the top landing, my head propped up against the old, wooden headboard sipping hot, sweet tea in the dark, listening to the silence. I imagined Helena two floors below oiling the guns, checking cartridges. She liked to have everything stowed in the Land Rover for the first drive of the day before making porridge on the stove. We would take coffee and sloe gin in the field before motoring back home for a serious fry-up and a couple of hours kip in the afternoon. Sometimes we planned a second drive as the crimson sunset drew the last of the geese inland for the night. If the weather held we opted for rough shooting on foot but none of us cared to waste birds for the sake of it. We only usually shot what we could eat.

Helena favoured her father's ancient Purdey but modern regulations outlawed lead shot. She judged Bismuth to be too light to get the job done and she didn't trust steel. Bore erosion, apparently. I told her time and time again that it was just a matter of using the right shotcup. Sophie swore by her old boxlock though her real preference was for smaller game. She left the big stuff to Helena. Sophie was, however, by far the most skilled of the four of us. She'd been a small bore enthusiast ever since her father taught her to shoot with his national service Enfield. A member of the Cambridge University Rifle Association, she won a Blue in '82. That put Theo's nose out of joint for a while. I tended to blast away with a Browning. Theo didn't always shoot. It depended on her state of mind. That is to say, how hungover she was. She couldn't bring herself to hunt fox though Helena was always going on about them being vermin and all. Sophie could be relied upon to bag a few rabbits. There was always a good supply of birds.

We'd set aside the afternoon for plucking and drawing, all cold hands and sharp bones. That was the time I liked the most, when I felt an earthy connection to the real life outside of books and ideas.

Shooting was often cold, frustrating and wet. It could unleash quite a competitive streak within me that was constantly frustrated by Helena and Sophie's superior skills. But with a nip of whisky and a newly sharpened blade I dressed widgeon, mallard, pheasant and grouse with atavistic pleasure, thoughts turning to those who had gone before when such quarry sustained whole families through the dark months of winter.

I listened to fresh, hot water trickling through the pipework behind the bedhead as Sophie showered in the bathroom below. It was time to wake Theo.

I pulled on my dressing gown and knocked three times on the wall. There was no answer so I went out onto the little wooden landing lit from above by shafts of moonlight through a narrow skylight. I knocked on her door and turned the doorknob, whispering 'It's only me.' The door flew open suddenly and I felt myself yanked into the dark and flattened up against the partition wall.

Boyd put his hand across my mouth and pushed his knees between my legs. I felt his hardness through the thin fabric of my robe and registered the strangest sensation, like a buzzing sound in my brain as I tried to make sense of the face in front of me. Boyd wasn't wearing glasses. Hs eyes were much larger now and very blue. And he was naked.

I swung my fists at him but he grabbed both wrists

and pushed my arms up over my head. He stared at me intently for a moment then he very gently lowered his head and kissed the base of my throat. His lips moved upwards with the lightest of kisses until he reached my jaw line and all the time I didn't make a sound. I should have shouted or screamed or pushed him away. But I didn't. Instead I went with him to the rumpled bed and let him inside me.

And it felt so good, good, good, not like Daniel constantly soliciting my approval, expecting me to verbalise every sensation, so intent on pleasing me, willing me to climax and then when it was becoming apparent that my body had no such intention, humbly asking for permission to come. I never understood how a man could be so driven to experience pleasure with a woman who couldn't respond in kind. It wasn't that I was naive or inexperienced. When we first met we couldn't keep our hands off each other. But latterly things had waned between us and I knew it was my own fault. Daniel persisted with all the subtlety of a mechanic in search of an oil leak. Inside, I knew it was hopeless. It was as if I had become the mountain. Nothing could penetrate the small frozen void within me. Not the breathy fumbling young men of my youth, nor the sophisticated older men of my middle-age.

But Boyd was something raw and unnerving. I experienced for the first time the utter purity of the act itself. This was coupling shorn of all relationship ties, uncorrupted by emotion and empty of meaning. Boyd didn't matter and I didn't care.

I felt myself gasping, uncoiling. He picked up the tempo and I shuddered then, my body in full spate as he tensed, his hips rigid, holding himself apart from me so that he could see my nakedness and watch himself in the act. I looked up into his face and saw no tenderness or pity and for the first time in my life I felt equal and whole. He pulled away and I lay there feeling the first chill on my skin, exhilarated to the core.

He leaned across me to switch on the bedside lamp and retrieve a packet of cigarettes. He lay back against the frame at the opposite end of the bed for his first nicotine kick of the day. I envied him.

'Where's Theo?' I said slowly. He grinned as if he'd known all along how this would play out.

'Sofa.'

'Helena made up another room for you on the first floor.'

'I thought it might be more interesting up here.'

'I think I hate you.'

'That's what made it so good, sweetheart.'

'*Foot soldier of the Great Class Struggle.*'

'What?'

'Nothing.'

My eyes traced the cracks in the ceiling where the plaster had sagged. The sprigged wallpaper was betraying signs of damp under the eaves. I wondered which of the Copeland brothers had slept here. It seemed too pretty for a boy and then I remembered the sister, Helena's aunt. It must have been her room when she was a girl.

'Theo was right about you,' he said indifferently.

'What do you mean?'

'Often chaste, seldom caught.' He stubbed out the cigarette and folded his arms behind his head with his eyes closed. 'Haven't you got birds to kill?'

I stood up to pull on my robe and went to the door.

'I don't want them to know,' I said.

'Fine by me.'

'I think you should go today.'

'We'll see.'

And then, just as I had opened the door to leave he said in a jocular tone, 'How about an interview? Daniel Forrest told Theo you could use some column inches.' His mouth split into an ugly smile. 'You know it's amazing what a few inches in the right place can do for a girl.'

My face flooded crimson. I went back to my room and grabbed a towel then ran down the stairs two at a time. The bathroom was empty. I turned on the shower and sluiced frantically between my legs scrubbing the sticky scent of him off my skin. The water pulsed in time with my heartbeat. *You stupid stupid stupid bitch.* I was ready to kill Theo.

***

That morning I shot more birds than ever before.

Helena congratulated me. Sophie kept proffering hot coffee, her usual chirpy self, whilst Theo sipped sloe gin from a hip flask, looking wretched. I couldn't bring myself to speak much to any of them.

After breakfast I was first up the stairs for a hot bath and a few hours' kip. I undressed slowly thinking through the events of the weekend. I returned to my room and for the first time ever, I turned the key in the lock before lying down on the bed.

A flat dreamless sleep enveloped me and it was around three o'clock in the afternoon when I woke again.

The house was silent. I rose and opened the curtains.

The sun was low in the sky. It was a day such as only an English Autumn can bestow. The fens stretched out beyond the farmhouse in all directions. Yellow sunlight seeped like molten gold into the water-logged ditches that bisect the land. A broken line of black furrows betrayed the man-made scars upon the earth, that would not heal until Spring. Beneath my window lay the maze of outbuildings now deep in shadow and beyond the stone dyke, the rich black peaty soil that had given its name to this place over five generations before.

I dressed and padded out onto the narrow wooden landing. What the hell was I doing? I loathed him yet here I was going back for more. I listened first, then cautiously opened the door to Boyd's room.

The bed was stripped. All his personal items were gone. It was as if he had never existed.

PART III

1

Now that I come to think of it, I'm certain it was Helena who first conceived of the idea of an expedition to climb Ausangate. I had done some Munro bagging with my brother Luke as a younger teenager; with Helena I had graduated to alpine climbing.

Luke had given me a bottle of Moet & Chandon as a sort of christening gift for my new life as a Cambridge scholar with strict instructions that I should *drink the whole bloody bottle myself.* At the time I thought it such a grown-up idea but now that I was finally alone it seemed utterly naff, particularly as everyone else went about with an air of smug detachment. The only thing that marked my achievement as worth celebrating was the pride and exhilaration felt by those closest to me. Nobody else cared. I saw my situation for what it was. Fate had determined that I should make up the numbers. Everyone else had been expected.

As a child I had never really known what it was to be at peace with oneself. Even happy moments were overshadowed by other emotions jostling for pole position: excitement, fear, shock, vulnerability, disbelief. Chief amongst them had always been *embarrassment,* rarely for failing to meet a challenge, always as a result of having succeeded. Success precipitated the on-rush of self-consciousness as surely as an Indian monsoon in June. I spent most of my formative years simply drenched.

But Cambridge was a privileged environment. Here it was cool to be smart. I didn't expect to soar but the sky beckoned and I couldn't wait to test my wings.

My personal self-doubts were less easily assuaged. I treasured my academic gown for it happily disguised my middle-income wardrobe. I aspired to the fashions of Lady Diana Spencer but couldn't quite pull it off. My pearls were unknotted and fake. They were easily scratched. I lived in dread of the string breaking. Those petty misgivings were, however, only superficial. The years of my adolescence were disturbed by far deeper currents of anxiety.

We were living at Four Minutes to Midnight, constantly on the brink. The world I had grown up in was dominated by the cold war, nuclear proliferation and the great Russian bear. The death of Brézhnev in November of the following year was to usher in a very different era leading to Glasnost, Perestroika, the crumbling of the Berlin Wall. But all that was undreamed of in my first term at Cambridge. All I wanted was to cloister myself within the stone walls of that ancient seat of learning and instruct myself in the nobler values of a more illustrious age.

I believe that first Michaelmas term was the happiest time of my life.

I fell in love with the smell of the place. Polished oak, ancient tallow, mildew, linseed and chalk, the sweetness of freshly cut grass and warm stone. I bought a classic black sit up and beg bicycle with a wicker basket on the front and pedalled madly, jarring my joints, bumping along the cobbled streets and narrow walkways. I sucked in the air around me, gilded with centuries of accumulated wisdom. As the seasons turned I relished the cold, scribbling in what I thought of as my garret space, pouring over books and manuscripts, drafting and re-drafting essays with a copperplate hand. I attended evensong at King's and went for bracing walks breathing clouds of vapour like a recovering consumptive. Toasted muffins and anchovy paste were the guilty pleasures of my day along with Gingernuts and peppermint tea, thick slices of buttered maltloaf, and late night discussions about hubris and revenge. I wanted to be a scholar. I quickly developed a crush on my tutor Dr Mackey, joined the Chapel choir and polished up my vowels.

A decade of reading Angela Brazil and fantasising about dormitories, tuck shops, lacrosse sticks and boaters had fine-tuned my expectations to such a pitch that nothing could have prevented me from becoming the most frightful blue-stocking. Nothing perhaps except my burgeoning friendship with Helena.

She was completely opposite to me in many ways, not least her sexuality which was loud and proud. Our rooms were on the same staircase and that first year we were in and out of each other's pockets on a daily basis. I had at first been rather wary of her. I didn't want others to think that I was her *special friend*. Nevertheless, it took a while for me to register that she didn't have the slightest interest in me sexually. Rather than relief, I felt an inexplicable resentment, but this eventually subsided into a companionable intimacy that I started to take for granted. I even found myself eyeing up potential partners for her. As if she needed any help in that regard. It must have confused the men of our year group considerably.

The day of the Ausangate conversation, a raw February morning as I recall, I was fretting over Pindar and declaiming silently whilst walking up and down with my eyes closed, a small leather bound volume clasped to my chest. I heard someone cough rather theatrically and

I swung round to find Helena watching me from the open doorway.

I hated being looked at and she had such a direct way about her. It really unnerved me at times. She used to say that it was a pity that I didn't see myself as others saw me: tall, hourglass figure, lovely chestnut locks, smoky blue grey eyes and a rosebud mouth. All I could see when I looked in the mirror were dumpy thighs and straight brown hair that refused to curl.

Helena took the opportunity to cast her eye around my rooms for what she termed 'evidence'. I was mystified.

'Theo must have gotten her wires crossed,' she sighed.

'About what?'

'Nothing.' She nodded in the direction of Pindar. 'If you're done with that, I've got an idea for an Olympian deed of our own.'

I smiled. 'Great. I need something to cheer me up. Lunch?'

We wrapped up and headed out to the Buttery.

I listened agog as she outlined her plan for Ausangate.

'Whatever made you think of it?' I asked over sticky toffee pudding and custard.

'You know it's the funniest thing,' she said in a dreamy faraway sort of voice that I had never associated with her before. 'It's as if it's always been there at the back of my mind – to climb in the Andes.'

'Yes, but why now?'

She turned her head away slightly as if considering her answer carefully. Finally she fixed her gaze on me and said simply, 'Last night I had a dream.'

I hesitated, not knowing quite what to say. Her cheeks flushed a little.

'I know it sounds a bit *weird* and I don't want you to

say anything to Theo or I'll never hear the end of it.'

I thought of Theo and her talent for mockery. It was better to remain silent. 'It's a big step up for me,' I said at last.

'Not really,' she sat back in her chair and sucked her spoon. 'It's really just a question of altitude and acclimatisation. Sophie will be up for it.' Sophie was a seasoned climber having spent childhood holidays with her father at Zermatt and Chamonix.

'The thing is,' she added, 'I know things can be a bit tight your end. Do you need some dosh?'

Money was a sensitive subject for me. My father was paying for my education, not my social life. I had to take a part-time job during the holidays to give myself extra funds. Nobody ever mentioned it but they all knew; Sophie and Theo were rather tactful, allowing me to pay for the small stuff, but always picking up the tab when there was a lot of cash at stake. Helena wasn't terribly sensitive in those days and had a brisk way of dealing with delicate subjects, which was to ignore the fact that they were delicate and somehow this tactic seemed to work wonders.

'I could tap my brother for a loan, how long do you think we'll be gone?' Luke had graduated with a Masters in Engineering and was already down in Chile working for an oil company. He knew what it was to feel out of one's depth financially, having suffered Dad's lectures on fiscal responsibility as I had, but a first class degree had kept the old man happy. He was the best older brother a girl could have. I knew he wouldn't see me short.

'Easter jamfest is five weeks. I was thinking three or four days to get there, then we'd have to wait four days or so at Cuzco to get used to the altitude and pick up supplies. It's about a seven hour climb to the summit, so base camp for three days or so to prepare, high camp for a couple of days, overnight ascent to the top and then back to town.'

'What about Theo? Is she game?'

I didn't want to disappoint Helena by staying home, nor did I wish to let the girls down by being the weakest member of the team.

'Chomping at the bit. By the way, she seems to think you did a bit of horizontal folk dancing with Le Featherstone last night.'

I blushed. Damn Theo and her big mouth. Certainly I had a bit of a crush on gorgeous Guy but jampot or no, he was engaged already. True, we'd had a bit of a snog at Alistair Throckmorton's anti-apartheid Jazz Supper, but it hadn't amounted to anything. In fact I wasn't entirely sure that he'd got the right girl. He'd seemed rather drunk. Kept calling me Estella and begging me to chill out so that Young Pip could snuggle against my comely bosom. But even worse was the idea of being ratted out by one of my friends.

'God no! Too rich for my taste.'

I could see she wasn't entirely convinced. Theo was obviously determined to create mischief.

Helena soberly inclined her head in mock impression of Professor Hewlitt, an earnest young Fellow from Trinity, and contemplated the problem before her with scant attention to the Socratic method.

'Well, no doubt if you *had* lost your virginity to Guy Featherstone, youngest son of a Viscount no less, and currently rumoured to be engaged to Figgy Leighton-Burrows, you surely would have told Sophie by now. It's almost midday, ample time for morning confession. No.' She wagged her finger. 'Clearly the deed has not been done. You are still vestal. Guy is in the clear. Figgy need never know and Theo is definitely for the high jump.'

'So sorry to disappoint,' I countered with heavy sarcasm.

'Never mind.' She shook her head sagely. 'I'm sure it's just a matter of time.'

That wasn't quite how I wanted to view the situation. It was all very well for Helena. Cambridge was littered with single women of a certain age who preferred a life of letters to what Helena described as 'wifely fetters'. Not that she was at all backward in coming forward. There were rumours that she had recently formed an intimate friendship with one of the Fellows at Trinity who shared her passion for shooting. As for me, I felt it wasn't so much a question of losing my maidenhood as trying to give it away. Well, that wasn't quite fair. Miles Cruickshank would probably do the deed for me if I asked him. I tried to picture him without his trousers on and felt slightly sick. Too ginger.

'What's the elevation?' I asked. Helena looked at me and raised an eyebrow.

'I mean the damn mountain!' I laughed in spite of myself.

'Just shy of twenty-one thousand feet. There are two peaks. South side assent up a steep icefall.'

'Okay, I'm in.'

'We'll need a guide and perhaps a porter or two. In the meantime you can brush up on your Inca mythology.'

'I'll leave that to Sophie,' I joked. 'And we can always rent out Theo if we run short of pesos.'

In our naivety it never occurred to us that external forces might come to bear upon our plans. Galtieri's decision to invade Les Malvinas in April of that year put quite a spanner in the works. My mother wouldn't countenance my departure. She fretted about Luke; would he be completely safe down in Santiago? Even if he came home, what were the chances of him being conscripted?

There were phone calls back and forth and in spite of much pleading, my parents were adamant. Sophie's mother was equally forthright. Our expedition was abandoned. It would be another two years before we tried again. In the meantime I settled back into my academic routine, studied hard and took my exams. I wonder if things would have turned out differently had we ploughed on regardless. I wonder what would have been Helena's response if I had told her the truth over lunch that cold February day?

That I, too, had dreamed of Ausangate the night before.

2

Sophie wanted to be a good Catholic. It was her habit to rise early and say prayers in the college chapel for Saint Agatha, patron saint of volcanic eruptions and wet nurses. Helena would have scoffed naturally, but the juxtaposition of volcanoes and breast-feeding was entirely logical to Sophie given the tortures suffered by Saint Agatha at the hands of her rejected suitor.

Saint Agatha, a virgin and an early Christian, had spurned Quintianus and defied his superior rank. Clearly unperturbed by any romantic sensibility, he responded by having her breasts sliced off and when that failed to quieten her revolt, she was rolled in hot coals. This history made a great impression on flat-chested nineteen year-old Sophie. If Agatha, who had suffered so dreadful a trial of faith, had risen to the occasion, then surely it was not asking too much of Sophie to satisfy her mother's wish for a good marriage.

She really wanted to believe. She described to me her earliest memories of Father Rafferty's sonorous chocolate brown voice intoning the Mass. She had felt the promise of a warm enveloping world of simple truths and natural consequences. But lately things had become complicated and unpredictable. Her understanding was no longer satisfied by familiar rituals and though it might have been easier had she chosen Oxford, where she would have been more strictly supervised, she had struck out on her own, her true love of Mathematics supplanting for once her first love of God.

Helena had no truck with religion. For her it was all 'Bells, smells and twoddle.' She couldn't get past the comedy of tortures so fiendishly inventive as to defy belief.

'It's all so ridiculous,' she argued. 'Severed toes and boiling oil. If someone said to me *will you renounce Jesus Christ or we'll toast your genitals*, I'd be screaming *where do I sign?*'

That Helena was an atheist pained Sophie but God had been known to turn even the most recalcitrant sinner into a faithful servant. I at least, baptised into the Church of England by two parents not disposed to attend services as a general rule, favoured a traditional liturgy and had been attending confirmation classes with the local vicar. I think Sophie took some comfort in the idea of me as a simpatico who understood the need for ceremony and ritual, hierarchy and paternity. None of this Jesus stuff for me, Sophie, it's Mr Christ as far as I'm concerned. Yet privately I was very confused. On the one hand, I was glad that I had not been born into the Roman Catholic Faith. Hell and Damnation were truly terrifying. Yet on the other hand, I couldn't help but feel that Sophie's religion was somehow the Real Deal. Even high church Anglicanism seemed a bit flabby by comparison. We didn't harp on about hellfire, never mentioned Satan, and frankly lacked any real incentive to be good at all. Being Church of England was like taking out student insurance. Minimum cover, but better than lying awake at night listening out for burglars.

Added to which, Sophie wasn't sure that Heaven would welcome a Christian who didn't practise confession. It seemed to her that Anglicans just wanted to cherry-pick the good bits. And I in part agreed with her. But it was Theo, our very own Magdalene, who caused Sophie the most agony. 'Pray for *me*? Sophie – darling, you're such a sweetheart! Now I'm bound to scale the heights of ecstasy!'

Sophie and I often spoke about these things when the other two weren't around. We used to pop next door to King's every now and then, and sit at the back listening to the choir and the great organ bellowing as if God Himself were about to make a guest appearance. I would feast my eyes on the gothic interior whilst Sophie sat with her head high and her eyes closed looking like a lost little angel swathed in her great coat and muffler. Afterwards, we'd slip out before the rest of the congregation and take a detour through the trees via King's Back and across Clare bridge. If it was dry we'd sit by the bank but most of our conversations were had on the hoof.

'The thing is,' she said, pondering the toe of her boot, 'I don't know if it's really possible to reconcile my love for God and how I feel about Mathematics. I mean, God's truly omnipotent and all-seeing. He is infinite and infinity is the most beautiful and elegant concept in Mathematics, Georgie. It's always just out of reach.' She sighed. 'Sometimes I feel so stupid.'

'Sophe – you're just about the least stupid person I know.'

'Well, brains isn't everything. I mean, God wants us to know Him, really feel Him, but then He goes and makes Himself unknowable – infinite. Almighty. It's like a cruel joke.'

'Catholicism is a bit beyond me. What does your priest say about it?'

She let slip a little laugh. 'Oh, he's very old-school. Mummy would adore him.'

'Isn't confession supposed to help?'

She studied the ground and then looked straight ahead, her jaw set in a firm line.

'But I don't want to confess,' she said. 'If I confess

it's like I'm saying it's a sin. But how can it be a sin?' She turned her face to me and it was so earnest that I didn't know what to say. I took hold of her hand, puzzling over her words.

'Each time I feel my heart pounding I have to suppress it, pretend I don't feel anything. It's tearing me apart Georgie.' Her voice was a dry whisper. 'I can't even bring myself to be obedient. I can't pray. I can't take communion unless I confess.' Her eyes were bright with tears and her bottom lip was trembling. 'All my sins are thick upon me like layers and layers of cobwebs. If I took communion it would burn like acid on my tongue. But I can't confess. I just can't do it. I'm not sorry – do you see? I just can't bring myself to condemn my own feelings.'

We leaned over the stone walls of Clare bridge and watched the water flowing beneath.

'I don't feel contrition. I'm such a hypocrite.'

I didn't quite know what to make of it. This seemed so extreme. I didn't feel compelled to turn away from God because of my passion for Classics. It was as if Sophie were caught up in a medieval mindset, afraid of the Inquisition.

'But nobody expects you to give up your love of Maths, Sophe – especially not here. C'mon, it's not as bad as all that is it?' She looked at me strangely. 'I mean, if what you're saying is right then God created infinity didn't He? He made Maths and Science possible. It's all part of some greater plan and we're just finding ways to understand ourselves better.'

She sniffed and pulled out a scrap of lacy handkerchief to blow her nose.

'Yes. Yes of course, you're right. I'm sorry Georgie. I'm making rather a scene, aren't I ?'

'No, of course not. It's just that you seemed so happy

to be here. I mean it's a dream isn't it? All this?' She followed my glance with such sad eyes, taking in the landscape around her without really seeing it at all.

'And there must be some famous Catholic mathematicians, surely?'

She nodded and wiped her eyes and nose.

'Most of them were excommunicated. I know I'm being silly,' she said.

'No, no you're not.' I struggled to find the right words. 'It's just that there's so much to be grateful and happy for. Look at me, and Theo and – well, look at Helena. We all think the world of you, Sophe.'

'Helena?'

'Oh, I know she can be a bit brusque. She frightened me almost to death the first time I met her, but she's such a good sport. Why don't you go shooting together some time? It would be good for you to get out and do something different for a change. All work and no play . . . ' I drifted off vaguely, completely at a loss as to what to say next.

'Helena,' she said softly.

'We ought to get back. It's getting quite cold.'

'Thanks Georgie, for listening.'

But it did no good. Looking back it was as if her soul plummeted each time she attained a complex understanding. She evaded endlessly. Although her tutors encouraged her to excel, Sophie could not bear to be the centre of attention. She had reached her own event horizon and with every affirmation of her genius she felt the pull of the invisible darkness within, the terrible gnawing despair swallowing her atom by atom.

Some weave words. There are those of us who seek oblivion in the company of others, or in drink or drugs. Sophie felt God all around her. She wanted to be blessed. She wanted to die. She desired to be everything that her mother wanted her to be. She asked for guidance again and again, for penance to take away her sin.

I watched my friend deteriorating and felt powerless to intervene.

I visited her rooms one night to find her sitting on the floor surrounded by textbooks and papers of complex formulae written in her spare elegant hand. She'd turned her room upside down. She'd been walking and her hands and feet were chilled. I lit the gas fire and made tea.

'I'm going to fetch someone,' I said.

'No, don't go.' She gripped my arm tightly with her bony fingers. 'I'll be all right, honestly. I'm all right now.'

But she wasn't. There was an anxiety eating away at her that I simply couldn't comprehend. It wasn't unheard of for students to go mad but not Sophie. Please God, not Sophie.

If this period induced a heightened state of anxiety for me then perhaps it's not surprising that my work was beginning to fall off. My tutor requested my presence.

Dr Mackey's rooms were intimidating. Sitting on a hard chair surrounded by curios and glass cases of 'interesting finds' made me feel clumsy and awkward. I wasn't much interested in archaeology; it was drama and poetry that inspired me, not scrabbling about in the dirt for potsherds and coins. He addressed me whilst looking out of the window, as if I had forfeited the courtesy of a face to face interview. Once I had thought him handsome, but up close he seemed pompous and unforgiving. Theo had been right, as usual. *Georgie's not really interested in men, it's the ideas that get her juices going.*

'You understand how fortunate you are to be here.' It was a statement not a question. 'I do not wish to have mine or the college's time wasted on undergraduates who are unwilling to meet the required standard.'

My gaze drifted across the cabinets crammed with tarnished bronzes and chipped clay figures, fragments of the Roman Empire that he hoarded like a schoolboy. I felt a bubble of hysteria rising inside me and pinched myself. He went on in the same vein but I scarcely heard him. A shaft of milky light stole in through the window and illuminated a small brown glass phial turning it from mud to amber. I felt a lump in my throat and a sudden desperate wave of homesickness welling up inside me. A little glass bottle. That's all it took, and I was ready to run out of the room and get the first train home.

Paul, my first crush, had collected glass. I watched him from my bedroom window as he performed bike stunts in the street with his mates, Bry, Kev and Mart. I couldn't figure why boys thought it was cool to shorten each other's names to one syllable until one tea-time when I heard my own mother shouting at my brother: 'Lucas!' Even worse of course would have been *Lu*cas *Ed*ward but that was reserved for serious misdemeanours and little chats after Parents' Evening.

I was an eight-year-old stalker, desperate to catch a glimpse of my intended. I had no doubt that one day Paul would fall off his bike and sustain a very bloody injury. I would nurse him back to health and then he would marry me out of intense gratitude. It could have happened. He'd gone over his handlebars once and bashed his jaw which made his teeth grow at a slight angle.

Every Saturday morning he cycled off with a flask and a duffel bag slung across his back to go bottle digging with his Dad. He was four years older than me, and his sister Deborah was my best friend. She and I used to play 'Charlie's Angels' which consisted of dressing up in her mother's kaftans and running in and out of the garden performing Karate chops in mid air. Exhausted by lunchtime, we'd eat jam sandwiches in her bedroom and listen to Tubular Bells on cassette tape, which inevitably led to trampolining on her bed. Paul's bedroom was on the corridor opposite Deborah's and whenever she had to go for a pee I would slip into his room. He kept the curtains drawn all the time which gave a blue cast to everything even on the sunniest afternoons. I was used to the smell of my brother's room – wet dog spiced with mouldy orange peel. Paul's room was different. Everything was tidy and clean. Even the posters were straight. It was the room of a boy on the cusp of teen-hood: a single bed, a desk and a chair for homework, Scalectrix and a big box of Meccano. He collected Dinky toys and kept them in their boxes. But the most amazing thing about this room was the shelves of glass bottles. Opaque, amber, blue, green, turquoise, milky, clear, ranging from two to six inches in height, carefully washed and displayed with pride. The most precious pieces he kept in an alcove beneath the window. There must have been some system at work but I never guessed what it was. I knew that if I touched one of his bottles he would be sure to know. I never got any nearer to Paul than hovering in his bedroom when the coast was clear. Once I sniffed his cotton pyjama top that was draped over the back of a chair. I felt giddy. It was still warm. To think that I was touching something that had been on his *actual body* whilst he was *in bed*.

By the time he turned sixteen he had a string of girls trailing after him. Everybody liked him. Paul wore his hair long so that it swept his shirt collar like one of the Bay City Rollers. He hung out with my brother during that long hot summer of '76. We had a paddling pool because of the hose pipe ban, and I nearly died when

Paul slipped his t-shirt off and lay on the grass drinking a can of Tab. By September Luke had found his feet academically and tended to stay in his room reading. Paul just shrugged his shoulders and took off on his bike. He was becoming quite an athlete so nobody was very surprised when he announced his intention to join the army. He looked amazingly handsome in his camouflage gear and beret. My Dad went out to shake hands with him before he left on his first tour of duty. I brushed my hair fifty times and leaned out of my bedroom window. *Hey Paul.* He looked up at me, squinting into the sun. *Hey Georgie.* That was the only time he ever smiled at me directly, a generous wide open smile like the sun coming out, and I'll remember it till the day I die. I never told Deborah that I was madly in love with her brother.

But even if I left now, I couldn't really go back. Deborah and Paul wouldn't be there. She was studying Art in London, and Paul, the lovely boy with the crooked teeth was long gone, shot dead by a sniper on the Falls Road just before his nineteenth birthday.

Professor Mackey was waiting. I mumbled an apology, said I would try harder, and left.

Sophie collapsed a week later. An ambulance was called and she was admitted to hospital. She was diagnosed with pneumonia and bronchitis. Lady Audrey wanted her to come home but the doctors said she was too ill to make the journey so she was moved instead to a private sanatorium near a village outside Cambridge. I looked up the bus timetable. I wished Helena could come with me but in my heart of hearts I knew that I had to make the journey on my own. I found a telephone box and took out the slip of paper with the number on it. An austere voice answered and said the name of the hospital. When I heard the pips I pushed in the coins and waited. Visiting hours were strictly limited. I could gain admittance at three o'clock for quarter of an hour.

I didn't take in much of the bus journey. Everything felt grey to me. After an hour the bus driver pulled into a lay-by and pointed to a side road that twisted up through some woodland.

'It's a fair walk,' he said. 'Should have brought some decent shoes, love.'

I looked down at the path which was waterlogged and muddy.

'Isn't there another way?'

'This is quickest, love, if you don't have a car,' he sniffed. I stepped down gingerly and gave a start as the hydraulic door closed behind me.

I checked the road but there was nothing but hedgerows and open pasture. I slid my hands under my slip and carefully undid my stocking tops. I stepped out of each court shoe in turn, rolled down my stockings and stuffed them in my handbag to keep them clean and dry.

It was a crisp golden afternoon. Through the trees I glimpsed a white stuccoed building that must have been a private country residence at some point. By the time I reached the grounds to the rear of the house my feet were freezing and my shoes and ankles were caked in mud. I crossed the gravel that had been raked into swirly patterns, looked around for a bench and took out some tissues to clean myself up as best I could. There was a small ornamental pond with a large hideous stone fish in the middle spurting water where I managed to wash off the worst of the dirt. I dried my feet with my scarf and slipped my shoes back on. I crunched my way around the side of the building towards the main entrance where a number of cars were parked in neat formation. I recognised the beautiful Jag that Sophie's father drove.

I wasn't sure what to do. I didn't want to interrupt his visit but I'd come a long way and if I didn't see her at three o'clock I wouldn't get another chance for a week or so. I was trying to decide whether to go in or wait when I saw Sir Peter coming around the corner from the other side of the building. He seemed to have aged terribly. I went to wave to him, and felt a bit silly. This was hardly a social call. He saw me and seemed to pull himself together. We shook hands. He looked down at my feet.

'Goodness me. Been on a bit of a hike?'

'I had to walk from the bus-stop,' I said.

He nodded slowly as if processing a piece of information of great significance. He ran his fingers through his hair and made a deep sighing noise.

'She's been asking for you,' he said, almost to himself.

He looked out over the gardens. 'I don't know what to say to her. I usually leave all this sort of thing to her mother.' His voice trailed off.

I snuck a glance at my watch. It was 3.05pm.

'Look, I really want to see Sophie,' I said.

'Yes, of course. How selfish of me.' He stopped and looked at me as if seeing me for the first time. 'You are a good friend to my daughter, aren't you?'

'I think so. I hope I am.'

'She needs a good friend right now.'

'I must go in.'

'Yes. Of course.'

I turned to go in and nearly bumped into two nuns who were shepherding a young chap in a wheelchair. I realised with a jolt that this was a Catholic institution.

'Don't let them bully you,' Sir Peter smiled at me.

It was a Sister Monica who met me at the front desk

and insisted on escorting me upstairs.

'You will find Miss Thompson-More feeling rather sorry for herself,' she said calmly. 'Please don't upset her by talking too much. You are rather late for visiting you know.'

The door closed behind me bringing a welcome silence.

It was a beautiful room in its simplicity. Yellow curtains against cream walls, walnut furniture, and a high narrow bed where Sophie lay ashen-faced, her cheeks wet with tears. The only decoration was a large wooden cross above the bed and a print of Bellini's Madonna and Child in a heavy gilt frame next to the door.

'Sophe?'

She turned her head slightly and gave me a weak smile. I walked over to the bed and took her hand in mine.

'Did you see Daddy?'

I nodded.

'Mummy wants me to go down. She thinks it's all too much for me. I tried to tell her the truth, but she won't listen. Georgie, nobody listens to me.'

'I'm listening,' I said feeling wretchedly ill-equipped to deal with Sophie's anxiety.

She looked at me. She was even thinner than before. Her cheeks were hollow.

'The doctor wanted to see my hands when I came in.'

'What on earth for?'

'He wanted to see if there was any evidence.'

'Evidence of what?'

'Self-harm,' she sniffed. 'Silly man. As if I'd do it where it shows.'

'Whatever do you mean *where it shows*?'

She struggled to prop herself up in bed. 'Here,' she

said pulling back the bed sheet. I did a double take. She pulled her left leg up and let it flop down like a frog, exposing her slender inner thigh which should have been smooth and white but was instead pink and scarred with what looked like deep scratches and minor cuts, some of which were obviously infected. I recoiled in spite of myself.

'Now you know the truth about me,' she said flatly.

'Does your father know about this?'

She pulled the sheet back over herself and turned her head away.

'I am nothing but a liar and a sinner and a fake,' she said.

'Sophie,' I pleaded with her. 'Please tell me. Does your mother know? What did the Doctor say when he saw this?'

'They think I'm mad. Maybe I am. They'd prefer that. That would be much easier for them to deal with.'

'You're not mad. Of course you're not. Why ever do you think that? Sophie – please, talk to me.'

'I can't bear it Georgie. I can't bear it anymore, knowing what I am. I can't change. I've tried. I really have. In my heart of hearts I know what I am and it's so disgusting.'

There was a knock at the door and Sister Monica bustled in to give Sophie her medication.

'You'll have to go now,' she said. 'You can visit again next week.'

I made a point of ignoring the interruption and leaned closer to Sophie. 'I'll come and see you next week.' I kissed Sophie on the forehead and felt her squeeze my hand so tightly, I thought my fingers would break.

'Thank you Georgie. Thank you for coming,' she whispered.

I stood in the corridor feeling bewildered and shocked. Was this her penance? If so, penance for what? It seemed that the more Sophie modelled herself according to the example of the blessed Saints, the more hypocritical she felt. I made my way back downstairs and out to the car park at the front of the building.

To my surprise Sir Peter was still sitting in his car staring out of the windscreen. When he saw me he waved, leaning over to open the passenger door. I got in and sat with my hands in my lap feeling foolish and overwhelmed and totally miserable.

'I don't understand,' I whispered, tears blistering my cheeks.

'Put your seatbelt on,' he said and handed me his handkerchief. We drove on through the countryside, me snivelling into his handkerchief, neither of us speaking until I realised that we weren't actually on the road to Cambridge, but heading further out into the country. I looked across at him but his face was blank.

'Don't worry,' he said.

We drove for a long time. The car was warm and comfortable. I was weary and drifted in and out of sleep, my head resting against the window. We stopped once at a little petrol station. I opened the car door and swivelled round in my seat to stretch my legs. I didn't think anybody was looking so I slipped off my court shoes and pulled on my stockings. On the opposite side of the pump was another car. A harassed-looking woman in her mid forties was remonstrating with an angry little boy who was jumping up and down on the back seat. The man I presumed to be her husband came out of the little shop just in front of Sir Peter. The man swept an envious eye over the Jaguar. As he caught sight of my legs his face twisted into a horrid little smile, and he winked at me. He glanced askance at Sir Peter, who seemed oblivious. As the man got back in his car I noticed his wife was staring at me and her expression said it all. *Little tart.*

'You must be hungry.' Sophie's father unwrapped some chocolate and handed me one half of a Bounty Bar. We sat there. I didn't have the heart to tell him that I hated desiccated coconut. I ate my half and he ate his.

'Better?'

I nodded. He started the car engine and we set off again.

I tried to make sense of Sophie's situation. I couldn't put it into words then but it was as if she couldn't take credit for anything except hurting herself. The burden of her 'perversion', as she saw it, was taking a huge toll. The more she tried to exorcise her need to express herself, the deeper it seemed to take root. I wondered if her father understood his daughter any better than my own seemed to understand me.

It was dark by the time we arrived back at Clare. Sir Peter stepped out of the car and came around to open the door for me. On the pavement he shook my hand. 'Thank you Georgina,' he said, 'for being there.' He drove away and I walked slowly back into college. When I got to the top of our staircase, Theo was waiting in Helena's room with the door propped open. They both jumped up and hugged me.

'Golly, we were about to call out the police. Where have you *been* all this time?'

'I decided to go into town,' I lied.

I never told them about my afternoon drive with Sophie's father. It would have been a betrayal somehow. I kept the handkerchief.

***

I visited Sophie often but she seemed such a lost figure, lying flat, arms straight by her side. I arrived one afternoon a little early and was horrified to see her lying upside down with her head and arms down on the floor, the Sisters slapping her back, making her cry out with pain. That was part of the treatment: loosening the build up of fluid in the lungs. It was medieval torture.

On my next visit the following week I recognised the college Chaplain coming out of her room. He was a rounded, bearded man in his mid-forties who smelt reassuringly of pipe smoke. He nodded at me.

'It's Miss Marsh, isn't it?' He closed the door to Sophie's room behind him. 'She's sleeping at the moment. Why don't you walk with me?' I hesitated. I didn't know if I wanted to talk to him.

We strolled through the garden and found a wrought iron bench. He filled his pipe and set about the arduous business of lighting it. Once settled he turned his attention to the blackbird overhead. Finally, when no doubt he felt I had had ample time to prepare myself he focused on the real reason for his visit, and by implication, my own.

'I believe you are very close to Miss Thompson-More.' He took my silence for confirmation. 'I wonder if I might therefore speak to you about a matter that has been troubling her?'

'I would do anything for Sophie. We all would, that is to say my friends and I. Is she very ill?'

'Yes,' he said. 'She is.'

The answer was so direct I didn't think I'd understood him properly. I bit my lower lip and held on to the seat of the bench with both hands.

'But the question is not entirely one of physical health, though of course the body and the soul are as one.' He paused as if to check himself. 'It is rather a question of spiritual suffering, I think, Miss Marsh. Miss Thompson-More asked to see me about a very delicate matter. I was surprised at first because she is of the Roman Catholic faith and I would have expected her to see Father O' Connell.' He turned to me and his cheeks were a little flushed. 'Well, in the circumstances, perhaps not.'

He patted his jacket pockets and withdrew his tobacco pouch once more. Then realising he had his pipe between his teeth he sat with the pouch in his hands looking rather defeated. He tried again.

'Miss Marsh, Georgina. May I call you Georgina?' he continued. 'Sophie has confided, but not within the sacrament of confession. You understand? This affords me a certain leeway. It is important to be discreet of course, but I think that only a loving Christian friend can truly help her at this time.'

'You're frightening me.'

'I am so sorry. It's simply that Sophie is deeply troubled about her relationship with God, that much I believe she has already discussed with you over many weeks now.'

'Yes.'

'There is another matter however, which she has tried to convey to you but she is too afraid to really talk about it, and she has asked me to speak to you about it instead'

'She's going to die, isn't she?' My voice cracked and I clenched my fingers together in my lap.

He looked at me in surprise. 'Good Heavens no! No. She will make a good recovery with time and care. No, the matter I speak of is of a more personal nature. Sophie wishes you to understand that she is . . . *different.*'

I stared at him.

'Different?'

He looked down at his hands again and folded them in his lap. 'She prefers the company of women to that of men.' He waited.

I registered the words well enough. Sophie wasn't unique on that point. I had to admit that I pretty much looked upon male company as tiresome unless I was in the full throes of a mad crush. Sophie didn't have any brothers so it was probably . . . I stopped in mid-train. Something in his demeanour suggested a far more serious interpretation. I swallowed hard and looked away. Had I been a complete and utter idiot?

The Chaplain gave me a helping hand. 'Your friend is of the Sapphic persuasion,' he said gently.

'Gay?' I blurted out, turning to him, my eyes swimming with tears. 'You're saying that Sophie is gay?'

He nodded slowly.

'But she *can't* be!' I said bluntly. 'She's practically engaged,' I added in a hoarse stage whisper.

'She has felt extremely uncomfortable lately, because she hasn't told you the whole truth and, as she put it, you have been so very kind and understanding to her.'

I let the words settle in my brain. Sophie – *gay?* Helena – yes – of course. She was tall and strong and just a little bit scary. But Sophie was, so, so . . . *feminine.* So *petite* and, God almighty, *Roman Catholic.* And to cap it all, there was a boyfriend back home wasn't there? Was that what all the marks on her thighs were about? Self-harm. Why, why would she do it? Why?

At twenty Sophie was on the cusp of her adult self. She was becoming truly beautiful. We all could see it. Though I felt positively abject on my own account, I had no wish to deny others the opportunity to know and receive love. Sophie should have felt love spilling forth like the blossoming fruit of a tree that both nourishes the self and gives seed to others, love begetting love. There should have been a sun-dappled clearing where all praise and love bestowed by a benevolent God or devoted parents could find safe soil. Seeds of love taking root, providing ballast for her soul when rocked by the currents of self-doubt. Instead of which she had been cutting herself with a razor blade.

I was beginning to piece together the clues that had been staring me in the face these last few months. I thought back to an earlier conversation in King's Parade. We were looking at silver antiques in anticipation of her parents' twenty-fifth wedding anniversary.

'Sometimes,' she said, staring into the window of the antiques shop, 'I feel like there's nothing inside me at all. Just a black hole.'

I followed her gaze through the plate glass to a large funereal silver urn with great wreaths of ivy and small bacchanalian figures dancing hand in hand around the fluted rim. Ghastly.

She was chewing her bottom lip and for a moment I thought she was working out how to get it home on the train when I realised that she was crying.

'Sophe? Whatever is it?'

'Nothing. Nothing at all.'

Then there was always that slight tension whenever Helena was around. I thought she didn't entirely approve of Helena's sexuality. Was that why she never seemed keen to be on her own with Helena? Was she afraid that Helena would try and seduce her?

'I have to go and see her,' I said standing up. The Chaplain stood up nervously.

'Georgina – Miss Marsh – Sophie's feeling extremely sensitive at the moment. I would suggest waiting a little while.'

'No, I have to see her right now.'

I went straight into reception and up the stairs two at a time. I knocked softly on Sophie's door and went in. She was lying in bed, her face turned to the wall. I knelt down beside her so that my face was at eye level with her.

'Sophe, it's me, Georgie.'

She looked at me sadly and tried to make a joke.

'So he told you. I'm Saint Sophie, Patron Saint of Sexual Deviants.'

'You silly goose. Do you really think I would think any the less of you? Or Theo, or Helena?'

'She's the very last person I can confide in,' she said.

'But she would understand, better than any of us!'

'But I can't! Don't you see? I have to fight this, this *perversion. I don't want to sin.*'

'But you can't go against your true nature!'

'I know, I know but there's no other choice. God made me this way so that I can prove my love for Him. It's a test of my Faith. If I give in to my feelings I let Him down, don't you see that?'

'No.' I shook my head. 'No I don't. It's not your fault. Are you telling me that this is your way of purging yourself? A razor blade? God doesn't want you to suffer like that Sophie, He can't do!' I was furious and upset. 'What kind of God wants that?'

'You don't understand,' she breathed. 'The Holy Father talks about dignity for those with 'disordered attractions'. What dignity,' she cried, 'could there be in so shameful a condition?'

'Do you think Helena is shameful?'

She shook her head, her face twisted in agony.

'Helena's an atheist. It's different for her.'

So this was her dilemma. Everything was conspiring against Sophie in her search for peace of mind. To accept her true self would mean losing the love of God. It was an algorithm of despair providing proof after proof of her own corruptibility, her own unworthiness to receive Him. If Hercules could re-route the rivers

Alpheus and Peneus to cleanse the Augean stables in a single day, Sophie did no less to purge herself of all impure thoughts. She scoured her soul with small acts of contrition, denied herself food, cut herself with a razor blade, branded her inner thighs with the sharpened end of a compass point every time she thought of touching herself. Had God been a Roman Catholic He surely would have raised her up in alabaster, so perfect was her imitation of the Saints.

'But it isn't your fault,' I kept telling her. 'God didn't do this to punish you. Surely love is love whether it's between a man and a woman or between two women?'

But there was more. Sophie snuffled into her handkerchief.

'It's Helena,' she cried. 'I – I can't bear it George. I can't bear it!'

And the realisation finally hit me. Whilst Theo gave herself up to nocturnal assignations with junior Fellows and I fretted over how best to divest myself of my maidenhead, Sophie lay miserably in her single bed and tried not to dream of Helena. All this time Sophie had longed for intimacy with Helena, to share herself with Helena. Our friendship, close as it was, couldn't stop her from harming herself. Whatever my friendship meant to Sophie, whatever *I* meant to her, was nothing compared to the love she felt for Helena. It was selfish of me, horribly, dreadfully selfish of me, but in that moment I *hated* Helena. I hated them both.

'But that's okay, isn't it?' I tried, 'you and Helena? Isn't that just a perfect situation? Does she feel the same way about you?' My words were wooden, but Sophie didn't seem to notice.

'No. I don't know.' She shook her head vehemently. 'Even if she did, it wouldn't work. My mother absolutely loathes her. My family would never accept the relationship. How could they? It's sinning against God in the most awful, degenerate way possible. I couldn't bear it.'

I didn't know what to do. I held her whilst she cried against my shoulder feeling utterly wretched and completely out of my depth.

'Then what about some sort of counselling? What about your parish priest, Father O'Connell? You must confide in someone from the Church – someone who can help you with all this.'

'But I'm telling you,' she sniffed, wide-eyed and tear stained.

Inwardly I groaned. What was I supposed to do? I racked my brains to think of something useful. I had studied *Brideshead Revisited* for A Level but nothing leaped out at me. Was the entire English aristocracy riddled with unnatural vices? I tried to think closer to home. There had been a couple of girls at school who walked around holding hands, but they had been a bit glam-rock. Black eyeliner and pierced ears. I hadn't been sure whether same sex hand-holding constituted definitive proof of lesbianism or public mourning for Marc Bolan.

I myself had held hands with my best friend from school. She had gripped my fingers so tightly I thought mine would never recover. But that had been at her brother's funeral and we never spoke of it again. I wasn't prepared. I just wanted to grasp the essential tenets of Roman law, contemplate the universe of Parmenides. I wanted order and logic and certainty, not this. Not chaos and despair.

'You mustn't tell her.' Sophie was adamant. 'You must swear it. Georgie! You must *swear* on your *life* not to tell her!'

I returned via the College Chapel where I lit a candle

for Sophie and reflected on the example of the Blessed Virgin, her eyes drawn upwards to the painting of the Annunciation above the altar. I sat at the back and wondered not for the first time whether any of us would ever truly find peace, love, make happy marriages, give birth. Enjoy normal family life.

By the time Sophie returned to college some weeks later she seemed to have made up her mind. I carried her things up to her room. Theo was waiting at the top of the stairs to give her a brief hug and a kiss before sweeping off to a lecture. The porter arrived a few minutes later carrying a large bouquet; Helena had sent Arum lilies. We went in and I made some tea. Sophie fingered the stems of the lilies and read the small card attached.

'They're beautiful,' I said.

She didn't answer.

'What are you going to do?'

She turned to me and her little face was unreadable, like a mask.

'I've decided Georgie. It's going to be a test of Faith. I'm going to pledge myself to Our Lady and attend daily Mass.'

'But what about Helena?'

She stared at me as if I were the most frightful idiot. 'Helena and I are just friends,' she said firmly. 'This has been just a passing phase for me. I never want to speak of it again. Goodness, I'm practically engaged Georgie! Dear Hugo – he must be so worried about me. I'm going to write to him this very minute. Do you have any stamps? Do you think I can catch the last post?'

***

Hugo was Sophie's mother's choice.

'Not exactly our class, but a good sort. Military background you know. Very decent family. Scots

Guards. *Another* piece of ginger cake Sophie? Are you sure that is such a good idea? Goodness, you girls. Such appetites you have. In my day it was all very different. Just after the war you see. Very different.'

Lady Audrey was a Justice of the Peace. When not sitting it was her habit to visit Sophie, and on those august occasions one of us would be invited to accompany them for either luncheon or afternoon tea. Lady Audrey derived a great deal of pleasure on these occasions as they afforded her an opportunity to sniff condescendingly at Sophie's choice of Alma Mater.

'The traffic system in Cambridge is positively feudal,' she declared, narrowly avoiding a collision with two chaps on a tandem in King's Parade. Passing by the porter's lodge she suddenly said, 'I am not convinced that the standard of cleanliness is all that it should be.' Sophie steered her mother up the staircase to her room, but sitting on the edge of her daughter's bed she pronounced the space to be 'positively cramped' and declined a cup of tea on the grounds that she didn't care for teabags no matter how convenient they might be.

Lady Audrey was a Somervillian and had long cherished hopes that her middle daughter might be persuaded to continue the female tradition. Somerville College was enjoying something of a renaissance of popularity among the middle classes, having nurtured a certain grocer's daughter from Grantham in her early days as a Chemistry student. Much like the Iron Lady herself, Lady Audrey was nothing if not a fervent campaigner for feminine autocracy; witness her domestic arrangements, in particular the house rule that forbade the smoking of cigarettes, cigars, or pipe tobacco, and outlawed the consumption of food between meals. Such deviant behaviour denoted frailty of character and worse, suggested a psychological dependency liable to induce slovenly self-disregard and moral laxity in later years.

She was, in short, a formidable woman of serious intellect, blindsided by references to cultural practices and norms outside of her own class experience. As a result she was frequently moved to comment aloud on the degeneracy of modern life as exemplified in the affability of politicians, the choice of font used for road signs, the new breed of independent television news readers or the relative length of hemlines. She was simultaneously apt to extol the virtues of civilised society, which typically included correct punctuation, the use of natural fibres in household and domestic textiles, deportment, deadlines and last but not least, familial loyalty.

For Sophie, the presence of a chaperone was a buffer of sorts. Lady Audrey presided at the dining table as if she were still on the bench. Every time she spoke, her unctuous vowels put me into a temporary panic as if she were about to send me down for cutlery-related offences. But it was Sophie who was admonished constantly for failing to 'sit up straight,' to 'slow down', 'lift her chin' and so on. And with each petty correction, it was becoming increasingly clear that Sophie was considered, by her mother at least, to be a Great Disappointment. Of course Sophie was no more of a slouch than I was, and that too caused me no little embarrassment for Lady Audrey had a way of undermining her daughter whilst simultaneously making all manner of allowances for her daughter's friends. I wouldn't have been the least bit surprised if she had taken me to one side and explained, 'Sophie is born to be something special, whereas *you,* Georgina, are not and therefore I have no expectations of your behaviour. *You* cannot disappoint me.'

I was never entirely sure why Lady Audrey extended her invitation to include Sophie's closest friends, unless it was in fact a devious attempt to spy on her own daughter. Had Sophie chosen Oxford, it would no doubt have fallen to her elder sister Eleanor to keep an eye on her goings-on and report back to Lady Audrey, or Chiswick Central as we referred to the family home in private.

We took it in turns to escort our friend but even Theo, who exercised a gift for winning over indomitable parents, failed to deflect Lady Audrey Thompson-More from the task of grinding away her daughter's self-esteem in order to 'make something of the girl'.

After the first couple of outings Helena refused point blank to go any more.

'What an insufferable witch!' she declared furiously. 'I can't stand to see Sophe made so bloody miserable. Frankly, I am not *so* desperate for a cream tea at the Copper Kettle as to be willing to put up with the antics of such a frightful old cow. You go George. I know you'll appreciate it much more.'

Was that a sly dig at my own pecuniary state or a careless reference to my dumpy thighs?

'And besides,' she added tartly, 'Lady Tawdry isn't going to pull that lemon face with you. You at least are safe on that score. You don't pose an illicit threat to the female youth of the nation.' But it struck me quite forcibly at the time that Helena was really cut up. She didn't usually give two hoots for the opinions of others. And that's when I realised the truth. Helena had fallen in love.

I had no doubt that Sophie was the beloved in question.

3

Sophie was the middle child of three girls. Her eldest sister, Eleanor, had already distinguished herself in the field of Egyptian hieroglyphics and won the heart of a 'simply brilliant' Junior Fellow in Anthropology at the Other Place. The youngest daughter, christened Prudence, an ironic choice surely, given the unplanned nature of the pregnancy, was a precocious twelve-year-old, a late child, who revelled in the adult environment and was simultaneously beastly to Sophie and sycophantic to her mother. Sophie wilted in this fetid atmosphere like a rare orchid under glass.

Her father was mostly absent. His work took him to Africa for months at a time. When he was at home he made a great fuss of all of them, and us too if we were visiting. He referred to his family as 'his flock of white swans', which seemed sublime and ridiculous all at the same time. I couldn't imagine my own father using such hyperbole. Here I am Duckie, surrounded by my nest of crows, my ugly ducklings, my cockatiels.

We liked Sir Peter. Theo thought he was a bit of a jampot. I saw the way she looked at him. She was not above a bit of flirting even with the parent of a close friend, but to my relief he seemed oblivious to her posturing. Looking back, I think he saw it for what it was, and took pains not to give Theo any encouragement. I think that was rather decent of him. Many a married don should have done themselves the same favour.

Sir Peter often motored up to Cambridge unexpectedly and surprised us all with bottles of bubbly, insisting that we join him for an afternoon at the races.

Then we would swap academic gowns and flat shoes for ra-ra skirts and court shoes. It felt so wonderfully decadent, being driven through the narrow streets whilst squashed in the backseat of Sir Peter's Jag, giggling like three little maids from school.

I used to fantasise that Sir Peter was my real father. Flamboyant, charming, generous and of course, handsome. A man at ease with himself regardless of the surroundings. That was a characteristic of upper-class breeding, something you couldn't fake. Money could take you a lot of places but the charming authority with which Sir Peter conducted his affairs, whether chatting with the scout on our staircase or ordering afternoon tea was as natural, to him as breathing. Sophie's father was bespoke; a pater for special treats and red letter days. My dad was off the peg.

It's not that I didn't love him, David Anthony Marsh, husband, father and businessman. I just didn't really understand him; all the lectures about working-class values and the importance of hard graft, yet he thought the sun shone out of Mrs Thatcher's backside. His politics seemed to me to be completely at odds with his class upbringing. We couldn't agree on anything. The more he bellowed on about the hardships of his youth, the less comfortable I felt about going up to Cambridge. How could I feel I'd earned the right to a privileged education when my own father had shovelled shit for a living?

When the time came for my father to start earning his keep, his elder brother put in a good word for him at the local tannery. Young Davey worked like a dog unloading hides to be soaked in urine, returning home every night stinking of piss and excrement. But he was determined to make something of his life. He saw the small opportunities afforded him when others would rather slouch around the yard. He had a keen eye and volunteered to fetch and carry, shadowing the bigger boys who were charged with scraping the fat and flesh from the hides. He watched and learned, practised his skills with a blade and worked his way from yard to shop floor and later from charge-hand to manager. Undaunted by the gibes of his former schoolmates, he cycled five miles every day to the outskirts of the Midlands' town to learn his trade. His goal of one day owning his own leather factory would not have been possible without the financial backing of his future father-in-law, who knew a grafter when he saw one, but in all other senses my father was a self-made man and proud of it.

He understood the economics of diversification without recourse to economic theory. Why pay a supplier when you could control the quality and consistency of demand by having your own livestock? Why ship wholesale when you could manufacture locally? Why boost local competition when you could open your own premises and sell direct to the customer? My father was a natural businessman. He understood market economics and common sense. Thatcher was a godsend. No-one but she could have persuaded him to vote against his class instincts. I never let him forget it.

We had enough money for my mother not to work but she insisted. She didn't want to end up like her mother, dependent on the allowance gifted to her by a self-satisfied husband of middle-income and middle-class morals. Rotary-club dinners and minor Masonic outings were my grandmother's lot. My father had no truck with the Masons. All that funny handshake nonsense. That wouldn't get you very far when I were a lad. Sweat and grit. That's the way to get on in life. You earn the respect of the workers and that's how you get ahead. My brother had been approached once or twice and didn't dare tell my father. Joining the Masons was on a par with voting SDP. Double standards were a fact of my early life.

We argued back and forth over the dinner table. Thatcher is not a true Conservative, he would insist. Forget all the Tory grandées. Her father was a shop keeper. That makes her one of us. *And*, he would add, she went to Oxford, which is just as good as Cambridge and a lot nearer to home. I didn't want to tell him the truth – that I couldn't bear the idea of being close to home. What if my parents took it upon themselves to visit me in college? The thought of my father striding through the gates of Clare whenever he fancied, passing comment on the state of the nation, dropping in on me, *spying* on me, was enough to bring on a fit of the vapours. I went on the offensive. But Dad, Thatcher's appalling. Look at what she's doing to the unions. But he had no truck with communists or the work-shy. Still less could he relate to the Labour Party and their call for uni-lateral disarmament. Madness, he shouted at the television whenever Foot showed his face. As for Scargill . . . the air would turn blue at the very mention of his name. It horrified me sometimes to think that my father's politics were so closely aligned to those of Sophie's mother. Sir Peter on the other hand, never spoke of such matters. His duties were in the service of the Crown. Party politics were necessarily beneath him. That at least was how I chose to see him.

When pressed, Sophie admitted that she didn't really know what it was her father did to maintain a wife, three daughters, a large house in Chiswick, a cottage in Cornwall, three red setters, a cook, a maid of all works, two cleaners, a BMW, a Jaguar, assorted in-laws, a yacht on the Solent, a couple of race horses and a mistress in

Dar Es Salaam.

'Oh surely not!' we chorused in a mixture of outrage and intrigue.

'The dirty old goat!'

'How do you know, Sophe?'

Sophie, Theo and I had been lounging on the back lawn at Camber House (Chiswick Central). It was the weekend of the boat race and we had spent the afternoon down at the river watching yet another dispiriting Cambridge defeat. Even Theo's selfless extra-curricular coaching of Nigel the wiry cox had failed to deliver a much needed victory. We headed back to Sophie's feeling out of sorts. A light rain was falling so we had taken refuge in the summer house with a couple of bottles of fizz and a large joint. Lady Audrey would have had a fit, so we took care to leave all the windows open to avoid recriminations.

Sophie twirled a thin lock of golden hair around her little finger and said sadly, 'I saw her once, the mistress. He used to visit her in town. He took Eleanor, Pru and me out to the zoo one afternoon and on the way back we stopped in Knightsbridge. He said he wanted to treat us all so Eleanor chose a book, Pru picked out a doll and I couldn't make up my mind. Then he got all huffy and impatient and bundled us back into the car. He drove around the corner to a quiet residential street with redbrick mansion blocks and beech trees and parked the car by a meter. He told us to be good and he would be back soon.

'My sisters just got stuck into their presents. It was quite stuffy in the car. Pru was only five so after a little while she fell asleep. Eleanor wouldn't talk to me. She just kept telling me to shush whilst she was reading, so I climbed into the front seat to pretend to drive the car and I saw him coming out of one of the buildings, and there was a woman's face in the window on the second floor looking out through the curtain. He didn't look back up at her. She looked very sad.

'He got back into the car and I slunk onto the passenger seat and he didn't say a word about it. I just knew.'

We all sat quietly.

'But that was a long time ago Sophe,' I said, passing the joint to Theo, 'and you might have been mistaken.' This new information rather tarnished Sir Peter's romantic image. I thought back to the man who had taken me for a country drive – perfectly innocent. Sharing a bar of chocolate with me, nothing more. A perfect gentleman. Had I been lucky? Or maybe he just hadn't fancied me. My dad may not have been a blue-blood but I couldn't imagine him ever being unfaithful. I started to see that having a bespoke father accustomed to the high life might have its drawbacks.

'How do you know she's in Dar Es Salaam?' asked Theo.

'We went out two Christmases ago to visit. He promised to take us on Safari. I was down in the lobby of the hotel and one of the desk clerks was chatting up this very chic woman in a big straw hat. It was her, the same face, smiling. Then the manager of the hotel came along and made a great show of kissing her hand and escorting her out to a limousine. When the manager came back in I heard him give the desk clerk a real roasting.'

'God, that's awful,' I said, taking the joint from Theo.

'Yes,' said Sophie. 'I suppose it is. That's why Daddy calls us his swans. It's the term for a white man's women in the town when everyone knows he's got a black whore stashed away somewhere in the Bush.'

Theo and I looked at each other and said nothing. It

wasn't like Sophie to use such language.

'I'll bet a pound to a penny that somewhere down in deepest, darkest Africa I have a whole family of half-siblings. Little brown babies with skinny arms and legs sticking out. A whole other family that knows nothing about me.' She sighed quietly.

'Do you think your mother ever found out?' I asked.

'I don't know,' said Sophie. 'It's not the kind of thing I can ask her, is it? I mean, if she doesn't know, then I couldn't possibly say anything, and if she does, then she must be pretending just to protect us. It's not as if he's going to leave or anything like that. And what could she do? Divorce is out of the question.'

'I'd cut off his balls,' I said with feeling.

'She's a magistrate you idiot,' said Theo. 'Come on,' she added, inhaling deeply. 'Take a big drag Sophie. At least your father comes home every once in a while, and he is jolly nice in spite of it all. I never even met mine.'

I looked at Theo through a haze of blue. *Never met her own father?* What about the cabin in the Rocky Mountains and the skiing trips? I had taken so much at face value when it came to Theo but it wasn't the first time I had noticed inconsistencies in her stories about her family and her upbringing. I bit my tongue. She shrugged her shoulders. 'It's not the end of the world,' she said.

Not the end of the world. I lay awake that night struggling to make sense of Theo's indifference. She'd never known her own father. Was that why she was so ready to go to bed with men? Was that why I couldn't keep up with her? My father came home every night. I don't think he had a faithless bone in his body. Was that why I couldn't bring myself to do the deed? Was I handicapped for life because my family was completely *normal?*

***

I gave up smoking dope after Peru. Theo still liked a joint on the odd occasion. Helena never really approved and I don't think Sophie cared much one way or another. It's more about the lasting effects than the actual hit with me. Bad dreams. Bad memories. They seem one and the same after a while. Difficult to tell apart so I take care not to indulge, not even when clients expect it. Daniel used to think I was just being prudish. Of course, I couldn't tell him the whole truth. What is the whole truth anyway, come to think of it? I wouldn't know where to start. I'm not suggesting that he had a habit. Of course not. But the odd line of coke at the end of a dinner party, that sort of thing I really couldn't buy into.

It was the source of one of our worst arguments. We had been to dinner in Chelsea at the home of one of his partners in the firm. It had been a rather dull evening and the window of opportunity for leaving was closing fast. Daniel was getting his second wind. I wanted to go home. Had we been entertaining at home I would have gone to bed and left him to it.

'So how about a little pick-me-up?' Daniel's partner in the firm was a striking redheaded divorcé called Deborah McNeil. I never really liked her and I certainly didn't trust her. She produced a small polythene bag of powder and proceeded to cut it on the dining table with her platinum American Express card. Deborah had that gold-plated vulgarity usually associated with footballers' wives and girlfriends. She divorced her second husband on the pretext of some extramarital affair but I knew for a fact that she was quite partial to a little ex-officio fornicating herself, her taste running to the lighter side of thirty.

Tamsin, my PA, was a mine of information on the

seedier side of publishing and although I did my best not to encourage spurious gossip, information was power and I saw no reason to deny myself every opportunity of being well-informed. There was, according to Tamsin, scarcely a junior male executive at Holder & Wishart who hadn't been stalked, shagged and bagged by the lady in question. 'A regular tufter,' I thought to myself as I watched her, nose down, snorting powder like a hound scenting blood. I half expected her to start wagging her tail. Daniel was just game to her. He knew I wasn't keen so he didn't even ask before getting his head down. I said I had an early start in the morning. He tried to make a joke out of it. She thought it was highly amusing and arched her eyebrow. Her half-smile made my blood boil.

'Daniel, don't tease Georgina. It's not for everyone. Darling, it's fine really – help yourself to another drink. I promise I won't lead him astray.'

Patronising bitch. It was like being back at school. Damned if you do and pitied for being too chicken if you don't. Vanilla. Wasn't that the current slang for not being a complete fuckwit? Still, this was the price I had to pay for living with a man twenty years my senior. A man who would do virtually anything to maintain the illusion that he was as virile as someone half his age. I went out on to the patio to have a cigarette. Daniel hated me smoking. Serve him right.

It was cool outside, a light breeze coming off the river. There were sounds of laughter from the open plan kitchen-diner. How long was this going to take? I took a stroll around the garden and found a moulded plastic bench. From my vantage point in the area outside the floodlit zone, I watched Daniel with complete disinterest. It was like being at a modern staging of a Harold Pinter play. Within the lightbox that formed the single storey extension at the rear of the house the two actors rehearsed their pantomime for my benefit. God Almighty. Who was that fifty-something man leering across the table? He probably thought he was irresistible. Well I could resist him. In fact, since I had the car keys I could drive home without him.

I wandered back into the kitchen and reached for my handbag and jacket.

'Well, I've had a lovely evening Deborah. Thank you so much.' I blew her a kiss and headed for the door.

'Where are you going?' Daniel's face was a picture of alarm. He knew he'd crossed a line but was too far gone to figure out how to fix things.

'Home sweetie. Don't worry, I won't wait up. Ciao.'

'Georgina, don't be like that!' Then muted, 'Deborah I am so sorry, it's just you know, probably her time of the month.'

'Oh Daniel darling,' Deborah's lip curled into an unpleasant smile, 'honestly, there's no cause to apologise on Georgina's behalf.'

'No indeed.' I was fuming. It was one thing for Daniel to behave like a prick, but quite another for her to pity me for it. 'Be an angel and stick him in a taxi when you're done with him,' I said, flashing a taut smile which fooled nobody. I blew Daniel a kiss, turned on my heel and left.

It was around five in the morning when he finally appeared back at the flat. I accused him of sleeping with her and when he didn't deny it I told him it was just as well because she was much nearer his own age. Actually, I didn't really care one way or another.

'Christ,' he yelled. 'All this over a line of coke? Why can't you just lighten up? It would probably do you good. Then you might be a little less hard on the rest of us. You never know, you might even get off once in a while.'

Perhaps I should have told him then. It wasn't really his fault. He had no idea what had happened to me. It was only when the dreams started that Daniel began to understand in part, but even then I hid the truth from him, as much for my own sake, as for his. Had I known that thirty years on I would still be suffering the after effects of what Theo euphemistically called 'a bad trip', I would never have consented to the ritual.

San Pedro, Wamani's spiritual guide turned out to be not one of the Catholic saints, as we had imagined, but a plant. A psycho-tropic hallucinogenic. A cactus named after St Peter, the keeper of the keys. A plant that would open the gates of Heaven. Or in the wrong hands, lead us down into Hell.

4

Wamani was as good as his word and sent his houseboy to collect us from the hostel. Miguel was a scrawny kid of about fifteen, who was clearly anxious about his mission, and no wonder. The battered red pick-up truck, streaked with mud and covered in football club stickers drew wary looks, not least because the dark blue emblems favoured Cuzco's rival team in the Peruvian league.

Jorge, our greasy-faced landlord, stocky, middle-aged with a cheerful round face and broken teeth was not entirely happy with the new arrangement and urged us to reconsider. Cuzco was changing, he said. We needed to beware of cholo, an unscrupulous new generation neither Indian nor misto. He gestured towards Miguel who shuffled back and forth, his head bent low as he quietly loaded our gear into the back of the truck.

'I worry for you girls,' Jorge smiled kindly. His wife was even more insistent. She made a point of spitting into the dirt right at Miguel's feet. Jorge slapped his hand on the door jamb and pulled his wife back into the hostel. She plucked at his sleeve, muttering the word 'ñakaq', over and over. He pulled a face and scolded her in his native tongue.

I was embarrassed for Miguel, who trembled and put out a tentative hand to touch my sleeve. He raised his eyes to the sky and gave me a beseeching look.

'It's fine,' I said. I turned and shook Jorge's hand. 'We have to go now.'

'Do not listen to this foolish woman,' he said apologetically. His wife scowled and curled her lips into a hideous snarl. He raised his hand to her and she backed away, cursing under her breath. 'She is of the mountains, the Queros people. They have strange ways. Very superstitious. Nothing to worry about.'

We took our leave. Sophie and Theo wedged in the front next to Miguel, so Helena and I hauled ourselves into the back, our rucksacks and equipment stowed under heavy canvas between us. We were excited and not a little nervous. This was becoming even more of an adventure than we had anticipated. Miguel levered the truck into first gear and Jorge stepped forward to wave us off but just as we were about to pull away, his wife came flapping out of the hostel like a crow with a broken wing, threw herself against the side of the truck and reached up with claw-like fingers as if to scratch the air. She let out a stream of Quechua, nodding her head at me, her eyes wild and staring.

'What does she want?' asked Helena, recoiling.

'I have no idea.'

There was spittle at the corners of her mouth and she seemed apoplectic with rage. She shook her fists and then clasped her hands together with such a pleading look that I couldn't resist, and stupidly knelt forward to reassure her.

'It's okay, really – '

In an instant the half-crazed woman seized hold of me with a strength I would not have believed possible, as if to pull me out of the truck. Her husband rushed forward to grab hold of her arm and shouted something to Miguel. His wife shook her fist angrily as he hoisted under her armpits and swung her round to face him. By now a small cluster of spectators had gathered at the roadside, laughing at the pantomime.

Furious at being thus thwarted his wife kicked him in the shins and made one last effort to reach me, heaving herself up to grasp my wrist and press a small object into my palm.

'Pishtaco, ñaqak! Hina Kuchun!' She crossed herself and clasped my palms together. The truck horn sounded and I caught a glimpse of Miguel's terrified face in the rear view mirror. In his panic he must have pressed down on the accelerator because suddenly the truck lurched forward pitching her back into the knot of onlookers, squawking and scratching at her limping husband who was striving to keep his balance up against the doorway with one hand and fending her off with the other.

Helena grabbed hold of my jacket and I fell back, winding myself against the canvas bags, as we bounced down the hillside, trailing dust clouds in our wake, the crowd behind us fully embroiled now in a domestic dispute.

'What the hell was that all about?' Helena yelled above the roar of the engine.

I shrugged my shoulders. I gingerly opened my still-clenched fist and stared at the small polished disc of bone with pyrographic markings. One side bore a rudimentary cross surrounded by a circle with tiny letters and on the other was etched a figure holding a staff entwined with two serpents.

'An amulet of some sort?'

'That looks like a caduseus to me,' said Helena. 'Serpents representing power over Death, guardians of the Underworld.'

'And the cross?'

'Who knows? Perhaps it's just a multi-purpose trinket.'

I turned the amulet in my fingers and felt the warmth of the bone. It was a crude piece of folk-art, yet I couldn't resist the feel of it against my skin.

I imagined Jorge's fury at his wife's defiance. What

would cause a Quechua wife to disobey her husband in such a flagrant way? She had turned him into a laughing-stock.

'Whatever it is,' Helena added. 'She went to a lot of trouble to give it to you.'

I tucked the amulet inside my jacket pocket and huddled down beside my rucksack. 'Yes,' I said slowly. 'She certainly did.'

***

Chincheros lay approximately twenty miles to the northwest of Cuzco. We bounced along the dusty roads, singing and cheering and whooping every time we hit a pothole. Sophie stuck her head out of the window at one point and made the driver stop so that she and Theo could join us. It was dark and smelly in the front, she complained and besides, we sounded as if we were having a lot more fun riding shotgun in the open air.

We waved to small children herding sheep and goats at the roadside, and marvelled at the greenery. High on the hillsides we could see the stone terraces where local families had cultivated the red earth using hand-held ploughs to produce the all-important potato crop. The glaciated mountains made a staggeringly beautiful backdrop to the high plains. The temperature was dropping sharply. We had climbed another 1200 feet. I wish I'd bought a chulla, the woven headgear used by men, to keep my head and ears warm. It was getting on for sunset by the time we came in sight of our new lodgings, a whitewashed hacienda on the outskirts of the village, shielded on one side by a rocky outcrop covered in dense thicket and bordered on the south side by a wide verandah above a terraced garden of small cacti, shrubs and magenta blooms.

Our host waved to us from the terrace. Wamani had swapped his western style dress for a more traditional woven shirt, waistcoat and woollen trousers. His smile was as broad as ever. He still carried the chuspa of coca leaves.

Miguel unloaded the truck and Wamani ushered us into the main part of the house where a wood fire had already burned down to the red hot coals needed for cooking. Miguel brought us hot macha and after a lazy tour of the rambling house and grounds we sat down to a feast of roasted chicken, corn bread and potatoes. That was the best time, when all lay before us and nothing had been written in stone. We felt free, untouched by the mysteries that were even then unfolding around us as we raised our cups in celebration of our good fortune and to toast Wamani; our new benefactor and friend.

***

On our first morning in the hacienda, I awoke to the sound of screeching.

I rubbed my eyes and looked around the unfamiliar room. Outside the window white clouds scudded across a crisp blue sky. I nestled down under the sheet. More screeching, definitely bird in origin. There was a modest hump in the other bed and a soft fringing of golden hair on the pillow.

'Sophe?'

There was no reply. I sat up and swung my legs out to let them dangle over the edge of the outsized carved wooden bed. The buttery yellow walls were covered with simple woven hangings. A plaster Madonna painted with lurid blue mantle gazed down from the chest of drawers opposite. A green painted door led into a small washroom with plain white towels and red tiled floor. The water was hot which meant I was probably first up.

I dressed and slipped out into the hallway in search

of the other guest room. I knocked softly. Helena opened the door and waved me in, still yawning.

'What time is it?' she asked, clambering back into her bed. The room she shared with Theo was an exact replica of mine and Sophie's. Even the Madonna had an identical twin.

'Not sure. I think that's the Dawn Chorus outside,' I said, perching on the end of her bed. The bathroom door was closed. By the sound of hissing water, Theo must have been taking a shower.

'Wamani said something last night about an Indian market. I thought it might be interesting. Do you want to come?'

'Sure,' she said. 'Is Sophie up?'

'Still snoring.'

I lay back against the footboard and chose my next words carefully.

'Sophie seems a lot more relaxed.'

'Thank God. Makes me glad to be an only child. All that nonsense she's had to put up with lately.'

Sophie's eldest sister Eleanor had recently announced her engagement to Lawrence Asherton and the whole household had been swept up in wedding fever.

'Still,' Helena continued, yawning and stretching her arms in such a way as to suggest total indifference. 'It'll be Sophie's turn next.'

'Well that's the thing – ' I broke off as Theo emerged swathed in towels.

'Thank God,' muttered Helena. 'I'm dying for a pee.' She hopped out of bed and disappeared into the bathroom, sliding on the wet tiles and cursing Theo as she slammed the door shut.

'Well?' Theo hissed in a stage whisper. 'Have you broken the good news?'

Sophie was no longer engaged to Hugo.

'Not yet,' I mouthed back at her.

'You're really not cut out for a life of espionage are you?' She smirked.

'And you're not suited to the Diplomatic Corps,' I hissed back at her.

'But now there's no impediment is there?'

'Only her entire bloody family you idiot!'

***

Wamani had risen early to attend to business so it was just the four of us at breakfast. Miguel ran back and forth from the kitchen with hot coffee, head down, trying to make himself as unobtrusive as possible. Poor boy. He seemed so young yet he was more than equal to the task. Did we make him nervous? I sipped my coffee, pondering the actions of the hostel-keeper's wife, turning the disc of bone over and over in my fingers whilst the others tucked in to fried eggs and corn bread.

'That's the cross of St Benedict,' said Sophie. 'You see the etched letters on the front? They form the basis of the Latin text.' Sophie scrunched up her face in concentration and then intoned in a deep voice 'Crux sacra sit mihi lux. Non draco sit mihi dux. Vade retro satana. Numquam suade mihi vana. Sunt mala quae libas. Ipse venena bibas.'

'Blimey. What was that?' Theo's taste for the dramatic had been well and truly whetted.

'It's a sort of lay exorcism.'

'By the Light of the Holy Cross, then something about a dragon,' Helena offered.

'Vade retro satana!' Sophie repeated with feeling.

'Get thee behind me Satan,' I translated.

Theo grinned. 'Wow. You Catholics have all the fun.'

'There should be a figure of St Benedict on the back. The story goes that he got bitten by a snake and

115

managed to survive by the strength of the prayer. He beat back Satan.' Sophie studied the reverse side. 'That's odd.'

Theo peered over her shoulder. 'Two snakes and a naked lady.'

'Definitely not St Benedict,' said Sophie.

'Not with tits like that anyhow,' Helena muttered.

I wondered about Helena's earlier suggestion – a multi-purpose trinket. 'Maybe it's a cult figure, a minor saint.'

'Trust me, I know them *all*. The closest would be Saint Patrick who banished the Evil One from Ireland.' She passed the amulet to Helena who frowned. 'She looks ancient to me, Greek perhaps, or Abyssinian.'

Theo shuddered. 'Reminds me of Medusa.'

Helena rolled her eyes. 'She had snakes on her head, silly. The motif of entwined serpents has had a lot of different meanings – the Minoan serpent goddess holds the power of life and death – she predates the Christian church.'

'Athena of the flashing eyes was associated with snakes,' I added. 'She had a cloak of serpents and Perseus gave her the Medusa's head in gratitude after he slew the monster.'

'Just the thing to put on her mantelpiece,' said Theo.

'After that she had the snake's head emblazoned on her shield.'

'My guess would be protection of some sort,' Helena concluded.

'Protection from what?' Theo's question hung in the air unanswered. We turned our heads to see Miguel hovering in the doorway. Wamani had returned.

5

Eleanor had big ideas. A horse drawn carriage, grey morning suits. Cream taffeta and Duchess satin, bridesmaids in burgundy and lots of bows. Sophie couldn't think of anything worse than being obliged to wear burgundy silk with a huge taffeta bow. She had wanted to climb the mountain with us, but Lady Audrey had declared that to be out of the question. She would be needed at home. Her sister's wedding must take precedence. Never mind that the day in question was still three months away. Lady Audrey could not countenance Sophie putting herself in mortal danger.

'And what if you should suffer some terrible accident? Everyone staring at you as you hobble down the aisle with your leg in plaster. Or even worse! Not being there at all! What would your sister have to say about that? It would be far too late to find another bridesmaid by then. Everything would have to be cancelled because you were selfish enough to get yourself killed halfway up some stupid mountain!'

In the face of such opposition Sophie had conceded defeat. She had applied herself with due diligence, going down for weekends to write invitations or practice napkin folding so that Eleanor could decide whether origami swans really were preferable to fans or lotus flowers. Sophie's good nature was such that none but a highly sensitive and loving parent could decipher the code of Sophie's misery. Alas, Lady Audrey was neither. She merely harped on endlessly about what a pity it was that matters had not progressed as far as an engagement where Sophie and Hugo were concerned.

'Really, Sophie. Do not imagine that young men like

Hugo wait around endlessly for encouragement. Could you not show a little more enthusiasm?'

I believe Lady Audrey could see that her daughter was unhappy, but rather than fathom the real reason for her sadness, chose instead to bully her. It was as if she couldn't commit herself to the full satisfaction of an eldest daughter married and settled at twenty-one, knowing that her middle daughter was still unattached. Sophie was spoiling everything.

This state of affairs also aroused a bitter jealousy in Eleanor, who was always intent on claiming her birthright to be first in everything and naturally expected her mother to be as fixated on the minor details of her trousseau as she was. Eleanor's wedding preparations had proceeded apace. Prudence took to twirling round and round in a fevered expectation of silk and taffeta and ice cream and champagne.

Things reached a head however, on one of Lady Audrey's visits.

Sir Peter had arrived unexpectedly at our little house off Mill Road and finding Sophie's room empty, had gone in search of Helena and myself. We were having a spell of fine, good weather for March. The daffodils were out in force. I was on chaperone duty with Sophie and her mother. We had driven into Granchester for afternoon tea. Sir Peter had evidently had the same idea. Finding Helena encamped in the back yard with Ovid's *Metamorphoses*, he had invited her to take a drive.

Lady Audrey was in a particularly foul mood. Eleanor wanted to have an audience with the Holy Father as part of her honeymoon but dates were few and far between. June was a popular month for young couples seeking a nuptial blessing.

Sophie and I were just about ready to throw in the towel when we saw Sir Peter and Helena coming in to the gardens. Sophie blushed deeply. Lady Audrey had her back to her husband. I wasn't sure what was for the best but it was too late anyhow, because Helena stopped dead and put her hand on Sir Peter's sleeve to warn him. At that very moment Lady Audrey turned to summon a waitress for more hot water. Her face froze when she saw her husband with one of her daughter's so-called friends. And it wasn't the blonde who wore rather too much make-up but the tall angular one whom Lady Audrey suspected of having 'disordered attractions'.

Sir Peter tried to make the best of it. He sallied over and kissed his wife on the cheek. Sophie and I stood up. He gave her a very fond hug and shook hands with me warmly.

'Well,' he smiled. 'How are my lovely swans?'

I winced inwardly. Helena just rolled her eyes. Poor Sophie.

Lady Audrey said rather tartly, 'How nice of you to find the time to visit.'

Sir Peter pulled up a couple of chairs and invited Helena to sit down. He waved the waitress over and ordered more of everything. A chilly silence ensued. I was about to ask Helena whether she had seen Theo, when Sir Peter threw down the gauntlet.

'What's this I hear about Sophie not going to Peru?'

Shit, that's torn, it I thought. I glanced at Helena, who looked very uncomfortable. Sophie was still blushing. The waitress returned bearing a tray of tea and scones. Lady Audrey bit her tongue. She was not well disposed to talk about family matters in front of servants and underlings.

'It's a great pity if you ask me,' he continued, helping himself to a fresh cup and looking for the sugar tongs. 'Young people should get out there and have experiences. That's what being young is all about. There's plenty of time for knuckling down. A whole lifetime in fact,' he grimaced. 'Aha.' He smiled brightly as his eyes alighted on the sugar bowl. He deposited two lumps in his tea cup and stirred.

I poured Helena a cup of tea and passed the plate of scones. She helped herself to jam and cream.

'Lady Audrey?' I hovered with the teapot, but she seemed not to have heard me.

'I should have thought it quite obvious why Sophie has chosen to stay in England for the time being.' Her voice was steely and tight.

'Are you part of this junket to the Andes, Georgina?' Sir Peter asked, as if his wife hadn't spoken.

'Yes, well, hardly a junket. It's going to be quite tough going I think. I mean, I don't have the same experience as Helena or Sophie. They're both much better climbers than me,' I flailed around trying to think of something to add.

'But you are going?' Sir Peter pressed home his point. 'Obviously you are,' he added almost to himself. 'You would have been and gone already had it not been for that unfortunate débâcle in the South Atlantic.'

I picked a hole in my paper napkin. Helena lifted the teapot and helped herself to another cup. 'I couldn't really see why we had to cancel at all,' she said bluntly. 'It's a completely different country after all.' I felt Sophie flinch ever so slightly. 'I think it will be a very exciting trip for all of us,' Helena concluded.

'That's capital,' said Sir Peter, looking around for a butter knife. Then he turned back to Helena. 'And Theo is very keen to go?'

'Yes, we've done all the planning. The route is fairly well laid down. Lots of trekkers and climbers have started to go out there. Ausangate is not a terribly difficult climb.'

'Is that so?'

And then I realised that Sir Peter had obviously had the whole story out of her on the drive up. This was a ruse to flush out Lady Audrey's objections and blast them to smithereens. Two barrels, twelve gauge.

'Well in that case, and seeing as you other girls are sensible types, I can't see any reason why Sophie shouldn't go with you.' Bang. One barrel. Lady Audrey's bird was pricked. Sir Peter drained his cup and took a big bite out of his scone. 'These are rather good Audrey, have you had one?' I thought she was going to explode. Sophie looked into her father's face so earnestly that I thought she was about to cry.

'Why Peru of all places?' Lady Audrey persevered. 'It's completely disloyal.'

Sir Peter tipped back in his seat, the picture of contentment.

'I mean,' she continued, her voice reduced to a vehement hiss, 'after the Falklands. Peru was no friend to Mrs T. Not in the least. Completely biased towards Ar-gen-tin-a.' The last word was mouthed in a stage whisper as if sinister forces were listening in and poised to swoop down like agents from the Ministry of Truth.

Sir Peter smiled his most boyish smile, crammed his mouth full of scone and licked his fingers.

'And what about the communist rebels?' Her mouth in a disapproving line. 'According to *The Telegraph*, Peru is completely at the mercy of Shining Light.'

'I think you mean Shining *Path*, Lady Audrey,' I tried helpfully.

She swung the full glare of her disapproval onto me. Pricked but still pecking.

Sir Peter folded his hands behind his head.

'I shouldn't worry, Aud.' She bristled at the familiarity. 'It's the Yanks that have to watch out. Brits don't pose much of a threat. In any case, I have a few contacts out there. Belaúnde is a decent man. Hell of a backhand as I recall. Of course being President, he won't have much free time for tennis. Still,' he whistled softly, taking in the afternoon sunshine. 'I'm sure he'll keep an eye out. Best insurance I can think of really.' Bang. Second barrel right between the eyes. He slid down into his seat with his long legs outstretched, tipped his head back and closed his eyes. 'D'you know, this weather is quite something.'

Lady Audrey's argument keeled over, like a buffalo hitting the ground. But I had the feeling that whilst Sir Peter might have won this battle, the war waged back and forth on other fronts.

'Sophie, I am leaving now. Your father can see you back to Cambridge. Georgina, give my regards to your parents.' She ignored Helena.

'Thank you, yes I will,' I said. She had never condescended to send greetings to my family before. Clearly I was in the doghouse too. We all stood as Lady Audrey gave her daughter a perfunctory kiss on the cheek before taking her leave.

'I'll walk you to your car,' said Sir Peter lightly.

'Golly,' said Helena after they had gone, easing back into her chair and doubling up on jam and cream. 'That was a bit bloody.'

I took hold of Sophie's hand. She was shaking.

'Are you all right?'

She nodded and tried to smile but it was all a bit too much for her and she burst into tears instead.

'Sophe,' cried Helena, leaning forward, 'don't cry. We are going to have the best time in the world – all of us! We'll climb that mountain then we'll fly back home and toast your bloody sister in her dreadful meringue get-up, drink loads of champers and get properly plastered. You see if we don't!'

And then the three of us started to laugh which puzzled Sir Peter somewhat when he reappeared a few minutes later looking rather relieved.

'Well,' he said. 'I must say that went rather better than expected. Is there any more tea in the pot?'

***

So Sophie did come with us to Peru in April of that year. Eleanor's June wedding was as ostentatious as she could have wanted, and we did all get royally drunk.

I had always longed for a sister. Sophie's family seemed to offer up the perfect equation but seeing her routinely corralled with her sisters, each of them apportioned such a small amount of time with their father, I couldn't help but reflect upon the seismic difference between a family of five and a family of four. I began to see that in spite of all his charm Sir Peter found it difficult to individuate his daughters. Perhaps Sophie was right, that there *was* another family out there on a different continent. I began to wonder if Sir Peter's use of the term 'swans' or even his tendency to call everyone 'darling girl' or 'darling boy' was less a feature of upper class gentility than a strategy to avoid discovery. The critical moment came during his Father of the Bride speech. Buoyed up on champagne and bonhomie, he stumbled to recollect his eldest daughter's names. I admit that the practice of giving your child four Christian names must test any parent's memory at times, but not, surely on *that* most auspicious occasion?

My own mother and father had kept our names to a neat middle-class minimum: Georgina Elizabeth and Lucas Edward.

Poor Eleanor.

Or should I say, poor Mrs Eleanor Rosemary Bernadette Claire Asherton, neé Thompson-More.

Toasting and cake cutting aside, Sir Peter's marriage

was obviously in its final death throes. Yet Lady Audrey's revenge upon her husband was greater than any of us could have imagined at the time. The killer blow, when it came, was decisive.

Lady Audrey received a visit one afternoon in early September the following year just a few days after Sophie had gone up to Cambridge to start her teacher training. Two gentlemen wearing dark suits and hand-stitched leather shoes were shown into the conservatory. The weather was unseasonably warm and Lady Audrey was quite glad of an opportunity to come in from the garden where she had been cutting back the clematis. Over Lapsang Souchong and homemade battenburg they informed her of the purpose of their visit. She listened, pale and silent, as they described in the most euphemistic terms the scope and nature of Sir Peter's indiscretions.

I had the story from a tearful Cook on the eve of the funeral, she who had plenty to say about men and their manners. *That battenburg was homemade and they didn't so much as touch a slice.* They left after precisely forty minutes without even asking to see the house.

Lady Audrey went to sit on her favourite stone bench in the garden for several hours, the air chilling around her and in the end it was only the threat of sending for Doctor Mitchell that persuaded her into the house. *Awful queer she looked*, said Cook. They didn't know the ins and outs of it all, but the police turned up the very next day to say that Sir Peter had suffered a fatal heart attack. That just about took the biscuit. It all seemed very fishy to Cook who would never say anything against the family but me being friends and all, there was some talk about another woman a few years back. *Terrible rows, screaming and shouting when the girls were away at school,* she said in hushed confidential tones.

Sir Peter was flown home with full honours. Lady Audrey accepted the condolences of Her Majesty's Government and services were duly held. His daughters grieved as daughters should. The three of us paid our respects. But unbeknown to all of us, the casket was empty. Lady Audrey had ignored her husband's infidelity whilst he lived, and clearly the state was content to draw a veil over the memory of a great man. Whether it was this final shame or the betrayal of her country that proved the last straw remains uncertain.

Lady Audrey had her husband's body transferred to a crematorium outside Amersham where, in total anonymity, she consigned him to the flames.

She did not pray for him.

Sophie knew nothing of the true circumstances of her father's death until some five years later when a *Panorama* researcher telephoned Black Farm, looking for 'background'. Helena glanced up from the paper to find Sophie standing like Lot's wife, the receiver held out in front of her like a diseased animal. *No*, Helena bellowed down the phone line, *there's never been any intimation of a sex scandal. Yes, of course he died alone. No, her mother had never received a visit from MI6, you silly ass.*

It was another ten years later that Lady Audrey died, leaving amongst the documents entrusted to the family solicitor a letter for Sophie's eyes only, in which she confessed the whole truth, expressing regret for what she had done, and humbly asking her estranged, unnatural, God-forsaken daughter to do the right thing.

'My God,' Sophie said as she read the contents over breakfast.

Helena had looked up from her coffee to see Sophie sitting very still and suddenly pale.

'Sophe?'

'I have to go to Amersham in Buckinghamshire.'

'What on earth for?'

'To collect my father's ashes. They're sitting on a shelf at an undertaker's premises on the Chesham Road under the name of *Lord Lucan.*'

6

At the Indian market in Chincheros I couldn't decide between a red chullo with a blue diagonal diamond weave or a blue one with a red diagonal diamond weave.

'They're the same,' muttered Helena, bored to tears.

'No they're not,' I said, gritting my teeth and smiling at the Indian vendor with tanned hide for a face.

'Well buy them both then,' she sighed, waving 'no' to a cluster of traders determined to fit her out in quechua pantaloons. They were exclaiming at the length of her legs, pulling faces at each other and striding around her like John Wayne without a horse.

I plumped for the red. I paid the money and put on my new headgear to the delight of the Indian traders who clapped and cheered.

'Oh for God's sake,' Helena said. She seemed unusually out of sorts. It was a beautiful day. I put my arm through hers and we picked our way through the square.

'What's up?' I asked.

'Oh, do take that thing off. You look ridiculous.'

'It's keeping my head warm. What's wrong, H?' I rubbed her arm affectionately.

She didn't answer. I followed her gaze to where Sophie and Theo were busy bartering over some woollen shawls.

'Why don't you just tell her how you feel?' I said. Helena pulled away and turned on me sharply.

'What the devil would you know about it?'

'Nothing,' I said, going red. 'It's obvious, that's all. You love her, don't you?'

She looked furiously back at Sophie and Theo, then

at me, then down at her feet.

'It won't do any good, George,' she said sullenly. 'Sophie's got God on her side. I'd only mess things up for her.'

'Perhaps that's just what she needs. A bit of mess might be good for both of you.'

Helena cocked one eye at me and smiled in spite of herself. 'Are you pimping now?'

'God, no.' Sophie was twirling around with her new purchase. 'Faint heart never won fair lady. You know she's broken up with Hugo Spencer.'

Helena tried to look disinterested but I had her full attention.

'She went to see him the week before we left to put him straight. Her mother's furious. Eleanor was very sore. Something about upsetting the table arrangements. Anyway, luckily Sir Peter was camped at Chiswick Central and he drove Sophie back up to college. Still, you're probably right,' I said.

'What d'you mean?' Helena looked flustered.

'Well, if I were Sophie I wouldn't fancy you either.' Helena stared at me so I punched her in the shoulder. 'Don't be such a tit!' I said. 'Go and tell her straight. What's the worst that can happen?'

She didn't look convinced but I knew from experience that blunt speech was about the only thing that would have any effect on her. She'd been moping around for weeks on end. Sophie was just the same. I really hoped that this would be one of those times when two people most suited to each other would actually get together, like in a film. I loved then both and out of love, I had betrayed them both. Sophie had sworn me to silence. Helena would probably have gouged out my eyes if she had known of it, but I had broken my word. Theo and I had hatched a plot between us.

I had watched Helena closely whenever she was with Sophie. I watched Sophie too for signs of deterioration. So long as she didn't harm herself I thought it would be fine. But deep down I knew that wasn't true. The trouble with holding a secret is that the more you think about how you mustn't speak about it, the more it burns a hole in your throat. I even considered asking the vicar at the ecumenical church if he would hear my confession. I desperately wanted to share my burden of knowledge with someone else. The logical choice was Helena, but that was out of the question. So finally I had settled on Theo.

Theo was practical, not given to heavy hypothesis or philosophical debate. As an English student with a dramatic bent she could however feel her way into different characters. Psychological motivation was right up her street. And she knew about sex. I decided therefore to approach the subject at an oblique angle.

'What do you think about lesbians?' I asked her one afternoon over coffee in town.

'Great. Less competition.'

'Seriously.'

'Seriously! Why do you ask?'

'It's an essay question I'm working on.' I shifted in my seat. I wasn't very good at lying in those days.

'Lesbians in Greek drama?'

'Sort of. Do you think being a lesbian is an innate character flaw, or is it just a mistake? Is it a question of a woman's own nature having already been corrupted and therefore she is powerless to be anything other, or something that she can actively choose not to practise?'

'Neither, I should think.'

'But if you had to choose between the two?'

'I don't.' She breathed out a lungful of smoke. 'Is this about Sophie?'

I sat upright in shock. 'What makes you say that?'

'Well she is gay, isn't she?'

'How did you know?'

'Well it's obvious, darling.'

'It wasn't obvious to me.' I stirred my coffee rather more forcefully than the occasion demanded and slopped brown froth into the saucer.

Theo tried to hide a smile and failed. 'Look,' she said taking another drag on her cigarette. 'Sophie's a big girl and if she wants to explore her sexuality a little then I should let her if I were you.' She grinned. 'Not that she'll get very far with you Georgie. You're too buttoned up for your own good.'

'*Me?*' I recoiled. 'I don't . . . I'm not . . . ' I floundered.

Theo laughed. 'Yes, I know you're not *gay*.' She pulled a face. 'Just teasing.'

I sipped my milky coffee for a while. I tried again.

'The thing is, she's really unhappy. I mean seriously. It's all tied up with her religion.'

'Naughty convent girls and wicked nuns I shouldn't wonder,' said Theo. She saw my face. 'Oh come on Georgie, everyone knows that repression is spice for the erotic. All those girl hormones cooped up, ready to be unleashed. The whole crucifixion thing is one massive sado-masochistic wet dream.'

Now she *had* shocked me. She stubbed out her cigarette and gazed at me kindly as if I were about six.

'Well,' she said lightly. 'What does Helena think about it all?'

I shifted uncomfortably in my seat. 'I can't talk to her about this.' Theo looked a little puzzled. I found myself going red. I was going to have to tell the truth.

'Sophie feels gay. She knows according to the law of her faith, being gay is unworthy. So she has to punish herself in order to be worthy of God.'

'Oh dear,' said Theo. 'That's not so good. I thought

this God of yours was supposed to love a sinner. Suffer all the children to come unto me and all that.' I looked at her askance. 'Yes, I know,' she laughed at herself. 'The whole C of E thing hasn't passed me by completely. Why doesn't she just confess the whole thing and then get on with having sex with women? It's what I would do.'

'She can't. I mean she does confess but the Catholic Church takes a really dim view of it all.'

'You could have fooled me,' she sniggered. 'There are plenty of good little Catholic boys out there just waiting for a bit of chastisement. Couldn't she just cut out the middle man and talk to God direct?'

'She asks Him daily to take away her sin. In her eyes she has to stop sinning.'

'Well then she would be a hypocrite if she pretended that she is straight when she is in fact gay.'

'It gets worse,' I said.

'Helena?'

I nodded.

Theo lit another cigarette. We both sat in silence for a couple of minutes. The cafe was filling up. We were hogging a table that could have seated four. I tried to ignore the pointed looks of shoppers bearing carrier bags.

'Well,' she said. 'Helena's an atheist. She's not going to give a damn about what God thinks. I think they should get together and see what happens.'

'They can't, that's my whole point.'

'Why ever not?'

'Then Sophie would be committing a double sin: giving into her own unworthiness by loving Helena, thus disappointing God, and continuing to sin by being her true self, thus being unworthy of God.'

'This God is really rather difficult to please isn't he? Maybe God is unworthy of her, and maybe Helena is better for her than God is, for that matter.'

This was dangerous territory for me. I was very sure that institutions could only operate, in the main, for the greater good. It had never dawned on me before that the powers-that-be might have their own agenda. It certainly seemed bordering on heresy to talk about it with the local clergy, but I had so many unanswered questions and Theo – atheist that she was – did at least give me some room for expressing my doubts.

'You think perhaps the church has got it wrong?' I said.

'Obviously.'

'I just don't know.' I slumped in my seat. 'Faith doesn't submit to logic, does it?'

'No, but surely your God has to take into account how you feel?'

'Why should He?'

'Because we are not perfect,' she concluded. 'We are just trying. My mother always said that God loves a try-er.' I was surprised to hear her voice falter. She recollected herself. 'If people didn't sin and confess and do penance, religion would be out of business. You have to keep sinning to keep the whole thing going. God's the ultimate loan shark. You can never pay Him back.'

I stared at Theo. I couldn't decide if she was barking mad or simply brilliant. Ten minutes with Theo and I was sure the Middle East, Northern Ireland and Apartheid could be settled all in one go.

'Take Easter for example.' She flicked ash delicately from the end of her cigarette. 'What would you think of a man who made his wife and children go through the whole grieving process every year on the anniversary of his son's death? A man who never lets up, never lets them get on with the rest of their lives. Two thousand years of grieving and no opportunity to move on. It's sick.'

'It's not the same,' I said shaking my head. 'We have to remember our sins and what Jesus did for us.'

'Why?'

'Because . . . ' my voice trailed off.

Theo laughed. 'Well, you're a brilliant advocate for Christianity, aren't you!'

'No, come on. I'm just thinking it through. It's about sacrifice. It's no *ordinary* death. It's the *best* death *ever.*'

'Like . . . in the pantheon of deaths, this is a really good one? One that gets an A rating?' she smirked.

'No.' I shook my head. 'It has to be the best death of all, because it defeats death itself.' Theo shrugged her shoulders. I pressed on. 'And we're grateful, forever grateful, because His death means the end of purgatory. No more damnation. It's fantastic if you think about it.'

'But Jesus doesn't have the monopoly on death,' she said. 'Your classical education has surely taught you *that.*' Theo leaned back and raised her eyebrows in mock surprise. 'What about Orpheus? Didn't he go down into the Underworld to bring back his wife? All the ancient civilisations have resurrection myths.'

'So?'

'I'm just saying that it's *all* hog-wash – saints, gods, monsters and heroes – what's the difference? Today's religion is tomorrow's folklore.'

'I can't believe that's all there is to it,' I said. 'God loves us. He forgives us everything.'

'Provided you repent, and say sorry and never do it again?' She folded her arms.

'Yeah, well. Obviously . . . '

She stubbed out her cigarette. Her face looked serious and I wondered what she was really thinking.

'It's just a get-out-of-jail-free card every time,' she said quietly. 'A licence to sin.' She saw my look of concern and gave my hand a little squeeze.

'Anyway,' she added brightly. 'I have just had the most wonderful idea.' She smiled, her eyes wide open. 'Much Ado.'

I looked blank. 'Shakespeare?'

'Benedick and Beatrice.'

The penny dropped. 'That would be dishonest, Theo.'

'And you have engineered this conversation with me because you're writing an essay?' The point was well made. I blushed.

'Okay, what's your idea?'

'You take Helena, I'll take Sophie. We gently suggest that the other is deeply, humbly, overwhelmingly infatuated with the other. If there is any genuine feeling between them it will come out. Love conquers all.'

'It sounds rather manipulative to me,' I faltered, although I did quite like the plan. Art seemed to answer a lot of human needs in those days.

'Like playing God?' Theo said 'If you ask me, He's not made a fantastic job of things so far. I think it's time someone else had a go, don't you?'

7

Playing God. We all do it from time to time don't we? Lady Audrey certainly did, and Sir Peter. My father in his own way sought to mould me and my brother. Theo transformed boys into men. I wanted two of my dearest friends to find happiness together. And that's why I persuaded the others to come with me and Wamani to visit the shaman.

We were supposed to fast the day before. No sex, which wouldn't be a problem provided Theo kept her hands off Wamani, no alcohol and no food. Only meditation, which none of us had a clue about, and a little water. As we were 'gringo', exceptions were made and we had a light breakfast in the morning. Theo was quite excited. Sophie was understandably nervous and Helena feigned complete disinterest in the whole ritual but said she was prepared to come with us in case we got ourselves into a lot of bother, but frankly the whole thing was ridiculous hokum.

'What goes on then?' Theo flashed Wamani one of her seductive sideways glances whilst he was picking herbs in the garden. Helena and Sophie had walked into the village which left Theo and I at a loose end. I had elected to sit on the verandah and was trying to focus on *Shindler's Ark*. Sophie said it was an absolute must-read. Helena said she'd wait for the film.

Wamani paused to delicately peel back a leaf to expose the bud. His hands were large yet his fingers seemed so gentle. I had a sudden fantasy of those fingers teasing open the buttons of my shirt.

'This shamanic ritual,' Theo continued. 'I suppose it's like an orgy.' She winked across at me. I glared at her then stared at the page in front of me.

'First of all,' he said, 'it is of course a sacred event. You will be some of the very first foreigners to be invited. This is not something that we invite tourists to come and see. You are about to experience something very special. It is not for weak and foolish people. The ayahuasquero – the shaman – must train for many years. The ritual has not been seen by many western eyes. You will be among the first.'

My eyes narrowed as I recalled the mythical Forrester party he had mentioned during our first encounter at the café in San Blas. Didn't he say he'd arranged all this for them already? Weren't they tourists just like us? What made us so special?

He broke a leaf off the stem and crushed it in his fingers. Then he held it out for Theo to try. She took hold of his hand and guided his fingers closer to her face then breathed in the fragrance. She held his gaze and took a step closer, pushing out her breasts slightly so that they almost touched his arm. I was horrified and embarrassed. I lifted my book up a little higher and the words on the page swarmed like ants. He said something that I didn't quite catch and I heard her coquettish laugh. Suddenly the boards creaked and Wamani was standing over me holding a little pot-pourri of scented leaves tied with a dried twist of bark.

'For you,' he smiled down at me. 'It will help to keep the bugs away and make your linen smell fresh.'

I took the posy from him and muttered a thank you. Theo was standing very still, watching me from the garden, twirling a rhododendron blossom between her fingers. She tucked it behind her ear, looking at me coolly. Wamani stood for a moment then he gently took the book from my hands.

'This is a strange book!' he said. 'You read about Nazis?'

'Sophie recommended it.'

'You are all very good friends I think. You trust each other, yes?'

'Yes, I think we do.'

'That is good. For the ritual, it is important to be with friends.'

'Why is that?'

He crouched down beside my chair and weighed the book in his hand.

'Trust. You need to trust if you are going to make yourself open. Like a flower, yes?'

'I suppose so.'

'When a flower opens to the light, it is a truly beautiful thing. It is like God touches the petals and then the flower knows what it is here for. It knows suddenly that it must open itself to the honey bee.'

I blushed. Theo was still in my eye-line, watching every move.

'You think that we need a lesson in the birds and the bees, is that it?'

'No, no.' He shook his head with a little smile. 'No lessons. But,' he laid his finger against his lips, 'when the flower opens, then the honey bee begins its journey. It goes in search of the pollen. That is how life is, that is how life begins. So beautiful, so simple. These things are not to be feared. The great mystery of life is there for us to discover. You will see, Georgina.' And with that he reached out his fingers and lightly pushed a strand of my hair back from my face and tucked it behind my ear. My mouth was dry. He smiled again, handed me my book and stood up. He stretched his arms above his head and sauntered into the hacienda whistling under his breath. I opened the pages and tried to read but my head was swimming. I knew Theo was still staring at me but when I eventually summoned the courage to face her she was gone.

***

We left the hacienda around six and walked about a mile up a narrow track away from the village.

'It is a full moon tonight. This is very auspicious,' said Wamani.

It was certainly romantic. My fantasies about our guide had multiplied since our encounter on the verandah. I pictured us lying naked on my bed back home, our bodies slick with sweat, limbs entwined, Wamani sliding his fingers through my hair, kissing my throat, stroking my breasts. I walked beside him whilst Theo danced back and forth, no doubt in the belief that this would afford him the best view of her comely figure.

He turned to look briefly at Helena and Sophie who were walking a little way behind.

'Your friends – they are Sapphic, yes? Not a couple – not together – but they like each other – yes?'

'Yes, very much. It's not easy though. Sophie's family. They're Catholic. They don't approve of Helena.'

He shrugged his shoulder. 'They want their daughter to be normal. They want grand children. It is what all parents expect.'

'Yes, but Sophie has two other sisters. One of them is getting married in June. I'm sure they will have children.'

'And what about you, Georgina? You have a boyfriend at home?'

'No, gosh. No. Not really.'

Theo reappeared suddenly with blossoms.

'Here, put these on.' She tucked a bloom behind my ear and leaned in close to Wamani to tuck one into his breast pocket. She twirled around and linked arms with me and him, bringing us together with a kind of forced bonhomie. I knew exactly what she was playing at. We walked on.

Wamani smiled and turned the conversation to natural

history and mythology, weaving tales and stopping every now and then to pick a leaf or point out the magical properties of a shrub. I tried to disengage my arm from hers but she just dug her nails in and held me all the tighter.

'Cut it out,' I whispered.

'What? You like him don't you? Well I'm just helping you along.'

'I don't need your help.'

'Oh, don't tell me you're going to do anything about it. You wouldn't say boo to a goose Georgie. You need me to chaperone you. I could have a word with him if you like. Tell him how much you fancy him.'

'Shut up. I don't. Really I don't.'

'You can't fool me, sweetie.'

'What do you care anyhow?'

'I just want to help, that's all. Give you a both a little push in the right direction.' She smiled but I wasn't fooled for a minute. She knew damned well that the more she encouraged me, the less likely I would be to act. She was shaming me.

'What's got into you?'

Wide-eyed and innocent, she looked shocked. 'Honestly Georgie, don't be such a klutz! Think of me as your fairy godmother.'

I fumed inwardly, but there was something else. It was as if Theo had taken it upon herself to play cupid, but at the same time wanted all the attention for herself.

'Tell us about the goddesses,' I said brightly, turning to Wamani. 'You know, the ones you mentioned in the café, the ones from your dream.'

He raised his eyebrows and a lovely smile deepened his dark features. 'There were four of them,' he said, his eyes glittering. 'The first who came to me was naked. She whispered love in my ear. She brought me coca leaves to chew. She was Cocamama.'

'Coca-mama, like the coca we chewed?'

'Yes. Legend says that she is like Venus – a goddess of health and happiness and very, very, sexy.'

'Is the coca leaf an aphrodisiac by any chance?' Theo giggled, turning back to our guide.

Wamani arched his eyebrows and looked at me. I rolled my eyes.

'Yes,' he replied slowly. 'Some are used by the local women to make their men strong. In fact Cocamama governs the coca plant.'

'How?' I asked.

'It is said that Cocamama had many lovers. They fought bitterly to have her and in the end, they cut her in half.'

'Golly.'

'One half of her body grew into the coca plant and no man was allowed to chew the leaves until he had satisfied the needs of a woman.'

I blushed. The conversation was taking a turn I had not intended.

'How did you know it was really *her*?' asked Theo pointedly.

Wamani smiled again. 'Such a goddess can make a man – stand tall – you understand?'

'Absolutely,' Theo said breathlessly, locking eyes with him. 'So these coca leaves, can you use them to make a love potion?'

For God's sake, I thought, can't you just keep your knickers on for five minutes? Theo saw my expression and hissed, 'Not for *me*, silly. I don't need any stimulant to get me going. I mean for *them*.' She nodded her head in the direction of Sophie and Helena who were deep in conversation behind us.

'You said we reminded you of four goddesses,' I persisted.

'Let me guess.' Theo cocked her head to one side. 'Helena is a warrior princess. Brünnhilde with a pitchfork.'

I looked back at my two friends, red-headed Helena and golden-haired Sophie and tried to see them as Wamani did.

'Helena is down to earth. Strong, reliable – a goddess of the fields,' I said.

Wamani smiled. 'Like Zaramama, goddess of grain and corn,' he said.

'This is a real hoot,' said Theo and punched my shoulder. 'What about Sophie?'

'Her name is associated with wisdom,' I mused aloud, trying to feel the truth of Sophie's being, the essence that she embodied.

'And virginity,' Theo sniggered.

'Like Mary, the mother of Jesus,' Wamani said simply. 'There are many examples of gods and goddesses being celebrated across the world with different names. The conquistadores brought Catholicism to Peru and in some villages the priests were delighted to find the people turning up for Christian services.' He laughed. 'What they did not understand until much later was that the peasants had made little wooden dolls of the Inca gods and placed them inside the hollow plaster statues of the saints. The priests even tried to stop us taking ayahuasca. So we called it San Pedro and then they could not complain! We are just seeking the wisdom of St Peter, the keeper of the keys. What could be bad about that?'

'They pretended to worship Christ but in reality they still believed in their own Gods?'

'The ways of the old religion could not be killed off so easily. It is still common practice to pray to the Madonna *and* give offerings to Pachamama, Mother Earth.'

'Just like the amulet!' Theo exclaimed, nudging me.

Wamani looked swiftly from me to Theo and back again.

'Go on, show it to him,' she said laughing.

I felt a funny hollow feeling open up in my chest as I fumbled in my pocket to produce the smooth disc of bone for Wamani to see. His eyes narrowed slightly as he held it up between his fingers. 'It is a crude piece of folk art,' he said. 'Not valuable.' He paused in contemplation of the naked figure wielding the stave of serpents.

'Is she one of yours by any chance?' Theo asked.

He cocked his head to one side and shrugged his shoulders. 'An ancient goddess associated with the moon. She holds the two serpents to symbolise life and death, light and dark, good and evil. The serpent sheds its skin and is reborn; it glides between the two worlds of the living and the dead. But it is all part of the eternal cycle. Just as the moon grows fat and then becomes eclipsed, so there can be no life without death, no light without dark. She is the eternal mystery. We call her Mama-Amaru.'

'What does she have to do with the cross of St Benedict?'

'It is supposed to be worn with a thin leather thong like a pendant; one side lies against the skin of the wearer, the other side is on display to the world.

'A true believer of the old faith who wants to appear respectable?' I said thinking of the hostel-keeper's wife and her husband's embarrassment.

'Yes, perhaps.'

'That's how religious practices spread,' I said. 'Icons become absorbed into different cultures. The Romans conquered the Greeks. They assimilated the ancient myths and created their own pantheon. Zeus became

Jupiter, Aphrodite became Venus.'

Wamani inclined his head. 'In Inca mythology we worship Chasca who brings light and warmth. She is a flower goddess who protects maidens. She is similar to a young Venus. I think this suits your friend Sophie. Together they are a good match.' Wamani opened his hands wide in a gesture of supplication. 'They nourish each other, like the sunshine ripens the corn. Then the sun sleeps well at night because she knows she is needed and wanted.' He brooded for a moment. 'It is important to find your true mate, the other half of your soul. All things become possible when this happens.'

'Is that the purpose of the San Pedro?' I asked. 'To find your soul-mate?'

'This, and many other things. San Pedro opens the gates of consciousness. Do not worry Georgina,' he added softly. 'San Pedro will guide you. He will guide us all.' He held out the amulet and I slipped it back into my pocket; safe, out of sight. Protected.

'Amen,' said Theo loudly, flashing him one of her most seductive smiles. I pinched her arm.

We arrived at the top of the track where a wider clearing revealed a small *pueblo* or settlement. There was a bonfire burning in the centre of a flat circular dirt area ringed with small adobe houses and huts made from local earth and stone. Several women and children were sitting on rush matting and there were low wooden benches covered with woven blankets next to some carved wooden stools.

We were greeted by Unay, a small dark skinned Quechuan who shook our hands and welcomed us into the circle. Unay sat down on one of the stools and tended to a small fire over which a kettle was steaming gently. It was all rather domestic and a bit disappointing. I had visions of bare-breasted natives swooning and swaying like dervishes. This looked more like a knitting circle.

Wamani indicated for us to sit on the benches and wrap ourselves in blankets.

'Unay is the chief ayahausquero, a wise man who brews the libation of the San Pedro cactus. Ayahuasca is our most sacred medicine. When you drink you become a sister or a brother of San Pedro. We are one family, one Earth. This will show you the truth of who you are. This medicine will heal you.'

'Is it dangerous?' asked Sophie.

'It is always a little dangerous when you open yourself for the first time. You must fight your fear. You must open your mind and let go of your mental conditioning. Unay is a great man but very humble. It is safe with him, completely safe. You will know yourself. You will see the great beauty that surrounds you.'

Unay motioned to Wamani, and they exchanged some words together. Wamani smiled and nodded. 'He says you will find your true names, your true selves. San Pedro will reveal this to you but for each person, the plant may have a different guide. You understand? For some it is the Jaguar, for others, the Condor or the Hummingbird. You will see.'

We sat close to each other, hugging our knees. Wamani had warned us that we would vomit as part of the process. Purging ourselves was an important stage. Sophie had packed wetwipes and proceeded to distribute them between us. It was very still. I looked across at the small children sitting on the ground staring up at us. What must they think of us, gringos turning up from the other side of the world, looking for the meaning of life? I had a sudden presentiment that we were witnessing the end of an age of innocence. What we brought with us, like the Spanish invaders, would catalyse an irreversible change for these simple people.

News of ayahuasca would spread. The trickle of tourism would become a flood. The more remote, the less likely they were to escape. And how could they refuse? A few dollars to us could pay for an entire family's education.

The brew took all day to make. Unay must have risen early in preparation for our visit. I wondered what exactly the costs were involved in coming here. We'd arrived on foot, the San Pedro grew abundantly and as far as I could see the only other requirements were a fire and cups to drink from. Yet Wamani had charged us fifty US dollars for the privilege. Theo must have been reading my mind.

'Well, I hope we get our money's worth,' she whispered to me.

'I don't know if I want to drink something that's going to make me sick,' said Sophie.

'It's probably just to make you feel a little light-headed,' said Helena. 'That's why they prefer you to fast first. It's just messing with your blood sugar level so you get a higher 'high'.'

'Shush,' I whispered. I didn't want to admit it, but I was feeling frightened. Suddenly I felt a long way from home. I was glad that my friends were with me, but Wamani had also warned us that our experiences would be ours alone. Once we committed ourselves to San Pedro, we would have to follow through to the end. I closed my hand around the amulet in my pocket.

'How long is this going to take?' Theo asked.

Wamani settled down between me and Theo on one of the benches.

'Unay will bring the libation for you to drink. Then you will be sick. You keep drinking. Sometimes people groan or pass out. It is not unusual. You drink many times. San Pedro will adopt you. Cuzco is the spiritual centre of Shamanism in the Andes. There are many who come looking for wisdom. The true Andean priests and Shamans guard their secrets well. They only share with people who are willing to open and receive the teachings of San Pedro. You understand, this is a holy thing.'

'Will you drink with us?' I asked. He looked at me a little oddly. 'Of course,' he responded and slipped his arm around my waist. 'Do not be afraid Georgina, San Pedro will take care of you.'

The women of the pueblo came to sit closer, and they began to sing soft lulling tunes in their native tongue.

'What are they singing?' asked Sophie.

'These are the icaros – sacred healing songs,' Wamani answered. 'They sing to raise the spirits and ask for their guidance.'

The darkness behind us was thicker now and the campfire cackled as more deadwood was added to the flames.

Unay reappeared with a cup for each of us. He breathed tobacco smoke over Theo who seemed quite entranced by the whole performance. She clanked her beaker against mine. 'Bottoms up,' she winked at me. Helena sniffed and made a face. Sophie crossed herself. I pinched my nostrils closed with the fingers of one hand and took a great gulp.

And spewed almost immediately.

Wamani laughed and patted me on the back.

'Good Georgina, good. Drink again.'

Theo, not to be outdone, had also taken a great gulp but neglected to swallow and sat there with a stupid look on her face. Wamani urged her. 'You must drink it down!' She shook her head and spat out the whole lot.

'Oh Christ that is dis-gust-ing!' she yelled. Wamani looked upset. That was what decided the matter. I drank and kept on drinking even though my body recoiled and shook with every swallow. Perhaps I had found the one thing that I could do that Theo couldn't. Wamani smiled. 'Good, Georgina,' he said, his arm around my shoulders. I drained the beaker. Wamani was stroking my hair. I felt like a warrior, a goddess. I could get through this. I was willing to open myself. Hell yes, I would do anything this man asked of me.

'My God,' Theo muttered. 'Look at love's young dream over there.'

I looked over to where Helena and Sophie were taking it in turns to sip from the same beaker. Helena held Sophie's hair back from her face every time she vomited.

Theo turned to me and Wamani, her mouth set in a hard line. 'Count me out.'

I knew she was going to sulk but I didn't care. I felt a burning beginning in the pit of my stomach and I didn't care. I felt fearless, light-headed, jubilant.

I noticed he wasn't drinking.

'Drink with me Wamani,' I said eagerly. I pushed the beaker towards him but he had other ideas and pulled me into an embrace. At first his lips were soft and caressing on mine. Then I felt his tongue dart into my mouth and I pulled away sharply.

'Whoah!' I laughed, shaking my head. 'You said you were going to drink.' He held me by my chin and looked into my eyes. 'Georgina!' he whispered excitedly. 'You are a queen, a goddess! I knew it, the first time I saw you. Munayki, Georgina, I *want* you. *Together – you* and I, *we –* '

'Oh no you don't!' I said, buoyed up on my new found goddess status. 'If you want to sleep with anybody, it had better be her!' I pointed my finger at Theo, who looked at me open-mouthed in astonishment.

'Georgie, are you okay? I think you're as high as a kite.'

I frowned. 'I feel,' I stood up and started to sway my arms around like a hula-hula girl, 'like a breath of wind.' I closed my eyes and felt the stirring of the air around me. 'I am flying. Oh God, I'm flying!' And pitched forward onto the ground in a crumpled heap.

***

My memory of that night is fragmented and confused.

I recall the heat of the fire and loud singing all around me. Helena and Sophie were dancing around the flames like savages. I lost sight of Theo quite early on. I drank more. This time I felt cold and alone. The fire had burnt down to red embers and there were bodies all around me on the ground. They reached out to me. Some of them were wriggling like snakes, their bodies oiled with sweat. Others lay still. I lay on the ground next to them and looked up at the stars kaleidoscoping back and forth in a dazzling light shower. I drifted in the half-dreaming and my brother appeared to me, shaking his head sadly and calling my name. I reached up my hand and he took hold of it, stroking the skin of my palm tenderly. Then he knelt over me and slid his hand under my head, lifting me to make me drink again. His eyes were soft and brown. He smiled and leaned over to kiss me on the forehead. I lay back and sank deeper and deeper into the pit of vipers.

The next thing I remember was waking up to a cloud of red mist that enveloped me and lifted me high above the earth. I had no mortal form. The stars retreated and the moon slid beneath the curve of the earth. I felt a drumming beat vibrating through me. My body felt heavy, clammy, pulled down to the hard ground, squeezed tighter and tighter. I tried to cry out but no sound came from my throat. The drumming sounds became louder and louder; something was twisting in my hair, like the tubers of a creeping vine, white flesh errupting from the black soil. I wrestled and struggled but my arms and legs wouldn't wake up. I was burning up, my throat and mouth dry, my body sweating as if with fever.

All the while I tried to escape but the more I twisted and turned, the tighter the space became. I writhed and gasped, squeezed within the slick coils of the giant serpent, fledgling wings unfolding, undulating with a steady rhythm that beat in time with my heart. The fear hit me right in the solar plexus as if a hand had reached in and taken hold of my heart; *I don't want this*. Other voices chorused around me as if the stones in the earth could speak, their muted cries rising up in fear and dread. But the sensations were too strong. I rolled and twisted, arching my back to meet each thrust, driven by a deeper darker need to commune, to connect, to lose myself completely. I was out of control, totally at the mercy of the figure who knelt over me all the while, watching with glittering eyes, softly crooning my name, wiping the sweat from my forehead with a steady practised hand.

8

I woke up in my bed in the hacienda.

The bed next to mine was empty. Sunlight streamed in through the window. There was a soft knock at the door and Sophie's head appeared.

'Good morning,' she smiled, and sneaked in carrying a tray.

I half sat up, rubbed my head and croaked out a good morning.

'How are you feeling today?' She poured some milk into a mug of coffee and handed it to me.

'I don't know yet,' I grimaced. I took a sip of the hot coffee and felt something revive within me. This at least was familiar. This felt like home. I looked at her, sunshine falling across her face and wondered at the change. Sophie had a look about her that could only be described as beatific.

'Sophie?'

She didn't meet my eye immediately but when she did, her smile lit up my heart.

'Sophie!'

She clambered onto the end of the bed and settled herself cross-legged like a little pixie. I felt tears come into my eyes.

'Tell me. No. Don't tell me. I can see it in your face. You and Helena?'

She nodded.

'Georgie, I had the most wonderful dream-time last night. Helena – ' she blushed. '*We* both felt this incredible connection – to each other, to the earth – Pachamama – that's what the Quechua call her. It was amazing.'

I felt about a hundred years old watching and listening to her.

'That's fantastic,' I croaked. I meant it, but I couldn't exactly feel it. I sipped some more coffee.

'How did Theo get on?'

Sophie's eyes boggled. 'She chickened out! Said she didn't believe in all that hocus-pocus.'

'Blimey,' I said. 'I thought of all of us it would be Helena who might have backed out.'

'Oh no, not at all. She felt this incredible flow of energy through her. She said it was like God was talking to her. In Squirrel.'

We looked at each other and doubled up with laughter.

'It was like everything suddenly made perfect sense.' Sophie had tears of laughter rolling down her face. 'And she said she loves me, Georgie. Can you believe it? She really loves me.'

'Of course I can believe it,' I cried. 'I can see it now. The two of you nesting somewhere like a couple of mice. Or *squirrels* perhaps.'

'She kissed me and it was the most beautiful, perfect moment.' Sophie's eyes were shining. 'I never thought, I never knew it was possible to feel so light, so happy. It felt so *natural* Georgie. All I had to do was just *be myself.*'

I felt the lightness of her words, yet within it was as if a dark shadow had fallen across my heart.

'And what about you?' she asked keenly. 'You were fearless! You swigged it down like it was going out of fashion. Honestly Georgie, if it hadn't been for you I think Helena and I would have thought twice about it. Wamani was ever so impressed. He said he'd never seen anyone so open.'

I nodded and sipped my coffee. The truth was I didn't have any clear recollection at that time. I ached all over and I had a sense of something just out of the corner of my eye, but nothing more.

'Anyway,' she jumped up. 'Wamani thinks we ought to make for base camp tomorrow. We need to take some pisco and coca leaves to pledge to the mountain. Helena wants to check all our gear. Do you want us to make a start on that without you?'

'Yeah, fine. I'll get washed and see you in a bit.'

'Okay.'

After she'd gone I slid my legs out of the bed and stood up too quickly. My head spun madly and I had to catch hold of the bed head to steady myself. I made it into the shower and pulled off my nightdress. I turned slowly, realising with horror the truth of what I already suspected. In the mirror I saw my pale flesh covered in welts and bruises. The hot water stung my skin and ran in rivulets down my body, washing thin streaks of blood from between my thighs. I shivered. I felt cold and lost and alone. I leaned against the wall of the shower room and let out a great gulping sob, tears smarting cheeks that were red with shame.

9

Mountaineering is a lonely business. Of course, there is a great deal of comradeship at the outset and plenty of huddling when you make camp. But the actual process of putting one foot in front of the other, each time you slide yourself along a traverse or let your fingertips cleave to the thin promise of a ledge, you are totally, unmistakably alone. The void opens up beneath you and the only sure-footed way to succeed is to go within and press on, committed to the moment. No future, no past, just total absorption in the here and now.

Helena was my climbing soulmate.

I had developed a deep unspoken trust in her judgement, and she had allowed me to partner her. I was predictable and ready to follow her lead. She was the more experienced climber and wise beyond her years. She seemed to understand the mountain in ways that I could not. Her senses came alive up in the clouds. She could smell a break in the weather. She didn't so much climb the mountain as let the mountain talk to her. It was as if she became a part of the rock face, attuned to the granite resonance, constantly listening to the heartbeat of the slumbering giant and moving in rhythm with its sighing breath.

She would have scoffed to hear me describe her in such terms but I felt in my bones the truth of her endeavour. Climbing for Helena was not about achievement, though she was rigorous and methodical in all aspects of her life and may have appeared to an outsider entirely focused on the practicalities of the task at hand. She never left anything to chance and always scrupulously packed and checked and rechecked the gear for wear and tear. Yet for all of her diligence and skill, she was the most intuitive climber I ever knew. She never once pitted herself against the mountain. She just didn't see it in those terms. Olympian deed? That was pure irony. Conquest was the very last thing in her heart when she climbed. Climbing was breathing. Breathing was life. She climbed because everything got stripped away on the side of a mountain. All that remained was your raw self, exposed, vulnerable and instinctive.

I watched Helena on that last morning before the ice climb to the summit. She had a breathy sense of purpose that was entirely new. The difference of course was Sophie. Whereas Helena and I had always paced ourselves, bivouacking at crucial intervals for sleep and rest, with Sophie and Theo included in the team, the dynamic had shifted. Helena's concentration was divided.

It was colder than we had expected. I had wanted to make the climb but now that we were so very close to the summit, I couldn't wait to get back down. I hadn't confided to any of the others about what had happened at the house of the shaman. I was still too ashamed. I couldn't even be one hundred per cent certain about who had attacked me. It could have been any of the men at the pueblo, it needn't have been Wamani. And yet he had kissed me, told me that he wanted me. I looked across at Theo. She had disappeared early on. I didn't even have a clear recollection of my assailant. How could Wamani have betrayed me like that? And yet there he was, smiling and chatting as usual, offering up coca leaves and humming to himself. I had tried to gather my thoughts about the night of the ritual but I knew better than to think about it out here on the mountain. I needed all my concentration and focus for the ice climb.

Sophie wasn't doing so well. She seemed to

dehydrate more rapidly than the rest of us and was complaining of a headache.

We reached an uneasy decision. Theo and Sophie opted to stay put whilst Helena and I would make the summit climb with Wamani.

I wanted to talk to Helena on her own but there was no opportunity. Sophie was in high spirits but happy to sit out the final push. I think Helena was relieved. She had never climbed with Theo before and there had been one or two tense moments between them. I wasn't as skilled a climber but that weighed in my favour. Helena and I knew each other's strengths and would fare better as a team. I trusted her decision to go, and if she decided that we should turn back, then I would have followed her without any argument. Though the weather was holding, things could change very rapidly at this altitude.

Wamani preferred to climb using the German method of front pointing, using ice axes to haul his way up, each toe digging into the ice at a right angle. He argued that as the strongest of the three of us it made sense for him to make a parallel assent so that he could be on hand in case of a problem. Helena and I were quite comfortable using our own belay system. It was slower and I daresay less dramatic, but safe.

We set off late morning. The going was tough. Pulling up on ropes, even with an ice axe, was as much a matter of rhythm as strength. Helena and I were taking no chances. Each screw had to be fixed tight. We used runners to protect each belay before making the next stance. We climbed in relative silence, signalling to each other by pulling on the line. Wamani kept a sharp eye on me, making occasional encouraging remarks. I wanted to tell him to shut up. I didn't need him patronising me. I had enough Alpine experience under my belt and besides, I trusted Helena implicitly. With her lead, I knew I could climb almost anything.

'Good Georgina,' he exclaimed. 'Relax now. Breathe.'

Already the adrenaline was beginning to kick in. I knew I was gripping too tightly. I tried to blot him out by keeping my nose to the ice, but there he was just at the edge of my peripheral vision, his red jacket stark against the brilliant blue-whiteness. I was holding my breath. I jerked my head to the side and closed my eyes. Nausea bubbled up inside me and I swallowed hard, panting. It could have been the altitude starting to play tricks on my mind, but I swear I heard a sound like rustling feathers, and the twitching of something out of the corner of my eye.

Helena reached the final pitch about thirty feet above me and was ready to haul herself up to the summit. She pulled on the rope. I wedged in tighter against the face and rested my head against the ice. There it was again. A fluttering at the corner of my eye. I turned my head to see Wamani traversing the vertical incline towards me.

'Georgina, are you okay?'

I watched him edging nearer, splinters of ice bouncing off the surface as he dug in with his axes. Then he was right next to me, attaching a V-thread into the ice to make a support.

I couldn't move. It was as if I were looking down on myself from a great height, everything clear, everything in its place.

'It's okay,' he said calmly. 'We'll take a rest here.' Suspended now on a safety harness, he hitched himself up so that he was level with me and put his hand on my shoulder.

'Georgina?' His voice was soothing, as if talking to a child.

I stared into his face.

'It was you,' I whispered, the fear coiling itself in my

abdomen, reaching up towards my heart.

His eyes narrowed. 'What are you talking about?' He smiled and rubbed my shoulder. I flinched and pulled away sharply. All I could think about was his arms pinning me to the ground, his breath hot against my cheek and his body moving inside me.

'The red mist. It was your jacket. The lining of your red jacket. You pulled it over my face, so that I wouldn't see.'

'The first time with San Pedro,' he shook his head sadly. 'It's not easy, but it will get better, Georgina.'

'That's not what you told Sophie.'

He looked away as if trying to find the right words.

'Georgina, why do you say these things?'

'Don't say my name!' I cried. 'Don't talk to me like I'm an imbecile!' I started to shout.

'You must calm down!' he hissed and I was pleased to see that there was a flicker of fear in his eyes. That was confirmation enough. He pushed off from the ice and swung himself over me, pinning me against the face of the mountain.

'Get off me!' I pushed back against him but he had me wedged tight against the hard ice.

'Calm down!' he rasped, 'or you'll get us both killed.'

I heard Helena's voice above me.

'She's ok!' he shouted up to her. 'She just needs a rest. It's the altitude. Give us a few minutes.'

I was shaking but whether it was rage or fear I don't know because his next words chilled me to the core.

'Now listen to me. Nothing happened that you didn't want, so don't pretend. You are all the same, you English girls. You tease and flirt and act as if you don't know what you are doing but you don't like it when a man treats you as a woman.' He pressed himself against me. 'Something beautiful happened. You were magnificent

Georgina! We can talk later, when you are ready.' He looked so earnest. 'All my life . . . I never really believed, until now, with you. Do you understand?'

I shuddered. 'Yes,' I said quietly, thinking of the bruises and the blood. *Don't listen to him.* He rested against me. I could feel his breath warm on the back of my neck. 'Now we will make the last pitch together, yes?'

'Yes.'

'And no more of this silly talk, okay?'

I felt hot tears running down my face.

'Okay.'

'Good girl.'

He must have guessed that I would recall that night sooner or later. Was that why he chose to climb next to me, to protect himself? And if anything had happened to me on that climb, who would have been able to prove anything other than an accident? Climbers die on mountains. I would have ended up as just another statistic. My fate would have been chalked up to any number of factors: inexperience, altitude sickness, hypoxia, panic.

I couldn't reach Helena so I would have to be on my guard. Our safety now lay in the hands of the man who had violated me. If I could keep up the pretence of everything being fine, he would have no reason to harm any of us. Sophie was already sick and needed to get off the mountain quickly. My only hope was to make a report to the police in Cuzco, and to do that I needed Wamani to believe that he had nothing to fear from me.

'Maybe I was mistaken,' I whispered.

'We all make mistakes,' he said lightly. 'It's still a little way up, and you know, Georgina, it's a long, long way down. If we can't trust each other, who knows what might happen?' Then he leaned in again, his mouth close to my ear. 'There is so much I want to share with you.' I felt the bile rising within me. 'Do you understand?' he demanded.

I nodded, my head pounding, the adrenaline coursing through me. 'I can't go any higher,' I whispered. 'I'll wait here for you both.'

He hesitated, weighing up the relative danger of greeting Helena on his own against his suspicions that I might do something in his absence. His ego won out.

'Okay.' He swung himself across from me using one of the ice axes, then kicked in with his right foot and hauled himself up to slip the knot free from the V thread support.

I couldn't say with any certainty exactly how it happened, but he must have misjudged the angle because his left axe suddenly gave way as he heaved himself up a fraction. He tried to hold on but it slipped out of his grip, toppling down a hundred feet or so, and he was left clinging to the wall of ice with his right axe. He was panting hard and made a grab for the rope threaded through the V section but it was no use, there was no knot to hold him. I shrank away from him, moulding myself to the ice, as his left arm flailed in mid air.

'Catch this!'

He threw the end of the rope to me, but I didn't move. *Stay perfectly still.* His face contorted into a sudden flare of rage at my incompetence. There was sweat running down his face, and he tried again to pull himself up so that he could attach himself to my support harness. Helena was calling me, her vision obscured by the overhang of ice above my head. Wamani tried again.

'What's wrong with you? Take the rope!'

He tried to find some kind of purchase with his fingers, panting through gritted teeth, but it was too late. Helena's voice above me was filled with alarm but I knew she would hold her position unless I pulled on the line. *Don't move a muscle.* I let the line slacken off almost imperceptibly.

Wamani's face was turned towards me, and I saw clearly for the first time the hatred, the pure venom in his expression. I fancied he had the eyes of a snake and let slip a giggle of hysteria. *Look at him! Not so powerful now, is he?* It must have been the altitude playing tricks on my mind. But then I saw the thin forked tongue dart from between his lips, and my insides turned to liquid. In that fraction of a second I knew that it was him or us. I chose us.

I watched him slide just a few inches.

He was breathing hard now, his eyes wide in fear.

'For Christ's sake!' Panic had set in.

He tried to pull up again, but with all his weight on one axe, he couldn't move any higher.

'Georgina!' The full terror of his predicament hit him.

He tried to side step up with his left leg crooked towards me, grimacing with the effort, the fingers of his left hand desperately feeling for the smallest crack in the ice-wall to gain a hold.

He slid another inch. He was way off balance. He tried to pull himself level again and made a grab for my right ankle. I slid my foot out of reach. *Let him go!*

'Help me!' he screamed.

He couldn't hold on forever. He slid and his chest must have jarred against a wedge of ice, knocking the breath out of him. The impact pitched him backwards and I watched him tilt headfirst into that great void, a slowly dissolving figure swallowed up in the vast whiteness below. No sound, no last cry of alarm. Just arms outstretched as if he were embracing the space.

Should I have felt something even then? A great chasm opened up within me. There was no God, no

Apu of the mountain, no retribution and no great truth, just a cool hollow space within. No time, no feeling, nothing. I felt as empty as the great sky above me and as cold as the ice to which I clung, eyes screwed tight shut, breathing ragged and fierce. *He can't hurt you anymore.*

Light snow began to fall in the stillness, wiping the mountain clean. It was if he had never been there.

As if he had never existed.

10

I awoke with a start. The room was dark. Sophie's bed was empty.

I slipped on some clothes and crossed the hallway. I put my ear to the door of Helena's room and heard Sophie's voice. I thought she and Helena might be having some private time together and was about to go back to my room when I heard Theo say something in reply. I had just put my hand on the door handle, resolved to go in, when I heard Helena say my name. I hesitated. These were my closest friends. Talking about *me*. I couldn't make out all the words but her tone was urgent, excited. Theo was angry. The other two tried to calm her down but she seemed intent on some matter. I heard the shifting of bodies within the room and steps towards the door. I flattened myself against the wall, unable to regain the safety of my own room in time. The door opened a couple of inches and I heard Sophie pleading with Theo.

'Let her *sleep*. She's in no fit state. Helena, make her see sense can't you?'

'Sophie's right. It can wait. The last thing we want to do is to alarm her.'

'But something has happened,' Theo hissed from the open doorway. 'Something that none of us is going to be able to explain.'

'I know, I know.' Helena was whispering urgently.

'It touches all of us. *All of us*. We're going to have to make statements to the authorities, don't you *understand*?'

'Yes of course I do. Look we're all in this together.'

'But *she* was the one – '

'I *know*, I *know* but we're all in the same boat.' There

was a horrible pause. 'Aren't we Theo? *Aren't we*!'

There was a muffled response and then Helena's whispered voice again, angry and insistent. 'Theo!'

'*Yes,* all right. All right. So what are we going to do now?'

'Come back inside,' Sophie said.

Theo hesitated. The door creaked open a fraction wider and soft yellow light spilled into the corridor.

'The important thing is that he's dead,' Helena whispered. 'He's dead and we are the only witnesses.' There was a terrible silence. 'He fell off the mountain,' she continued. 'We make a pact right here, right now, okay? It wasn't anybody's fault.'

'Okay.' Sophie sounded relieved. Theo hesitated.

'Yes, but what if she suddenly remembers? She could incriminate all of us.'

'You saw the state she was in,' said Helena crossly. 'She's been out of it ever since we got back, sleeping round the clock. She hasn't spoken a word in two days. Not a single word.'

'But what if she *does*?' said Theo and closed the door.

I let my breath out slowly and crept back to my own room. *Two days?* I had been lying there for two days? I lay back down on the bed. So it *was* true. Wamani was dead. I could have saved him but I let him fall to his death. I turned onto my side and curled myself up into a ball. We were strangers in a foreign land, alone except for each other, dependent on our friendship and committed to a single course of action. They had made their vows and so must I. I squeezed my eyes tightly shut and prayed to a God I had long since lost faith in.

***

I heard the voices crying out from the earth. I looked down to see Wamani's face and the wordless screaming coming out of his mouth as he coiled around me, trying to save himself, clawing at the dirt, sliding into the gaping pit: Uku Pacha, Hades, the Underworld from where there was no escape and no redemption. Only darkness and pain and fear. My head was pounding.

Sophie was kneeling beside me.

'Shall I call Helena?' Theo was hovering.

'No, she's coming round.'

'Sophie,' I croaked, my throat dry and tight. 'Am I insane?'

She shook her head firmly.

'It's just a bit of altitude sickness, Georgie.' *She's lying.* 'We've all felt a bit light-headed these last couple of days. Just rest now.'

'I'm feeling very tired but every time I close my eyes I see things.'

Theo's face was pale over Sophie's shoulder. She looked anxious but Sophie was so calm, so gentle. So insistent. I swallowed hard and gripped her wrist.

'When I wake up properly, I want you to tell me everything. Do you promise? We have to talk about everything. Will you do that for me?'

'Yes, yes of course. When you wake up.'

I closed my eyes as she leant over to kiss my forehead. Theo moved across to the door, her face in shadow. *Theo. Why don't you say something?*

'He's never coming back is he?'

'No.' Sophie gave my hand a little squeeze. 'He's never coming back.'

Oddly reassured, I slipped into a deep dreamless slumber.

11

Helena elected to go on ahead with me to Cuzco by truck, whilst Theo and Sophie packed up all our gear in Chincheros. It was a mostly silent journey, punctuated only by Wamani's houseboy Miguel who seemed intent on whistling the whole way.

'What's he got to be so bloody cheerful about?' asked Helena.

'Perhaps he's just trying to lighten the mood?'

'Or just delighted to see the back of us,' she answered.

Police Headquarters was a grand, colonial style whitewashed building that had seen better days. Helena and I were shown into an anteroom to wait our turn. The ceiling fan turned slowly on a wobbly circuit that made me wonder if it might spin off altogether if switched to a higher speed. A family of Quero Indians was sitting quietly in one corner. They spread woven cloths on the floor and unpacked baskets of bread and corn. Their faces were wreathed in smiles as they invited us to share their meal. Clearly they expected to be kept waiting a long while. There was no obvious queuing system. You simply waited until all the people who were there before you had gone. An older man was sitting next to the open window, holding the hand of a younger woman with a plain face who we took to be his daughter. When the door of the Chief of Police opened however, expelling a young couple carrying a small baby, neither party made a move. They looked at us expectantly. Then when we continued to sit, one of the family elders bowed and waved his arm, motioning us to go into the office. We were embarrassed. We would wait our turn. The Chief, however, had other ideas and barked from within for his next customer.

We stood and nodded our thanks to the family and stepped cautiously through the doorway. The room was large, wood-panelled and heavily corniced. Above the large mahogany desk hung a photographic portrait of President Fernando Belaúnde Terry. *One hell of a backhand.* He must be over seventy. What were the chances of him recalling a Paris semi-final match against a young English diplomat in 1958? I hoped against hope that we wouldn't need to call in any diplomatic favours.

Belaúnde's aristocratic bearing contrasted sharply with the stout, balding public service official seated below, who regarded us with barely concealed boredom. He waved his hand at the two wooden chairs in front of his desk which we took as an invitation to sit. He opened a folder in front of him that bore a large photograph of Wamani, clipped to formal-looking, closely typed documents, two inches thick. Some of the documents had thick black lines underlining the text and what looked like handwritten annotations in the margin. My seat was warm from the previous occupant. I wondered fleetingly which bottom had recently graced my seat. I hoped it was the wife's.

The Chief of Police fanned the documents out on the desk in front of him and cast a practised eye over the contents. It was not clear to us exactly what the status of this interview was intended to be. We had already made formal statements in Chincheros and again on our arrival in Cuzco. Nevertheless, we waited silently until he gave us his full attention, and signalling with his index finger, invited us to speak.

Helena told our story the best she could.

We had nearly reached the summit. About fifty feet from the top, Wamani had called up to her to say that I needed a few minutes rest. Helena had called down but could see nothing. The next thing she knew Wamani had pitched off the side of the incline. She rappelled down to find me completely locked up, hands gripping my axes, unable to speak or move. Obviously I had been in shock. She eventually managed to lower me down and once we had rejoined Theo and Sophie, we rappelled down the mountain as quickly as we could and made our way back to the meeting point. Miguel was encamped with the truck at the base of the mountain. His face, formerly wreathed in smiles, twisted into total disbelief when he saw that we were only four instead of five. It had taken several minutes for us to persuade him that Wamani was never coming back.

The Chief of Police listened carefully, his hands folded over his stomach. His English was precise, delivered slowly with a thick accent.

'Were there any signs of altitude sickness in the party?'

'Only Sophie, but she had stayed behind.' He nodded slowly.

'And what about the señorita?' He gestured towards me.

I felt Helena look across at me but I could say nothing.

'No, at least . . . Well, he did say that it might be the altitude kicking in. He said something about needing a break.'

The Chief patted his stomach in a gesture that seemed to say These Things Happen. If you will be foolish enough to go up a mountain, then sooner or later you're going to get yourself killed.

'This man.' His fat finger prodded the photograph. 'You have known him for how long?'

'About two weeks. We met him here in town and he offered to guide us.'

He sighed. 'And your other friends, they stayed below while you were doing the climb to the top of Ausangate?'

'Yes.'

'So they saw nothing,' he concluded to himself, his hands flat upon the table.

My eyes flickered towards Helena but she continued staring ahead.

'This is a most tragic accident,' he said finally. 'But not without its compensations.'

That caught me off guard. I looked at Helena, who was equally non-plussed.

He cocked his head and his next question took us both by surprise.

'Your husband let you travel here?'

'I'm not married. None of us are.'

He exhaled sharply in a way that conveyed faint disgust.

We sat quietly.

'Will the body be recovered?' Helena asked at last. 'It's awful to think of him lying out there.'

'That will be a matter for the local people to decide. In such cases it is not always possible.' He paused. 'It is a sacred place to the Quechua. It would be better perhaps if it were respected as such.'

His rebuke was unmistakeable. We must have seemed very foolish to him. Ignorant young foreigners, out for a good time, trying to prove ourselves at the cost of a man's life.

'When do you return to England?'

'We're booked for the nineteenth, unless you need us to stay.'

'Have you spoken with your Embassy?'

'Yes. They advised us to co-operate fully.'

'We have your details and statements on record.' He considered the photograph of a younger Wamani fresh out of college.

'This man has been known to us for some time. You

have heard of *Shining Path*?'

We nodded mutely.

'Someone in the Cuzco district has been able to acquire significant funds, travelling backwards and forwards into the States. We think this man may have been involved. He is what you English call *a slippery customer*. We have had our suspicions for a long time, but – ' he sighed heavily. 'No evidence.'

'What about his family?' I asked quietly.

'There is not much family. An uncle in Cuzco. A step-mother in Florida.'

Then he looked me squarely in the eye and said sternly, 'You have been very lucky.'

There was a horrible silence. I thought for one awful moment that he had seen right through me. I half expected him to add that my father was very disappointed and I had broken my mother's heart.

'And now,' he added, more matter of fact, 'you must put everything behind you.'

'We will,' Helena said. 'Thank you.'

'One other thing. This Wa-ma-ni,' he added as we were about to leave. 'It is a girl's name.' He chuckled. 'It means *sacred mountain peak*. This man had many names. A different name for every purpose. Perhaps if you knew more about the language of the country you are visiting?' He left the rest unsaid. Suckers. There's one born every minute. He grunted and waved his hand in dismissal.

We left the office building and made our way back to the hostel where we had arranged rooms for the last few days of our stay. It was the same place we had left so casually to go to Chincheros. The patron had greeted us with a wary smile of relief. His wife remained silent, half-hidden in the doorway to the dark interior, her eyes fixed on me like a crow. Two double rooms. Sophie and

Theo would join us tomorrow with all the gear. In the meantime it was just me and Helena.

That night we took a late stroll around the city. We chatted about home and joked about Eleanor's forthcoming nuptials. We drank beer and I could see the load lifting from her shoulders. Something had shifted for me too. I had a sense of purpose. We returned to the hostel and let ourselves into the little room with two narrow beds. I lay in the dark and waited until her breathing gave way to little snores. Then I went down the passageway and locked myself in the bathroom. I didn't recognise the face in the mirror, so drawn and grey. I swilled down the contents of a bottle of painkillers purchased that afternoon whilst Helena was sorting out our laundry. I didn't give her or the others, or even my family, a second thought.

12

I should have died. I hadn't counted on Helena being so alert. She had woken to find me gone and hunted me out. The hostel manager had bust the door open. He wanted to call for a doctor, but his dark-eyed wife Nina persuaded him to keep quiet. They took me into a room at the back of the building where they had private living accommodation and gave me ayahuasca to purge my system.

How ironic. The very stuff that had brought me to this wretched state, ended up saving my life.

She must have sat up with me all through the night. In the morning Helena went to fetch me a change of clothes. Nina brought me water to drink. I recognised her dark pinched features. She looked at me for a long time.

'You and the Fernandez man?'

I was surprised. On the previous occasions we had met, I had had the impression that she only spoke Quechua. She repeated the question. I wanted to pretend but I couldn't. I didn't have the energy. I nodded.

She shook her head sadly and kissed the crucifix she wore on a thin gold chain around her neck.

'Naqak. Bad man,' she muttered. 'Pishtaco.'

'What do you mean?' I croaked. She had said it before when I told them we were leaving for Chincheros. Her husband had scolded her. Cuzco was a conservative town. The men didn't care for their women to speak out of turn with strangers.

She pulled her chair a little closer and cast a glance over her shoulder before speaking.

'Naqak is the devil,' she sighed, shaking her head sadly.

I swallowed hard, trying not to let the fear seep into my heart.

'He has the *snake* inside him. He take white women. He make sex with them.' She pinched up and down my arm as if she were looking to fatten me up. 'He take the white out of you and sell it to make other people white like him.' She simulated washing her face and hands. I raised an eyebrow. Surely this was just another naive folk tale? 'They make cream and cosmetic from human fat. They take a needle and put it here,' she slapped her backside. 'He make you thin, like ghost.' She shook her head sadly. I was rather pleased that she thought I'd lost a bit of weight. 'Naqak do this to you. Bad man.'

'He's dead.'

She crossed herself and clapped her hands together like a child at a birthday party. 'You have the protection, yes?'

'The amulet?' I reached into my pocket and pulled out the disc of bone to show her. She nodded furiously and lowered her head, pushing the amulet back towards me.

'Naqak still come in the night and feed off you. You must be strong now. You must make him *go away*!'

She stood up and went over to a small wooden chest covered in tea lights and the same small carved wooden figures that I had seen on the Indian stalls at Chincheros. It was an altar of sorts. 'Naqak works by dark magic. The brotherhood of the Laika.' She crossed herself. 'Evil ones . . . '

'What do you mean?'

She was whispering now, almost talking to herself. 'You must push the dark away.' She muttered as she gathered her medicines and herbs.

I wondered what could be taking Helena so long. I wasn't exactly frightened. I knew that this woman meant well, but it was unnerving, the presumption that dark forces were at work, that somehow the man we had known as Wamani could still hurt me. I didn't want to believe. I wish I'd done as Theo had and spat out the vile liquid.

'What are you doing?' I asked.

She shuffled back and forth, passing her hands over me. Then she sat next to me and closed her eyes. When she opened them again, her expression was sharp and excited.

'You have the dark.' She placed her hand lightly on my lower belly, and then on my heart. 'Here, and here. He is inside you. You must clean your body, send him out. You understand?'

'But he is dead,' I insisted. 'He fell from the mountain.'

She shrugged her shoulders.

'The Apu was hungry,' she said. 'The Apu sees inside this man's heart. This man is bad in his heart, not worthy. The Apu take the life of this man.' She spat on the floor.

Then she leaned forward again, her brown eyes searching my face. She pressed a small piece of paper into my hand and closed my fingers around it. 'You must see the curandero,' she plucked at my sleeve. 'You must send out this darkness. You no want pishtaco in your life.' She wagged her finger sternly.

'What do you mean?' The tears started to roll down my cheek. I was tired and cold. 'I don't understand.' I wanted Helena to come back. I didn't feel right. This woman was beginning to frighten me. I wanted to be away, far away. I wish I'd never come to Peru. I just wanted to go home.

'My sister is curandero, a healer. I will take you to her. She will help you,' she urged, her eyes shining, excited. She put her face very close to mine and stroked my hair. I could smell the pisco on her breath, see the rotting yellow teeth, the spittle at the corners of her mouth.

'You must pray to Pacamama, goddess of the Earth. Go to the curandero, she will help you.'

She paused and nodded slowly, squeezing my hand. She sighed deeply and I saw pity in her eyes. I looked over her shoulder to see Helena pale and still, standing in the doorway.

'Nakaq make child in you. Now you must take it out or this darkness will spread through your whole life. A life for a life. You understand?' Nina stroked my hair again sadly. 'A life for a life.'

13

Helena and I went out for breakfast. Sophie and Theo weren't due in on the local bus until four o'clock. The day yawned ahead of us. I didn't want to be the first to talk about it. Neither did Helena, but talk about it we must. Our friendship depended upon us being truthful now. Our friendship and so much else besides.

Helena looked more tired and lean than I had ever known her. All this time I had her pegged as the strong one, the person least likely to fall apart, the unelected spokesperson of our group. Adept and worldly, reliable and, to a large extent, infallible. I saw sadness now in her eyes and the downward turn of her mouth. She was out of her depth, a frightened twenty year-old. Just like me. We found a quiet cafe off the main drag and slumped, bone weary, in a corner near the window. Despite having already ordered coffee and fried eggs, Helena continued to study the menu as if it were an arcane manuscript that could tell her the secret of life.

'I don't know what to say.' I picked at the cuticle around my nails.

She was silent for a minute. I thought this was by way of punishment but when I could bring myself to look at her again, I saw that it wasn't that at all. She was biting her lip, trying not to cry.

'I'm sorry H. This is all my fault,' I blurted, burying my head in my hands, elbows on the table.

'How can you say that?' She sounded aghast. I looked at her through my fingers and shook my head.

'Because it's true. If I hadn't insisted on the ayahuasca ceremony, if I'd been more careful, thought things through . . . ' I was buckling under the weight of it all.

She took a deep breath. 'He raped you, didn't he?'

I covered my eyes again and felt the shame welling up causing me to tremble and sob. I nodded.

'He betrayed all of us,' she said flatly. 'If anyone's to blame it's Theo. If she hadn't been so quick off the mark, so determined to make another conquest, we'd never have gone anywhere near him!'

I wanted it to be true. In that moment I would have loved to have blamed Theo. If she hadn't made it quite so obvious how much she fancied him, if she hadn't flirted on the way up to the pueblo asking all kinds of stupid questions about aphrodisiacs, if she'd only drunk the ayahuasca like the rest of us, then it would have been her name notched up on the bedpost so to speak. It would be her fault for being such a tart. It wouldn't have mattered if he'd had sex with her because she wasn't a virgin. Even rough sex couldn't have hurt her as much as it had hurt me. Even if he had held her down and ground himself into her, it wouldn't have been a crime because she'd had half the male population in college already. Like prostitutes plying their trade. You couldn't rape a prostitute. Everybody knew that. The Yorkshire Ripper had proved it already. It was only when he killed a student that the police woke up to the fact that they had a serial killer on their hands. Wamani couldn't have *raped* Theo. He could only have raped somebody like me. Or Helena. Or Sophie. Somebody innocent.

But it wasn't true. Rape was rape. I remembered my grandmother's habit of reading *The News of the World* out loud, her prurient sensibilities simultaneously outraged and satisfied by the grotesque parodies of justice meted out daily in her tabloid universe. *The alleged victim admitted under cross examination, to wearing purple knickers on the night in question.* Well then, she was asking for it. My grandfather's look of embarrassment. My mother shuffling her feet. Another cup of tea, Dad? My own indignation welling up, ready to sweep all before me on a tide of self-righteousness, stemmed only by my mother arching her eyebrows in silent admonition. Don't start, love. Please.

Theo wasn't to blame. Helena was wrong. But there was more to it.

'It wasn't an accident,' I said under my breath, wiping the snot away from my nose with one hand. 'Not really. It was me. I could have saved him.' *Let him go* . . .

Helena looked at me in horror. She shook her head and put her hand out to my shoulder.

'None of us could have saved him.' She let her head drop forward, trying to get eye contact with me. 'Don't you remember?'

'Yes,' I sniffed, trying to find a find a dry patch on my tissue. 'He slipped. He threw me a rope and I didn't help him. I couldn't move. I just watched him, and he couldn't hold on any more. I saw his face, the fury in his eyes and then this terrible panic, the sudden comprehension that he was going to die if I didn't help him. That's when he fell.'

She was leaning forward; her grey-green eyes never looked so serious as at that moment. She sat back in her chair slowly. We were both silent, reliving the moment. Suddenly I understood the meaning of purgatory. A terrible grey heaviness settled on us both as if everything else had receded and all that was left was a yawning chasm of guilt and nothing but Judgement on the horizon. Never had I needed empty reassurances more than at that moment.

'It wasn't your fault, George.'

'You couldn't see. I didn't pull on the line. I could have got you to lower another rope. I could have saved him.'

'So why did he push you against the ice? Why did he try to grab your foot and pull you down with him?'

'What?' I looked at her in shock.

'Theo saw the whole thing. She was watching through the binoculars. She saw what happened. She was giving Sophie a running commentary. They were frantic apparently. Said that you were completely frozen, that it was him all over you. He pushed off from the ice and dropped his axe. Yes, he threw you a line but you were locked up. Altitude, remember? When I got down to you, you were in a hell of a state. I thought I was going to lose you there and then. There was nothing you could have done. He was unlucky. Too bloody macho for his own good. He didn't want to rope up, remember? Insisted on a parallel route. All the time he was patronising you, telling you where to put your feet. For God's sake, I would have pushed him off the mountain too, if it'd been me.'

'I didn't push him! I didn't!' I looked at her in terror. 'He fell, I – he . . . ' My heart was hammering inside my chest.

Her face coloured.

'I'm sorry, it's just that – ' she broke off. 'I'm sorry George, I'm sorry. I didn't mean that.'

I was shaking. *Calm down. Think clearly. Be strong . . .*

'I didn't really remember the attack clearly until I was there on the ice. It was like a flashback.' I still felt confused about the sensations I had felt, and the small voice inside me, guiding my every move. *Let him go . . .*

'I confronted him. It was stupid of me. I should have waited until we were all down safely.' I bit my lower lip. Helena rubbed my arm gently.

'At first he denied it. Then he threatened me. Said how easy it would be for me to fall. I was shit scared Helena. I was so scared of what he might do, I couldn't move.'

'Well fuck him! FUCK HIM!' Helena squeezed my hand tightly. 'You don't have to talk about it anymore. He's gone. That's the only thing that matters. He's gone and we're alive.'

A middle-aged couple at a table near the counter stopped talking and turned to stare at us. The wife looked particularly aggrieved. I shifted uncomfortably in my seat.

Helena took no notice.

'I am mad at you about the pills, though.'

'I'm sorry. I just felt so wretched. I didn't think about anybody else.'

'That's okay,' she mumbled but I could see that it wasn't. She exhaled deeply. 'I might have done the same in your shoes.' This was astonishing coming from Helena.

'Really?'

She nodded silently without looking at me.

'Did I ever tell you about my parents?' She broke off for a moment, her eyes staring into the middle distance. I could see she was unsettled, and the effect was deeply unnerving.

'No. You said your grandmother brought you up. Somewhere in Hampshire. Winchester.'

She nodded.

'I was born in Singapore.' She sighed as if she had won the inner battle and decided to unburden herself.

'You're kidding?'

'My mother met my father at an army dance. Her father was a brigadier so most of the chaps were too scared to ask her up on the dance floor. My father, Stephen, had gone along with a friend, not expecting much. He was fresh out of Downing College, destined for a blistering career in the FCO. They were completely smitten with each other.'

I was quite surprised by this revelation. What a romantic vision. I suddenly had an image of a young couple whirling around, all the uniforms looking on with envy.

'They courted, even planned to get married but the situation there was becoming quite dangerous. Rioting in the city. My father thought it was too dangerous so he packed me and my mother off back to England, intending to follow soon after.'

She was looking straight down at the table now.

Her words slowly registered with me. Something clicked into place. Helena was telling me that she was illegitimate.

'My mother kept a diary, wrote letters. She described the journey back to England as the most miserable of her life. She didn't want to leave but her father insisted. There were a lot of Cold War tensions in the Far East, military escalation on all sides. Grandfather was none too chuffed with my Dad, but they both thought it best that my mother should go home and take the baby with her.'

I imagined a willowy red-headed woman gripping tightly onto the deck railings as the port slipped away from her. How old was Helena then? Did she stand there on the deck waving goodbye to Daddy? Or did her mother hold up a tiny bundle of life in her arms for Stephen Copeland to see? Mouthing *I love you* as she waved goodbye to her lover standing on the quayside.

'My father's official duties were ostensibly to do with trade but his real purpose was to gather covert intelligence. That meant spending time in Geylang. It was full of racketeers and prostitutes, a popular destination for off duty soldiers. Rich pickings for Soviet agents looking for an edge. Singapore wanted independence. The Konfrontasi were out to sabotage the state. My father was part of the establishment drafted in to safeguard British interests.

'There was a second wave of rioting in Geylang in September 1964. An eye-witness for the official report stated that Stephen Copeland, British citizen, tried to help a Malay woman whose market stall had been overturned by four Chinese men. They smashed and trampled her goods into the dirt, poured oil from her wok over her head and arms and set fire to her.'

I stared at her.

'Oh my God, that's terrible.'

She sat very still.

'Then they beat him to death.'

It was awful. Her face was drained of colour. I blinked, my mind trying to take it all in. I looked down at the table. She still had hold of my hand. It had never before occurred to me that Helena's stoicism might have been the result of private tragedy. In my naivety I had assumed nature, not nurture, was the true cause.

'My mother received a cable about two weeks into the voyage and she just collapsed. There was an elderly ship's surgeon on board, used to gastric cases – not a clue how to help someone like my mother.' She sounded angry.

'He told her to go for long walks on deck, said that fresh air should do the trick. Put some colour in her cheeks. Told her she'd be back on the plum duff and custard in no time.'

I squeezed her hand.

'Helena.'

'By the time they got to England it was too late. I think she would have done it on board if I hadn't been with her. Nowadays they might have diagnosed post traumatic stress. I don't know.'

I pictured Helena's mother overwhelmed by grief for

a man she couldn't even call husband.

She lifted her shoulders and let out a deep breath. When she resumed, her voice was more matter of fact.

'The coroner's report said that she went for a walk one evening through the village neighbouring her parents' estate. It was quite a warm night for April and people were busy in their gardens. She was seen by several locals. It is a matter of public record that she stopped to admire Mrs Farncombe's forsythia.'

My mother's voice came back to me. How many times had I heard her talking to herself in the garden. You have to be right firm about it, snip. No nonsense, snip. If you want a good flowering next year, snip.

'Apparently they discussed the slug problem.'

Our neighbour Mrs Ainsworth leaning over the hedge to offer free advice. Guinness, duck. Never fails. Better on the garden than inside my old man and that's a fact. My mother gritting her teeth, a tight smile plastered on her face. Very sound advice, I'll be sure to remember that.

'The fool of a coroner asked a woman in her garden *did the deceased give any indication that she intended to do herself any harm*? As if any of them had a clue what she must have been feeling.'

I held Helena's hand in both my own and listened to the rest of her story.

'The postman found her the next day floating face-down in the river, her body jammed beneath the weir. She was fully dressed except for her shoes and stockings. Sling-back silver dancing shoes, a gift from my father. She left her small gold confirmation cross and chain in the toe of one of the shoes on the grassy bank, about fifty yards upstream and her overcoat neatly folded as if she had only intended to sit on the bank, and let the minnows nibble at her toes.'

I felt the tears well up. I couldn't help it. Whether it was tears for Helena or for her mother, or her father, I couldn't tell. Probably each of them. Probably all of it. The whole bloody tragic waste of life.

'She didn't leave a note,' she said. 'The coroner recorded a verdict of mis-adventure. That was to save my grandfather's family the embarrassment. Of course she killed herself. She killed herself because she couldn't live without my father. I must have been a daily reminder of what she had lost. Imagine that.'

I couldn't. I couldn't imagine my mother taking her own life. I couldn't imagine being left like that. I felt a tremendous swell of love inside for my parents, my brother, and for my friend who sat before me, her hand limp like a dead thing between my palms. She could give comfort in her own way, but was scarce able to receive it.

'The coat she was wearing that night was a navy blue gabardine. I've often thought about that coat. Plain and practical. I think she thought it was a shame to get it wet, that it would do for somebody in the village after she'd gone. That's why she took it off and folded it up and left it on the river bank.' Her voice was flat. 'I think she gave more thought to that coat and what was to become of it, than she ever did about me.'

Helena didn't cry. There wasn't an ounce of self pity in her. Was this the blueprint for her emotional life? The recognition from an early age that utility was to be prized above personal need? In despair, one still had to soldier on, do the right thing, sacrifice oneself. Endure. My escapade with the bottle of paracetamol seemed so cowardly, shameful, mean. Maybe Helena had at times been too hard on herself, but I in turn had been too soft. Too much given to blaming others, too ready to let others lead, too unwilling to take proper responsibility for myself and my actions. I had thought all families were pretty much like mine. Save the truly awful fictions on television that must have been derived at least in part from the reality of northern wastelands and inner city sink estates. I was coming to realise that nobody's family is like anybody else's. We are all unique in our suffering. It's not pain that unites us. You can never really stand in another man's shoes. The only thing that really brings us together, the only thing that we can truly share, is love. All the rest is separation. All the rest is meaningless, without love.

We sat in silence. The couple from the table next to the bar stared at us as they squeezed past to leave the cafe. The space had filled up. I hadn't noticed other tourists coming in. Our coffee was cold in our cups. The untouched food lay congealed in its own fat on our plates. Helena gently removed her hand from mine.

I signalled to a hovering waiter. He shrugged his shoulders, and swept up our plates. Helena cocked one eyebrow at me.

'You know if I hadn't found you in time, Sophie would have been up shit creek without a paddle.'

'Eh?'

'Bloody Eleanor's bloody table settings.' And then, in near perfect mimicry of Lady Audrey, she added, 'How selfish of Georgina to go and die like that. Really Sophie. I do wish you could choose some *reliable* friends for a change.'

We both laughed a little but it was forced, uncomfortable.

'I'm so sorry,' I said.

'Why do people always say that? My mother did what she did. My father thought he was doing the right thing even though it got him killed.' She looked at me very earnestly. 'Georgie, people occasionally do the right thing for the wrong reason, but mostly they do the wrong thing for the right reason.'

She leaned forward.

'You did what you *had* to do,' she said. 'We all do what we *have* to do.'

It wasn't the redemption I was looking for, but it was a comfort none the less to hear her say it. The voice inside me was insistent, seductive: *she's right!* I flailed around for something to hold on to. *I know she is, so why can't I feel anything?*

Was it the life I had taken that troubled me or the fact that so far the authorities had not punished me for it? Could I really live with a man's death on my conscience? Was this what Sophie meant about contrition?

But I'm not sorry. That's it! I'm not sorry at all!

I was really only terrified of being found out. How could I ever expect forgiveness when I couldn't bring myself to repent the loss of a human being? *Had* I done the right thing? *Yes! I saved us – all of us.*

The only clear memory I had was of his face, full of hatred and then him falling, arms outstretched, embracing his fate. *Let him go . . .*

The waiter returned with fresh offerings and we turned our attention to food. I wasn't hungry but eating gave us both an opportunity to regroup. Perhaps we had come through the worst.

'What about the other thing? Lord, I suppose it's too early for a pregnancy kit,' added Helena rather unnecessarily.

'God, I don't know.' I pulled the piece of paper that Nina had given me out of my jacket pocket and laid it on the table between us. It was a shopping list of sorts: cuy negre femenino (seis mes), coca, pisco.

'I have a bad feeling about this,' I sighed. In the course of a week my life had gone from the sublime to the ridiculous. What could I possibly want with a bottle of pisco, some coca leaves and a six month old black guinea pig?

'Something else happened up there on the mountain.' It was a statement rather than a question. I took it as a cue and opened my mouth to respond, reluctantly. I hadn't mentioned what I was beginning to think of as my 'visions' to anybody. Not even Nina.

'I saw something,' she said. 'Something that couldn't have been there, but it was.' Helena carried on eating.

'What did you see?' I asked tentatively.

She sliced into her eggs and took a great gulp of coffee.

'You,' she said.

14

I stared at her. She looked up at me and saw the surprise in my face.

'I know. It sounds ridiculous.' She carried on eating.

I put down my knife and fork and raised my eyebrows. She took the hint and finished chewing her mouthful.

'I was ahead of you by about thirty, forty feet. I could see the summit about twenty feet above me. That overhang of ice gave me enough purchase to fasten an ice screw so I knew I was totally secure. I couldn't have fallen more than about twenty feet and you were anchored so there was no real risk. So I climbed up.'

'What, to the summit?'

'Yep. I know I shouldn't have but I just had this sudden urge to get to the top. As if there was something drawing me.'

'And?'

'And there you were.'

I screwed up my face and took a sip of coffee.

'Where?'

'On the summit. You were already there.'

'But I wasn't. I was below, with *him*.'

'Like I said, I saw something that couldn't have been there, but it was.'

We resumed our meal in silence.

'What was I doing?'

Helena paused and her face took on a softer, more wistful expression.

'You were praying,' she said.

'Praying?' I repeated stupidly.

'Yes.' She drank some coffee. 'Out loud,' she added

as an afterthought.

I was finding this revelation almost as difficult to digest as the breakfast in front of me.

'So, a hallucination then?'

'Obviously.' She lifted her fork. 'Bloody real though.'

'What was it?'

'What?'

'The prayer?'

'Oh, I don't know. It was in Quechua.'

'Well that's not possible, is it? I mean, I don't know any prayers in Quechua.'

'Well, I don't think *you* were actually up there, so it's probably immaterial.'

I could see her point.

'Altitude playing tricks on your mind, no doubt.'

'Mmmm. You took a step backwards. You had your eyes closed and I thought you were going over the edge, so I shouted.'

I frowned. 'I thought you were calling down to me?'

'No.' She sounded surprised. 'I thought you were going to step off the ridge. I put my arm out to stop you.'

'Did you hear Wamani shout up to you?' I winced inwardly. It was the first time I had used his name since our return and it felt unfamiliar, alien, like him as it turned out.

'Yes. No – well, I heard someone below. I glanced down and when I looked back, you were gone.'

'The other me.'

'Yes.'

I hesitated then decided to take the plunge.

'I saw something too,' I confided.

'It wasn't me by any chance was it? Levitating in the air beside you?'

'It was like the night we drank the ayahuasca. I had a string of hallucinations but the one I remember most vividly, the one that keeps coming back is, well – it's actually rather difficult to describe – it was a beating sound, like drumming, and a crushing feeling round my hips and my chest like I was being held tightly in the coils of a snake. A sort of huge snake.'

Helena swallowed hard.

'A huge snake?'

I nodded. 'With wings.'

She didn't speak for several minutes. Perhaps I was going a bit mad and she wasn't sure how to tell me. In the end she shook her head decisively. 'That sounds, forgive me, horribly Freudian. Are you sure that's not your mind trying to shield you from the truth? It's not him doing this to you, it's a fantastic creature. Easier to deal with. Sublimation and all that?'

'Well it could be. I had the vision, before I knew what it meant, before I remembered that it was him. But, in my dreams, and on the mountain, I keep seeing *it*, not him. I mean, I know he raped me. He more or less admitted it. But it's like it was him, but not in human form. It was him, but he had taken the form of something else.'

'A huge snake?' she repeated, looking at me as if I had lost my marbles.

'*Amaru. Quetzacotal*, South America is full of references to feathered serpents.'

She considered the possibility.

'He said San Pedro would show us our true selves. Maybe it showed you the truth about him?'

It was possible. Wamani had seduced us with his smooth talk, and he had reeled us in, coiled himself around us. Then when he was ready, he had struck when I had been least expecting it.

'What did you see that night? Sophie mentioned something about Pachamama.'

'It was quite startling. Sophie looked so radiant. I knew it was her, but she looked so soft, all lilac and silver – like Eliot's violet hour.' I was amazed to hear Helena speak so poetically. 'You know how the winter sky looks first thing in the morning before sunrise, and last thing after dusk?'

'*Chasca*, goddess of twilight and dawn,' I said quietly. 'What about you? How did you seem to her?'

Helena frowned. 'She kept calling me *Zara*. I have no idea why.'

'*Zaramama*, goddess of corn and grain.'

'How do you know all this stuff?'

'Wamani. He told me and Theo about his dream of the four goddesses. Chasca, Zaramama, Cocamama – '

'Who's she?'

'A promiscuous goddess of love who gets pulled apart by jealous lovers, then grows back as the coca plant. Theo rather fancied herself in the role.'

Helena sniggered. 'Now *that* I can believe.' She paused. 'Who was the fourth goddess? Who did he think you were?' She kept her voice light but I wasn't fooled. *She knows something.*

'He didn't say.'

I picked up the scrap of paper. What did it mean? I felt unclean. I wanted to scrub the memory of Wamani from my very soul. I still didn't quite believe that I could be carrying his child. But at the very least I wanted to put an end to the matter, to draw a line under the whole episode.

'Come with me,' I said urgently.

'Where?'

'To the curandero. I have to know the truth. *Please.* Nina will take us, but I want you to be there. I need a witness so that I can be certain.'

She regarded me closely. I could tell she was trying

to make her mind up about something.

'You really think there's some sort of powerful force at work here?' she said.

'I don't know.'

'But you feel it's possible?'

I sat back in my chair. 'I don't know, maybe. Everything is jumbled up inside me. I lost two days Helena – two days where I can't remember anything.'

'What's the last thing you *do* remember?'

I put my head in my hands.

'It was very white, very cold.' I closed my eyes but it was just the same as before. I opened my eyes again. 'His face,' I said. 'Just before he fell, the way he pitched backwards. That's the last thing I remember.'

'You don't remember coming down the mountain?'

'No.'

'Or getting back to the hacienda?'

Helena's expression was so strange. She seemed almost nervous, excited even, yet tender at the same time as if she were willing me to understand her. *What is it?* Her eyes were green, fiery. She seemed exultant somehow, passionate.

'No, it's a blank.'

She lowered her eyes again and fiddled with her napkin.

'Is there something you want to tell me?' I asked.

Her eyes flickered.

'Something about you and Sophie?' The excitement ebbed. The moment had passed.

'It doesn't matter,' she said, shaking her head.

'Is it important?'

She squeezed my hand. 'It can wait.'

15

We purchased without too much difficulty the items on the list. The guinea pig was in a cloth bag with a drawstring. It squeaked from time to time. It was a cute little thing. The vendor at the market where we had bought the little fellow was at great pains to point out its pedigree, and the fact that the pelt was completely black.

'Very rare, very special,' he insisted.

I nodded my head and smiled, anxious to get the whole matter concluded.

'Whatever does he mean?' Helena hissed at me. 'Very rare indeed. Does he take us for fools? They eat them here all the time.'

That much was true: guinea pigs were part of the staple diet, often bred as miniature livestock in back yards and dirt gardens. Yet he had wanted a considerable amount of money for such a fine specimen. In the end we settled on US dollars and obtained a meagre discount. We went to meet Sophie and Theo off the bus from Chincheros.

They looked dusty and weary, but pleased to see us. We unloaded the gear and took our time walking back to the hostel. How different from when we had set out ten days before, bouncing around on the back of the pick-up, spirits high, looking forward to climbing the mountain. Our lives had changed irrevocably since then. But our friendship had deepened.

Helena and I had edited our version of events, leaving out my suicide attempt and the stuff about her seeing my doppelganger on the summit. They were both chastened by the revelation of Wamani's real identity.

At first Theo had not wanted to believe me. However, Helena insisted on me showing Theo the cuts and bruises, which were still blue black and purple. Sophie threw her arms round my neck. Theo sat down heavily on her new bed in our little dorm and unscrewed a bottle of pisco.

'No,' said Helena firmly. 'It's important that we're all clear-headed.'

'Did you see anything that night?' Sophie asked.

Theo shook her head.

'Where did you go?' I asked her. 'My last memory of you is spitting out the stuff. I woke up in the hacienda. I didn't know how I got there. Where did you go?'

Theo pulled her legs up and leaned back against the wall. She seemed defensive.

'Nowhere. I didn't go anywhere.'

'Did you watch me and Sophie dancing like a couple of banshees?' Helena propped herself against the door frame.

'No.' Theo shifted. 'Why are you asking me? I didn't do anything.'

'It's okay,' said Sophie reaching out her hand to pat Theo's foot affectionately. Helena however, wanted to get to the point.

'Did you see him attack George?'

'Of course not! Don't you think I would have done something? What do you take me for!'

'Helena, that's not fair,' Sophie glared up at Helena. This was going nowhere. I tried a different tack.

'Did he try it on with you?' She looked uncomfortable. 'Theo, look at me. Did he try and force you?'

'No, I told you.' She bit one of her nails, something I'd never seen her do before. *She's lying . . .*

'So where were you?'

'I went back to the hacienda.' She breathed a deep sigh and looked at Sophie. 'You and Helena were having a great time together. Wamani was talking to George, so I just decided to go back.'

'Just like that?'

'Yes! How many more times?'

I regarded her carefully. There was something else. I knew it. And so did she. We were all waiting for the truth.

'I don't believe you,' I said coldly. 'I think you know something or you saw something that night.'

Theo looked agitated. 'Think what you like!' she shouted and pushed herself off the bed, towards the door. Helena shifted sideways and blocked the doorway.

'Get out of my way, Helena. You can't keep me here.'

'Not until you tell the truth,' she said calmly.

Theo gritted her teeth. She looked back at me and a little cat smile crept across her face. She folded her arms in defiance of Helena.

'The truth? The truth, now let's see, what *is* the truth? Five people go up a mountain and only four come back down again. How long are we going to carry on pretending that it was an accident?'

'Theo!' Sophie jumped up and pulled her arm but she was having none of it. Theo turned her attention back to me, spitting with fury. 'You *knew* I liked him, you just couldn't bear it could you? Could you! You just wanted him for yourself didn't you? Didn't you!' she screamed.

Helena slapped her hard across the face. Theo put her hand to her cheek in shock. I didn't know what to say. Sophie put her arm around Theo's shoulders and made soothing noises. She settled Theo on the edge of the bed.

'I'm sorry,' Helena mumbled. Sophie looked up at her in exasperation over Theo's shoulder as she hugged her tightly.

'I really fancied him, Georgie,' Theo sounded miserable. 'I wanted him and all he could do was talk about you. He kept asking me about what you liked and disliked, how long had we been friends, did you have a boyfriend? I told him I'd go with him, that once the rest of you had taken the San Pedro, he and I could go back to the hacienda together.' She looked wretched. We all looked at her in silence.

'He laughed at me. Said I was a common little whore.' She was crying now. 'So I told him you were a virgin,' she said fiercely, her face red with shame. 'I didn't know he was going to hurt you. I thought he would lose interest in you! I didn't imagine for one minute that he was going to do that! I swear I didn't. I swear.'

'Oh Theo.' Sophie hugged her tightly whilst Theo sobbed against her shoulder. Helena lowered her eyes.

'How could you be so mean?' I whispered.

'Mean?' Theo stared at me, her make-up streaked down her face. 'Mean? Well I wasn't the one who decided to kill him, was I?'

Sophie put her hand to her mouth.

'We made a pact, *remember*?' Helena was livid.

'I didn't kill him,' I said, suddenly feeling worn-out. 'He fell, that's all. One minute he was there, the next he was falling.'

Theo looked at Sophie who turned her face away. 'Fine,' she spat out. 'What's the difference anyhow?'

'So what now?' asked Sophie.

I looked at her and Helena, and Theo. There seemed to be only one course of action open to us now.

'Now we go to see the curandero,' I said. 'All of us.'

***

Nina's sister lived in a respectable neighbourhood about two miles away. Nina didn't want her husband to know what we were up to. He evidently did not approve of his sister in law, or her activities, fancying himself to be a modern man, not one of these unsophisticated cholo who clung to the old ways instead of embracing modern medicine, modern science. There had been words earlier and he had left us to it, choosing for himself the relative sanctuary of the bar on the corner where he could smoke his pipe in peace.

I had wanted to go to see the curandero straight away but Helena persuaded me to wait until later that evening. We had a quiet meal in a local cafe where Nina joined us a little after seven o'clock. Theo was very quiet and chain-smoked her way through dinner, the bruise on her cheek blooming nicely. *Serve her right.* I had packed everything necessary in my backpack. As I walked through the streets I could feel the guinea pig scrabbling around from time to time.

Cuzco by night was just as busy as during the day. Cafes and restaurants spilled out into the streets, pan-pipe music and Quechua folksong made a constant blur of sound, against which the pitch of gringo laughter seemed a little too loud and incongruous. The local men of the town smoked their pipes, chewed coca leaves in doorways and on street corners, watchful and curious as we walked by. We passed through the city and on into the suburbs where granite stone gave way to adobe and each house boasted a dirt patch large enough for a few chickens to scratch around.

The house of the curandero was a simple brick and stone affair, set back from the road. There was a largish garden neatly tended, and steps leading up to a first floor balcony. We followed Nina up the path, our conversation petering out once we had entered the property. The place had a stillness that made talk feel somehow redundant as if the house were beckoning us kindly with one finger against its lips in silent welcome.

I was astonished. There must have been at least twenty five people of all ages waiting quietly in the anteroom. The most elderly or infirm were seated on benches, the youngest sitting cross-legged on the floor. Men leaned against the walls or crouched down with their children. Many of them carried a draw-string bag that made occasional rustling sounds and tiny squeaks. But there were other ingredients too set down at their feet as they waited their turn, wax candles, eggs, San Pedro plants, coca leaves, agave leaves, fruit. The room was bare of decoration, lit from above by a central strip light that conferred upon the space and all its occupants a jaundiced pallor. A single neon blue u-shaped tube zapped unsuspecting insects. And once again, no obvious queuing system for us to go by.

Nina ushered us in, though there was nowhere for us to go. Then an inner door opened and a smart looking young woman dressed in a shirt with a brightly coloured woven waistcoat and skirt, signalled for us to follow her. I looked at the people sitting patiently. They would be waiting for hours. This was all part of the process, a necessary show of commitment. Some of them would have driven all day to come here. Why should we be granted an audience ahead of them?

I turned to Nina and shook my head. It didn't seem right.

'I want us to wait,' I said holding her back by the arm. 'It's not right. These people were here first.'

She peered at me. 'It will be many hours,' she whispered. 'I have to go home. If I am here all night my husband will be angry with me.'

'It's fine,' Helena said. 'We'll wait on our own. You have brought us here. We can wait.'

Nina wasn't satisfied. She obviously thought this was

some kind of trick. She shook off my hand angrily.

'I do not believe you,' she said savagely.

'No, it's not that,' I said, bewildered by her change of tone. 'Look, I have everything here. Everything you told me to get.'

I slipped the backpack from my shoulders and undid the straps. I reached inside and lifted out the black guinea pig to show her, proof of my intention. As I revealed the creature there was a collective intake of breath from the assembled clients and fierce mutterings. Several of the women crossed themselves and started to rock back and forth. Nina put her hands out to grasp the animal. She thrust it back into the bag and pushed it back to me. The woman in the doorway said something in Quechua and the rest of the room nodded nervously and pointed towards the doorway.

'They want us to go in,' Sophie said, looking around at the concerned faces of the people around us.

'I think we should do as they ask,' said Theo. Helena nodded.

I turned back to Nina. Her eyes were full of distrust and what I took to be a sort of angry satisfaction. It was only afterwards I realised how much her sudden flare of rage towards me was born of fear.

We went through into a consulting room that seemed dark and cavernous by comparison. Nina followed us in. The door clicked shut behind us and a gentle voice welcomed us from the shadows.

***

Once my eyes had adjusted to the light I saw that we were in a room much the same size as before. There were no windows. The walls were covered with blankets and woven cloths in luminous colours of greens, gold, purple and blues that depicted Ayahuasca – the sacred vine of souls – San Pedro, the moon and stars, the sun, streaming clouds of cosmic energies, sacred vessels and representations of the divine powers: Inti the Sun God and his beautiful wife, Viracocha the creator, Cocamama the sexy goddess of health who presided over the coca plant, Chasca the goddess of twilight and dawn, Zaramama goddess of grain and corn, Copocati who liked nothing better than to destroy the temples of other gods, Urugary the god of hidden treasures. There was row upon row of glass jars containing herbs and plant extracts, incense, spices and salt. Every surface was covered with wax candles and carved wooden figures, plants, vines, flowers, bottles of pisco, and eggs. The only illumination was candlelight. It was oppressively warm and smelled of sage and jasmine. The effect was intoxicating. I felt light-headed and gripped the back of a chair for support.

The assistant who had shown us in, retreated slightly, ushering us all to take a seat. We sat in a rough semicircle, nervous and uncertain.

The curandero was of average height, her features dark like those of her sister, but she had a kinder face. She spoke no English. Nina was to translate for us. The curandero smiled and seemed to be asking Nina a question. Nina pointed a bony finger at me and said something under her breath.

The curandero nodded to her assistant who took the backpack from me and withdrew the pisco and the coca leaves. She handed the leaves to Nina who in turn divided them between Theo, Sophie and Helena.

'You must help your friend,' Nina said. 'The coca increases the spirit. It brings more energy to the healing. Here, chew this.'

The curandero fixed me with her expression and put both hands on my shoulders. Then she sat at a small table and produced a deck of cards, so well-worn that I could hardly read the images. She laid the cards out in front of her on a woven cloth and tapped her fingers. She made several deep sighing sounds and focused on each card before turning to me and placing her hand on my stomach. Her hand was hot, and I noticed that she was sweating quite profusely. She shook her head and muttered again.

She pulled me up and her assistant laid a woven blanket on the floor. I took off my shoes and stood on the blanket. Then she invited me to strip. When I did not move, the three Quechua women all laughed and nodded, gesturing with their hands for me to go ahead and undress down to my underwear.

I looked at my friends but they were already starting to relax under the influence of the coca. Sophie nodded at me, her eyes bright.

'It's okay, we're here with you.'

I took off my clothes slowly and folded them up to put on my chair. I was shivering even though the room was stiflingly hot. There was an uneasy silence in the room as the women took in the full scale of my injuries. I folded my arms over my breasts. The bite marks were still horribly visible as was the bruising around my arms and thighs.

The curandero poured pisco into a jug of water and stirred it. Then she took a large swig of the liquid and sprayed it over me with her mouth like a human sprinkler. Theo's jaw dropped. Helena and Sophie giggled in spite of themselves. She motioned for me to rotate, and continued to spray pisco water over my head and body until I was completely wet.

'Limpia,' Nina smiled knowingly. 'Cleansing the body.'

I was then required to lie down. The blanket had been sprinkled with flowers, the heady scent filling my nostrils. I rolled on one side then the other. After that Nina produced the black guinea pig.

'The curandero uses the cuy negre to help you. You will see.'

I stood still as the curandero held the animal by the scruff of the neck and gently rubbed it over my head and body. The sensation of a warm pelt on my skin might have been mildly erotic had the circumstances not been so bizarre. The animal was mostly silent until she reached my abdomen. Then it started to squeak and wriggle around. The curandero turned me around and rubbed the animal all over my back and shoulders, the backs of my legs and arms. But when she came anywhere near my pelvis, it squeaked and became agitated again.

Helena was agog. Sophie and Theo had stopped chewing and were rocking back and forth trying to suppress their laughter. They didn't laugh for long.

Satisfied with the proceedings so far, the curandero seized the guinea pig by the head, stood it on its hind legs, picked up a small knife and slit its throat. Then with a single fluid movement she turned it upside down and skinned the creature down to its hind legs and plunged the still quivering animal into a large bowl of water.

I nearly fainted. Sophie and Theo were shocked into silence. I saw Helena roll forward to put her head between her knees.

The curandero lifted the warm quivering body and displayed the neck which was yellow and pustulated.

'Susto,' Nina clapped her hands together. 'You have the fright. You see how the cuy trembles? And the neck. Brujeria. Black magic. You are not yourself. Espanto. Your body is here,' she pinched my arm, 'but your spirit wanders, no longer part of you, yes?'

I didn't dare look at Helena. She had seen my spirit

on the mountain. The susto was real enough.

The curandero grunted, flipped the body of the guinea pig over and sliced into the abdomen. Nina moved forward to see closely for herself but there was no doubt in her mind. Even I could see the truth. The womb was bulging. The assistant crossed herself.

The curandero shook her head sadly and looked me straight in the eye. She held my chin with her fingers lightly as she spoke and then smiled and gave my cheek a little pat.

Nina listened and nodded. There was excitement in her expression, a beady intensity that was repulsive.

'You have the dark seed inside you. This dark energy must be healed. You understand?'

The curandero pulled the skin back over the warm body and gave it to me to hold. Then she swigged the pisco water and sprayed me up and down to complete the ritual.

'You must take the cuy and bury it where no-one can see. Then you will be free. Your body will wash out this dark seed. After, your spirit can return to your body. Until then, your spirit will wander. You will grow weak.'

I nodded, still clutching the dead animal. The curandero took it from me and wrapped it in a cloth filled with the flowers from the blanket.

The assistant packed it in my backpack whilst I dressed. Nina took the others out ahead of me to get some fresh air. I thanked the curandero. I handed her the money and lifted up the backpack. She gripped my hand suddenly as I turned to leave.

'This man who hurt you. His spirit wanders. He has no peace. He died before you could forgive him. This is only the first part. To complete the healing you must open your heart and forgive him.'

I stared at her. She could have spoken to me all along

and yet she pretended to have no English. Instead I had to suffer Nina with her beady black eyes and her foul breath. I shook my head vehemently.

'No,' I said.

'You are young, inside you are hurt and your heart is broken.'

'No, there's nothing wrong with my heart,' I said.

She took a step closer to me and her eyes were wide and dark.

'Not *him*,' she said. 'Your heart is broken because of one of *them.*' She gestured with her head and I swallowed hard because I knew she spoke the truth.

'This man he has come among you like a fox. He has turned you against each other. You must make your peace with him – and with your friend.'

'I don't know how.'

'You must forgive them *both* or this hate inside will destroy you.'

I lifted my chin and looked her straight in the eye. 'That's asking too much,' I said. I held out my hand in goodbye.

She looked at me with a little half-smile and shrugged her shoulders. 'You have powers within you. You can use them for good, or for evil. The choice is yours.'

She has no idea.

'I can see why he chose you,' she said.

I blinked at her. She put her hands on her hips and made a little coquettish swivel of her hips. Was she making fun of me? I wanted to hit her.

'How dare you!' I walked away from her and yanked open the door.

'Señorita,' she said wagging her finger at me. 'You cannot hide anything from *me.*'

***

We made a small detour on our way back to the hostel

so that I could bury the guinea pig by the river. The others hung around, their backs turned whilst I found a suitable spot for a rodent grave. The coca leaves were wearing off and a sense of despondency hung over them. Nina was standing a little way apart from us, smoking a cigarette. I wondered whether her sister paid her a commission for conning tourists into killing small furry animals. What fools we had been.

I said sorry to the guinea pig and her unborn litter and laid her in a shallow pit. I covered her with loose dry earth and vegetation, knowing full well that some yellow dog would be bound to dig her up for breakfast.

Sophie came up and handed me a couple of twigs lashed together with a hair band to form a rudimentary cross.

'Thanks.'

I laid the cross over the grave. It was an awkward moment. A sort of X marks the spot. I picked it up again and sneaked it into my shirt. I would keep it as a reminder.

'You know there must be thousands of guinea pig graves all over this country,' she said, taking hold of my arm.

'I suppose.'

'In fact,' she said warmly, 'they ought to have designated cemeteries. That's what we would have in Britain, if . . . you know . . . ' She squeezed my arm. 'You weren't to know what would happen.' She was right but it didn't make me feel any better. A life for a life. Was that it?

I turned back to see Theo remonstrating with Helena, but they were too far away for me to hear the words. Sophie squeezed my arm tightly. I supposed we were all pretty much done in. Nina spat on the ground, impatient now to get home. Sophie and I rejoined the others and walked through the quiet suburb back to the city streets where the party continued on late into the night. Back in our dorm I climbed into bed and crashed out, bone weary with the exertions of the previous few days.

I awoke a little while later, to feel a seeping warmth beneath the sheet. I put my hand between my legs. My period had started. Wamani's seed was no more.

PART IV

1

My relationship with Theo never really recovered after Peru. Serving me up on a plate for you-know-who had brought our friendship to an all-time low. We'd let that one lie for so long that it seemed churlish to bring it up. But *he* was always there between us like Banquo's ghost. I had never entirely forgiven her, not really, and she knew it.

At Cambridge we drifted apart in that final term. Helena and Sophie settled back into college life as a confirmed couple and I got my head down for the final push. A respectable upper second was all that I needed for the job market. Sophie claimed her first. I saw Theo's name on posters for the Footlights, even considered going along with Helena and Sophie, but instead took pleasure in one scathing review which described Theo as 'destined for soap.'

I could not forgive; a small piece of grit remained lodged in my heart. All was not lost, however. I had my writing. Over time something pearlescent began to emerge. I slogged away. My first slim volume of poetry, *On Virgin Slopes,* made a modest appearance, garnering some encouraging responses. I acquired an agent. I felt happy. My life was gaining momentum.

We probably would all have gone our separate ways entirely after graduation had it not been for Sir Peter's untimely demise.

I had a job at the University Press and was in the

habit of taking sandwiches to eat by the river to eek out my salary. There was a telephone message from Helena waiting for me when I returned to the office, asking if I would go round that evening. She and Sophie had digs in town and I found the address easily enough. I parked my bicycle and knocked on the front door. I hadn't seen Helena for about four months and I was afraid that I had let the friendship lapse beyond the natural limit when relations might be re-established without embarrassment. I need not have worried. She flung open the door, grabbed me in a bear hug and kissed me on the cheek.

'It's so good of you to come,' she said ushering me inside and telling me the whole story over tea and ginger cake.

Lady Audrey had arrived to break the news to Sophie in person. She hardly commented on Helena's presence, which was proof enough for me that she could not have been entirely herself. It was agreed that Sophie would return with her mother and that Helena should go by train to stay at Chiswick Central for the weekend of the funeral.

'Thing is, I'd – we'd – really be grateful if you could come along.'

I put down my tea cup.

'Of course,' I said. 'Anything for Sophie. How is she?'

'Absolutely gutted. They're all in total shock. He was as fit as a flea apparently. Nobody can quite believe it.'

'Perhaps the high life was catching up with him.' I thought back to the last time I had seen Sir Peter on Eleanor's wedding day. You would have thought him the proudest man in the world. And he had always been jolly nice to us.

'I wonder what will happen now?' I pondered aloud.

'How do you mean?'

'Well, Sophie always thought there was another

woman somewhere out in the Bush. Possibly a family. Do you think they will be there?'

'Good Lord! I hope not. That would be taking the biscuit.'

We sipped more tea, contemplating the worst case scenario: Father Rafferty intoning mass in his Irish brogue and Lady Audrey in magisterial robes, fending off a bunch of jumping Maasai.

Helena seemed perturbed.

'What is it?'

'Sophie wants Theo to come too. I know the two of you haven't seen much of each other lately. Would you mind awfully?'

'No.' I sighed. 'I can't help it H. The way I feel about her. But I wouldn't make a scene or anything like that.'

Helena breathed a deep sigh of relief.

'Oh, that's brilliant. Sophie will be relieved. I told her I thought you'd probably tell her to take a running jump!'

I blinked at Helena's splendid lack of tact. As if. Poor Sophie. It was her father's funeral, for goodness sake.

My mother always said that funerals brought out the worst in people. Driving to my grandmother's service in Hythe had born out that truism. The crematorium was about four miles from the Church, down a dual carriageway. An impatient motorist behind us cut in front only to find himself ramming on the breaks so as not to rear-end my grandmother's hearse.

I was more concerned that Theo would take the opportunity to shag a curate.

Helena and I took the train. Lady Audrey drew the line at Sophie and her lover sharing a room, but was content for the two of us to bunk together in the guest wing. I had no great desire to be at home with the whole family during this period of concentrated mourning; however, one look from Sophie and I banished any thought I might have entertained of ducking out to the nearest B&B. She looked ghastly.

The three of us slipped out that night down to a riverside pub. Over gin and tonics in a cosy corner, we discussed Theo's latest news.

'She's engaged to be married,' said Helena pulling a face. 'Douglas Allenson. Duggie to his friends. Worth an absolute fortune. We're all invited.'

I shook my head. I didn't suppose that a gilt-edged invitation would be hitting my doormat any time soon. Sophie put her hand over mine.

'You *are* invited Georgie. You can come with us if you like.'

'I wouldn't bother if it were just me,' Helena added by way of encouragement.

Sophie rolled her eyes. 'That's just mean. I'm sure it will be fabulous. Plenty of jam-pots. She knows practically everybody on the arts scene.'

'She's slept with practically everybody on the arts scene,' Helena responded, finishing her drink and heading for the bar. Sophie squeezed my hand.

'Don't take any notice. You *will* come, won't you? She'll be so disappointed if you don't.'

I didn't like the idea but now was not the time to deny Sophie.

'Yes, all right. What does this Duggie do anyway?'

'That's a bit vague. Some sort of entrepreneur. Investment broker, I think.' Sophie was always vague about anything to do with money. It must have been a product of her upbringing. I could imagine Lady Audrey thinking cash a rather vulgar entity. I had a fleeting image of some scrawny youth up before her, awaiting judgement for sandbagging an old lady for her pension money. *Off with his head!*

I didn't want to bring up the subject of Sophie's

father but the pause in our conversation had become a silence and then a chasm of unspoken thoughts against the background of clinking glasses and boorish Hoorays.

'These city types are becoming a public menace,' I said. 'Let's take our drinks outside.' I signalled to Helena.

We found a table recently vacated. We were having one of those Indian summers. The river flowed past, a silken skein of silver and lilac threads. We let the outdoor splendour of it all wash over us.

'I don't think mummy will ever get over it,' Sophie murmured almost to herself.

'I suppose he was still in his prime,' I said carefully. 'She probably thought they would have time together once he retired.'

'Not that,' she frowned. 'Dying in Africa. You can't imagine all the red tape she's had to cut through. They're sending someone down from the Foreign Office to attend. HM government offered to arrange the whole thing and give him a proper send off, but mummy wouldn't hear of it. Said she wanted a private service. Still, I think they'll be bound to make a posthumous award or something.'

Helena picked her way through the beer garden with a tray of glasses and tonic bottles.

'A toast,' I said when we had settled again. 'To Friendship, Life and all that She can throw at us.'

'To Friendship, Life, and all that She can throw at us,' they chorused.

We clinked glasses in the dying sunlight.

***

Theo was happy.

The shock of it hit me like a wrecking ball but there was no mistaking the genuine article. Douglas wore an immaculate suit of charcoal grey and held Theo's hand throughout the service. She had put on a little weight and it suited her. She trembled slightly when she caught my eye but I felt the fight drain out of me. Here we were standing beside the grave of a beloved man and no amount of recriminations for past indiscretions could disguise Lady Audrey's obvious distress. I had never seen her so quiet and still. Sophie held her mother's arm. Eleanor's husband supported his wife and her younger sister Pru. Eleanor and Prudence made a point of ignoring Sophie. It was savage behaviour when you came to think about it and I hoped it would pass. Surely the death of a parent was supposed to bring siblings closer together? Helena stood next to me and I knew she was thinking only of Sophie.

Afterwards, we returned to the house where Lady Audrey had arranged afternoon tea for guests in the drawing room. Helena and I took refuge in the summerhouse. We were shortly followed by Theo, desperate for a cigarette.

'Christ, what a palaver,' she uttered between draws. 'I've never been to a Catholic send-off before. It's very camp isn't it? All that incense wafting about.' She picked a speck of tobacco from her teeth.

'Is that Douglas?' The man in question was standing on the lawn looking up at the house. Calculating square footage, no doubt.

'He's an absolute darling. I adore him. You will come, Georgie, won't you? It wouldn't be the same without the four of us. I've told Duggie all about you. He's dying to meet you – honestly.' She stubbed her cigarette out on the ground and opened the door to call him inside. Helena raised her eyebrows but said nothing. Douglas rubbed his hands and let Theo link arms with him. He looked so earnest and chuffed as punch at the same time. I wondered if he had any idea of his future wife's appetites.

Theo looked at me and I felt her silent need. *Please don't, Georgie. Please don't spoil it for me.* Did my opinion really weigh that much? Could I ruin it for her if I really wanted to? I realised suddenly that I wasn't second fiddle after all. I was a solo artist, just like her. I could scale my own heights, create my own music, perform on my own. From time to time, the four of us might get together, reform the band, have a jamming session. I smiled to myself. Sophie would like that idea. But I no longer needed to blame Theo. I could meet her on equal terms. She had suffered the loss of my friendship. Perhaps that was punishment enough.

'Sounds really great,' I said, shaking Douglas by the hand. 'Congratulations to you both. Of course I'll be there. Wouldn't miss it for the world.'

She hugged me tightly. We all looked at each other. We were entering into a new era: our very own perastroika. A new entente cordiale.

'Let's go in and rescue Sophie,' I said.

PART V

1

I stood in the doorway of Boyd's room and considered the options.

Had Sophie driven him into Cambridge to catch the London train? Had he decided to go for a walk and was even now sitting in the kitchen below sipping coffee, smoking a cigarette and droning on about his future career as a television pundit? I'd asked him to leave and seemingly that's what he had done, so why did I feel a surge of resentment now that he had? Surely I wasn't hoping for anything more?

I padded back to my room and sat on the edge of the bed. *How about a few column inches.* Theo had been in cahoots with Daniel all along. So that was what this weekend was really about. Daniel and Theo getting me to agree to an interview with Matthew Boyd. Daniel, you silly arse. I bet you didn't expect me to sleep with the bugger. Or Theo. I bet that was the very last thing either of them thought I was capable of. Poor Georgina. She's not herself you know. Quite lost without her writing.

It wasn't my fault. He forced himself on me. Just like the first time. But that wasn't really true. I picked at the duvet cover, overwhelmed by contradictory feelings. Boyd had grabbed me in the dark but he hadn't been violent, just assertive. And I'd rather liked it. I'd responded in kind. Boyd had surprised me but it hadn't been rape. Thank goodness I'd never had full recall of that night at the pueblo. I had been spared the horror of that. It was quite enough suffering the dreams. My visions and the bruising on my body were proof enough of what had been done to me. Wamani had even admitted it. He had threatened me on the mountain. *It's a long way down. If we can't trust each other, who knows what might happen?* I was glad he was dead. Glad that he couldn't threaten women any more. He had deserved to die. He was a hustler, a fraud, a violator of women, and probably a terrorist to boot. The military would have caught up with him sooner or later. That would have meant torture and, almost certainly, execution. All things considered, he was probably lucky to have died the way he did.

Fuck it. I didn't want anyone to know that I'd slept with Boyd. Especially not Daniel. I wanted a cigarette. I knew in my heart that he hadn't actually slept with Tufter McNeil. I was pretty sure that she wouldn't have lowered herself to that. Not out of any consideration for me, or regard for him. She had her own reputation as a cougar to maintain and Daniel was far too grey and stiff of hip to meet the criteria of young stud. I felt a sudden pang of remorse.

Sitting on the edge of the bed in that little attic room I conjured up happier memories from our time together: Sunday afternoons at *The Renoir*, a fortnight climbing in the Western Isles, weekends in Berlin. But that inevitably brought me to the end point; the last time we'd been truly intimate, the last time he'd made love to me.

***

I had arrived home after the usual Northern Line commute-fiasco to find Daniel nursing a malt whisky in the sitting room conducting *Madame Butterfly* from a prone position on the sofa.

'I've had a genius idea. Why don't we celebrate the Queen's Jubilee by travelling to the nearest republic so we don't have to deal with all that bollocks? You've always wanted me to whisk you off somewhere romantic.'

That was true. In all our years together we seemed permanently at odds on the best way to spend our *quality time* together. Personally, I had never had any trouble enjoying quality time without him, but this was at least a gesture. I would have preferred it if the thought had been truly about pleasing ourselves, by which I meant *me*, rather than a strategy for expressing his contempt for royalty. He twisted his head round.

'What do you think?'

I stood in the doorway and stared at his feet hanging over the armrest. I was wet, cold and petulant, wondering how it was that he always managed to corner me at the most inopportune moment. Was it some sort of radar? A kind of male intuition? I caught sight of my reflection in the hallway mirror. No matter what I put on in the morning, by evening I looked and felt like a bag lady. I couldn't even begin to imagine Paris. I could still smell the underground in my nostrils. I wanted a hot shower, take-out Thai and a stiff gin and tonic, not necessarily in that order. I kicked off my heels and headed for the kitchen.

'Well?'

Christ, did I have to give him an answer right there and then, that very bloody second?

I gritted my teeth and reached for a glass. 'Fine.'

'What? What do you think?'

'Could you perhaps just turn down the volume? Then you might be able to hear me.' I poured myself a large measure of Bombay Sapphire. I opened the freezer compartment door.

'There's no ice,' I said.

'What?'

'I said there's no ice, Daniel. Where's all the ice?' I slammed the door shut which made the fridge vibrate.

'It's in here.'

I squeezed my eyes tight shut and did a mental count to ten, then exhaled sharply. I'd sent an amusing retro birthday card to Theo a couple of years back that had a picture of a smiling fifties housewife and a speech bubble that read 'yoga, meditation, reflexology and still I want to beat the living shit out of somebody'. I'd thought it really funny at the time. I slipped my coat off and rubbed the back of my neck.

'Well?' Daniel was standing in the doorway with the ice bucket and a pair of tongs. 'One lump or two?'

I held out my glass.

'Fine, sounds fine. Really.'

I walked past him and turned on the lamp on the hall table, where we kept the take-away menus.

'Well if you don't want to go, we don't have to go.'

'I said it's fine. Can we talk about it later?' I picked up the receiver and dialed the number. 'Are you okay with Thai?'

'Actually I'm rather in the mood for Italian.'

I cocked my head to one side as the line cut in at the other end. '*Hallo, Golden Lilly Restaurant – can I take your order?* 'Sorry,' I said into the receiver and was about to put the phone down, when I was suddenly seized with a cold fury. 'Hello, hello? Yes mm, I would like to order please.' I scanned the menu even though I knew exactly what I wanted. 'Number 32, number 12 and a 10 please. Yes, that's for one. Thank you.'

I put the phone down and took a swig of gin. He stared at me in disbelief.

'I'm going to have a bath,' I said as I walked past him

and up the stairs.

'Well what the hell am I supposed to eat?' his voice echoed behind me.

'Open a jar of *Dolmio*,' I shouted and slammed the bathroom door shut.

I lay in the bathtub and pictured Paris in June. I imagined mornings spent viewing antiquities and sculpture, candlelit evenings pouring over menus together, lovemaking in the afternoons on fresh linen sheets. The trouble was, the lover in question wasn't Daniel. It was a faceless, dark, handsome waiter with narrow hips and bags of stamina. I stroked myself as my fantasy lover brought me to a quivering climax.

The doorbell rang. That was the only problem with *Golden Lilly*: they were so bloody efficient. Guaranteed delivery within thirty minutes or a free meal. I shouted down for Daniel to get the door for me.

The strains of *Madame Butterfly* grew louder and louder. Bloody hell.

'Daniel!' I shouted. 'Get the door!'

The bell rang again. Cursing, I hauled myself out of the tub and pulled on a bathrobe. I trundled down the stairs dripping just as Daniel appeared.

'For God's sake,' I hissed at him, fumbling in my handbag for cash. My purse was empty. I'd forgotten to get cash-back at the Tesco Metro. 'Oh, shit.' I pulled open the door to the shiny faced Thai delivery man.

'Good evening.'

'Good evening. Thank you.' I took the bag from him. Daniel leaned against the wall with a smug look on his face.

'Need some cash, darling?'

I scowled at him.

'Yes. Please. Thank you.'

I turned on my heel and headed into the kitchen

whilst Daniel engaged in multicultural chitchat. I heard the door close. I picked up a spoon and fork, stuck the Bombay Sapphire under one arm and a bottle of tonic under the other and headed back upstairs.

'Are you going to eat that in the bedroom? You'll get fat on the pillow cases.'

'Yes. I probably will.'

I curled up in the bedroom and flicked channels until I found an old episode of *Top Gear*. Downstairs Madame Butterfly had sung her last note. I picked at my food and let the gin do its work. I watched Jeremy Clarkson whinging on about Chinese imports and felt all the toxic shit drain out of me. My thoughts drifted back to Paris. At work everyone was already rolling their eyes in horror at the thought of bunting and street parties. It was bad enough staging the Olympics.

By the end of *Newsnight* I was ready to kiss and make up. I padded downstairs to find him asleep on the sofa, the television on pause, half a plate of congealed spagbol on the carpet next to an empty bottle of Shiraz. I studied the lines of his face, every grey hair, the wrinkles in his neck, the tuft of grey chest hair poking up where he had unbuttoned his shirt. Perhaps Paris was just what we needed to re-kindle the passion in our relationship. I knelt down and kissed him. He made a face like a sulky five year old so I kissed him again.

'Paris sounds great to me.'

He smiled without opening his eyes.

'Those royals are just a bunch of fucking parasites,' he mumbled.

'I'll remind you of that when you get your invitation to the Palace.'

'What would they want to give me a gong for?'

'Oh, I don't know. Courage in the line of fire? Services to uptight, ugly bitches who can't even pay for their own takeaways?'

'You're not ugly,' he grinned.

I punched him in the shoulder and lay my head on his chest. 'I'm sorry,' I said in a small voice.

'It's okay kiddo,' he said stroking my back. 'You can't help it.'

***

For an extra couple of hundred quid, we upgraded our Eurostar tickets to first class. Fat seats, complimentary beverages including biscuits, breakfast on the way, dinner on the way back. Adjacent, a more sophisticated, absorbed sort of traveller, screened by the pages of a large broadsheet, so that we could pull faces at each other and stare out of the window like a pair of day-trippers.

Our room in the 14th Arrondissement was large by Parisian standards. The windows looked out across the rooftops of neighbouring embassies. Even the air seemed just a touch more refined in this district. We walked and walked. The warmth hinted at the dry heat to follow. We sat in the sun and ate in the shade. I sampled five different crème brulées that week. Daniel, not big on deserts, sampled French onion soup, declaring each bowl to be superior in either flavour, presentation or texture than the one before. We gorged ourselves like children on a school trip. It was one of the happiest weeks of my life.

On our last full day we set off for the Rodin museum just around the corner. The chateau and gardens were a delight, but despite wearing my most comfortable sandals, my feet ached and burned in equal measure. My mother said that London had the hardest pavements in the world, but she had never been to Paris.

'It's only a few hundred yards back to the hotel.'

'Why don't your feet ache?' I sounded petulant even

to my ears.

'Well, sit down then and I'll give them a rub.' He led me to a stone bench shaded by plane trees. 'Give me your foot.'

Naked, the puffy white flesh was striped with red welts. Pink blotches now threatened to blister. Daniel gingerly picked off a few blades of grass and some gravel that had become embedded. I flinched. Then he grinned. 'Ticklish?'

'Not today, no.' It was a half lie. True, my feet were sensitive, but they were too sore to feel anything other than irritation, or so I thought.

'Hold on a minute.' He got up and sauntered down to the small café stand across the grass. He returned a couple of minutes later with a litre of water, a cup of ice and some paper napkins. Instead of sitting back down on the bench he squatted down in front of me and broke the seal on the bottle. 'Careful,' I said. 'Squashing grass is practically a capital offence in this country.'

'Ready?' he asked with a smirk. I expected him to simply pour cool water all over my foot but instead, he started to run an ice cube in small circles around the base of my heel. Then he swept the cube slowly up the sole of my foot and then down again in figures of eight, never touching my toes. The ice melted in seconds, but he kept on stroking my foot, sending a thin current of excitement up to my groin. He lifted my foot and placed it against his chest, using both thumbs now to knead more rhythmically. I hardly dared look at him. When I did, I saw that he was watching me intently.

'Someone has a fetish, I see.'

'Shut up,' I groaned.

His hands stilled and he lifted my foot away from him and for one awful needy moment I thought he had finished with me. But then, still watching my eyes, he pulled my foot towards his mouth and licked long and slow along the side of my instep and up over my big toe. I closed my eyes, silently begging him to do it again. And he did. With each sweep of his tongue I felt myself loosening inside.

Daniel gave me a look.

'Scared?'

I scowled at him, but I didn't pull my foot away.

'People are looking,' I hissed, hoping rather than knowing this to be true. He grinned up at me.

'Coward,' he said.

I considered this carefully. Inside something was shifting.

He looked puzzled. 'What is it?'

'I was just thinking of what you said to me the first time we met. Do you remember?' Theo's second wedding party; lots of balloons and streamers, a tall good-looking stranger bearing down on me with two glasses of champagne and a rakish smile.

He reflected for a second. 'You look like a friend to steal horses with.'

We looked at each other for a long moment.

'It's still the best chat up line I've ever heard.'

He grinned.

'Do you love me?' I asked.

'What?'

'Do you love me?'

His jaw dropped a little as he made a sort of gasping, slightly exasperated sound combined with a manic smile. That was classic Daniel. Evasion dressed up like a schoolboy misdemeanour.

I pulled my foot away.

He rubbed his chin and sat back onto the grass as I stood up and reached down to put my sandal back on.

'Georgina.' He sounded tired. 'Georgie – wait. Wait!'

But I was off and moving fast back through the park to the main road and the relative seclusion of the hotel.

He caught up with me and held me roughly by the arms, forcing me to look at him. I couldn't. I felt about six years old. I couldn't even understand it myself but suddenly the cold hard reality of our relationship was exposed. I had asked the question without thinking. I hadn't even suspected the truth. It would have been so easy for him to let slip a white lie – 'Yeah, Babe, of course.' I would have believed him. Didn't he even trust me to believe his fictions? Why did he have to tell me the truth? Whatever had possessed him to own up to the truth after all this time?

'Stop, Georgie. Listen, I'm – ' He groped for the right words.

'I'm what?'

'I'm – God – you don't make this easy do you?'

'I'm *what* exactly?'

'I'm *very fond* of you. You *know* that.'

It was like I'd just taken a blow to the solar plexus.

'*Fond?*' I said, the tears sliding down both cheeks. 'You're very *fond* of me? Like a pet? Like a German Shepherd?'

He looked frightened. 'Georgie, that's not what I mean. You *know* how I feel about you. We're good together, aren't we? We've never pretended. But after all this time, surely you know I'm really happy with you. I – for Christ's sake, Georgie – I left my wife for you.' He let go of my arms and ran his hands across his face. I stared at him. Did he expect me to offer him some comfort?

'Fond,' I whispered hoarsely. 'You're fond of me.' I took a step back from him and turned slowly to walk away. Until that moment, until those words were uttered, I never knew the power of them. I never before understood how deadly that four letter word could be. Fond. Such a small, innocent, little word. An old-fashioned word, a nursery phrase, a term of affection. Ted's awfully *fond* of golf you know. Mary's very *fond* of a tipple at Christmas. Words inside a birthday card from a spinster in the family: *Fond* Regards, Auntie Dorothy. But never ever a word to be used between lovers. I'm very fond of you, he had said. Of all the words my erudite, intellectual, publisher-lover could have summoned in that moment, but there it was: fond. A word that felt so foolish, so improbable and so out of joint. A phrase that so adroitly summed up the reality of our relationship. He was an aging man-child with grown-up children living with a woman twenty years his junior. A woman – not the mother of his children – a woman of whom he was *very fond*. Like St Augur cheese, or the novels of Dostoyevsky. I was just one of his appetites. A tit-bit, a morsel. What will I indulge myself with tonight? A slice of Georgina or a bit of Vivaldi? The humiliation was overwhelming. I felt my insides shriveling. I couldn't bear to look at him. I left him in the street and walked back to the hotel.

Up in the room I slipped off my clothes and climbed naked between the cool, freshly laundered linen. The door opened quietly a few moments later and Daniel drew the curtains closed against the heat of the afternoon and stripped off his clothes. He slid into bed beside me and wordlessly folded me into his arms.

He made love to me – tenderly, but we both knew it was the beginning of the end. I lay in the crook of his arm and felt the love in my heart seep out like blood from a flesh wound. Paris was the last time we kissed like lovers do. It was the last time I let him touch me.

2

I stood up and paced around the little yellow bedroom.

Why did I have to push him away? Why couldn't I have accepted Daniel just as he was? We had a good life together. He was faithful as far as I knew. Why couldn't that be enough?

Saturday afternoon. Where was he? I pictured him mooching about the British Film Institute bookshop filling in time before a retro screening of some black and white classic. I'd surprised him last year with tickets for a Humphrey Bogart double bill: *The Big Sleep* followed by *To Have and Have Not*. We even dressed up. He wore a crumpled mac belted round the middle and a trilby. I had put on my sharpest black suit, a fox fur and a fedora. We met in the bar, grinning sheepishly at each other. It might have been sexy had not every other couple in Christendom had the same idea. Still, Daniel could be a lot of fun and I did still love him. Bugger. I still loved him.

I picked up my phone and pressed the key for his number. There was a brief interlude. Reception was patchy. The best place for getting a signal was close up to the window at head height so I hitched myself up onto the sill of the alcove and kneeling on the bare wood, tried his number again.

'Hello?' He sounded surprised.

I felt a wave of relief wash over me.

'Daniel, it's me.'

There was an audible intake of breath. I waited. Perhaps he couldn't hear me.

'It's Georgina.'

'Oh.' There was a pause. 'Hi.'

'How are you?' I asked.

'Fine. Fine.' There was another pause. 'Is anything wrong?'

I'm a complete fuckwit. I slept with that working-class oik you and Theo set me up with. I know I told you to go back to your wife but I didn't mean it. I don't want to be alone anymore. When I get home will you be there?

'No, I'm fine.'

Another silence. I let my gaze wander over the roof slates of the kitchen below me.

'Have you seen much of the kids?'

'Ah, yeah. A bit. You know. Busy. Everyone's very busy.' I could hear some rustling noises. A woman's voice humming in the background, the sound of cutlery and plates. The penny dropped.

'Are you at home? With *her*?'

'Oh er, yes. I think the papers are on my desk.' He made a sort of chuckle. *He's talking to me like a client. He wants her to think I'm somebody else.* I could hear canned laughter on television. I wanted to vomit. Saturdays at home with Imogen: take away dinner, plates on laps, followed by *Casualty* and a half-hearted hand job if he was lucky. That's how he had described his married life before we met. I had been *such a revelation* to him. A woman willing to give him the full works any night of the week, and never dropping hints about biological clocks or ticking wombs.

His saintly wife was *so* understanding, so maternal. He was so undeserving, so *weak*, but he didn't have the heart to leave her even though he had found me maddeningly irresistible. *It would kill her Georgie, if I ever left.* Good! Shoot the sanctimonious bitch! Put her out of my misery! The years I had wasted, waiting for him. But in reality it was time for me to face up to the truth.

That he wanted to have his cake and eat it. So Imogen had taken him back, though I dare say, not without a dizzying number of conditions, and with a great deal of martyred satisfaction. That was Imogen's trademark.

'Let me guess. Egg fried rice, sweet and sour chicken, spring roll, chips and a bottle of Bud?' I shrieked down the phone before hurling it across the room where it bounced off the wall, splintering into three sections.

She must have heard that.

That was her *on the phone wasn't it? That publishing slut! Why's she calling you? Are you still seeing her, is that it? Don't even try to deny it! I should never have taken you back! You lying cheating bastard!*

No hand job for Mr Winky tonight. Old One Eye would have to make do with the spare room. There was some satisfaction in that.

But that wasn't the end of my problems. I wasn't too sure how Theo would react to me and Boyd. Jealous? Supercilious? Outraged?

I slid off the window sill, bruising my hip, and hobbled over to where my phone lay in bits. I couldn't hide up here for the rest of my life, though there was something terribly appealing about the little yellow room under the eaves. Everything complicated and wretched in my life was stripped away in this room. Like Clarissa Dalloway escaping the party, or was it herself? Who had that line about a narrow bed? A truckle bed. Wasn't that Shakespeare? How I longed for fleecy sheets like I had when I was a kid. Being tucked in tightly with teddy bears on either side. Lying perfectly still so the plumpfy satin eiderdown wouldn't slide off during the night. Always waking up cold to find it heaped on the floor at the foot of the bed like a sulky débutante after too much gin.

Tomorrow night I would be at home in my own bed.

A great big Ikea monster designed for couples with kids and pets. I could order Thai food and smear coconut oil and mono-sodium glutamate over the pillowcases to my heart's content. It should have been a fantasy space for splurging with Sunday supplements, or indulging in Olympic sexathons. Except now I had no-one at home to share it with. It would just be me feeling terribly alone under a dove grey, nine-hundred thread count, Egyptian cotton duvet from John Lewis. Tastefully miserable.

I dressed and trotted down the stairs.

The weekend wasn't a complete loss. We still had dinner ahead of us tonight, and, from my point of view, the best part of any weekend at Black Farm. Sunday roast slow cooked in the Doric with farm vegetables. Bread and butter pudding. An afternoon snooze followed by a brisk walk and then the Sunday evening commute back into London. Staving off the inevitable return to my achingly dull routine, and an empty nest.

Sophie was chopping vegetables in the kitchen.

'Georgie!' She smiled. 'Help yourself,' She indicated the open bottle of red on the table. She took a sip from her own glass. She poured olive oil into the casserole dish on top of the range.

'H is still flat out upstairs.'

I poured myself a glass of wine.

'Any sign of Theo?'

'She took Mattie into town.' She added the chopped potatoes and onions to the casserole dish and stirred vigorously. *Mattie?* Had he worked some sort of charm on her? She had loathed him the night before.

'Well that's a relief. I for one am glad to see the back of him.'

'Oh, he's coming back. They only went for cigarettes and booze.'

I sighed inwardly. Fucketyfucketyfuck. What chance

227

was there of Boyd keeping his mouth shut, if indeed he had no intention of leaving?

Sophie popped the dish of vegetables into the range to slow cook and closed the door into the hallway before sitting down opposite me.

'I wanted to have a quiet word with you, before the others get back. Daniel's been on the phone, asking if I knew where you were. He said he tried to phone you on your mobile but there was no answer. He sounded really worried. Do you want to ring him? You can use the house phone.'

Dear Sophie. She had an unflagging belief in the course of true love. She didn't much approve of Daniel but her own romantic history with Helena had taught her to hope and trust in love when all else fails.

'He's back with his wife. I spoke to him earlier, lost my temper a bit. He can stew in it for all I care.'

'I just want you to be happy, Georgie.' But I could tell that there was more on her mind than just that.

'I loved him.'

'I know.'

'I asked him once if he loved me,' I said. 'He said he was very fond of me.' I felt tears pricking my eyes. Sophie put her hands out and held mine. My voice was barely a whisper. 'It's so humiliating to hear a man say that. I can't tell you how much it shamed me.'

She squeezed my hands tightly.

'I think men can only love once,' she said.

I looked at her in surprise.

'Do you remember what I told you about my father and his mistress?' I nodded. 'It took me years to understand that it made no difference. I thought it meant that he didn't love *me*, you see. I thought he was trying to replace us – my mother, Pru, Eleanor and me, but it wasn't that at all. I don't think he loved her. I don't think a man can ever truly love the second woman, the one who comes after. Oh, I know you'll say that there are lots of second wives out there and mistresses and what-have-you who are really loved by their husbands, but I think it's a lie. It's one of the biggest lies there is. I think that when a man loves a woman he is somehow *undone* and if they have children together, well even more so. A man can never allow himself to feel that vulnerable ever again with anyone else. A mistress or a second wife is another chance, a lifesaver perhaps, often a really safe companion but I'm convinced that it is *she* who does all the loving. All she can really hope for is that he will take what she gives him and find it sufficient. But he'll never let himself be undone like he was the first time. It's asking too much.'

I flinched and tried to take my hands away but she held on.

'You need to find your own man, Georgie. Don't settle for somebody else's.'

'I can't believe you're saying this! I know lots of women who have settled down with divorced men. Their husbands don't tell them that they're *fond* of them!'

'He told you the truth. You're one of the lucky ones.'

'How can you be so cruel? I didn't expect this from you.'

She sighed and let go of my hands.

'I'm only saying this because I love you Georgie, and I can't bear to see you throw your life away on a man who just can't love you. It's not his fault.'

We were silent for a moment whilst I tried to take it all in. Sophie poured some more wine.

'People are what they are. And what about you? Can you look me in the eye and tell me that you were your *whole self* with Daniel?'

I opened and closed my mouth. It was useless to

pretend with Sophie.

'I don't think I've been my *whole self* with anyone, ever. I feel more at home with you and Helena and Theo than I ever have with anyone else. Christ, I'll be fifty in a matter of months. What have I done with my life?'

Sophie's face brightened. 'Even recognising the problem is a start. Do you remember in our second year how far gone I was when you came to see me in hospital?'

I hadn't thought about it for a long time. 'Yes,' I said.

'If I hadn't been able to admit the truth, if you hadn't been there – to hear my 'confession', if it hadn't been for you and Theo and Helena whisking me off to Peru – ' she shivered. 'I dread to think what would have become of me.'

'You don't have any regrets?'

'How could I? I know it's a pathetic cliché but I *found myself* out there. I suddenly knew what I was, what I wanted. If it hadn't been for the three of you, I would have probably topped myself.' She grasped the coloured beads she wore around her neck, and had done ever since Peru. 'Either that or married Hugo Spence and made both our lives miserable.'

'Your mother would have been over the moon. She never liked Helena.'

Sophie thought about this for a moment.

'You know there's something I never told anyone before, not even Helena. Mummy wrote me just before she died. She wanted to make her peace with me.'

'About your father?'

'Not just that. There was something else in the letter. It made me so angry. It's taken years for me to truly forgive her.'

I wondered what it could be. Lady Audrey's passing had seemed momentous at the time; a resolution of old hurts and conflicts, the end of the cold war for Sophie and her family. Eleanor was just as entrenched as her mother but Pru had softened over the years. There were nephews and nieces who occasionally came to visit. The threat posed by Aunt Sophie had been downgraded. She and her same-sex companion were viewed as eccentric, bordering on *cool* rather than degenerate.

'She wrote me about a friend she had when she was sixteen. She said that she didn't want to recognise the feelings she had then. She'd married my father partly to get away, to convince herself that she was completely normal. The marriage was a success in that she bore him three children but she knew she couldn't make him happy. She knew he couldn't make her truly happy either. She turned a blind eye to the affairs. She couldn't blame him for seeking out company when she herself was such an inadequate wife. She never regretted giving up her friend, but she never quite forgot about her either.'

'Good grief.' I sat back in my seat and took a large sip of wine. I thought back to the mockery of his funeral. 'So why on earth did she punish him like that? Sending him to the crematorium?'

Sophie shivered. 'Because she was capable of great cruelty.' There was a long pause. 'Daddy was a great disappointment to her in the end. I think she thought he was going to leave her. For good.' She tucked a lock of hair behind her ear. 'The more she tried to hold on to us, the further we wanted to run away – me, Daddy.' She shrugged her shoulders. 'All that time she *knew* what I was going through, how desperate I was, and yet she said nothing.'

'How did she explain herself?'

'She said she hoped that with me and Helena, it was just a phase – an adolescent crush – she didn't want me to be excluded, to miss out on marriage, children, 'a *decent* life' – as she put it.'

'She must have suffered, Sophie. In her own way, I mean,'

'Yes, I think she must have. That has given me a little satisfaction over the years.'

'Why didn't you tell Helena?'

'I couldn't betray Mummy, even in death. God knows what it must have cost her to write those words. I wondered if she'd ever confessed. It made me wonder if she'd died with a clear conscience, if she made a good death – that's how the Church sees it. That's not something that Helena could really understand. It bothered me once, but now – well, now I think we make our own judgements.' She paused. 'That's why I'm telling you now. My mother tried to be somebody she was not and she had to live with that lie her whole life. Once I gave up the struggle Georgie, once I accepted myself, life began to have real meaning for me.'

'I can see where this is going and I know you mean well, but I gave up on religion a long time ago – '

'Listen, there's a part of you that you've never come to terms with – isn't there?'

I stared at the table, uncomfortable, not wanting to acknowledge the truth of her words.

'This is about Ausangate,' I said quietly.

'I want to help, Georgie. We both want to help you. We thought we'd do something a bit special tonight. We've been thinking about it for a long time and we'd love you and Theo to share the occasion with us. It's easier if I just show you.'

She took a key from the dresser drawer and pulled on her wellingtons. I followed her out of the kitchen by the back door and across the yard to the nearest outbuilding. It took a couple of minutes for my eyes to adjust to the darkness inside. I trailed after Sophie through the maze of internal byres and storage areas until we came to a sturdy wooden door padlocked on the outside. She unlocked the door and pulled it open, ushering me inside.

Sophie closed the outer door behind her and pulled a light cord. Then she unlocked an inner door in front of us and pushed it open. I stepped over the threshold and found myself bathed in moist tropical heat. The light was almost blinding. She handed me a pair of sunglasses. I could hardly believe my eyes.

The room itself was only about twelve feet by eight and sealed floor to ceiling with light-reflective tiles. A central raised area partially obscured the water tank where the plant roots derived their nourishment. There must have been around twelve or so fully grown, and I could see that they were fine specimens, carefully cultivated. On the benches on either side were seedlings and infant plants, polystyrene cups and four large sunlamps.

'We started off with some seeds off the internet and tried them in the greenhouse, but they didn't survive. We had to do quite a bit of research and in the end the only answer was this.'

'Hydroponics.'

Sophie nodded.

'We found a guy in Amsterdam who was importing from the Amazon so we paid him a visit and brought back some seedlings on Eurostar. It was such a lot of fun, Georgie. Can you imagine? Me and Helena – the most unlikely international drug smugglers!'

My God. My two most beloved, respectable friends growing Ayahuasca in an outbuilding.

'When did you start?'

'About ten years ago.' She perched herself on a stool.

'When I found out the truth about my father and what mummy had done to him . . . It was such a breach of trust, I really couldn't cope. It felt like the universe was caving in on me. All my life my mother had been staunch in her beliefs. You remember what she was like the day after the funeral?'

I remembered. There had been a terrible scene. Helena and I had a taxi booked to go to King's Cross. Lady Audrey had thrown down the gauntlet to her daughter. *You either stay here with your family or leave now with that ungodly creature and never come back.* Sophie didn't hesitate. She got into the taxi with us and never looked back. She chose love in the face of cruelty. And then to find out all those years later that the hypocritical old bitch had broken faith with all of them.

As it turned out, her father left her a separate annuity, perhaps suspecting what might happen should he ever fail to return home. Or perhaps it was simply guilt for having fulfilled his own desires at the expense of his wife and children. He must have seen how it was with his middle daughter and her friend with the red hair and sad grey-green eyes.

'Helena was terribly worried about me, wanted me to go to the doctor. He prescribed a mild anti-depressant but once you're on them . . . ' she hesitated. 'It's so hard to wean yourself off again.' She seemed nervous, almost agitated.

'I understand, of course I do.' I wanted to reassure her. I wasn't so sure about Helena. She had never suffered fools gladly and I could imagine her having plenty to say on the subject of pill-popping. Poor Sophie. It couldn't have been easy for her.

'I kept thinking about that night in Chincheros, when we bonded with San Pedro.' She flashed a look at me and I felt uncomfortable. Our experiences that night had been so very different. I didn't like to think about it.

'I wanted to feel that way again, to experience the intense love, the feeling of being strong and confident again.' She slid her hand along the edge of the bench as if feeling her way with the conversation. 'Helena got busy on the internet and, well, here we are.'

My mind filled with the obvious questions: what about the electricity, the utility companies, the police? Instead I said, 'What do you do with the stuff?'

'We made a pact that we wouldn't get into selling. It's just for our own use. Once we got the hang of cultivation, no need to involve anyone else.'

I nodded as if this was the most normal past-time in the world. She seemed to derive some confidence from my response and got into her stride.

'We applied for an energy efficiency grant for the farm a few years ago, put in some under-floor heating, solar panels and an emergency diesel generator. We're looking into a wind turbine. Helena's awfully good at that side of things. Did you know her great-uncles used to grow marijuana in the old turnip shed? It was to help their sister. She had fits, seizures. Apparently the local GP recommended it. I suppose he was in love with her.'

I wondered at Sophie and Helena's ingenuity. All these years I had believed them to be living quiet rural lives in retreat from the world.

'Has Theo seen all this?'

'Yes. We weren't sure how reliable she would be under the influence of alcohol but it turns out she's a fellow traveller in her own way.'

'How do you mean?'

We broke off conversation as the door opened and Helena appeared.

'Thought I might find you in here.' She stretched her

arms above her head. 'What do you think?'

'It's amazing. I can't believe it.'

'Have you asked her yet?' Helena looked at Sophie.

'No, I was just getting to that.'

'Asked me what?'

Helena and Sophie looked at each other and then at me.

'We want to hold a ceremony. Tonight.'

I stared at them both.

'Whatever for?' But I already knew the answer. Helena's face cracked into a broad grin, her green eyes twinkling, as she put her arm around Sophie's waist.

'For you George, of course. For you.'

3

I needed to sit down. We returned to the kitchen and Helena made coffee. The three of us waited for Theo in the kitchen.

'Can I be frank with you?' Helena looked quite solemn. When had she ever been anything else?

'We have to talk about Peru.'

Sophie nodded. I didn't know what to say, so I said nothing. It was obvious that Helena meant 'I' not 'we'.

Helena leaned forward with her elbows resting on the table. 'You've always blamed yourself for Wamani's death.' She looked at Sophie who dropped her gaze. There was a strange hush in the room. 'But the truth is that the Apu of the mountain took him. It was a good death.'

I looked at them both squarely.

'He would have hurt all of us eventually,' she continued. 'He violated you. The Apu saved us, don't you see? It was *our wayward guide* who made the offering for safe passage, and *he* was the only one to fall.'

'There's more to it than that,' I said. I recalled the words of the curandero. 'Nina's sister said I had to forgive the man who hurt me. She said that his spirit wanders, and that I would grow weak if I didn't complete the ritual.'

They both looked at me sharply.

'You've never mentioned that before.'

No, I hadn't.

Nor had I ever told them that he was a regular visitor to my bedside, his large brown eyes sad and accusing. The Queros Indians believe that when they die they wander the mountain. It's like their Valhalla. But he

237

doesn't walk there. He doesn't stand with his ancestors. He can't enjoy the sacred paths of Ausangate because he must walk where I walk. I let him fall to his death and he is bound to me forever.

Sophie looked absolutely petrified.

'She said it after all of you left with Nina. It was as if she was waiting to tell me on my own. She seemed very definite about it. She said something else. It was about me and Theo.'

'What exactly?'

'I can't remember. I was angry and upset. You must admit it was a fairly bizarre encounter. She told me I had *powers within me* – very theatrical.'

Helena shuffled her feet impatiently and looked from me to Sophie and back again.

'We must ask San Pedro,' Sophie blurted out, squeezing my hand in encouragement.

I sighed again. 'Look I know you mean well, but – '

'Please Georgie. What have you got to lose?'

She had a point. I didn't want to admit it but my life had spiralled down into a well and I couldn't see any way out. Perhaps the only way forward now, was to go deeper within. Then a thought struck me. Theo. And then another. Boyd.

'Look, I'll do the ayahuasca ritual but not this weekend. We can't do anything while Theo and her toyboy are here.'

Helena cocked her head to one side. 'I think you underestimate Theo,' she said.

'That's as maybe but she hasn't exactly acquitted herself so far has she? This was supposed to be a girls' weekend and she turns up with someone almost half her age, gets completely legless and makes a right tit of herself. I bet he doesn't even fancy her,' I spat out before realising that the couple in question had returned. Theo was standing in the doorway bearing an ASDA carrier bag, red in the face. Boyd was smirking behind her.

'Well, hello to you too George,' she muttered savagely.

Sophie was the first to speak in an effort to rescue the situation.

'Mattie, would you be an absolute angel and go and fetch some wood? There's a wheelbarrow in the yard outside and the logs are in the woodshed – red painted door round to the left?'

Boyd shrugged his shoulders and winked at me before leisurely squeezing his way round the kitchen table and chairs to make his exit.

Helena poured Theo a mug of coffee and pushed milk and sugar in her direction. Sophie pulled on her coat and boots and took the dog lead from the hook next to the dresser. Ralph wiggled his backside in anticipation of rabbits. Theo pursed her lips and sat down without looking at me. I shrivelled inwardly. Helena paused for a moment.

'Sophie and I are going to take Matthew and Ralph for a long walk.' Boyd gave a little snigger. Helena glared at him and he raised his hands in mock surrender. She fixed her gaze on me and Theo. 'We're leaving the two of you in peace for a bit,' she continued. 'I think it's time you had a proper talk,' she said firmly. 'When we get back I hope you will have made a decision about the rest of the weekend.' It wasn't a threat but it soundly awfully like one.

***

Theo fetched a saucer and lit a cigarette. I sipped my coffee in silence. Helena hated people smoking in the house. Theo knew it and looked at me with one eyebrow arched as if daring me to comment. I didn't

239

want to be the one to start a conversation that had been nearly thirty years in the making. I hadn't realised until that very moment just how far our relationship had deteriorated. She noticed that one of her nails was chipped and scowled, then ferreted around in her handbag for a file. She seemed on the verge of tears and I couldn't blame her for feeling peeved but I had other reasons to be angry with her for my current situation. Starting with Daniel and the plot to hook me up with an interviewer. I knew I'd hurt her feelings so rather than apologise I opened with a front-loaded attack.

'What's all this about Matthew Boyd and an interview?' I watched her expertly tackle the offending nail, her cigarette hanging from her mouth like a charlady and felt a fresh wave of revulsion wash through me.

She paused to breathe in a lungful of smoke, looking at me as if I were congenitally stupid.

'The *Sunday Telegraph* and *Elle* magazine want to do features on you. Surely Daniel told you?'

Yes, no, sort of. I decided to gloss over that one.

'Anything else you haven't told me?'

'There's the chance of a spot on *Culture Now*. It's very late night but about as high-brow as telly can get.' She started work on the other nails, clearly reluctant to focus her full attention on the conversation at hand.

I knew she was only trying to help me but I was still smarting from the humiliation of it all. I tried a different tack.

'Why *him*?'

'Why *not* him?' She stubbed out her cigarette. 'God George, you're such a snob. Don't you read anything in the media? He's just the sort of academic-bit-of-rough that gets noticed. If you want to salvage your career as a poet at the age of forty nine then you're going to need some help. Frankly I agree with Daniel. *What Georgina needs is the editorial equivalent of a jolly good seeing-to* is how he put it. Matthew Boyd is just the kind of rough-diamond intellectual male totty that women's magazines and features editors are falling over themselves to sign up.' She emptied her mug into the sink, reached into the carrier bag and pulled out a bottle of merlot. She unscrewed the top, grabbed a glass from the dresser and poured herself a large one.

I was gob-smacked. How dare Daniel speak to her about me like that?

'The way you carry on,' she continued, 'you're still living in the Dark Ages. Cambridge aesthetics, snide little comments. I heard you last night. What the fuck difference does it matter where Matthew went to university, for God's sake? What makes you so superior? Got to have a little bit of sandstone in the blood, do we? Christ!' She sat down and rummaged around again in her bag for her lighter.

I had never known Theo so cross. She lit another cigarette, and leaned forward with her elbows on the table.

'You know, the day I left that sanctimonious, smug little village of effete, small-minded, boorish elitist thugs was the happiest day of my life.' She exhaled and took a big gulp of wine.

I sat back in amazement.

'You loved it!' I insisted. 'You swanned about like Lady Muck. You just sailed on, not caring what anybody thought. You had a pretty good time from where I was sitting.'

'I couldn't wait to get out,' she snapped, her head erect. 'To get to London, somewhere where I could breathe, be myself. I couldn't wait to get away, George. I couldn't wait to get away from Cambridge and I couldn't wait to get away from you.'

'*Me*? What have I ever done?'

She cocked her head, her eyes half-closed as if in dreamy reflection through the haze of smoke.

'At the beginning I thought you were so sweet.' She pulled on her cigarette, her wet red lips staining the paper. 'The way you tried to improve your accent by copying Helena. And Sophie. You were always trailing after Sophie because she was the real deal, wasn't she George? A real bone fide piece of the English aristocracy. Sucking up to her mother at every opportunity. Do you know, I think you might even have converted to Catholicism if you'd had more guts. But then if you'd had more guts you would have dropped your knickers and slummed it like the rest of us.' She flicked ash onto the saucer. One of Sophie's Denbyware set. 'Who exactly were you saving it for anyway?'

'That's a horrible thing to say. Just because I didn't sleep with anything with a pulse.'

'There you go again!' Her face twisted into an ugly smile. 'I have a healthy interest in sex and you have to denigrate it. All I ever did was follow my instincts. It's supposed to be about pleasure. But you never understood that, in your little virgin enclave, constantly fretting about God and sin with your petty bourgeois morality.'

'Oh really? You were such a prima donna. I just did the clearing up and the sorting out. How the hell did I ever hold you back?'

'With your school-monitor mentality, that's how!' she shouted. 'I put up with all the hostility from the blue-stocking brigade. I worked my arse off for my degree. But as for you, you were the worst of all. Rolling your eyes, constantly picking up the pieces, looking after me, treating me like some wayward child – God, you made me sick!' She pushed back her chair and paced up and down, one arm crossed at her waistline, her shoulders hunched, and trembling.

I felt paralysed. I wanted her to stop but I knew there was more. And some deep-seated part of me needed to hear all of it.

'You judged me.' She jabbed her cigarette hand towards me for emphasis. 'You took pity on me. You! The grammar-school virgin with your great doe eyes and bleating Church of England rhetoric. What the hell did you know about life? When had you ever suffered? What made you think you were in any position to look down on me? All you wanted was to feel superior because underneath all that classical scholarship, the Latin quips and the Greek references, was a silly frightened little girl, out of her depth and desperate to curry favour with the middle class contingent. You had to have a whipping boy to feel good about yourself, to enable you to have some sort of identity. So you became my keeper like some Victorian governess. Poor Georgina, so long-suffering, so patient, so self-less. You didn't have the slightest idea about real life.' She paused to take another deep draft of nicotine. I was rooted to the spot, my insides almost liquid with fear and loathing.

'So when you fed me to Wamani, you were just trying to show me a bit of real life, is that it?'

She stopped dead and shook her head, her tone suddenly much more serious, sad even.

'That was a *mistake*. I told you that at the time. I was stupid. I *didn't know*, okay? They don't all wear signs round their necks.' She tipped ash into the sink. There was an awkward silence, both of us lost in the past. 'Anyway,' she collected herself. 'It's not as if he got away with anything, did he?' she smirked. 'We all saw to that.'

I looked at her sharply.

'It was an accident!' I hissed, my fists clenching and unclenching.

'Yeah, yeah. You keep telling yourself that, Georgie.' She had a strange superior look on her face that I couldn't quite place.

'You weren't there! You don't know how it felt, how terrified I was!'

She gritted her teeth and gave me a long hard look.

I felt buoyed up with indignation. How could she be so crass?

'I was a *virgin*. Do you even remember what that felt like? It was my *first time* and he ruined it for me. He *ruined me*, Theo.' I was shaking.

'You really believe that, don't you? I must admit I have had my doubts all these years but Helena always insisted . . . ' She shrugged her shoulders.

I regarded her with utter contempt.

'Helena *what? What!*'

She shook her head again. 'I never know with you,' she said quietly.

We looked at each other for a long time. I was missing something and it frightened and confused me in equal measure. She looked away. When Theo spoke again it was as if she had resigned herself to a situation not of her making. Her tone was more matter of fact. 'Afterwards. When we returned to the hacienda you didn't speak for two days. It was like you were in a trance. And then when we came back to England,' she frowned as if the memory was painful, 'none of us could reach you.'

'I don't remember that time very well.'

She took a step forward and her expression was suddenly very earnest.

'Try.'

I stared at her. The seconds ticked by. Try. I

understood the word but I couldn't grasp her meaning.

'I don't know what you want from me,' I said.

Her mouth twisted into a grimace. I had made her angry again and I didn't know why.

'Do you have one single authentic bone in your whole body? Can you feel anything? Can you imagine what it's been like all these years, watching and waiting for the smallest sign that you might be ready at last to rejoin the party?'

So that's what this was all about. I was supposed to feel gratitude for their silence.

'All those feelings and passions,' she picked a speck of tobacco from her sharp white teeth. 'They're just words on a page to you, aren't they? You never truly dived in, did you? Never took a risk and said bugger the consequences. Never just jumped into the great sea of life and started swimming.' She blew out a plume of smoke. 'It's obvious to anyone who's ever read your verse. *On Virgin Slopes*. What a frigid joke!' She sniggered, taking another drag. 'Behold the intellectual clitoris at work. I bet you've never even had an orgasm.'

She had breached the unspoken golden rule of friendship. She had told me the truth about myself and she wasn't going to stop any time soon.

'All you've ever done Georgina, is play the critic.' She waved her cigarette in mock imitation. 'Observing, making notes on others' performances, having the final word, making the final judgement. And what roles have you assigned the three of us, your best friends? I suppose Helena is the backbone, the foundation. The Great Mother. Let's face it. We're all just a little bit scared of Helena, aren't we?' She smiled again. 'And Sophie,' she paused and considered the question. 'I suppose she's the baby, the darling girl if you like. We all *adore* Sophie don't we? Then there's me. What am I

Georgie? What am I in the pathetic pantomime of your life?' She clicked her fingers as if the thought had only just occurred to her. 'I know. I'm The Bad Girl. The Jezebel. Bette Davis in *The Letter*.'

'Norma Desmond actually,' I spat out. 'Bette had class even when she was being a total bitch.'

I swallowed hard and tried to out stare her but she just started laughing.

'You have always been jealous, George. Jealous of me. Jealous of Sophie for her blue blood. She's a member of the club you wish you'd been born into. Even jealous of Helena because at the end of the day she's Sophie's choice, isn't she? They don't need you. I don't need you. That's why you haven't written anything in over twenty years. You are not in a position to judge anymore. And without that you have nothing to say. You're petrified. Eaten up with fear. You don't know how to live. You're a coward George, a pathetic, long-suffering, fool. And to think you waited all those years for Daniel to leave his wife and then when he couldn't live up to your high-brow expectations, you threw him away.' She crushed her cigarette in the sink and turned sharply, her arms folded tightly across her body.

'Do you know what I think?' She leaned towards me, her eyes narrow. 'I think you have surpassed yourself this time. I think you are the stupidest cunt I ever – '

I wasn't intending to wound her. It was more of a slap really but it caught her off guard and she pitched sideways onto the floor. Next thing I knew I was kneeling, straddling her waist, my hands tight around her neck banging her head repeatedly against the side of the dresser. She went limp. I didn't move. I thought I'd killed her and the idea was strangely pleasing. I let go of her neck and her head slumped against the wall. I stood up. She looked like a broken doll. I went to the sink and stared out of the window into the yard. I washed my hands. I felt nothing. A few more seconds passed, my mind a complete blank. I heard a small groan. I went over and knelt down and shook her by the shoulder. Her eyes flickered open and focused on me with a wild mixture of awe and confusion.

'Jesus. That really hurt.'

'Then we're even, aren't we?' I said flatly.

'I suppose.'

I helped her back onto her feet and sat her down at the kitchen table. She rubbed the back of her head and gingerly felt around her throat. I poured wine for both of us. Her hand was shaking as she took the glass from me. I leaned back against the sink and took a long gulp.

She looked at me with a wary eye over the rim of her glass.

'I didn't mean what I said about your poetry.'

'Yeah you did.'

The seconds stretched into minutes.

'You've had every opportunity Theo,' I said.

She looked at me, bleary-eyed.

'Marriage, kids, career. Everything.' I let the truth drain out of me. There seemed no point in holding back now. 'I've envied you all these years. It's always been about you. You risk everything you have for the sake of a quick shag but you're like *inviolate* or something. Nothing ever sticks. You still go home and there's Douglas waiting for you,' I felt my voice breaking, 'and those two lovely boys.' My voice was just a whisper. 'That's the life I always wanted – that's the life I should have had. It means nothing to you, does it? You squander everything and your life just bounces back. *You* just *bounce back* every single time.'

The tears broke from me and I was so unprepared that I found myself gasping for air. I leaned over the sink, my arms rigid, and for a moment I thought I was going to pass out. I felt her suddenly beside me, one hand upon my back and I arched away angrily. 'Don't,' I hissed.

The crisis passed. I felt a cold raw ache inside me. *Children at home and a hearth so fine.* It was the line from an early poem inspired by a childhood holiday in Orkney. *Love has you caught in a double-bind. Grieve for the life that you left behind. Children at home and a hearth so fine, Selkie Wife you must make for home.* Was that what I had done? Chosen the freedom of the deep blue sea, and in so doing sacrificed any chance I had of becoming a wife and mother? I sat down at the table. Theo put out a hand to cover mine but I pulled it away. We drank in silence.

Theo hadn't lost out. She'd somehow managed to have it all. She was a Selkie who had learned to walk on dry land. I could still feel the texture of her skin on my hands, the smooth heat of her body. She was a plump, smooth, smug Selkie wife and I had been seized by an urgent desire to crush the very life out of her. I tried to figure it out. These were sensations hitherto unknown to me: exhilaration and blind cold seething hatred. The minutes ticked by. Everything she said had the ring of truth about it. Everything I had ever wanted from life gnawed at me with sharp little teeth. What a fool I had been. Self-pity swept over me.

'Why did you even bother being friends with me at all, if I was such an obnoxious individual?'

She nursed her jaw. 'You weren't *always* such a prude. Sometimes I really quite liked you. It's habit mostly though, isn't it?' She looked at me squarely. 'When you come to think of it, would we be friends now if we'd only met last week? Do we have anything in common other than the past?' She shook her head sadly. 'We're different from our parents' generation because we look outside the family for kinship. We build networks and contacts and spend our working lives spinning webs of association to make ourselves feel like we belong somewhere. It's such a joke really. I know where I belong. I grew up in a council flat with my mother and three brothers. I never told you that, did I?'

'No.' I thought of her marriage to Douglas. 'You said they were overseas. They weren't at your wedding.'

'I didn't invite them.'

I was deeply shocked. Even in my most selfish moments I couldn't have envisaged marrying someone without my family being present. Even if only to prove my mother wrong.

'What about Douglas and the twins? Do they know about your mother?'

'I didn't want my family to have anything to do with my kids.'

'But your father,' I blinked. 'You said they had a cabin in the Rocky mountains. You said that's where you learned to climb.'

She stuck her chin out. 'And you never thought much of my acting skills.'

Was it all a lie then? Had I really known anything about her? 'Theo! For God's sake.' I looked at her, waiting for the rest to unfold. She rested her glass on the table and began.

'My father left when I was a baby. After that my mother had gentlemen callers from time to time when the rent was due. I couldn't wait to get out.'

I leaned forward and rubbed her arm. She shrugged and took another sip of wine.

'You asked me if I remembered what it was like.' She pursed her lips together. 'The truth is, nobody ever forgets. They just lock it away somewhere and pretend it happened to somebody else.' She looked up at me and I saw the little girl she must have once been. Her voice was flat, matter of fact.

'When I was nine, one of my mother's boyfriends,' she bit one of her nails, 'said he'd buy me a Sindy doll.'

The seconds ticked by. 'Did you tell?'

'Never.'

I looked at her and put my hand over hers. She squeezed my fingers. There was nothing I could say.

She gathered herself and topped up our wine glasses.

'I used to lie awake at night imagining all kinds of monsters in the dark. Then I thought about running away. I saved bits of pocket money. I packed Teddy, my nightie and a toothbrush and went to the local depot looking for the bus that had 'Daddy's house' on the front. A very kind bus conductor phoned my mum and brought me home at the end of his shift. He let me give out the tickets. It was an adventure of sorts.'

I slumped back in my seat.

'How did you get out?'

'I used to do this thing – I know it sounds silly but I pretended that everything bad that had happened to me was 'old Theo' and any time I wanted I could be 'new Theo'. 'New Theo' was powerful, in control. I just switched off, detached myself. I was quite the little tart by the time I reached secondary school, but there was one teacher who thought I showed a lot of promise. She cast me as Shakespeare's Juliet in the school's end of term play. That changed everything for me. I never felt so powerful as I did on that stage; everyone looking at me, hanging on my every word. I felt like a goddess. I was 'new Theo' every day. And the language! Such noble sentiments, such passion. Then there was Keats, and Coleridge. John Donne, Webster, the whole canon waiting to be explored. She coached me after school, told me about Cambridge, what it would be like. I thought it would be Heaven on Earth.'

'I wished you'd told me. I felt out of my depth so many times. I had no idea you hated it so.'

'Oh, it wasn't all bad. There was one person in particular who was very kind to me.'

'Sophie's father,' I said.

'Yes! How on earth did you guess? He was about the only man who never made a pass at me.' Theo's words drifted over me as I recalled that afternoon so long ago; Sir Peter driving through the countryside whilst I snivelled into a hanky. 'Of course by then,' Theo continued, 'I'd discovered that what I lacked in social pedigree was more than made up for by the male totty on offer.' She grimaced. 'Talking of which, I still think you should do the interview with Matthew. I think he really quite likes you.'

'I slept with him.'

Theo's eyes widened.

'Well, you are full of surprises.' She raised her glass in a mock toast and took another swig. 'The little bastard. No wonder he was so coy with me this afternoon. Was he any good?'

'Yeah,' I grinned sheepishly. 'Really good.' I hesitated but it seemed churlish to hold back. 'In fact, that was my first time. The big O.'

'Ah.' She had the good grace not to laugh or say *I told you so.*

'Well, I'll drink to that.' She clinked glasses with me.

'That looks sore,' I indicated her neck which was reddening nicely. 'Do you think they've got any ice?' I went over to the fridge. There were some old looking cubes in the freezer compartment with bits of broccoli and a couple of peas sticking to them. I made up a makeshift icepack with a tea towel and handed it over to

Theo who grimaced slightly.

'Were you planning to have sex with him yourself?' I asked.

'Eventually.' She sounded defeated. 'Spending the weekend with two lesbians and a frigid poet, I didn't think there would be much in the way of competition.'

'Sorry. It was a spur of the moment thing.'

We drank some more and the edges started to blur a little.

'All those times I thought I was saving you from yourself,' I mumbled.

'I was hoping you would join in. We would have had much more fun together if you'd been less uptight.'

I thought about all the missed opportunities that would never come again.

'But there were so many times when if I hadn't been there, you would have been sent down.'

'I think subconsciously that was rather the point.'

'I thought one of us had to be sober and responsible.'

'Ah,' Theo nodded sagely. 'That's the formula for marriage, not friendship.'

I thought about Douglas and the Volvo. My own mother and father. Helena and Sophie. Could Daniel and I ever have survived together as a married couple? Would I have been the sensible one? What happens if neither wants to assume that role?

'I'm sorry,' I said. 'For trying to throttle you, and everything.'

She smiled at me.

'Not too much humble pie please. It's not me you need to apologise to, anyway.'

I looked blank.

'I gather our hosts have plans for tonight. It's time you were brought up to speed.'

'I didn't much care for it the first time. And you

didn't even drink it as I remember.'

'True. I've had my own psychedelic experiences since, though.'

'Where?'

'Here of course. I don't much care for the San Pedro bilge-water though.'

'What did you see?'

She put down her glass and stared at the table for a few seconds as if weighing something up.

'Let's just say that our mountain guide was genuine on one point. He really believed. I think you should take the ayahuasca tonight, George. I think you will understand. The Fates have gathered us here this weekend for a purpose, and it's time for you to face up to the truth of who you really are.'

I looked into her face. I would not have pegged Theo as the romantic type yet she too seemed taken with San Pedro in a way that surprised me.

'You think taking the drug will unblock my creativity so I can write more rubbish poetry?'

She laughed in spite of herself. Then she looked at me with an earnest expression.

'I think it will do you good. We all of us have to face the truth about ourselves at some point, don't we?'

I pulled back slightly. 'Are you trying to frighten me?'

'No, no. God no.' She sighed, taking my hands in hers. 'It's time to wake up George, that's all. Just time to wake up.'

4

'I thought you had to brew this stuff all day,' I said looking over Helena's shoulder.

'That's the beauty of modern technology,' said Sophie.

I gazed in wonder at the jug of ayahuasca orbiting on medium heat inside the microwave. Theo had escorted Boyd out into the back yard again for a cigarette whilst we made final preparations in the kitchen.

'Whatever happened to fasting and abstinence?'

Helena shrugged her shoulders. 'To be honest, so long as you haven't had a heavy meal, the purging effect is largely the same. I wouldn't say that you get a bigger hit on an empty stomach. There's a lot of pseudo-mysticism about the whole process. Frankly, all that is quite unnecessary. The most important thing is to know when you've had enough, and to be clear about the questions you want to ask.'

'How do you mean?'

'Well, what is it you want to know?'

Sophie stuck her head in a cupboard and re-emerged with five large plastic bowls, a pile of old tea towels and some plastic beakers.

'That's obvious H,' she smiled. 'Georgie wants to remember who she is so that she can start writing again.'

Helena winked at me. 'I think George might have something else in mind.'

'Whatever do you mean?' I said, then following her gaze out through the window, I saw Boyd watching in awe as Theo blew smoke rings at him.

'*Him.* Oh, you're just crazy.' I mumbled. 'Theo thinks he would be good to interview me for one of those women's magazines with pretensions to cultural capital,' I said airily. 'Beyond that I have no interest in him. None whatsoever.'

'So that's what all the squeaking bedroom noises were this morning then, was it? You and Matthew figuring out his angle for an interview?' She pulled a wry face.

I stared open-mouthed. Sophie giggled and put her arms around me.

'Ahhh, poor Georgie. Don't tease her so!'

Helena took the jug out of the microwave to give the libation a stir.

'Nothing wrong with a bit of rough. From what I hear there's nothing so good for getting over a man as getting under the next one.'

'Unbelievable,' I muttered under my breath. Sophie laughed. I shook my head in disbelief. 'I'd have thought you would have disapproved entirely.'

'Why ever would you think that?' they chorused.

I felt stupidly contrite.

'Well it's not the kind of thing proper feminists get up to, is it?'

Helena looked at me with amusement. 'For goodness sake, George. We love you in spite of your political aspirations not because of them. You're so stuck in the seventies. I don't love Sophie because I hate men you nitwit. Not even a Johnny-come-lately like Matthew Boyd. I don't care for his politics. Frankly I think he's a complete wanker, but if you find him amusing, I daresay we can overlook his more obvious short-comings.'

'He's not bad looking,' Sophie added by way of encouragement.

'I distinctly remember you saying that he gave you the creeps,' I blurted at Sophie.

'Well,' she smiled benignly. 'That was before you had sex with him.'

The door opened and the man in question came into the kitchen stomping his feet.

'It's brass monkeys out there,' he said. 'Mind if we come in now?'

'Sure,' Sophie smiled like an angel and waved him in the direction of a chair.

'I think we're ready,' said Helena.

Whereas during our first ritual together it had been necessary to puke or defecate outside the circle of truth, in the bushes adjacent to the pueblo, Helena and Sophie had refined this practice somewhat. We made use of the outside lavvy in the courtyard and puked into plastic buckets.

'To *Zaramama* my beloved!' Sophie took a swig from her beaker.

'To *Zaramama*!' We toasted Helena. Helena stood up, our Goddess of Grain and Corn – the giver of the feast.

'To *Chasca* !' she gave a flourish with her beaker.

'To *Chasca* !' We toasted Sophie, our Goddess of Dawn and Dusk.

I stood up and swung the jug of ayahuasca like a baton. 'To *Cocomama*!' We nodded to Theo, our Goddess of Love, Health and Wellbeing.

I thought Theo might once again abstain from the proceedings, but whether out of solidarity or a desire to redress the balance between us, she gamely drank the vile liquid and puked merrily along with the rest of us. Matthew Boyd had wanted to observe but we insisted that he partake. Helena nodded in his direction.

'To Matthew, welcome to our Huaca de la Luna.'

He looked completely blank.

'Temple of the Moon,' hissed Theo in a loud stage whisper.

'We goddesses welcome you to our ritual,' they chorused.

We raised our beakers to Matthew.

'Bottoms Up!' he sneered before gulping it down. Clearly his body had other ideas and it was only a matter of seconds before he heaved it back up again, spraying San Pedro juice all over Theo.

***

After half an hour or so Sophie and Helena took themselves off to the sitting room and lay down on cushions, holding hands like a couple of love-struck starfish. Matthew declined any further part in the ceremonies and, complaining of stomach cramps, retired to bed with an aspirin and a bottle of whisky. Theo passed out on the kitchen table and I, possessed of a sudden and intense need to commune with the elements, slipped on her coat and swept out into the night.

It was a full moon. The ground was hard and crunchy underfoot as I trudged beyond the grey stone dyke at the rear of the farmhouse, into the hinterland of peaty fields and stubble. The air was still. Perfect conditions for a hard frost. Sound travels differently by night as if the air itself were thinner, less densely packed with the routine noises of daily commerce. There was a purpose burning within me like a beacon at sea, urging me onward though I could see no destination. Some internal compass was navigating me and I ploughed on, indifferent to the cold, my eyes straining toward the horizon, seeing but not seeing, like a dog that catches a wild scent, pulling at the leash. I fell to my knees and stretched out my arms like a blind beggar and closed my eyes to see the truth within.

The whiteness was dazzling. I opened my eyes again to see the dark, then closed them again and looked around me at the crisp frozen wasteland.

It had taken us most of the day to rappel safely down

the mountain after Wamani fell. It was important that we made camp before nightfall. We knew it was only a matter of time before we came across his body. My hands and feet were cold. Sophie's headache had improved as we made our descent but we were a tired, aching, miserable little party as we set up our final camp. We had food but no appetite. The weather had turned. Light snow continued to fall, obscuring our tracks, causing us to slow down. We boiled snow to make tea and huddled together in the largest tent, each of us reluctant to be alone. It seemed our greatest strength now lay in staying together, planning and executing our route back to warmth and safety as one.

I slept fitfully, the wind outside rustling the tent, making small moaning sounds. My last image of Wamani falling seemed to be burned into my retina, so when I closed my eyes all I could see was the red jacket tumbling into the white space beneath. Theo lay next to me, her breathing ragged and shallow. We must have slept for an hour or so.

The first cry was barely distinguishable from the wind. I knelt low and spread my hands out across the ice sheet, the coldness seeping through my finger tips as I crawled forward. Complete white-out all around me as I edged nearer and nearer, my heart hammering in my chest as I stretched out my hand to touch the dark motionless figure lying below.

'Georgina.'

My eyes snapped open to see Helena leaning over me, her face deathly white in the glow of her torch.

'There's something outside.'

I stared at her face, trying to make sense of her words. There could be nothing outside except ice and snow and rock. Nothing and no-one.

'What do you mean?'

'Please get up. There's something outside in the dark.' She pressed her cheek close to my ear. 'I can hear it,' she whispered.

I scrambled out of my sleeping bag and searched for my own torch. Sophie and Theo were sitting up, huddled together, frightened. We sat, straining to hear any sounds above the wind. And then I heard it. High-pitched, terrifying, distant. Like an animal caught in a snare.

'It's nothing.' I swallowed hard, not wanting to own the truth. 'It's the wind. Our minds are playing tricks on us.'

'No, listen!' Helena put her hand up to quieten me.

'It's nothing I tell you, nothing!' I grabbed her hand tightly. 'Nothing could be out there. Do you understand? No living thing could be out there.'

'But I can hear it.' Sophie was gripped with fear. 'I can hear *him*!'

I swivelled round to Theo. 'It's not him,' I insisted. 'We aren't low enough yet. His body will be further down the mountain.'

Theo had her arm round Sophie. She too looked terrified. 'What if it *is* him?' she whispered. 'What if he's coming for us? Coming to find us here?'

'Don't be stupid!' I yelled. 'He can't find us. He couldn't have survived that fall. It's not possible. You're just imagining things. It's this place. This cruel, frozen mountain.'

'We should never have come,' Sophie wailed.

'It's the altitude,' I said directly to Helena. 'We're all stressed out and tired. It's just a hallucination. You know that! Helena, look at me! It's not real! It's not him!'

She was shaking. She shrugged off my hand and made for the door of the tent.

'Helena!' I shrieked at her, my own fear getting the better of me. 'Helena, come back!' I flung myself at her and tried to pull her back into the tent. Theo made a grab for her leg but she kicked back and half staggered, half fell out of the tent, leaving the opening flapping in the wind. I launched myself after her and landed on the snow outside. I raised my head to see a figure loping off into the middle distance.

'Helena,' I breathed, and set off, snow whirling in my face, catching in my throat. I thought my lungs would burst with the effort of keeping up with her. I was so cold. The ground kept rising and falling around me, causing me to slip and fall. All the time I was trying to keep up with her I knew we were getting farther and farther away from the tent and safety. It was madness to be out like this. I shouted after her but she wouldn't stop. Then suddenly I saw a grey shape kneeling on the ground in front of me. Helena was within reach. I grabbed her arm and pulled her back towards me. And then I heard it. A high-pitched keening sound. I looked at her and we both pitched forward onto the snow.

His body was lying a few feet below us on a wide ledge. His arm was broken underneath him and his leg jutted at a strange angle from the hip where it had shattered. His breathing was fierce and rattling and a strange whistling emanated from his chest via his broken nose. He couldn't be alive. He had to be dead. Yet there he lay before us, making that awful sound, still breathing, still living. Beyond recovery but not yet gone.

'We have to get the others,' I shouted. She shook her head.

'There's nothing we can do for him,' she yelled back. 'He can't make it through the night without shelter.'

'We have to go back.' I pulled her and she resisted at first but it was madness to stay any longer. 'It will be dawn in an hour. Come on,' I cried.

We struggled back to the tent and collapsed inside. I

didn't want the others to know the truth but they saw it in our faces without either of us speaking a word.

'It's him, isn't it?' Sophie screamed. 'He's alive isn't he? Oh my God, we have to do something, we have to help him.'

'We can't.' I shook my head. 'There's nothing we can do for him.'

'We can't just leave him out there!' Sophie was becoming hysterical. 'We can't do that to another human being! Helena, we can't leave him out there alone!'

Theo was crying. It was the worst possible situation imaginable at that time. Sophie was right. It was inhumane, but leave him we must.

I looked around the tent. We had Wamani's sleeping bag and the extra tent, but moving him was out of the question. Even if we made it down the mountain, we couldn't have raised the alarm any more quickly. He wouldn't live beyond morning. But for now, we had the night still ahead of us. We lay back in the tent, trying to block out the sounds of the wind and the half-dead man lying a hundred feet away.

I felt like I was sucked into a living nightmare. I would always be haunted by the whistling calls of a dying man. I couldn't bear it. I gripped Helena by the shoulder. Her expression was one of dread and resignation.

'I have to go,' I said. 'You don't have to come with me. But there's something I must do.' I felt around in Wamani's sleeping bag and gear for the package I knew would still be there.

'I'll come with you,' she said quietly.

I glanced at Sophie.

'It's okay,' I said. 'We won't be long.'

Sophie was shaking but whether it was with cold or fright I couldn't tell. Helena and I left the tent once more and made our way back to the ledge.

It was still dark as I settled myself to kneel in the wet snow, Wamani's head in my lap. Rocking gently back and forth making little soothing sounds, I cradled his head firmly and reached for the quilted sleeping bag. I saw his twisted shattered limbs, the juncture where the left femur formed an unnatural angle with his hip joint, and felt the sweat breaking out on my forehead. Helena stood above me, her head bowed down, her hands clasped together. Suddenly Wamani opened his eyes and his good hand gripped my wrist.

'There, there,' I stroked his forehead, even as he had stroked mine on the night of the San Pedro ritual. He pushed against me, his chest straining as Helena knelt down and pinned his arm to the ground.

'Shush.' I pulled coca leaves from the small package and stuffed them into his mouth. 'For the pain.'

I felt a movement beside me and Theo appeared. She drew a sharp intake of breath and then settled herself at Wamani's feet. I saw Sophie over her shoulder, white and trembling. Sophie reached out her hand to me. I was puzzled. Then I understood. I gave her coca leaves. We each took the leaves and started to chew.

He stared up at me. 'You can't let me die here! The apu will not be pleased with you. I will wander the mountain. I will have no peace!' He was drifting in and out of consciousness. I kneeled close to his face and whispered in his ear. 'Do you know who I am?' He blinked and nodded, his face creased in pain. 'You nursed me on the night of the ritual.' I pulled the sleeping bag towards me and kneaded the padding between my fingers. 'I will guide you now, as you guided me.'

Helena and Theo wept and prayed in a strange tongue that seemed both alien and familiar to me, like a language once learned and then forgotten. Sophie began to rock on her feet, a strange moaning sound coming from deep inside her. The keening sounds of our voices rose up, stronger and stronger as we pledged the life of the broken body before us to the great mountain spirits, an honourable offering, a human sacrifice, that we, the Daykeepers, the embodiment of the Divine Feminine, the sisters of San Pedro, might be avenged.

The grey dawn was breaking. My hands seemed to move now of their own accord. A greater urgency flooded through me as the day was almost upon us. He struggled, his body twisting against me as we pressed him down into the snow, our hands joined in the single task of taking his life. My own voice took strength from the voices of my sisters and I felt the power of the great serpent uncoiling within me. An irresistible rhythm pulsed within my breast and my hips. I arched my back, each vertebra articulating in unison as my feathered wings unfolded, no longer a fledgling, and beat against the frozen air. I watched my sisters illuminated from within, their bodies vibrating, possessed by the divine spark, infused with the anima of the gods: Cocamama, Zaramama, Chasca. We were transforming, stretching, pulsing as one entity; communing with the energy of the stars and the moon, the vast sky above us and the frozen earth beneath. My silver scales flashed in the moonlight. My head reared back and forth, tasting the air with my forked tongue, all my senses attuned to the wonders of Creation, no longer separate, but fused with the Divine. Such revelations I enjoyed in those brief moments as if the book of the world had been opened up to me and I felt tens of thousands of years of wisdom singing through me. You cannot imagine the passion, the joy, the terror of it all!

Wamani screamed, his face frozen in horror, for

now, at the moment of his death, he saw us as we truly were. Helena burnt orange and red like a flaming torch in a dry cornfield; Sophie, garlanded with flowers, burned white-hot and violet, her silken shift rent apart to show her pale nakedness beneath; Theo sprouted tubers from blood-soaked wounds where her limbs should be, every orifice erupting with snaking tendrils of coca leaves. I pulled the sleeping bag over his head and weaved the drawstring tightly around his throat, my own hiss of rage rising to join with the crackling, moaning, shrieking sounds that pervaded the air around me.

'Can you feel it?' I hissed in his ear. 'Uku Pacha, the Underworld, opens up to swallow you whole.' I drew back, triumphant. 'I will show you the way to Hell!' I cried aloud in vengeance, every ounce of my strength driven to take the life of the man who had wronged me. 'Did you really believe I would not take my revenge? Did you really believe I would surrender my power – to *you*?'

***

I opened my eyes.

The full moon shone down, casting silver light upon my skin and I remembered. I remembered everything. Wamani's death, our ritual song, our purpose and our prayers: take this man, we give him to the Apu of the mountain. This man cannot live for he has offended us. We make this sacrifice, we the Daykeepers, for we are four: Chasca – protector of maidens, Zaramama – goddess of fertility, Cocamama – goddess of sexual freedom, and one other: Mama-Amaru – Defender of Women.

5

I sat up in the middle of the ploughed field and shivered. I understood the meaning of the nightmares. No more repression. San Pedro had shown me the truth all along but I had not grasped it. All these years I had blocked the memory, unwilling to accept it. I had thought Wamani himself was the serpent god. 'San Pedro will show you the truth about yourself.' How could I have been so mistaken? But now the truth of what I had done, what we had done together was no longer a mystery to me. It was the essential link that re-united us as friends and sutured my life together again. No more nightmares. No more blankness. No more forgetfulness. I was emerging from a grey cocoon into the light of the present. Re-born once more.

I stood up and surveyed the landscape. I saw yellow lights ablaze at a distance and headed back to the farmhouse, the cold biting through me to the bone. It took me a good half an hour to reach the stone dyke. I paused despite the chilliness of my surroundings. The farmhouse seemed so quiet, like a woodland cottage in a children's fairytale. Within I would find my sisters-in-crime. I stepped lightly through the courtyard and waited. Through the window I watched my three friends gathered in the kitchen. Sophie was pouring a pan of hot milk into mugs. Helena was pacing up and down and Theo, well Theo looked positively abject. The biscuit tin was lying open. Kit-kats and digestive biscuits were normal late evening fare. I felt a strange coldness run through me as if I were being watched. I turned sharply but there was no-one there, just the black earth frosted with silver moonlight, my own shadow falling behind me as the soft yellow light spilled from the kitchen windows.

Sophie started as I came in through the back door. Helena stopped dead in her tracks.

'We thought you must be upstairs with lover-boy.' Theo faltered. 'I listened at the door about half an hour ago. He's snoring for England.'

I shrugged off Theo's coat and sat down. Sophie hesitated then rushed over and folded her arms around me. 'You must be frozen!' She rubbed my arms. I let her kiss me on the cheek. I couldn't see Sophie's face but Helena's wary expression and Theo's restlessness were confirmation enough.

'You've known all along.' I flashed accusing looks in all directions. Sophie hovered, tears welling up.

'We made a vow,' Helena responded. 'We wouldn't speak of it. Not until you remembered the whole truth.'

'To save my blushes or to spare your own?' I spat at her.

'Georgie, please,' Sophie bit her bottom lip. 'It's been ever so hard on Helena – well, on all of us.'

'How is that exactly?'

Sophie hesitated and I saw a small tear roll down her cheek.

'It's my fault,' Theo shuffled to her feet. I turned on her, feeling a cold fury seething through my body. 'I badgered and begged them to talk about it. I wanted to have it out in the open but Helena said you weren't ready. All these years I've been nagging them . . . ' she let her shoulders drop. 'Maybe I should have ignored them. Just told you everything. From the beginning.'

Helena spoke and her voice was grave. 'That night, on Ausangate, something incredible happened.'

'I remember,' I looked her straight in the eye. 'We strangled Wamani.'

Sophie put her hand up to her throat and grasped the coloured beads as if to ward off some presentiment of evil.

'Yes.' Helena nodded. 'We killed him, all of us.'

'And you decided that you were going to lie to me, treat me like a child! Was that it?'

'No!' Sophie shook her head, tears streaming down her face. 'We love you Georgie, we only want you to be safe!'

'Safe? *Safe*?' I gritted my teeth. 'It's *you* who don't feel safe isn't it? In case I spill the beans? You think I'm going to do – *what*, exactly? Call the police? Is this what our friendship has been about all these years? Fear of what I might do if I remembered what happened?'

'Of course not!' Helena bellowed. 'Now SIT DOWN and LISTEN!'

I regarded Helena coolly. Theo had already regained her seat and Sophie dropped down like an obedient puppy. 'Georgina,' Helena tried again, her voice more level and conciliatory. 'Please.'

I obliged her. There was a moment's rapprochement, a kind of ceasefire between us though I watched them all with a good deal of wariness, my so-called *sisters*.

'Of the four of us, you were the only one who didn't have perfect recall of that night.' She paused to let the words sink. 'We returned with Miguel to the hacienda and you went to lie down. But later Sophie couldn't wake you. You were still breathing but it was as if your whole body had gone into some sort of shock.'

'I remember waking up and hearing you talking about me in the next room.'

'We were trying to decide what to do. Sophie and I thought it best to let you come out of it yourself in your own time. Theo,' she searched for the right words, 'thought differently.'

'Okay!' Theo threw up her hands. 'Look George, I wanted to wake you up. I admit I was frightened that you'd get a crisis of conscience, that maybe you'd want to hand yourself in.'

'And turn you in at the same time?'

'Yeah – well, okay.' Theo sank back into her chair. 'I admit it. I was worried.'

'The thing is,' Helena continued. 'When you did come round a couple of days later, you had no memory of killing him. It was as if your mind had re-booted itself and wiped the incident completely.'

'You could have *told me*!'

'There was more to it than that. It was as if you'd gone into some sort of hibernation,' Sophie added. 'It's what reptiles do in winter. They slow down, digest more slowly to conserve energy.'

'You think it was my body's way of healing itself.'

'And then there was the guilt,' Sophie said.

Guilt. Sophie's speciality. But not mine. Not any more.

'You should have told me,' I whispered. 'You really don't get it, do you?' I let a bubble of hysteria break free. 'Thanks to you I've been in hibernation ever bloody since!'

They stared at me, the penny dropping.

'I never felt so primal, so powerful, as I did when the life force drained out of him!' I slammed my fists on the table. 'It's not *guilt* that's kept me from forging a life for myself! It's the three of you!'

It was only as I spoke the words out loud that the full truth seemed to erupt from within me, the full weight of the past, heavy on my shoulders.

'Wamani took advantage of us from Day One. He played us off against each other, tricked his way into our confidences.' I turned to Helena and Sophie. 'We trusted him.' I looked at Theo. 'He crushed you,' I said.

'And he raped me.'

*He raped m*e It was the first time I'd said those words out loud. My eyes brimmed with tears that splashed onto the table like tiny silver raindrops. My throat contracted. I let out a great heaving sob and gulped in the air. I rocked back and forth. A great sea of grief for a half lifetime of crippled desires, all my suppressed rage towards the evil that men do, the totally overwhelming truth that I had been living a lie my entire adult life to date; all this and more besides, flooded through me now.

How does the Moon feel when she is eclipsed by the Earth? The Incas believed her to be under attack, eaten up by a predator of the night. They screamed and shouted, howled and threw spears to draw the hunter from its prey, for fear that the world would be left in total darkness.

I howled that night.

I cried and screamed and heaved my body back and forth with the great terror of it all. I wept for every woman who has ever suffered at the hands of a cougar or a wolf. For every abuse, every slight, every taken-for-granted she-doesn't-understand-me thought, word or deed that eviscerates the soul and heart of a woman until she cannot bleed any longer. Until her very entrails are powder and her Will, nothing more than a whisper. Until she is hollow inside, not for want of courage or duty but because without love, she is reduced to servitude; a vessel for men's disappointments. In her grey eyes and sallow cheeks they see only a defeated girl, her very bones a ringing bowl that sings to them a song of betrayal. For was not woman put upon this Earth as companion to man, and has he not blamed her every night and day for his own weaknesses?

How was it that Eve was all alone and undefended? Was Adam lost in deeper thoughts? Had he retreated from her side even then? Had he retired to his garden shed?

Did he already see his work in the garden as more important than her? Had he told her to run along, he would be there in a minute, just a couple of things to sort at the office? Don't wait up. When the evil serpent first appeared next to Eve there should have been such a mighty hollering from young Adam as to freeze the blood. Then would the serpent have turned away in fright and Eve would have been saved. And how the world would have rejoiced! My God, how different the world would have been.

I had fought the serpent and I had won. The evil in Wamani was dead. But it had not ended there. He was not alone. This hatred of women, this need to betray the feminine, the continual seduction and violation of women's rights, the violence towards their bodies and their work, the perpetual undermining and sabotaging of women's achievements: none of this had been erased by his death. He had the serpent within him, but the serpent lived on in others.

How had men come to be so afflicted? Did it really start with the Creation myths, or were the legends told in the dark many aeons ago, the distillation of a darker truth? An unseen energy that threatened men, even as it worked through them to violate and subjugate women?

What if every minute spent in overtime at the office, away from the heart of his wife and daughters were a heartbeat lost from the life of a man? Would we still sacrifice our sons to the same mill, breed more and more to conquer death or would we in fact conserve? Might we forgive instead, relate to the other, return to share our own little Edens once more? Woman has been trying to recreate the garden ever since that terrible exodus. All that frantic house-making, nesting, sowing and planting, all to try and kiss it better. And man has been intent on fleeing *Her*, the scene of his crime, at every opportunity. Nothing can stop a man in his tracks as much as a disappointed woman. It's guilt that overwhelms men more than anything else.

The Ancient Greeks knew a wronged woman when they saw her: Ariadne, Cassandra, Clytemnestra. The Fates, the Moirai – the women who determined the destiny of each god, each human being; Clotho – she who determines the birth, Lachesis, – she who measures the allotted thread of life and Atropos – she who determines the point of death and severs the thread with her dreaded shears. Even the gods could not defy them. I saw them now before me in the faces of my friends.

'We are strong,' I said. 'Stronger than any mortal man.' I touched their cheeks and held hands with them. 'There is nothing we cannot achieve, if we work together.' We sighed with the relief that comes from finally arriving home, to a place of sanctuary. We wept and hugged each other.

A darker part of myself crystalised into being that night. The grief lifted like a vapour cloud and a larger purpose started to take shape; an irresistible vengeance that would not be denied any longer, filling the void, anchoring me to the Earth. My heart broke into a thousand tiny shards and I crossed a line I never realised existed. I now understood the true nature of my longings, and from that point onward I would never look back.

6

Helena lit the fire in the sitting room. I sat on the floor, leaning back against the sofa, a blanket around my shoulder and watched the flames leap. Sophie sat with her legs tucked up under her. Theo was painting her nails.

'He was filled with terror at the end – I saw it in his eyes,' I said. 'I wanted him to know, in that moment before he died, how much he'd abused and violated me. How he'd broken trust with all of us. He destroyed our innocence, didn't he?'

'Like it must have been in Eden,' said Helena quietly.

Sophie stroked my forehead. I sighed deeply and huddled against her knee. Helena reached out and put another log on the fire.

'When we came back to Cambridge and you started writing, we hoped that your unconscious mind would release the truth,' said Theo.

'I think my poetry was a way of keeping the truth concealed. The way dreams allow you to stay asleep. All these years I thought you were just needling me about my writer's block. Teasing me about my short-comings,' I said.

Theo shook her head sadly. 'I know we haven't always seen eye to eye. The thing is Georgie, it's like I was saying to you earlier, it's much more fun being wicked in partnership, than on your own.'

'But you were so angry after Wamani died. You *blamed* me, you were so angry at me for killing him.'

'I was furious with you because he liked *you* more than me! As for killing him, I was only worried that you'd come over all sanctimonious once your memory came back and want to confess to the authorities. I don't regret him dying, not a bit. I agree with you; I never felt so powerful as I did on the side of that mountain.'

'What about Douglas?' I asked her. 'Did you ever tell him the truth?'

Theo shrugged her shoulders.

'It's nothing to do with him. He's a good father who's never done me any harm. It's just that we have different appetites. I suppose that's the goddess in me. I always need more. It's funny, but I wouldn't have married Douglas if I hadn't already married him. Do you know what I mean?'

'No,' we all chimed together, laughing at her.

'He's part of me. Probably the better part. It's comfortable, familiar, like coming home, and he gives me my freedom, and God knows with my appetites, I jolly well need it. The last thing I want is a jealous man! It might look like weakness, the way he puts up with me, but Douglas is one in a million. How many men are willing to accept their wives as they truly are? What more can I ask for than that?'

'A man who truly loves women,' Helena said. 'That's rare, Theo, really rare. You're very lucky.'

'Yes,' she bit her lower lip. 'I am.'

'But you feel the same way I do?' I asked.

'Oh God, yes!' Theo said. 'All my life I've known that I could be anything I want. The only problem is that it's men who have always been the gatekeepers. Promising stardom on the basis of a blowjob.' She blew on her nails and held her hands out to admire the end result. 'Sex has been the only means of control that I've ever known.' She cocked her head and smiled. 'I think it would be fascinating to see the shoe on the other foot, don't you?'

'We all do!' Helena laughed.

'Can I do anybody's toes?' Theo shuffled round and

Sophie nodded and slipped off her crocs.

'We've all talked about it, dreamed about it,' said Sophie.

I turned to face her and saw a keen burning intensity that I had only ever witnessed once before.

'Every day I have to go into school and pretend that Helena doesn't exist. I spend my whole working life second-guessing my every action in case it's misconstrued by the so-called moral majority. It just wouldn't do for one of the parents to discover that their precious boy is being taught by a *dyke*.'

I was horrified.

'But surely your private life is your own business? It's just not legal to discriminate against you.'

She shook her head. 'Do you really think that makes any difference? It may not matter to the Head or the Governors what I do at home, but they're never going to promote me. I can't tell you the number of times I've been passed over by a junior male member of staff with a stay-at-home wife and a bun in the oven. I don't fit the mould. The last school I worked in, the male staff ran a book on which of them would be first to get into my knickers. When it became apparent I wasn't interested in any of them nobody sat with me at lunchtime. It was miserable. I used to take a flask of coffee for break-times and sit in my classroom.'

Helena gave the fire a fierce poke.

'That was the least of it,' she said. 'Once the boys found out they made her life a living hell. I keep telling her to give it up, go for a fellowship instead. College is full of progressive dykes and queers. I can't be doing with this bourgeois education bollocks.'

'Yes, well then I would have to live in, wouldn't I?' Sophie sighed. This was obviously a well-worn argument between them. 'And besides, the money's terrible.'

'Bugger the money,' Helena said. 'I just want you to be happy.'

Sophie reached up and took her hand. 'I am,' she said.

'It's all so fucked up,' I said. 'Whatever happened to women's liberation? Here we are in the prime of life, still fighting the same bloody battles for equality and recognition. It's still a man's world.'

I thought again of Boyd and his ilk: so certain, so confident of their place in the grand scheme of things. So unapologetic, so confirmed in their inalienable right to rule, lead, conquer and deny. Men didn't second-guess themselves. But I had never yet come across a woman in public or private life who didn't suffer self doubt and anxiety, or harbour second thoughts about succeeding in her chosen field lest she undermine her husband or fail her offspring.

Even my most liberal male friends, those with the career wives without whom the middle-class lifestyle would have been a wet-dream; men who flinch at the very idea of a sexist quip yet blanche at the prospect of dirty nappies and school runs; men who may on occasion stoop to scoop up dirty laundry from the bedroom floor but sense the crippling emasculation that would follow if they ever cleaned a toilet or unblocked the bath plughole of human hair – even their own. The educated, charismatic, intellectual, enlightened, post-feminist professors, pundits, artists, consultants and journalists of my generation; scratch the surface and you will still find the Kipling gene; it's man's work filling the unforgiving minute with sixty seconds' worth of distance run. Man's work, so much more weighty than the work of women, in every field of endeavour from Genetics to Philosophy, Cookery to Economics, Poetry to Law.

'It's all so bloody disproportionate,' I said angrily. 'Men's achievements on the one hand, women's sacrifices on the other. There's a tipping point and I feel I've finally reached mine.'

'We need to balance the books, somehow,' said Helena.

'Swing the pendulum in favour of women for a change,' said Theo.

'What we need is a proper execution,' said Sophie cutting across all of our thoughts. Theo was just finishing the last toe and looked up in wonder. I sat up.

'Sometimes, in departmental meetings, I fantasise about lopping the head off my head of department,' she continued. She looked at Theo. 'Who would be top of your list?'

'Long list or short list?' said Theo with a crooked grin.

'You have a long list?' I said incredulously.

'Don't *you*?' She shrugged her shoulders.

'I'd nominate the patronising little shit who works in Customer Services at our local *B&Q*,' said Helena.

'That's too random,' said Theo. 'If you start with *B&Q*, you'll end up executing every spotty oik who's ever sold an electrical appliance.'

'Helena and I talked about it quite seriously once before,' said Sophie. 'Before Amsterdam, we fell in with a couple of chaps on the internet and you should have seen the spiritual claptrap they were spouting about Mother Earth and their need to commune. It's always so egotistical, the way men describe this need to fulfil themselves.'

'Ask not what Mother Earth can do for you, but what you can do for Mother Earth,' I said.

'Exactly. Even the ones who have tried ayahuasca before are so macho about the whole process. They never seem to join the dots and look at their motives for seeking higher spiritual contact. One minute they're desperate to commune, the next thing, their girlfriend doesn't understand them.' She sighed. 'They don't really live their so-called beliefs. It's depressing.'

'Just like Wamani. Remember his dream version of the four or us?' Theo sniggered. 'Completely different from the real thing!'

'Men love the big idea but they can't seem to translate it into the domestic sphere,' I said, admiring Theo's steady hand with the nail polish brush. 'Daniel was always spouting stuff about women's equality in the work place but if he ever cooked a meal it had to be a big hoo-ha. I was supposed to be *grateful*.'

'I think there's a lot to be said for just leaving them to it,' Theo said, her face screwed up in concentration. 'Men are babies. You have to admire what they've been up to and always say *well done*. That's where so many wives go wrong. Trust me.'

'Like saying *what a clever boy* when the cat brings in a dead sparrow?' I said scornfully, my incredulity vying with an uneasy feeling that had I done that more with Daniel, he might be home right now instead of sleeping with his ex-wife.

'Exactly. There!' Theo sat back on her haunches. 'All done.'

'H was all for inviting one of these internet chaps down here, but we chickened out at the last minute,' Sophie said admiring her new red toenails in the firelight.

'Why?'

'For one thing, we didn't know how discreet he'd been about us,' Helena explained, 'and we hadn't figured out a foolproof system for disposal of the body parts.'

'Yes,' Sophie nodded. 'And I think you'd agree that the whole endeavour felt incomplete somehow unless it involved all four of us.'

I brooded over the matter a little more.

'It needs to have meaning, doesn't it? It's not just

about killing someone. I mean it's more important than that. It's about re-balancing the Earth. Saving her from the endless machinations of masculine fuckwittedness.'

'Isn't it interesting how the most potent symbol of women's betrayal has just been absorbed into our culture?' said Sophie. 'I mean it's right *there* in the story of St George and the Dragon.'

'You mean *man fighting the demon snake to rescue the fair maiden?*' I said.

'Yes. He has to defeat the snake to be worthy of her.'

'Yes, but how often does a man even recognise his own complicity, and even *try?*' I added.

'True,' said Theo. 'I mean take that horrible big snake in the *Harry Potter* books.' We all looked at Theo. 'Nagini?' she said impatiently. 'You know, the big python-y thing that kills what's-his-face.'

'What on Earth – ?' Helena started.

'I'm just *saying* . . . that's all. *Snakes*. You know? They're everywhere.' She finished bluntly. There was a moment's silence. 'Not like you, Georgie,' she mumbled. 'You're lovely and . . . slinky.'

'A ritual offering,' suggested Sophie lightly.

'Yes. Properly purified. A sacrifice. Just the four of us, when we are together,' added Helena.

'We would be ridding the world of evil.'

'Making it a safer place for women. No more sexism, or patronising or being put on a pedestal.'

We paused in silent contemplation of the noble task that lay ahead of us.

'We could make a start tonight.' I looked up at the ceiling. The others followed the direction of my gaze.

'Of course!' Helena said with a little smile. 'I'd rather forgotten about him.'

***

We debated the pros and cons.

'My name is Matthew Boyd,' I said. 'I am a film maker, an intellectual and an academic. I'm on the brink of stardom, and you – ' I pointed to each of my sisters in turn ' – have no right to stop me.'

'That might be all well and good,' said Helena, 'if you were just content to go about your ordinary life, but there's every chance that you will become a star, particularly with Theo representing you.'

'Oh don't worry about me,' said Theo. 'I've just resigned as his agent.'

'Well,' I conceded, 'what if I do become a star? Why should I not enjoy the freedoms of anyone else to express my views?'

'You are quite simply not the masculine role model any of us would choose to have on screen,' said Sophie.

'You don't even watch television!' Theo cackled.

'Oh c'mon!' Helena ran her fingers through her head of short thick curls in mild frustration. 'He's a living example of why we don't bother with television.'

'Stick to the point,' I said.

'Take something as anodyne as gardening,' said Helena. 'Look at what happened to that strawberry blonde whatever-her-name-was.'

'Charlie Dimmock?'

'Nobody gives a sod if Alan Titmarsh is wearing a bra or not. Who wants to see another generation of young women hectored, botoxed and air-brushed just so that they can compete in the ratings? How many O levels do you think Kim Kardashian has? What kind of message does it send out to young women when the apparent female winners of our society are still judged on the size of their arse?'

'I don't think Kim Kardashian has any O levels,' I said.

'Exactly!'

'She's American for one thing. I'm surprised you've even heard of her,' I added.

'*Women's Hour*,' Sophie said. 'And our local hairdresser carries *Hello Magazine*.'

I couldn't help myself.

'You read *Hello Magazine*?'

Helena scowled at me. 'We *all* read *Hello Magazine*,' she said emphatically. 'When's the last time you went into a hairdresser's and found anything but?'

'Anyway,' said Sophie. 'It's not just TV is it? Our whole society is riddled with inequality. I sometimes think when I'm at school that the boys are just acting out the whole time. It's like they're so terrified of being thought weak or feminine that they have to do the exact opposite. I think they hide it their entire lives and it comes out in either actual or latent aggression; the Old Boy Network or Freemasonry, for example.'

'Well, let's give them something to really be terrified about. We have to start somewhere and upstairs we have a fresh specimen on the cusp of a stellar career. Now. What, if anything, are we going to do about it?'

I looked over to Theo who had been rather quiet throughout the latter part of the conversation. She'd brought him here. I wondered how much she felt compromised now.

'Theo?'

'Girls are very tender, vulnerable creatures,' said Theo wistfully. She paused for a moment, her face unreadable. She turned her head towards the fire as if thinking aloud. 'I think on close reflection, the idea of a swaggering Boyd beamed into sitting rooms across the nation, inspiring idolatry and sexual fantasies in mothers and daughters alike is beyond the pale.'

We all looked at her in quiet acknowledgement.

'So we're decided then?' I asked slowly.

Theo nodded and put her hand out. I gripped it firmly. Sophie put her hand on top of mine and Helena grasped all with both hands.

'Shouldn't we say something?' asked Sophie.

'I'm trying to think,' said Helena.

I took a deep breath.

'Acta non verba. Deeds not words,' I said.

They smiled, echoing my sentiment: 'Acta non verba,' we chanted together.

'Am I interrupting?' We swivelled round to see the man himself standing in the doorway. Mathew Boyd yawned and patted his jacket for his cigarettes. 'Any chance of a drink?'

***

Sophie was the first to recover. She sprang up lightly and headed down the hallway to the kitchen for another glass. Boyd sauntered into the sitting room and helped himself to a light from the fire.

'Did you have a good sleep?' Theo gave him a brilliant smile and patted the sofa next to her by way of invitation. He ignored her.

'I'll get some logs for the fire,' Helena muttered, heading for the back of the house.

It was as if he hadn't heard her. Theo glanced at me and opened her eyes wide in speculation. I gave a tiny shrug of the shoulders which was just the visual clue he seemed to be waiting for.

'I've been mulling over a few ideas upstairs,' he said slowly. 'Theo's keen on *Marie Claire* but I'm thinking something more hip.'

Theo mouthed the word *hip* at me and pulled a face. Boyd straightened up. 'Blogging's the thing. Podcasts.' Then, turning to face me, 'You do tweet I take it?'

I blinked and bit my lower lip. Was he serious?

'No.'

'Shame. You can build up quite a following online if you take the time to Twitter.'

Theo let out a sort of piggy snort and keeled over in a giggling heap.

'What's so funny, darlin'?' he asked mildly but there was something about his eyes that looked all wrong to me. He leaned over Theo, his mouth very close to her ear and repeated the question. 'I said, what's funny?'

She uncurled herself and crooned his name, raising a tentative hand to his cheek. He twisted his head round to smile at me.

'You know modern technology is an amazing thing.' He put his hand in his pocket and brought out his mobile phone.

'All I have to do is press 'send' and everything I know about your misdemeanours appears online. Imagine that.'

I stared at him. Theo sat up swiftly and made a clumsy lunge for the phone.

'No, no, no,' he said softly and covered her face with his hand to push her roughly back down onto the sofa. I started forward but he waved the phone at me.

'One text message,' he said. 'That's all it takes these days.'

My mouth was dry and my head was spinning.

Sophie entered the room with a glass and a bottle of cognac. She stopped dead when she saw my face.

'What do you want?' I croaked.

'What everyone wants,' he grinned. 'Money. Lots and lots of money, sweetheart.'

'How much?'

He took a drag on his cigarette and cast a glance at Sophie. 'You'd better get the other dyke in here. We've got business to discuss.'

Sophie flinched.

'Fetch Helena,' I said. Sophie slipped back into the hallway and ran back through the kitchen.

'I should think ten grand for starters,' he said. 'Each.'

'You're mad!' said Theo, sitting up swiftly. He punched her hard in the stomach. She rolled off the sofa like a dead weight, clutching herself, doubled up in pain. In one stride he was right in front of me, his hand around my throat.

'You tell your friends the price just went up. Fifteen grand a piece or you get to be famous. Very, very famous, only not quite the way you dreamed you would. I press this little button,' he jabbed the send key with his thumb. 'And everything I know sits patiently in my email account waiting for me to decide what to do with it.'

He glanced at the screen and his expression froze. Then suddenly he was pushing me backwards. I cracked my head against the plaster and went out like a light.

7

I could only have been unconscious for a matter of seconds. Sophie was kneeling over me, her lip bleeding and her face swollen.

'We can't let him get away,' I stuttered. 'He's got stuff about us on his phone. He tried to send a text. All he needs is a signal.'

'We're in a bit of a black spot here. No reliable signal for about a mile. He can't get very far on foot.' Helena pulled on a jacket and unlocked the gun cupboard.

And then we heard it – the unmistakeable sound of a car engine starting up: Theo's Volvo.

'Shit!' Helena launched herself back down the corridor out to the Landy that was parked behind the kitchen. 'I'll try and cut him off.' She would have to close the gap between Boyd and his escape route via the side exit away from the house, along the single track that lead to the bottom gate.

I stood up and made for the gun cupboard. 'Look after Theo,' I said.

'What are you going to do?' Sophie looked dazed. I loaded the Purdey and grabbed a torch.

'It's all over, Sophie,' I grabbed her shoulder. 'He's not going to let it rest here, you can be sure of that. I have to help Helena track him down.'

'I'm going to call the police.'

'No! You can't do that. He'll tell them everything about us and what we did to Wamani.'

'Oh God,' she gasped. 'Be careful.'

I pulled open the front door. The house was ablaze with lights. The ground was hard with frost and crunchy underfoot. I ran blindly out of the front gate and down the track in pursuit of the Volvo. It was very cold. I snatched deep lungs of frozen air and felt the adrenaline spiking through my body urging me on in spite of the danger.

He'd played us. He'd heard everything. My heartbeat was hammering in my chest by the time I reached the road. About half a mile up ahead I saw two sets of red brake lights at odd angles to each other. Then with a jolt I realised that one vehicle had crashed into the other and both had come off the road. I picked up speed and flung myself at the driver's side of the Landrover.

Helena was slumped at the wheel. She was deathly pale. The Landrover looked like a write-off. The Volvo was intact but tilted at a steep angle in a three foot ditch, the engine still running.

'Helena!' The car door was wedged shut. I smashed the window with the butt of the gun. I laid down the weapon and reached in, lifting her under the arms so as to pull her free but I couldn't get enough purchase. I felt her pulse. It was strong. I guessed she was concussed but in no immediate danger. I looked back towards the house. I would have to get help.

I turned to leave and swung the torch around to see Boyd staggering towards me. I made a grab for the Purdey but he was too quick, knocking the wind out of me as we both hit the ground. He was heavy and I kicked out but he already had his hand on the barrel and elbowed me in the face. There was a horrendous snap which brought tears to my eyes. He'd broken my nose. He hauled himself to his knees, and pulled me up by the hair, smashing my head against the door of the Landy. I saw stars and all my limbs just collapsed as if the strings had been cut. He was breathing hard and spitting blood.

'She tried to kill me!' he wheezed. 'Fucking bitch drove straight at me!' He sounded offended.

Then he was up on his feet, kicking my legs. 'Get up,' he said. 'Get the fuck up now.'

I rolled over and shuffled onto my hands and knees. He brought the butt of the shotgun down on my left hand and I howled in pain and shock, rolling over onto my side again, clutching my broken fingers to my chest.

'That's for planning to kill me,' he said, his breathing coming in fierce gulps of air.

He brought the barrel of the shotgun down and pushed it under my chin. 'Get up, bitch.'

The blood was streaming down my face, blocking my nose making it difficult to breathe. 'Get UP!'

The safety catch was on but I still didn't dare try anything. Guns are made to measure. He was a different shape entirely from Helena and not used to handling firearms. That made him even more dangerous. I stood up, holding my hand tightly as he waved me back towards the house. I looked towards the lifeless body of my friend.

'What about Helena?'

'She can bleed to death for all I care.'

He prodded me in the back and we limped back up the track towards the farmhouse.

'What are you going to do?'

'Keep walking.'

My mind was racing. Theo was hurt, Helena was out of action. I was walking wounded. That only left Sophie. I had to warn her somehow before we got to the house.

'Keep moving.' I felt the barrel jabbing me between the shoulder blades.

We were within a hundred yards of the house when I saw the front door open. Theo was standing in the doorway.

Boyd pushed me again.

'Tell her to get where I can see her with her hands in

the air.'

Theo was rigid with fear.

'Where's Helena?'

'Tell her to get where I can see her!'

I used my good hand to wipe away the blood from my face. 'She's in the car. I couldn't get her out.'

'Oh, Christ.' Theo put her hands up over her mouth as we approached the doorway and light fell across my face.

'Where's Sophie?' I asked.

I felt the end of the barrel jab me in the small of the back. 'Shut up and get in.'

Boyd ushered us both inside and herded us down the corridor to the kitchen where Sophie was nursing a black eye. She had hold of Ralph and started when she saw me, tears running down her face when she realised that Helena wasn't with us.

I wanted to reassure her that Helena would be fine, but at that moment I didn't know for sure and I didn't want to give Boyd any reason to go back and finish the job.

'Car keys,' he said hoarsely. 'Where are they?'

'Upstairs,' I said.

'You lying bitch!' he shouted and clipped me across the face with the barrel of the gun. Sophie shrieked and I toppled backwards, landing on the floor with a crunch, my broken hand under me. I rolled around on the floor whimpering with the pain. Ralph barked hysterically, pulling towards the threat whilst Sophie held tightly onto his collar.

'I am going to shoot someone unless you give me your fucking keys right now!'

Theo knelt down to help me sit up and held me tight making little shushing sounds. My head was spinning. If I gave him my car keys it was over for all of us. He must know that.

Theo tried to reason with him. 'Matthew, you're not thinking straight. It's the drug you've taken. You're just having a bad trip. We can sort this out, Matthew.'

He spat in her direction.

Theo swallowed hard and her expression was pained rather than scared.

'Matthew – ' her voice was quivering. 'I – I never planned this, we – '

'You stupid ugly cow. Shut your fucking mouth. I am so sick of your whining.'

She tried again. 'We can work something out, just you and me. We can just walk away and strike a deal. I'll give you what you want – all of it, I'll find the money somehow. We can put all this behind us and you can have the career you've always dreamed of.'

He looked incredulous.

'You're plotting to *kill me*!' he yelled. 'Don't you think it's a bit late to be offering me endorsements and a television contract? You should have played ball when you had the chance. Fuck you and your money. I don't need you or your hand on my thigh or your mouth around my cock. You know you're quite a legend in your own lunchtime.' He smiled savagely. 'I bet you were quite a good shag about a hundred years ago.'

Theo's face was red. I felt her trembling beside me.

He continued in the same vein.

'I couldn't give a shit about you or your fucked-up friends. I don't know why you killed the poor bastard on the mountain and I don't care, but I am going to salvage something from this fucking weekend.' He laughed almost in spite of himself, shaking his head. 'Goddesses my arse! Look at you! You know, you couldn't make it up.' He slid back the safety catch. 'Now Give Me The Fucking Keys!' he screamed, pointing the gun straight at me and Theo.

'They're here!' Sophie screamed at him from across the table and he turned his attention to her, swinging the barrel wide. Sophie put up one hand instinctively as if to fend him off and dropped to her knees, pulling Ralph into her chest and holding him tightly. Boyd lowered the barrel and aimed it directly at her head. He was going to shoot her. In that split second of terror I knew he was going to kill her and there was not a single thing I could do about it. The moment seemed to stretch into an infinite time and distance. I saw in Sophie's frozen expression the realisation that she was about to die, glimpsed Theo's arm stretching out towards her as if to save her and heard my own protesting howl of agony.

But all that was nothing compared to the terrible sight of Helena; bloody and magnificent, rigid with pain, she stood silently behind him in the kitchen doorway. Boyd swivelled his head, sensing the danger too late. She carried something in her hand. She brought her arm down hard and fast, across the top of his shoulder breaking his collarbone with a sickening crack.

Boyd staggered backwards against the dresser with a high-pitched scream. He lost his grip on the Purdey which hit the ground, blowing a great hole in the plasterboard above Sophie's head. Theo screamed. Helena dropped the tyre iron and sank to her knees, all her strength gone. We froze, deafened in the aftermath of the gun shot for a matter of seconds, as plaster dust settled all around us.

Boyd groaned. He shunted forward on his knees, holding his arm at the shoulder and pulled himself up. I thought he was going for the gun, and scrambled out of Theo's embrace, but he had other ideas and shuffled towards the back door.

'No!' I shouted, my voice high-pitched, agitated. He

kept moving. 'Stop!' I yelled again, fumbling for the gun, but he was already out of the door and limping across the back yard towards open fields.

I knelt across to touch Helena. Her head was bleeding and her face was like a mask. 'You have to finish it,' she croaked.

***

I could barely see with all the dust in my eyes and everything throbbed with pain. One barrel gone. I had one shot. Just one shot to stop him. I headed out of the door. The cold air chilled my face. I clutched the Purdey across my chest and staggered after him. The ground had frozen hard. Beyond the glare of the kitchen light I stopped, and let my eyes adjust. To the east I could see a blood red line appearing on the far horizon. The moon was slung low, giving me just enough light to see a dark figure moving awkwardly about fifty yards ahead of me.

I called out to him again but he just kept running. I was finding it harder to breathe. Dried blood was clogging up my nasal passages. My hand was swollen and throbbing like hell. It was all I could do to try and keep pace with him. I reached the dyke and closed my eyes, leaning against the damp cold stone. *One shot.* If I could line up the barrel on top of the wall I might be able to bring him down. I remember thinking *this is madness* when I felt a familiar rush of air. I opened my eyes wide, sensing the drumming fluttering sensation, like wings on glass in my peripheral vision. I pushed myself away from the wall just in time as Boyd's first blow glanced off the stone where my head had been. The rock skittered out of his hand and landed somewhere on the earth. He launched himself at me and the next thing I knew I was flat on my back with Boyd on top, his good arm locked tight, hands around my throat, squeezing the life out of me. I clawed at his hands but he was too strong. I groped around for the gun but it was out of reach.

'It's a shame,' he said, leaning in with a twisted little smile. 'I like older women. They're so *grateful*, if you know what I mean?'

I brought my knee up straight into his groin and felt a satisfying crunch of bone against flesh as he keeled over in pain. I rolled to one side and drew myself up onto my knees. Boyd clutched himself, whimpering like a dog. I sat flat back against the wall, breathing hard, drawing the air into my lungs like a drowning woman. I cast around for the gun and reached for the end of the barrel that was lying just inches away. My hands were trembling as I checked the barrels and brought the stock up, nestling the butt into my shoulder. It was a comfortable fit. Even with three broken fingers, I could hardly miss from this distance. I brought the barrel down and lined up my sights. Boyd was still rolling around on the ground, retching. He looked up at me, his face twisted in pain, the hatred oozing out of him.

'You haven't got the fucking nerve!' he screamed at me.

I felt moonlight flooding through my body and took a deep breath.

'Haven't I?' I answered calmly. And pulled the trigger.

***

The sun was just rising as Theo and Helena wrapped him in an old carpet and moved him to an outhouse.

I sat at the kitchen table hunched over a glass of brandy. Sophie had the Doric lit. She shuffled about making coffee, toasting bread. I smelt bacon cooking. It was all so normal. I wanted to help but all I could do was sit and rest my aching body.

I don't know how long it was before Theo and Helena returned. It was getting light when I heard my car pull up at the back door. Helena came straight in and went down the hallway to take off her jacket and gloves. Theo followed suit. Nobody spoke. After a few minutes Helena returned and stood by the range, warming herself. Theo slumped onto a chair and buried her head in her hands, elbows on the table. Sophie squeezed her shoulder as she leaned over to put the butter dish on the table. Ralph raised his head from his basket expectantly and then lowered it again. No-one looked at me.

Sophie had hot plates in the oven. She dished up breakfast as if nothing untoward had happened. She poured strong tea into mugs and fetched fresh milk from the pantry. I watched her in a bemused state. Her left eye was swollen and purple.

'Did you get the Volvo out?' I asked. Sophie placed a plate of bacon and eggs in front of me and proceeded to cut the food up into bite sized pieces. The three of them settled themselves and started to eat slowly, passing ketchup and salt up and down the table. I looked down at the food in front of me and felt nausea rising.

'Yes, the body work is a bit chipped but it's structurally sound enough,' said Helena evenly, pouring herself another mug of tea.

'I'm not sure what I'm going to say to Douglas,' said Theo, lighting a cigarette. 'He absolutely adores that car.'

'What about the Landy?' I sipped tea tentatively, the steam making my eyes smart.

'Tough as old boots,' Helena said. 'I'll need a new window for the driver's side though – ' and turning to Theo rather tersely added, ' – look, must you smoke in here?'

'Sorry,' Theo took a deep lungful of smoke and glared at her. 'But yes, I think I must.'

Helena glared back.

Sophie glanced over at my plate. 'Eat up. We all have

to keep strong now. It'll be all right,' she added brightly.

I pushed my plate away, a sudden rage flooding through me. 'Well it's not bloody all right is it? It quite clearly is anything *but* all right!'

Sophie reached out a hand to cover mine, but I pulled away sharply and stood up, knocking over my chair as I did so.

'What are we going to do?' I shouted. Everything hurt.

Nobody spoke. Theo looked embarrassed. Sophie bit her lower lip. Only Helena kept on eating breakfast.

'I would have thought that was obvious, Georgina,' she said. 'We keep calm and carry on.'

I stared at her, every bit of my body furious and aching.

'But he's dead,' I said. 'He's really dead.'

'Yes,' she answered me, with a finality that brooked no opposition. 'He's dead. You killed him. If you hadn't killed him he would have strangled you first, and then come back to finish off the rest of us. Now, sit down and finish your eggs.'

'What about the police?' I said.

They all looked at me in shocked amazement.

'There's bound to be an investigation.'

'Are you going to tell them what went on here?' Helena appraised me narrowly.

'And say what exactly?' Theo cocked her head at me. 'Awfully sorry Officer but I killed a man in self defence because he found out we were planning to kill him and tried to blackmail us instead? Oh, do use your head, George.'

'She's right. Look, I made scrambled eggs for you,' Sophie led me back to the table and I sat down again awkwardly.

'Honestly Georgie,' said Theo. 'Are you going to do this every time?'

'Do what?' I prodded my breakfast and took a bite of toast.

'Go all indignant on us, or *worse*.'

I sniffed, feeling rather sorry for myself.

'It just hurts, okay? Everything hurts.'

Helena softened and put her hand out to me.

'Look,' Theo said in a placatory tone. 'We'd already decided to kill him. It was just a bit of a cock-up. We didn't expect him to try and blackmail us. Chin up, Georgie.'

There was an unhappy silence.

'It's a lot more messy and unpredictable than we thought though, isn't it?' Sophie said quietly.

I nodded. No-one spoke.

'Perhaps we're just not cut out for a life of crime. I mean that's two men I've killed and I can't honestly say I feel that much better for it,' I added.

Theo made a face. I stared at her. 'What?'

'What about the rest of us? ' She demanded.

'What do you mean?'

'Well, when do *we* ever get the chance to do the dirty? You with your bloody cloak of righteousness – I would have killed him if you hadn't got there first!'

'I don't have a *cloak* you moron! I'm not a fucking superhero!'

'What about the fluttering wings? Isn't that like your *spider-sense* or something?'

'Shut up, the pair of you!' Helena pushed her plate away. 'You're right,' she muttered, nodding in my direction. 'We draw a line here and now.' Sophie leant forward and wrapped her arms around her shoulders and gave her a kiss on the cheek.

'What? Just like that?' Theo was fuming. 'A few hours ago you were all for mounting a crusade against the tyranny of male oppression.'

'A few hours ago we were all under the influence of a psychotropic drug,' I said flatly.

'No balls,' Theo said. 'That's the problem George – you've never had any balls.'

'*Balls*? If anyone here lacks balls it's you, Theo. You couldn't even face a weekend without a fuck-buddy in tow, could you?'

'I hardly knew him!'

My jaw dropped. 'But you *brought* him here, boring us to tears about his work, how you thought his career would develop in television. You tried to seduce him on the sofa, for God's sake!'

'But I wasn't the one who *actually fucked* him though, was I?'

Hissing furiously, I raised myself up to my full height and batted my wings. Theo sprouted coca tendrils and lashed out at me with her tuberous limbs like a hysterical eggplant.

'Oh for Christ's sake! ' Helena shouted, combusting on the spot with flaming orange hair.

'Enough!' Sophie screamed. 'Stop it! All of you!' I blinked at her. Theo blushed. Even Helena looked surprised.

'Don't you get it? Every time a man enters into our little group, we end up tearing each other apart! First Wamani – Theo you egged him on, you know you did. And George – you never stood up for yourself. He fancied you. You fancied him. Where did it all go horribly wrong? And now with Mattie. He was a horrible, self-centred pig, so why did you bring him here when you knew it was supposed to be a girls' weekend?' She glared at Theo who, rather crest-fallen, drew in her tendrils and looked down at the kitchen table.

'Just showing off, if you ask me,' mumbled Helena, her head now a mass of smoking embers.

'And as for you – ' Sophie pointed at me next. 'You slept with him even though you detested him *and* you had every reason to think he was already involved with Theo!' I folded my wings and slid down into my chair feeling my legs once more, desperate for a drink of water.

Helena allowed herself a little smile so I stuck my tongue out at her.

'Don't think you're getting away with this either,' Sophie snapped at her.

'What did I do?' Helena sounded miffed.

Sophie looked at her with what could only be described as a Paddington Bear hard stare.

'It's because of you that there's a bloody great hole in the ceiling.'

'I thought he was going to shoot you,' Helena muttered.

There was a couple of minutes' silence during which we all reflected on how stupid we'd been.

'It's so easy to blame men, isn't it?' said Sophie folding her arms and glaring at us each in turn. 'But it's not really them that are the problem – it's us. Bring a man into the equation and we all just seem to go daft or something. So much for sisterhood. I'm sick of it. When the hell are we all going to grow up and wise up? Men wouldn't get away with half of what they do if we didn't hand it to them on a plate, and I know that I am one of the worst offenders.' She placed her hand over her heart and shook her head slowly. I opened my mouth to say something but she cut me off.

'It's not the fact that I'm a lesbian that stops me from getting promoted at work,' she sighed. 'It's because deep down I feel I'm just not good enough. My sexuality has nothing to do with it. If I had more self-belief I'd be in the running for a headship. Governors don't have confidence in me because *I* don't have confidence in me. You sleep around, Theo, because you think that's all you're good for. It's not who you really are – it's just what you believe about yourself deep down.'

She was right. About Theo that is. I didn't feel entirely comfortable with the notion that I was the architect of my own misfortune, yet there was something niggling at the back of my mind nonetheless. Something she was saying was chiming with a deeper resonance within me.

'What did it feel like?' asked Helena.

'What did what feel like?' Sophie sounded tired.

'No,' She turned towards me. I pretended for a few seconds not to understand her but she saw it in my eyes. I knew. I knew what she was asking and that everything depended on my answer. 'What did it feel like?'

'It felt different this time.'

It was true. Boyd's death had not been sanctified.

'Wamani was an evil man and it just seemed like the right thing to do. It felt like the Apu of the mountain was singing through us, all of us, disposing of his spirit. He wasn't going to survive – you could call it a mercy killing if you like – he couldn't have lived much longer. But what made it a good death was that we were ridding the Earth of a dangerous man.'

'A good death is better than a bad conscience,' said Sophie.

'What about last night?' Theo's voice shook. 'Haven't we done a good thing in ridding the world of another arsehole?'

'I thought so at the time,' I said. 'This morning I'm not so sure.'

'It's still self-defence,' said Sophie.

'How could anyone say differently?' Theo added.

'But they would,' I said. 'Helena brought the tyre iron into the kitchen from outside. That looks like intent.

And as for me,' my words trailed off. 'I went after him. I hunted him down.'

The seconds ticked by.

'What are you saying?' Sophie cried in dismay.

'You know what I'm saying. It's murder.'

'But you only have to look at our injuries,' Sophie cast her eyes around, 'and the state of this kitchen to see it must have been more complicated than that,' she pleaded.

'And besides,' countered Theo. 'We *know* what happened. We're witnesses.'

'*Witnesses?*' I laughed in spite of myself. 'Witnesses don't truss the body up in a carpet and then have a full English breakfast in the middle of a crime scene.'

'I just thought we all needed to keep our strength up,' shouted Sophie.

'I *know!*' I shouted back, but it hurt so much I nearly keeled over.

'Sorry,' Sophie bit her lower lip.

'Look,' I took a couple of deep breaths. 'I remember someone once said to me that most of the time people do the wrong thing for all the right reasons,' I said slowly. 'And that's what happened here.'

'So what now?' asked Helena.

I managed a half smile at my friend. 'We keep calm and carry on,' I said.

'Okay.'

'Theo?'

'Yeah.'

I looked at Sophie. She had tears in her eyes. She nodded.

'I don't know if I'm cut out for this goddess-lark, ridding the world of evil. It's bloody hard work if you ask me,' I said wearily.

8

Spring is almost upon us. Helena has gone out for Sunday papers. The signature tune for the Archers has just played out. Eddie Grundy's in the kitchen talking up his new sure-fire get-rich-quick scheme for Valentine's Day: a job lot of red plastic roses. *Honest Clarrie love, better than the real thing. Completely life-like but never die, see? That's what they call a unique selling point.* I help myself to coffee and milk and stir in some sugar.

It's just a normal Sunday morning at Black Farm. The roast is in the oven. Theo's upstairs in the bath. Sophie's just popped into the outhouse for spuds. I'll put my wellies on in a minute and go out for a stroll. The days have just started to lengthen again after what has been a dry crisp winter. I'll get Helena to show me her crop rotation for Spring. We'll take Ralph for a run and then later we'll all sit down to lunch with roast potatoes followed by petty squabbles over the supplements and an afternoon kip. I'll avoid the traffic by leaving a bit after six. Home by eight, then work in the morning and a meeting with an agent from Reykjavik.

Icelandic crime fiction. The next Big Thing.

Not so different from the Scandinavians, but much more difficult to pronounce. Just a normal day, the beginning of another normal week.

I worried that Boyd's sudden disappearance would cast suspicion on Theo. But I hadn't banked on her years of expertise as a duplicitous wife. She'd covered her tracks well. She'd already told Douglas that she was spending the weekend with me in town: *Poor Georgina. She needs me now that Daniel has gone back to his wife.*

We checked Boyd's mobile phone and there it was;

the message that would finish us all, lying in the outbox waiting to be sent. Proof positive that smart phones really are lethal in the hands of stupid people. Thank God for poor reception. I pressed delete. There was nothing else to link him to us. What's more, Theo had only picked him up at the last minute, which is why he hadn't so much as a toothbrush on him.

Theo telephoned Douglas to say that I'd had a bit of an accident and that she would be staying on with me for while. The Volvo needed a paintjob. Helena was able to reset my fingers and nose but the bruising was so severe that all I could do was take pain killers and rest. Theo phoned my office and said I'd been in a car accident at the weekend and would be taking a few days' leave. I couldn't drive so Theo thought it best if she drove me back to town at the end of the week. Helena had suffered cuts and bruising but was as resolute as ever about disposing of our little problem.

As we were rather shaky on modern forensics, having only the odd episode of *CSI* and *Lewis* to go on, we decided that immolation was the best way to dispose of Boyd's body. Taking him to another venue was risky. Too many surveillance cameras around these days. Besides, there was nothing to connect Boyd to Black Farm. Nobody would think to look for him here.

Sophie's form had done a project on the Vikings so she knew a surprising amount about burial customs. Building a pyre requires real skill. Matthew's body burnt awfully well. And it sort of completed the weekend. We huddled together in the chill of the evening, sipping cognac, watching the flames lick ever higher as the burning embers floated up into the night sky.

'Should one of us say something?' I pondered.

'Good riddance you nasty man,' said Sophie prodding the pyre with a large stick.

'There's no going back now,' Helena said. 'We're all in this together.'

***

In the weeks that followed I gave serious thought to all that had happened.

We had been very lucky. There can be no doubt that something had watched over us. There really was no other way to explain it. When Theo returned to work she heard the rumours: Boyd had disappeared off the face of the Earth. The police had their suspicions: his apartment was clean, *too clean* they reckoned. As if someone had cleaned up after themselves, if you know what I mean. Then there was the small matter of Boyd's cocaine habit; he suffered bouts of paranoia, he was heavily in debt. He frequented underground gambling dens and had formed liaisons with some rather unsavoury members of the Estonian mafia.

The emerging consensus was that Boyd had gotten into something way over his head, ruffled a few Mafia feathers in his pursuit of *avant garde* documentary realism. The BBC even issued a statement subtly pointing the finger at Boyd's unusual technique whilst lamenting the loss of a promising new talent. Theo was impressed. 'That's a publicity coup if ever I saw one,' she laughed on the phone to me. 'I come to bury Matthew Boyd not to praise him.'

There was talk of dragging the river because the phone company said the last recorded location for his mobile phone was on the banks of the Thames, but a budget-conscious Assistant Commissioner intervened at the eleventh hour. It stood to reason that if Boyd had finally got his comeuppance at the hands of experienced killers, the police were never going to find his body.

At least that part was true. Case closed pending further evidence.

Theo and I took a trip just before Christmas, ten days in Mauritius. There was plenty of sun, white sand and deep blue water and she managed not to have sex with anybody.

'I think I'm getting old,' she sighed mournfully as we packed our things on the last evening.

'Older or wiser?'

She stared into the middle distance. 'You know, I eyed up that gorgeous young waiter when we first arrived and then it suddenly hit me. He's the same age as the twins.'

'Oh.'

'That means he's probably got a mother my age.'

'Yup.'

'And how would I feel if one of my boys was being shagged senseless by a woman like that?'

It seemed the wisest course of action was to say nothing.

I shed my former life like the proverbial snake. I had my hair cut and highlighted, my apartment re-decorated, cleansed the space of Daniel-esque vibrations and picked out a new wardrobe. I took to wearing the amulet that Nina gave me all those years ago. I think she tried to show me who I was. At the very least, she must have hoped it would invoke the goddess to protect me from the man she called 'ñaqak'. Poor Wamani. I think he really was astonished to find himself in the presence of a goddess, but as with so many foolish mortals, he overreached himself. Like the heroes of classical mythology he thought he could mate with a goddess, and become god-like himself. I daresay he thought I would protect him from harm, help him in his business, support the cause of *Shining Path*. The irony is that given the option, I might well have chosen him. If only he hadn't been so impatient. If only he hadn't forced himself on me. If only he could have waited and helped me to understand my true nature.

I pretended not to notice Tamsin, my PA, admiring my change of image, and biting her tongue. Though it's common knowledge that Daniel left me, people are remarkably discreet. Of course the real scandal was that Imogen threw Daniel out. In a fit of indignation he rented an outsized penthouse flat and threw some rather wild parties. He phoned me a couple of times, lonely and miserable, locked inside his own bathroom while some young posh totty lounged on the sofa drinking his best Merlot. Sophie's words echoed still and I told him that I needed a clean break. He's a hand-me-down man and I can do so much better. Besides, I couldn't have better support than the love of my closest friends. It's them that I turn to because they know me inside out. They understand the truth about me – that I am a woman and a goddess. Not necessarily in that order.

***

Sophie's career is starting to take off. Whenever a pupil gives her an insolent look, all she has to do is fix him with a stare and think deadly thoughts. Her colleagues are in awe of her discipline. A deputy headship beckons.

Frankly life has never been better. Black Farm continues to thrive. Helena is expecting to make quite a tidy profit with beet and barley. The wind turbine application has been accepted and the foundations will be laid in early summer.

Theo is channelling her energies into family and work. When Douglas asked her what she wanted for her birthday she never thought twice. She's looking very sleek these days. She found a wonderful Lithuanian cosmetic surgeon who specialises in fat implants. They give the skin a natural smooth finish without loss of feeling; infinitely more desirable than botox and of course far more expensive. Most women run out of fat deposits and draining adipose cells from the buttocks inevitably leaves mild pitting. That's her one regret. Sophie thinks it's terribly gross but as Theo put it, *Georgina's got a bun in the oven. Why didn't I think to save a piece of his ass?*

I talk to him sometimes on the spot where we laid his bones to rest, in the shadow of the dyke where the earth is black and fertile. I describe to him the sensations I feel as the little life we inadvertently made together grows and feeds inside my belly. The GP thinks it's madness at my age but I have made up my mind to go to full term. The girls are delighted. Helena has already made over the little yellow bedroom for me and I'm planning to spend my maternity leave at Black Farm. It seems the natural choice for me now.

My Muse has returned. Wamani sits at the end of my bed and watches me while I sleep. He is a second shadow making the dark just that little bit darker. When he opens his mouth I hear the East wind keening over the dank fenland towards the horizon. Darkness falls like spindrift rolling down the side of the mountain. Ausangate calls to me; it is the lullaby that rocks me to sleep, the breath of the Apu cool upon my cheek.

I write furiously; dark acerbic cantos, blank verse, mock epics. The *Sunday Times* critic described my latest volume 'as if penned by the imaginary lovechild of Sylvia Plath and Charles Bukowski'. My agent is astonished. He can't get over the change in me and keeps making crass little jokes about *late flowering talent*. It's mildly annoying.

Perhaps I'll invite him up to Black Farm for the weekend.

Acknowledgements

Thanks go to Pat, Louise and Anna who listened to the story in its embryonic form. I am particularly grateful to Nasrim and Ceri, who read the first fifty thousand words and offered helpful criticism and lots of encouragement.

Several sources have helped me to get an historical and cultural perspective on Andean beliefs, rites and rituals including Mary Weismantel's *Race Rape: White Masculinity in Andean Pishtaco Tales* and *The Guinea Pig: Healing, Food and Ritual in the Andes* by Edmundo Morales. The internet yielded hundreds of first hand testimonies on the effects and experience of taking ayahuasca, for which I am also grateful.

Whilst Andean spiritual beliefs are well-established, I have been a little creative when it comes to specific gods and goddesses. The goddess mostly closely aligned to the moon is Mama Quilla, wife and sister of Inti the sun god. However, I wanted my principal character to embody a more sinister energy so I invented Mama-Amaru.

The Myth of The Goddess by Anne Baring and Jules Cashford, and *Women Who Run with the Wolves* by Clarissa Pinkola Estés were both influential and a joy to read.

I would like to thank Seonaid at ThunderPoint Publishing for her detailed editorial work. Any mistakes are my own.

And finally, thank you to Jasper and Thomas for constant support and to Simon for being so patient, and always believing in me.

More Books From ThunderPoint Publishing Ltd.

Mule Train
by Huw Francis
ISBN: 978-0-9575689-0-7 (kindle)
ISBN: 978-0-9575689-1-4 (Paperback)

Four lives come together in the remote and spectacular mountains bordering Afghanistan and explode in a deadly cocktail of treachery, betrayal and violence.

Written with a deep love of Pakistan and the Pakistani people, Mule Train will sweep you from Karachi in the south to the Shandur Pass in the north, through the dangerous borderland alongside Afghanistan, in an adventure that will keep you gripped throughout.

The Birds That Never Flew
by Margot McCuaig

Shortlisted for the Dundee International Book Prize 2012
ISBN: 978-0-9575689-3-8 (Kindle)
ISBN: 978-0-9575689-2-1 (Paperback)

Battered and bruised, Elizabeth has taken her daughter and left her abusive husband Patrick. Again. In the bleak and impersonal Glasgow housing office Elizabeth meets the provocatively intriguing drug addict Sadie, who is desperate to get her own life back on track.

The two women forge a fierce and interdependent relationship as they try to rebuild their shattered lives, but despite their bold, and sometimes illegal attempts it seems impossible to escape from the abuse they have always known, and tragedy strikes.

More than a decade later Elizabeth has started to implement her perfect revenge - until a surreal Glaswegian Virgin Mary steps in with imperfect timing and a less than divine attitude to stick a spoke in the wheel of retribution.

Tragic, darkly funny and irreverent, The Birds That Never Flew ushers in a new and vibrant voice in Scottish literature.

www.ingramcontent.com/pod-product-compliance
Lightning Source LLC
Chambersburg PA
CBHW070917260626
47162CB00007B/2705